KENTUCKY
STAND

KENTUCKY
STAND

By

JERE WHEELWRIGHT

NEW YORK
CHARLES SCRIBNER'S SONS

To
the Masters of the Gilman Country School
and to
JOHN FRANCIS CAULFIELD

KENTUCKY
STAND

I

JIM CHESTON WAS SHAVING. He made as much ceremony over it as a young Shawanoe warrior preparing for his first wartrail. The case of razors which his grandmother had given him was open upon the washstand, seven razors, one for each day of the week although his requirements had not as yet extended beyond a single one for that period. The ball of soap hung by a string passed over the cloudy mirror set in a frame upon the wall; steam arose from the basin and the pitcher. At nineteen, shaving under the angle of the jaw was as yet an unfamiliar exercise and he screwed his face into a grimace, tightening the skin with the fingers of his left hand as his right brought the blade cautiously into position.

There was a murmur of excitement from the half-dozen small boys who clustered admiringly behind him as the lather was scraped away.

Feeling more relieved than he dared show, Jim wiped the blade carefully upon a two-months-old copy of the *Maryland Journal and Baltimore Advertiser* bearing the date of April 1777. The other angle of the jaw must next be attacked and the task would be harder, for he must bring his right hand under his left to have proper play. He held his breath unconsciously and came down with a short stroke. There followed disaster. Either the edge was not exactly at the proper angle or else the skin

1

slipped a trifle under his fingers. There was a quick pain and the blood began to flow.

"Damme!" exclaimed Jim with feeling, and a voice squeaked, "Lord! He's pinked hisself!"

Jim tried to staunch the tiny dribble with a rag. He dabbed at it with furious annoyance. This evening he was taking Mary Raeburn to the ball at William Sterrit's and he foresaw an unsightly scab, with its invitation to teasing. Unable to do anything about it, he expressed his feelings by saying "Damme!" again with even more emphasis.

There was a sound of feet scuffling in panic and a stern voice intruded in rebuke.

"James Cheston, you'll oblige me by not cursing and swearing before these young minds."

Master Blackthorne, the grim old schoolmaster, stood in the doorway. The Scottish burr that was usually submerged in the softer accents of Maryland had swum to the surface, as it always did when he was annoyed or excited.

"By good fortune you damned yourself, which is your Maker's privilege and not your own. Had you chanced to damn one of these others I would ha' had words with you."

The old man whirled upon the boy who had squeaked. "William Decker! A great oath was in your mouth too and an equally great offense against the King's English. 'He's cut hisself,' aye, I heard you cry that. I'll not ha' the language of slaves, potwallopers and sailors brought into my school, not whilst I can wield a cane. By the Lord, I—"

He stopped short with a grimace of dismay. "Forgi'e us all! The cursing is in my own mouth now." Then his face hardened. "But 'hisself'! That I can cure with no smarting of conscience."

He seized little Decker by the ear and drew him downstairs whence loud lamentations soon resounded.

Jim, released from his audience, finished his shaving with no further casualty. He began to dress, stopping occasionally to admire himself in the glass, although it gave him a fore-shortened view and made his legs more spindly than they were. He had no reason to be ashamed of his clothes. Grandmother Dorsey had made sure that they were of the finest quality, and cut perfectly for her grandson's figure. She had even taken him to Annapolis to the Governor's own tailor to be fitted. Royal Governor Eden had departed, but the tailor, although he might have changed his politics, had not lost his skill. White knee-breeches, white stockings, white smallclothes and long, loose-cut blue coat went on above the silver-buckled slippers; the linen ruffles at the throat were spotless. He felt right elegant. Maybe he didn't get to many balls or dinners, Grandmother still kept him in school though most everybody else he knew of his own age was managing his place or starting off in business or in the army, but he wouldn't be ridiculous—unless that damned scab made him so.

He smeared powder on it, thinking all the time that he was sick of school, sick of studying Latin and mathematics and ontology with Master Blackthorne. Grandmother had said that Master Blackthorne was a mighty smart man who'd ought to be a professor at the college at Princeton or at William and Mary, but that didn't compensate Jim for sitting around on scholars' benches as a sort of uncommon student when there wasn't anybody older than fifteen to associate with. He'd have gone to Nassau Hall three years ago, but the troubles with England had started then and Grandmother Dorsey had asked his father to keep him home another year so he could have a better grounding. Then had come the war, and the colleges were mostly closed, and Grandmother wouldn't let him go into the army, because his father had been wounded and captured at the Battle of Long Island. His mother had died soon afterward, so that was another reason in Grandmother's mind for his staying close and getting still more grounding.

And if there was anybody in all Maryland better grounded than he was right now, he'd admire to meet him.

The sun was getting low and he wondered if Caesar would have the horses ready on time. Grandmother had sent in Justice and Ladybird, with a sidesaddle on Ladybird, so he and Mary could ride to the ball. He knew that Caesar was proud of the horses and always kept them looking clean and well turned-out. He'd cut a pretty good figure coming to Mary's door with such mounts, and the ride wouldn't be far enough to stain his stockings much. It was clever of Grandmother to coach him to send his invitation written on the back of the Queen of Hearts. Of course everybody used playing cards to write invitations on, but

3

not everybody got the Queen of Hearts. It kind of made a girl think that you'd thrown away the other fifty-one in the deck just to use that for her.

Old Mamie rang the dinner bell, and Jim took a last look at himself and went on down to Master Blackthorne's meagerly furnished parlor, conscious of the big eyes of the little boys and the occasional snickers of the larger ones who had lingered for a glimpse of him. Master Blackthorne was waiting for him in the microscopic room, with the five pupils who lived at the school and didn't go home after hours. The old schoolmaster in his dingy black was inspecting faces and hands for traces of soap and water, and he gave Jim a dry smile as he entered. His ill-humor was gone and likewise the predominance of his Scottish burr.

"Here's one of my lads I'll not worry over tonight, though surely, James, there is a modicum of lather which still clings behind your left ear. My kerchief, sir, and you can clear one evidence of your shaving though I fear the other will linger. Such a bloody assault upon yourself!"

He ignored Jim's frown and tendered him a glass. "Sherry, sir. You'll drink with me in honor of the occasion. It's seldom that an old pedagogue has a chance to see how splendid a butterfly can emerge from—your pardon, Mister Cheston—a rather unprepossessing caterpillar."

Jim, completely surprised at these unusual attentions, could not find a ready reply. The parlor with its scrap of carpet, the tiny sideboard and the single mahogany secretary-combined-with-bookcase was familiar enough, even to the polished rack in which were set the canes of punishment. Here the teacher did execution upon erring scholars and occasionally entertained visitors, mostly parents who sipped carefully measured sherry and discussed the failings of their offspring—probably there-after seeking their own sideboards for other wine to wash out the taste of Master Blackthorne's. Never before had Jim been advanced to the position of an equal, and he could not account for his unexpected promotion.

However, if the master's attitude seemed changed, the supper was not. Crabcakes, hominy swimming in butter, overboiled greens and undersugared berries were usual for early June and fitted precisely into the schedule of meals which Jim by long

4

residence had grown to anticipate, not necessarily with enjoyment. The Chesapeake worked hard for Master Blackthorne, he thought, fish and terrapin and oysters and crabs marched up like one of General Washington's regiments to lay down their lives upon his table, and crowded out all the flesh meats. Lord how he was sick of terrapin. Just because it was cheap they had it three times a week when it was in season. Then a drop of butter fell from the forkful of hominy he was raising to his mouth and he clawed with his napkin, fearful of the safety of his ruffles.

Master Blackthorne talked very little; he kept watching Jim with an expression that was a compound of amusement and something else the youth could not fathom. The little boys who sat in neat rows on either side of the table ate fast but didn't say anything at all, being well schooled in the policy of being seen but not heard. It was warm in the room what with the June night and the heat of the candles, and he began to sweat in his close-fitting, formal dress. His revulsion against the berries became acute when he saw that they weren't particularly ripe, but he was spared the trouble of eating them when the sound of hooves outside showed that Caesar had arrived with the horses.

Master Blackthorne nodded his permission and Jim excused himself, seeing five spoons suspended at five mouths and ten envious eyes following him out. His tricorne hat was hanging on the hook and when he took it down he found the schoolmaster beside him.

"I still stand *in loco parentis* to you, James," said the old man, using a favorite and familiar phrase of his. "You'll not take it amiss then that I caution you to avoid the cards and the dice and thereby shame the devil?"

Jim nearly dropped the hat. What had got into the old hunks? This wasn't his usual caution. There was nothing about minding his manners and being sure to make a leg to his elders before speaking to them. Now he was being as grave as if Jim had more than his none-too-abundant pocket money to lose at Loo or Fox in the Warner. Then he remembered his finery. By God, it had made an effect even on Master Blackthorne. Feeling a little unreal, he made a bow and stammered out that he would do his best to avoid temptation.

5

"Here is the key and I'll not shoot the bolts," continued the schoolmaster, opening the door. "You'll do me a favor, James, if you'll dismount at the end of the street and not have your horses waking us by their stamping when you come back. Have a care of the hogs and see you don't get a fall in the dark. The watch, the lazy loons, have let them stray about again, and it would be hurtful to your braw clothes as well as to yourself should your horse chance to blunder over one."

The light from the open doorway showed Caesar waiting with the horses and a candle lantern, reins looped over one hand and lantern in the other. The silver-gilt buttons on his dark-blue livery matched the flash of his teeth as he allowed that his Marse Jim looked mightly elegant. Before he had finished the compliment Justice chimed in with a whinny and the horse's iron shoe clicked on a stone as he pawed a welcome. Jim slid unconsciously back to the life of his holidays when he, as eventual heir to the great Dorsey place, "Happy Return," was being trained in the management of men and of broad acres. One swift glance assured him that Caesar had not been at the rum, that the satiny hides of the horses reflected back the candles as a sign of good grooming, and that breastbands, saddles and cruppers showed the soft brown that only soap and oil could give. "They look well," he said as he mounted the sidling Justice, and never realized how eagerly the slave had been waiting for the compliment.

He led Ladybird himself, letting Caesar ride ahead with the lantern. The burghers of Baltimore had not bothered to light their streets, since most honest men stayed home after dark, but the candle would at least give some warning of those roving impediments, the pigs. The dust rose in gritty clouds under the hooves and he looked anxiously towards the reassuring moon. Hope the dry spell holds, he thought, if it rains there isn't going to be anything on wheels stirring for the mud. He'd heard that there were people like the Stevensons and the Smiths of Calverton who were coming six or seven miles by coach for the ball.

Going up Calvert Street he saw the first signs of activity. A sedan chair carried by four brawny Negroes swung by, escorted by a stout gentleman with powdered hair who raised his hat in passing. Jim couldn't see who it was but swept down his own in return, though Ladybird rather marred the effect by shying

6

as the hat went past her nose. There were horses in plenty and lounging servants in front of David Rusk's tavern, every window aglow with a prodigious display of candles, but this he knew was because the Whig Club met there. Politics, public affairs and Madeira were their chief preoccupations, the Madeira by now probably being predominant.

Then came the dancing of other lanterns like the one Caesar carried, the creak of leather, jingle of bridles, quick-flung greetings, young voices and soft laughter as his own generation in Baltimore went on horseback to the ball. He'd better hurry or they'd miss the grand march, and Mary wouldn't like that.

He called to Caesar to trot and Justice arched his neck and pulled on the bit. They clattered along while the lantern flickered uselessly and a riding couple shouted gaily in unison: "Mend yo' pace, mend yo' pace, Miss Mary's going to be awful mad." He was pretty sure it was Henry McKim and Anne Turnbull—where one was the other was pretty sure to be. That was all right, Henry was a good friend of his. Then, even as a member of the much-maligned watch was about to shout to him to moderate his gait, they reached the Raeburn house.

It was four stories and of brick. That in itself was a good beginning towards establishing social position, but the Raeburns had the essential steps further. Mrs. Raeburn was a patrician lady, one of whose distant cousins was an aide on General Washington's own staff. Mr. Raeburn fitted out privateers and would unquestionably be hanged did the King come to his own again. General Burgoyne was operating roundabout Ticonderoga against a few Continentals precariously assisted by the local militia, and if he got through to Albany Mr. Raeburn might have plenty of cause to worry. Right now, though, it made him mighty respected.

Jim dismounted where the lighted half-oblongs showed that there were candles burning in the front parlor, and before his foot touched the ground the butler had the door open. That statue in ebony was the final proof of the Raeburns' social position. Rich people might keep a butler, but a proud butler was a stamp of quality, since he reflected in himself how he felt about his white folks. He ushered Jim in to where were waiting for him Mr. and Mrs. Raeburn, showing unmistakable

7

approval, and their eldest daughter, showing something less.

Mary—she was goodlooking enough to pour over corncakes. She was blonde and tall and well-schooled. She swept him a stately curtsy with a smile that would have fooled any northerner and almost fooled Jim. Mrs. Raeburn was saying nice things; yet he could look at nothing save Mary. In a dream he heard the compliments and the kind inquiries about his father. There was nothing to tell, for there had been no word from him beyond his name in the lists, and the exchanges were being abominably mismanaged.

"Your mother would be pleased to see you, James. You look so much like her." Mrs. Raeburn was being tactful, but he did not respond, though he appreciated it. Still, it was pity and he was getting sick of pity. Stealing glances at Mary, Jim realized that what counted was not what his father had done nor what older folks thought of his dead mother, but what James Cheston could do right now to attract a girl into smiling at him and meaning it.

Mary was murmuring the proper things, but she was restless. What could be more important to her than going to the ball, no matter whom she went with? Jim knew, coldly within himself, that it was her parents who had sent her with him, not her own desire.

She swung up on Ladybird like a Maryland girl, toe catching the stirrup deftly as his lift under her foot sent her to her seat. The mare danced and Mary took her up on the reins no harder than was necessary to make her behave. They rode together, Caesar now behind them, and Jim (keeping an unnecessary eye on Ladybird) proudly pretended not to notice the wayfarers they met who stopped to stare approvingly.

They came to the warehouse where the ball was to be held, with the horses and the coaches drawn up before it. One or two torches were burning and throwing off resinous sparks, but the spermaceti candles from inside sent out a softer and more consistent glow. Jim did not know who had contributed the slaves who took Mary's cloak and his hat, but he walked a little straighter when he saw people turn to look.

That was the last time he was happy that night. He had a few good friends and at the beginning they kept him from feel-

8

ing too much alone; but as the dances were set with the slave orchestra doing its very best, he began to feel more and more out of things. He could dance and dance well—Grandmother had seen to that as well as to his swordsmanship, importing teachers to Happy Return so that Jim could be schooled in those two prime necessities in society. But the young ladies did not seem to want to test his skill. Of course Anne Turnbull did, and Mary Ringgold, but they were old playmates and his eyes were blinded to how lovely and attractive they were. Instead he saw with envy his own Mary's success, and even quarreled a little with Anne when she called her "spoiled and high-walking, not much like her mother."

It had never happened to him before and he did not know what to make of it. Some observant oldster might have pointed out that his still being in school counted hopelessly against him; that these young people had in the last year passed over the line between youth and maturity (or so they thought) and that he had been left behind, still chained to the old interests that now were stale for them. Unfortunately no one took the time to do so. It left him with a frozen smile that brought pity from the understanding Negroes who were carrying glasses of punch and fans to the older women. To them he was Marse James Cheston, a mighty kindly young gentleman, but to Mary Raeburn he was a stiff and awkward bore with nothing to recommend him.

He gravitated at first to the alcove where was the huge punchbowl. He saw Mary squired to a glass or two (the spermaceti candles made the air very hot) and took a couple of dips himself. A few of the younger men were already above themselves with liquor, but heavy drinking at a ball was frowned upon and Jim had the good sense to leave it alone. He prowled restlessly away.

Another room, close and hot, held the gamesters, mostly the elders who smiled at him in a recognizing and preoccupied fashion but never gave him the opportunity of casting the dice or of having a hand at the cards. Friendly though they seemed, he knew that if he offered to participate he would have been met with a frozen refusal. In spite of Master Blackthorne's concern he was safe enough from such temptations, unless of course he went back and joined the over-jolly group at the

9

punchbowl. Pretty soon they would meander to a back room and start a game of their own. The older men might gamble hard enough among themselves but they would keep a boy out of it. That was the custom.

He looked again at the big ballroom. The warehouse was swept and garnished and bright with color. It was a most perfect party—and he was as much a part of it as if he had never been there.

Forlorn and alone he drifted along the walls until he stood alongside the alcove which held the punchbowl. Given encouragement he might have come out of his shell, but he was too unskilled to demand his fair share of dances from Mary, or, failing that, to draw out any of the young ladies who shared the wall with him. He envied the bright talk and the laughter which drifted to him in snatches from the alcove.

Then, inevitably, he overheard the worst about himself.

He wasn't the main subject of conversation, not by any manner of means. People were falling in or out of love every few minutes as overheard by the involuntary eavesdropper. It was only when his Mary appeared, warm and flushed, with three or four would-be partners trailing along with her, that he heard what his generation thought of him.

"You're with the schoolboy?" asked Philip Holmes, whose property was no more than slave quarters as compared with Happy Return.

"La," said Mistress Mary with an upturn of eyes. " 'Tis purely a question for the future. My mother and his grandmother hope for the best and hopefully fear the worst."

There was a roar of laughter from the group which had collected about them.

'What would he do if the worst were presented to him?" asked a reckless soul. Then, as he saw from Mary's conventionally shocked expression that he had gone too far, " 'Ods body, he would conjugate *amo, amas, amat* and deem it a pantingly passionate offer of marriage."

"He could do the conjugating even if he didn't realize the implications," chuckled a militiaman on leave from the harbor batteries. "The man has fame of a sort. The oldest schoolboy in the state is assuredly a reputation to be lived up to. I reckon he'll be champion too in the number of birchings he receives.

10

I'd have been willing to match him on that, but only some years ago."

"Better watch yourself," said another, whom Jim recognized as an old schoolmate. "If Master Blackthorne should hear what you've said he might wear out his cane upon Master Cheston's hide to prove you wrong and make him champion for all everlasting. The old man's right fond of him. He might want to do one last favor for his petted pupil."

"Well, champion or no champion, Master Cheston leaves us with Mistress Mary," broke in another, also in militia uniform. "Reckon we all owe him our thanks for that."

Jim never knew which fool it was that clapped his hands and set them all to clapping. Through the pain and disappointment he saw Mary standing with a half-smile of gratified vanity on her face. "You are awarded the next minuet," she said and led the militiaman from the alcove.

Before the others could disperse Jim strode in among them. "You've talked a little too free," he said. "You'd have done better to have looked first in the corner." He turned upon the one he resented most. "I'll conjugate it for you. *Amo, amas, amat*, does that suit you as well as—this?" He slapped the other across the face and watched the fingermarks spring out and then fade upon the cheek. "Sword or pistols, I'll be waiting for you."

It left them gaping until they remembered who he was. Then there was more laughter, cruel and biting. "It came pretty close to the truth, didn't it, Cheston? He's going to duel with you, Tom. You better guard yourself close, a chalked ferrule is a pretty deadly weapon." And a scornful voice crying, "Get out of here, schoolboy, or you may get hurt."

Jim faced them, but the mob urge was stirring. Though they might talk contemptuously, he had shocked them and they were reverting to their own schoolboy instincts, reinforcing their contempt by their numbers.

Then there came a drawling voice from the back of the alcove where the servants had retreated.

"Seems to me that this gentleman has a good deal to say on his side."

It was a battered officer in the buff and blue of the Continental Line. Propping him up was a crutch. He shook himself

11

free of the frightened Negroes and bowed as well as he could to Jim.

"Your name, sir?"

The question steadied Jim, brought him from blind rage to determination.

"James Cheston, sir," he replied.

"Not the son of Captain Cheston of the Maryland Line?"

"Yes."

The drawling voice subtly hardened. "Then, gentlemen, if this schoolboy chooses to be a schoolboy even if he must maintain his right to education with sword or pistols, it seems to me he is quite right in his contention. A challenge was passed. I heard it. If Mr. Cheston will have me for his second for his father's sake, I would admire to hear which one of you will second your man."

There was a dead silence. Duels were sufficiently uncommon as to be left almost entirely to the elders. Jim's challenge with so formidable a backer rocked the group upon its collective heels. A peacemaker, remembering what his family would think, rushed into the breach.

"We didn't know, sir, that Jim would take it so hard. An apology . . ."

"A most complete apology and from all of you," said the drawling voice.

Jim got the apology and was left alone with his new friend. He turned to give his thanks but the crutch was stumping out of the room.

"Don't want to hear any more, don't want to have thanks. Your father was my company commander. I left him when the British overran us. Yes, I had the use of my legs then and I was right quick to use them after the third charge. Just tell him if he ever comes back that Ensign Wilson got shot afterwards at White Plains, and that time I didn't run."

Jim had too much good sense to follow. He went back to propping up the wall until the ball was over. Mary had her dance and she didn't dance too often subsequently—not with Jim glowering from the side. She complained a little, riding back on Ladybird, but he didn't say much and she must have been aware that something had happened. Probably she was wondering why she should have been so popular at first and

12

so ignominiously unpopular afterwards. He saw her to her door without explaining, and in a sort of glum elation rode back to the corner of the street where the school was situated. There he dismounted and handed the reins to Caesar.

"You have a good time, Marse Jim?"

"A right good time, Caesar, but now I'm going back to school."

And, treading quietly so as not to wake anybody, he walked to Master Blackthorne's door.

II

Master Blackthorne finished his exposition of the philosophy of John Locke, set his book down upon his knees and looked under his brows at his inattentive pupil.

"James, I might ask you to argue *per contra* had I thought you had listened to a single word."

Jim straightened his slumping backbone. "I'm sorry, sir," was all he could say. He could not have repeated for the life of him anything Master Blackthorne had set forth.

The old schoolmaster rubbed his hands slowly together, his face immobile.

"I gave you yesterday a purging dose of the propositions of Euclid that you might rid yourself of the notions you acquired at that ball. You solved three out of ten, though we considered the subject two years ago. I have had great patience with you, James, but my patience is at an end." The Scots burr was becoming predominant. "Ye'll follow me to my parlor."

Jim looked at him with an open mouth. The pedagogue had given the sentence of execution. Was he mad? It was three years since the last caning. Did he expect Jim at nineteen to submit to being whacked like a grubby-nosed "Yessir-Nosir"? By God he wouldn't stand for it—but he was following Master Blackthorne.

They were in the parlor now with the doors shut and Master Blackthorne was selecting a cane. "Your coat, James, off with

13

it and hang it over the chair." There was no compromise in the assured voice and Jim obeyed in spite of himself. He stood like a bullock, blazing with anger and humiliation but held immobile and helpless by two restraints which he did not stop to analyze. One was the habit of obedience ingrained in him by these past years, the other, more subtle, the honest respect and affection he held for his master.

"Thwack!" the hazel rod whistled down upon his shirt. They were standing before a wide window which opened upon the street, but hardly a passer-by turned his head. The sight of a schoolboy being basted was too common to warrant any attention.

"Shift ye a pace to the right, James," directed the pedagogue in a level tone. "The light is over bright and I would not welt you too grievous."

The hazel rod splatted again upon the cloth but Jim was bewildered. Surely either he had overrated his memories of previous thwackings or age was overtaking Master Blackthorne. These were hardly more than taps.

"This is a beating withouten warranty, James Cheston. Yet there's reason for it, reason for it," cackled the schoolmaster. "Ye'll keep in mind that I stand to you *in loco parentis.*"

For the third time the cane tapped him, then it sailed into a corner and Master Blackthorne grasped his arm and pulled him around.

"Does that assure you the birching championship?" he asked, a trace too fiercely.

"Championship?" wondered Jim. Now where the devil did he hear of that?

"Is it strange, lad?" inquired the master with the glimmering of a smile. "Ye need not think that I have of a sudden gone mad and rush into the streets for aid to restrain me, though upon my soul forty years of instructing the young has sent me parlous near to that state. Did you not think that people would talk? Did you not think that the tale of your fierceness in that alcove would not reach the parents of those overgrown louts you defied and send those same parents to me in a fright to know if you were a devil—or merely a high-spirited lad?"

He went over to the secretary and made a selection from a formidable bunch of keys which he drew from his pocket. Inserting one in the lock he opened the door and exhibited an array of bottles and glasses.

"This is my private cabinet, d'ye see, not the one where I keep refreshment for my ordinary visitors. Here is consolation in moderation whereby I do thank the vintners for the first and the Scots Kirk for the second. Here is brandy, Monongahela whiskey, and a single flagon of *usquebaugh* which I'll uncork for this occasion."

Setting out the bottle and the glasses, his conscience overtook him. He darted a cautionary glance at Jim. "One stoup and one stoup only, lad. I wouldna' stun ye."

He poured the liquor and touched glasses in a toast. "Ou aye, a bloody-minded laddie ye are indeed. A fine defender of education you made yourself, and, had you but known it, all unnecessarily. You may have noticed that I've not been too cheerful of late. Your grandmother wrote me that she'd call for you this noon."

Master Blackthorne had shed his pedagogical shell. Beneath the vanished armor was a man, patient, self-governing, even a little sentimental. He mustered his voice to steadiness as he continued:

"Your school days are over, James."

His bright eyes were humorous and all his wrinkles were kindly. "I've had Mamie pack and cord your trunk for you. 'Deed it is just as well that you leave me, for I fear I've made myself as much of a fire-eater as you in coming to your defence." He drank down his liquor at one gulp and chuckled as Jim choked and gasped over his.

"Oh, laddie, laddie, I should be angry at you but I canna' be. Here was I, doddering fool that I am, cautioning you against the gambling and you calling for sword and pistols! It takes me back to my own youth and my own folly."

Jim had heroically swallowed the *usquebaugh* but he nearly missed the table in setting down the glass. Old dry-as-dust talking about youth and folly? What did he know about either as applied to himself? Master Blackthorne was allowing himself another touch from the bottle.

"I was in the '45, lad, and I followed Prince Charlie, though I was well-spoken of as a rising advocate. Call me a fool if ye will but I couldna' see the good cause go down and me strike no

15

blow for it. After Culloden I was taken prisoner. It was all my friends could do to have me sent out here as an indentured servant, and not to the West Indies to slave my life awa'."

Jim stared, but believed. The little, dried body had taken on blood and force, the voice had almost challenged.

"I'm sorry, sir, real sorry."

Master Blackthorne shrugged his shoulders and in so doing relapsed into his humbler self. He drew his chair up to that of his pupil and tapped him confidentially on the chest.

"Aye, lad, you're sorry and I am grateful for it. Many people are sorry for you, James. It is very pathetic—your dear mother dead and your father a prisoner—but you must not be sorry for yourself. You must *never* be sorry for yourself. Never whine, lad, never whine, else you'll find yourself friendless." He rubbed his hands together. "Ye've made a good beginning, though I should not be the one to tell you. Ye've made some others sorry for themselves."

There was a clatter of hooves and a grind of wheels from the street and he started guiltily.

"I had forgotten the hour. 'Tis your grandmother come for ye."

Master Blackthorne scurried about hiding the glasses and the bottle in his cabinet while Jim looked out through the window. The dusty street was filling with Grandmother Dorsey's arrival. Two outriders, tall Negroes in blue liveries and mounted upon gray horses, trotted ahead and shouted warnings to any pedestrian who might be endangered by the ponderous coach which looked like a blue-and-white house set upon wheels. It was drawn by more grays, four of them—heavy, powerful animals matched to a hair, whose silver-mounted harness winked back at the sun and at the statuesque coachman and footman side by side upon the box. Another outrider brought up the rear except for a rabble of little boys who ran shouting and capering behind.

The coach ground to a halt and his grandmother thrust her head from one of the side windows.

Grandmother Dorsey matched perfectly the splendor with which she surrounded herself. She sat as tall and as straight as a grenadier in spite of her seventy years, and her complexion

16

was as young and pinkish as that of his own dead mother whose mother she was. Although her own hair was snowy she invariably wore over it a white wig, flared out and powdered in the old-fashioned style. Now she was busy giving orders.

"Jupiter, lower the steps and then in with you and bring out Master James' trunk. Augustus, your horse is smearing your livery with his foam. Give him to Moses to hold and carry in this case of wine to Master Blackthorne with my compliments. It will not save you from having to clean your clothes tonight, but I hope it will save me from feeling that I am utterly surrounded by incompetence." Her tongue was far more savage than her nature, and there were few within ten miles of Happy Return who had not shared in her goodwill and wide-flung charity. Even the humbled Augustus said no more than "I'se sorry, Mist'ess," as he picked up the wine in his brawny arms and transported it across the rutted space to the schoolhouse door.

Jim ran out and kissed her. Grandmother Dorsey was swift and decisive. "Not so hearty with your kisses, James, I beg of you. There is a certain amount of art in keeping rosebud cheeks at my age and I fear you may mar me. Master Blackthorne, your many kindnesses will not be forgotten, I can assure you. James, you may join me, but first wipe your boots. I have no intention of transporting Baltimore dust eighteen miles into the country where we have an abundance of our own. Is the trunk safe stowed? Now be quick with your farewells, for I will not have my horses catch cold from standing heated while we chatter uselessly."

There was time for no more than a swift handclasp with Master Blackthorne, who trumpeted into the handkerchief to hide his emotion; then the steps were folded up and the horses given their heads. The streets resounded with the roll and the rattle echoing back from the house fronts.

Baltimore householders ran occasionally to brick in their dwellings, more often to wood painted white, blue, or yellow, but they had a tendency to climb skyward even to four stories. Passing a familiar one of these, Grandmother Dorsey caught her grandson's unwilling eye.

"How is Mistress Mary Raeburn?"

Jim scowled. "I don't know," he answered shortly.

17

Grandmother Dorsey scorched him with a look. "Here is no language to me!" Then she relented. "Yet you had provocation, as I heard. Damme!" she snapped suddenly. "The girl's a chit!"

"Lord!" said Jim to himself. "She's heard too. Can you keep any secret in Baltimore?"

He wondered miserably what sort of a wigging to expect, but Grandmother forbore to bother him further, occupying herself instead with stately bowings of her head to the solemn salutes of such old friends as she chanced to espy in passing. Meanwhile she kept up a running comment.

"Will Paca walking with an assured tread and the uptilted chin of a statesman now that he is in Congress. How changed his manner since election! And there is Anne Rideout in pink satin, tambour muslin and Brussels lace, unprettily arranged. She has her slavegirl behind her to carry her umbrella. No rain in sight and the worst drought in years but if her clothes fail to astonish, then perhaps that rag and stick contrivance may do it for her. The wise man will keep his eyes on the umbrella and pass over Anne."

Soon they were clearing the town and the road was growing rougher. Conversation would become impossible, for each time a wheel fell into a rut or struck a rise the passengers must cling to the leather supports which dangled from the roof or run the risk of being thrown to the floor. Even now she must half shout to be heard over the hooves and the creaking.

"It seems to me, James, that you were in high feather last week at the chance of going to the ball at William Sterrit's. Now you turn up your nose when you pass the Raeburns' house. Didn't you escort Mary Raeburn?"

"Yes, Grandmother," said Jim. He was pretty sure she knew all about it. This was merely the Grand Inquisitor asking a few preliminary questions.

"Did you send her the invitation on the Queen of Hearts as I told you?"

He nodded. "The horses were well turned-out too," he added with defiance.

Grandmother Dorsey half smiled. "You needn't be so firm with me, James." The keen old eyes invited confidence. "Tell me, if you like, though it's something I won't press.

18

Did you pick a quarrel with her at the ball or she with you?"

Jim looked away. "It wasn't her fault. Looks like she didn't want to go at all," he said.

Grandmother's teeth snapped together audibly. "You've answered like a gentleman, James. I had wondered if a squabble could account for everything I've heard, though I did not believe it. Looks to me as if fine blood has produced a pretty scrawny filly. It can happen both with people and horses." Her voice dropped until he could hardly hear her over the noise of the coach. "I'm the one to blame. Yes, I had heard some of the talk from older people before the ball but they are gentler than young ones. That is why I had planned to take you away from school."

She thrust her head out of the window and adjured Augustus with unaccustomed ferocity to sit straight and not slouch in his saddle like a sack of grain. When she sat back her whole manner had changed. It was almost as if she were pleading with her grandson.

"I have kept you beside me too long, James. When your mother—" She paused and then went on firmly. "I was wrong and I see it now. I should have left you to fend for yourself as a man should."

"It's all right," said Jim awkwardly. He hated to see her punish herself like this.

"Thank you, Grandson. You are more like your father than you realize. He used to stick out his lower lip that same way when he wasn't going to be pushed any further. Seems to me you've shown that you can be pushed just so far. I stayed last night with the McKims and I heard a story much to your credit, according to young Henry whose one sorrow was that he couldn't be there to act as your second. It was probably just as well, since this Ensign Wilson seemed thoroughly competent for the job. After that I entertained in procession the mothers of Baltimore whose offspring you had trompled on. It's a curious part of human nature that if some woman's son gets himself into trouble through picking on somebody who looks harmless, the woman screeches that it's all the harmless one's fault. I lost some acquaintances last night but I surely got a relief from my feelings."

She spread out a fan and made a couple of swift strokes to hide her face. Jim didn't say anything. There didn't seem to be much he could say.

"Trouble is," said Grandmother after a while, "you've been too fierce too young. They're not going to forget that for a year or so, but sooner or later some young fool is going to quarrel with you over the wine or the cards and he's going to be afraid to back down, just because of your reputation. Then you've really got to fight. If you go out and fend for yourself away from Baltimore for a spell they're going to forget the quarrelsome part and only remember that you bore yourself pretty much as a man."

The coach pitched like a schooner and she clasped the dangling leather just in time. The road had taken charge and Jim could not ask any question. They drove on their way, Grandmother Dorsey alternately peering at him and then at the condition of her horses. He was consumed with curiosity. Ever since his father marched away with Smallwood's battalion his duty had been to his grandmother, but her dominance had become irksome even though he would not have admitted it to any third person. Still he was bound by his father's last command, which was to obey her.

How was he to fend for himself as Grandmother had said? The army? He had wanted to join, but on that Grandmother had been adamant. Not until he was twenty-one could he go into the Maryland Line. She had made him promise that. She had given her son-in-law to his country, she had said. She would give her grandson too if it were necessary, but not until he was a man grown and ready to stand campaigning. Grandfather Dorsey had been in Amherst's army and he had talked in his sleep sometimes—or that was the way she put it. She must have heard some unexpurgated tales. What else was there? If it was to learn farming and horse-breeding and to squire girls like other young Marylanders did who hadn't gone to war, he would rebel—especially against squiring girls. Of that he was certain. Mary Raeburn had broken his heart and he wasn't going to trail around after others like a nice little lapdog.

Then Grandmother shouted an order to her coachman and

the cavalcade turned into a tavern, the kind you'd meet with on any road and which served also as a resthouse.

It was a fairly substantial one of close-mortised stone, two stories high with windows deep enough to be embrasures, an ell for a kitchen and the long range of sheds which served as stables forming a yard behind it. He didn't recollect ever having stopped here before.

Grandmother stepped out of the coach and met the proprietor, a long, shambling man in a once-white apron. She looked at the apron and sniffed audibly.

"John Tendergrass, see that my horses and my men are fed."

Her order was acknowledged by a brief nod accompanied by a smile that was hardly more than a lip-wrinkle. The proprietor showed them in to the whitewashed main room, indicated a couple of chairs, and shuffled out towards the kitchen, leaving Jim staring amusedly at his grandmother.

"What was it you called him—Tendergrass?"

"Certainly, James. It is a perfectly respectable and respected name, but it requires a courageous man to bear it."

"He seems a sour fellow."

"Not sour, but shy." She chuckled a little. "Now that I think of it perhaps it is the name that makes him so."

John Tendergrass came back into the room. Jim saw with amusement that he had changed the soiled apron for a clean one.

"What'll you eat?" he asked, in what was meant for a pleasant invitation but which sounded more like a doorhinge squeaking. Grandmother Dorsey snorted.

"You've kept this tavern for ten years and you've never offered me anything else but cornbread and fried pork. Why waste words, man?"

"This time we got boiled pork," announced the proprietor drily.

Jim spluttered with laughter but Grandmother drew closer to Tendergrass and sniffed suspiciously.

"High time you made a change," she said.

"Reckon you're right, Miz Dorsey, in more ways than one. Shall I fetch it in to you?" The proprietor winked solemnly at the surprised Jim. "Just to show you how progressive I'm a-gettin', I'll fetch some boiled greens along with it."

Grandmother Dorsey stood up in her place like a frigate's topmast. "John Tendergrass!" she thundered. "Have you been drinking?"

The proprietor shook his head solemnly. "No ma'am. Reckon I'm a little above myself. I'm going to Kaintuckee."

There was something about the way he said it that disarmed Grandmother. Her rage dropped from her.

"Kaintuckee!" she exclaimed. "When you came here ten years ago you said you were on your way to the Shenandoah valley and stopped to rest your team. Your team should be well rested if it hasn't died of old age."

Tendergrass agreed gravely. "I advances step by step," he said. "I'm that kind of a man."

Grandmother paid no attention. "Now you're talking about going to Kaintuckee! I've heard a little about that country across the mountains. Those hunters Daniel Boone and James Harrod and some others have been traipsing around there the last few years, one hand on a rifle and the other on the top of their heads to be sure the scalp is still there. A fine country indeed!"

"So I've heared, Miz Dorsey," answered Tendergrass with a totally different inflection. "A real fine country with black, rich soil, plenty game and plenty timber. Well-watered too."

"And jam-pack with Indians! The Cherokees are bad enough but the Shawanoes are worse, and yet neither of them has been able to hold the land against the other."

"Yes ma'am, but I got a wife and two children to fend for and I reckon I can better myself out there. My farm ain't much and I'd never be able to make a crop if it wasn't for this here tavern. Seems to me I got a duty to better myself for my children's sake. Don't seem right somehow for a bunch of indins to keep all that rich land and use it only now and then for huntin' over."

"But I keep telling you those indians are mighty dangerous!"

"Miz Dorsey, I ain't so harmless myself when I got a rifle and an axe."

Grandmother sat down and folded her hands in front of her. Jim watched her with interest. He'd never seen her like this. She looked like the judge down in the courthouse, only she seemed to have a queer mixture of respect and anxiety in her face.

"I've always liked you, Tendergrass," she said in the deep, considering voice she used when she was talking seriously with men. "There's a lot more to you than I ever suspected—if you really mean this. But you never got those stories about Kaintuckee from anybody living around here."

"No ma'am, I did not," answered the proprietor respectfully. "Of course I've heard a word here and there from travellers who've stopped, but the most of it I got from a feller named Loudy Jack Timms who stayed here a couple of nights. He says he got his name 'cause he was born in Loudon County, Virginia, but I reckon if you listen to him you can judge the truth of it. Never heared a man talk so!"

"And you believed him?"

"Only part way, ma'am. Even a braggart may have a word or so of truth in him. Seems that Boone and Harrod and Logan an' a few others are back in Kaintuckee to stay. They've planted settlements and cleared fields an' they're tryin' to make a crop though the indins rage against 'em cruel. There's Boonesborough now and Harrodsburg and . . ."

Grandmother slapped her hand upon the table like a man. She pointed to Jim. "Boonesborough! This boy's father has land near there."

Jim exclaimed in astonishment, "He has? I never heard him speak of it."

"Probably he never thought to mention it. He bought it as a speculation in the Henderson Patent when Boone first opened the Wilderness Road."

She meditated, chin on fist, Tendergrass standing silently in front of her, while a riot of excitement boiled up in Jim's brain. Kaintuckee! Master Blackthorne had talked about it one night when he had temporarily relaxed from his pedagogical severity and for once had thrust aside the geography of Greece and Rome. The carelessly mentioned names, brought again to mind, trumpeted adventure. Kaintuckee—rightly or wrongly he had been told that it meant "the dark and bloody ground"; the "Wilderness Road"; "Rockcastle"—was that a town, now, or the name for a district; "Boonesborough"—the vision of a mighty wooden fortress looming defiantly above a lowering

23

forest. Other phrases, just heard, trooped up, "plenty game and plenty timber," "jam-pack with indians." And now to find that his father owned land there!

Grandmother Dorsey was looking at him through narrowed eyes. "Your father owns the land, lad, not you. If you're doing like John Tendergrass and reaching for a musket and a tomahawk, then lay them aside. You're not going to Kaintuckee. Furthermore you'll learn a lesson by not believing all you hear, particularly from such gentry as this Loudy Jack Timms who you'll never see and never hear of again."

Then John Tendergrass said a surprising thing. "Beg pardon, ma'am, but the boy is goin' to see him an' right soon. When he left here this morning he was bound for your place Happy Return 'cause he had a message for you."

Grandmother fairly jumped. "A message for me? And pray tell me who this message is from?"

"I don't know for sure, Miz Dorsey, but he let drop that he was workin' for this boy's uncle, Treville Cheston, who's settled down on the Holston River in southwest Virginia. Seems that Mr. Cheston is aimin' to go to Kaintuckee to see about takin' up some lands for his own self an' he's gatherin' a company to go up the Wilderness Road with him. Matter of fact I'm thinking of trailin' along."

Grandmother Dorsey's mouth set tight.

"And I suppose he also let drop that James Cheston's uncle wanted James to go too?"

Tendergress nodded gravely. "Yes, ma'am, he did make mention of something just like that."

III

Loudy Jack Timms was waiting for them when the coach reached Happy Return. All the way down the long, maple-lined driveway, with the leaves showing silver bellies to the breeze, Jim had been searching for him. But he was heard before he was seen. The clack of his voice was plain as the

24

team slowed under the big copper beech which shaded the entrance. He rose from a cluster of Negro servants and pickaninnies, striding to meet them with an easy, swinging walk. He was a fairly tall man, a trifle bald, with the tan spilling high from his face into the temple patches. Either from habit or from a weakness in his sight he carried his head perpetually uptilted, as if he were stepping high through a tangle of fallen timber and were watching out for branches.

But what immediately fascinated Jim was his dress. He wore a fringed and beaded frock of buckskin which stretched almost to his knees and was girded in by a broad leather belt, from which hung a powderhorn, a knife, a hatchet and a collection of small pouches, all more or less blackened by handling. Buckskin leggings tied by beaded thongs ended in moccasins so encrusted with the same bright beadwork that they resembled red leather. Neither he nor his dress was particularly clean and he smelled faintly of woodsmoke, grease and sweat. He seemed very conscious of his appearance, giving little sideways glances to see that he was appreciated, and fondling the long rifle which he carried in the crook of his arm.

He swept off his coonskin cap and gave an uncouth bow. His assurance was fortified by a loud voice and by a booming laugh which shook him all over when he let it loose as he was doing now.

"I'm right glad to see you, Miz Dorsey, an' right glad too to see that boy with you who I reckon is Jim Cheston. I've come a long way for you, Jim, so's you and me can go back and shoot some indins."

Jim blushed red at this patronizing bellow. Then he stifled his resentment. If he wanted to step out on the road to adventure he couldn't be too persnickety about his guide. It was Grandmother Dorsey who answered for him.

"It is my impression that the indians unfortunately have a nasty habit of shooting back."

Loudy Jack tilted back his cap, which he had already replaced. "Well they do, ma'am. Yes they do now and then, but us frontiersmen we gets used to it. I'm Jack Timms, ma'am."

"Loudy Jack?"

"Yes ma'am, yes ma'am. They name me that every now an' again 'cause of where I come from, down in Virginia."

"Of course," said Grandmother Dorsey in a smooth purr. "I hear you have a letter for me?"

"So I do, an' while you're readin' it an' thinkin' it over I'll take Jim here an' show him something his Uncle Trev sent him."

Grandmother climbed out of the coach, and the man handed her a letter which he took from one of his pendant pouches. She spoke to Jim and not to Timms.

"I am interested to see what this present is. Your Uncle Treville is capable of very odd generosity. His wedding gift to your father, as I recollect it, was a bale of dressed deerskins. I hope and trust that this won't be another example of border humor or of border taste."

"Haw, haw, haw!" the laugh boomed out and set the Negroes to chuckling sympathetically. "No ma'am, 'tain't that, though I reckon Trev was a-bragging just a bit when he sent that bale. 'Tain't every hunter that could kill enough deer to make one up. Trev's an awful good hunter, just about the best there is. What he did send was a rifle, a reg'lar Kaintuckee rifle jus' like this one 'ceptin' it's got a plain stock without these fufarraws I worked into mine." He turned his weapon to show the silver stars sunk into the wood. "Want to have a look at her, Jim?"

Jim was familiar with firearms and had heard of those famous rifles. For the moment his enthusiasm over the thought of owning one submerged his embarrassment at Loudy's overheartiness.

Grandmother Dorsey darted a commanding glance at her coachman, who was relaxed and grinning on the box while the footman was edging forward to see better. Whatever was going on, her horses were not to be left standing, and the coachman hastily straightened his shoulders and picked up the reins. The coach rumbled off and she came around with a stately swirl of skirts. One glimpse of the bottled eagerness on Jim's face and she relented, leaving unsaid what she had had on her tongue's end.

"Of course he wants to see it. Take it, James, and I'll read your uncle's letter while you're looking it over." Her youthful smile stole back. "Also you had better try it out. Of what use is a rifle unless it is fired? But I beg of you to remember that my horses are famous and my cattle almost equally so. Have a care when it comes to moving targets."

"Oh, ma'am," said Loudy Jack, overcome by mirth. "He won't shoot no horse or no cow with me along."

"I gave him the warning only because you were along," answered Grandmother Dorsey in a tone of sweetened vitriol, and she went on into the house without looking back.

"She's a puzzlin' lady,' said Timms unabashed, and went over to his pack.

The new rifle was in a buckskin case and he drew it forth with proper reverence. The browned barrel was supported by wood almost to the muzzle, while the stock curved downwards so as to bring the line of sight nearer to the eye. When Jim, taking it eagerly, happened to lower the butt to the ground the muzzle came as high as his chin. Holding it there while he listened to Timms' explanations he crossed his hands over it, unconsciously assuming the classic posture of the borderer whose rifle also served him as a staff upon which to rest.

Loudy Jack was quick to notice and roar approval.

"We'll make a hunter of you yet, boy. You'll stand thataway many's the day and look for game across some hollow. It's a lovely piece, much better'n a musket. It'll carry further an' hit a lot closeter to where you aim. Right name of it's a Deckard. They're made in Pennsylvania for the Kaintuckee trade. Now heft it, Jim."

Jim weighed it and found it amazingly light for the long length of it. Loudy laughed again.

"It makes a right handy club if you've fired and hain't got the time to reload. You can kill an indin or a bear or a catamount thataway. I tell you I know. Now let's try a shot or so with her. Where's the best place?"

"Down by the springhouse," said Jim. "It's in a dip that'll stop a bullet."

Privately he was wondering just how many "indins, bears and catamounts" Loudy Jack had mowed down with his clubbed rifle. Jim was no fool, and in spite of the newcomer's novelty and self-confidence, he was beginning to put a good peck of salt on whatever he said.

Jim had to admit, however, that Loudy did walk quietly in

27

spite of his flood of talk, more quietly than Jim himself could with his city boots on; but he resented it when Loudy told him in front of a half dozen Negroes who had trailed along that he'd have to walk a lot quieter than that in the woods. He'd shot deer himself and had been on a couple of hunting trips, so he wasn't such a raw ignoramus as Timms made out. Then he watched the way Loudy put down his feet, not breaking a single twig and not squelching at all in the marshy spot near the branch, and he realized that he had much to learn.

His enthusiasm was rearoused when Loudy showed him how to load. "First you put in your powder. They's people do that with a measurin' cup but you can't stop for that when they's game about, so you got to judge with your eye just how much to put. Now you wraps your bullet in a greased scrap of cloth—we calls it a 'patch'—and then you rams it home. No, no, not so hard! Just use force enough to let it grip the grooves in the riflin'."

Step by step he made Jim go through the motions, discoursing loudly on how to "pick" a flint so that it would be sharp and give off a good spark when the pull of the trigger sent it down on the steel of the lock. The priming must lie just so in the pan, so the spark would ignite it and thereby fire the main charge. There was a torrent of other comments and precepts. How, if your rifle missed fire, to snap the trigger several times in the hope that the charge would finally catch and the weapon "fire clear"; how to draw powder and ball if your rifle got wet in crossing a stream or in damp weather—until Jim got back a certain amount of respect for him as an obviously knowledgeful rifleman.

Best of all was when Jim cuddled the stock to his shoulder, the sights lining up, and heard the sharp cracking report so different from the bellow of the old familiar musket.

"She's nice, ain't she?" said Loudy, who seemed to appreciate how he felt. "Now when Trev shows you some game, you'll know what to do about it."

"Will it kill a buffalo?" asked Jim after several shots. The bullet seemed so small after the heavy slugs he was used to.

"Surely. Trev'll teach you how to hunt one. I tell you he's a mighty good hunter. Why he's even better'n me."

They were walking back to the house, the rifle having been

28

carefully wiped, while the Negroes followed chattering and ump-umming over the new firearm. Loudy was lounging along in high good humor. Jim had come to like him more, but he couldn't keep from asking him a sly question.

"Have you ever shot a buffalo, Loudy Jack?"

"A buffler? Well, now, you've got bufflers in Kaintuckee but there ain't none 'round the Holston River settlements where we've been livin'. Leastways if there were they've been shot out."

Timms was flushing under his tan and Jim felt a twinge of compunction. If this fellow didn't know he was a braggart it wasn't his place to tell him so. He asked a quick question about shooting with so much deference that Loudy's good humor was restored.

"Yes, Jim, you're right there. You've sure got to be able to shoot good on the border or else get laughed at plenty. Don't you miss no squirrels less'n you wants to set up the liquor for every man who sees you. I'll show you how to hit 'em."

Jim smiled again. Uncle Trev was going to teach him to hunt buffalo while Loudy Jack would attend to the squirrels.

Grandmother Dorsey had arranged that Loudy stay with the overseer, but she was waiting for them in the high, shadowy library with its rows of calf-bound books. She looked very grave, and got rid of Loudy as quickly as she could and with less than her usual courtesy. Then she sat down next to the big table and fluttered Uncle Treville's letter in her fingers. Her face was very thoughtful and Jim noticed that her eyes were red. It startled him.

"Grandmother," he asked in quick alarm, "how're you feeling?"

"Not so good that I'd set out for a ball and not so bad that I'd begin taking more than a middling interest in the cemetery," she replied, and walked over to the window where she stood looking out at the fading sunset and at the strong young pines which whispered on the lawn. "I persuaded your grandfather to leave those trees be when we built the house," she remarked irrelevantly. "Sometimes I wonder if they don't remember that I did and comfort me because of it. James, do you want to go to Kaintuckee?"

Jim told the truth. "Reckon I do, Grandmother, but I hate to leave you."

"And what of your father?" she shot at him with sudden asperity, and then softened as she saw how she had hurt him.

"I could bite out my tongue," she said. "That was a mean thing to throw in your face."

They sat in a forgiving silence until she gave her deep man-like chuckle. "I was going to exile you to your Virginia cousins down on the Pamunkey."

Jim grimaced. She meant Cousin Oliver and Cousin Anna, whose chief interest seemed to be genealogy. He had visited them before and he had sympathized with the girls, whose parents had always debated the family tree, even unto the fourth generation, of any young man who came a-calling. It had taken plenty of strength of character for them to get husbands for themselves. The son of the family, Cousin Lewis, had stopped by on his way to Washington's army last year. Cousin Lewis had been in a sort of a happy daze like Jim had seen on the face of a freed Negro. When Virginia people decided to be straitlaced they sure could straiten their laces. Involuntarily he drew an anxious breath, and Grandmother chuckled again.

The last of the sunset was gone, and Simon, the butler, came in with the candles. He was descended from a Congo chieftain and looked it, with his dark, sharp-cut face. Jim watched him until he went out and then let his eyes move round the library, where even the lettering on the backs of the books spoke of solidity and comfort. Grandmother Dorsey's voice brought to the surface the current of his thoughts.

"Beads and buckskins, James? Are they better than this? Well, I reckon they are when you're young and haven't had a bridle on you yet. When you're older you'll turn to linen and plate and things done just right. Before that unfortunate ball I had planned that you would stay with me and learn the management of the place, since this will all be yours some day. Well—beads and buckskins and a long rifle have their rightful place too when you've been kept too long at school and have a broken heart into the bargain."

30

Jim felt a rush of shame mingled with hope. "But about Father . . ."

She would not let him finish. "There's no sense in your waiting your life away here for him. If he comes back—" she checked herself so swiftly that Jim hardly grasped the change in words, "when he comes back, a post rider can bear you a message. Meanwhile there's that land near Boonesborough which ought to be seen to. Is it worthless or is it valuable? Now your Uncle Treville is going to Kaintuckee and it is right for you to go with him. I owe you something, James, for nearly strangling you with learning."

Jim took her in his arms but she pushed him away. "It is not easy for me to say this to you, Grandson, but your Uncle Treville has the first call upon you at this stage in your life."

She waved him back to his chair and went on talking, very slowly and seriously.

"You have a right to wonder why I say that. I fear I have sacrificed you to my own fears and I thank you for the patience you have displayed towards an old woman's demands. Your Grandfather Dorsey would have been short with me. He belived that a young man should have his head. A year on the frontier with your Uncle Treville will shape your manhood far better than my clucking care."

She picked up Treville Cheston's letter and Jim heard it rustle in her fingers. "Do you remember your Uncle Treville, James?"

Jim thought hard. "Of course I saw him, but I was just little then. Seems to me he was tall and very kind to me."

"Yes, Treville is a kindly man and fond of children, although given to eccentricities. He was the older son and he got the Cheston place under the will. Your father had been trained for the law and was just starting in to ride the circuit. I'll never forget when he came to me and told me that Treville was putting up Balcombe for sale. Your father was born and raised on Balcombe and he was fond of it. Your Grandfather Cheston and his wife were both buried there too, which made a difference. But that didn't seem to sway Treville at all. He was mad for land speculation."

She seemed to remember the letter all over again, and, holding it to the candle, read a few passages to herself.

31

"He hasn't changed," she said finally, and lighted it in the flame. She carried the blazing paper across to the fireplace and threw it in as if she threw a memory and a regret with it. When she came back to her chair, she was more herself, talking with her usual inflection.

"Land's a funny thing, James. It seems to affect people two ways. Take your Grandfather Dorsey and me. Here's Happy Return. We built it up and we spent our lives making it better. You know the old house; Mr. Bates the overseer uses it now. We built that when we were just married, used my marriage portion to do it with, since your Grandfather was spending his money towards improving the livestock. Thirty years later we put up this house, but we'd planned it when we started the other. That's why we kept the hilltop free. We spent a mighty happy life together, raising cattle and horses. Breeding thoroughbreds takes time—you haven't got more than three animal generations at the most to prove your theories. I recollect when your Grandfather managed to get hold of a daughter of Selima, Governor Tasker's great mare, he was happier than when Lord Amherst made him a Major."

She smiled across at Jim. "Oh yes, the horses are part of the family and if you ask me Selima's got better breeding than we've got and that applies to most of the peerage as well. Her mistakes weren't hushed up—Lord no."

She paused an instant, still smiling. "It made us complete, your Grandfather and me. We put down good strong roots and we allowed to stay. I know your father feels the same way. Happy Return goes to him and then, I know, to you."

Jim was much moved, but he could not stifle that underlying elation—he was going out to see for himself what the world looked like.

Grandmother probably sensed his feeling for she grew more brisk and business-like. "Your Uncle Treville was different. Now buying land is a good thing. That was why I encouraged your father to come in on that Henderson Patent. You can buy it, develop it and sell it again or provide for some of your younger children that way. It's like putting a cargo into a vessel. But—whatever comes out of it must be shared with Happy Return.

"Treville, though, bought and sold land for the joy of it,

like some people are all the time trading horses. He's bought in Pennsylvania, bought in York state, in the Valley of Virginia, in North Carolina, and now apparently he's having a look at Kaintuckee. He hasn't kept land, hasn't developed it, and what he's got out of one he puts into the next. He leads a gypsy life and he's collected about him the oddest set of humans I ever heard of. Your father told me that and I thought maybe I'd better discount what he said a trifle until I saw this Timms, who's one of them. Wherever Treville has been, there he's picked up some hanger-on who tells him what a great man he is and waits around for hog and hominy when feeding time comes. Treville isn't an utter fool. He probably knew at first what was going on, but Treville's a masterful man and when you're told day in and day out that you're the finest fellow ever foaled and know everything—well, after a while you begin to believe it."

She stopped abruptly. "I'll talk myself out of letting you go," she said. "No, we'll try it for a year and see what it does for you." Then she laughed outright. "I reckon a year even with Treville is more to your taste than a year with Cousin Oliver."

She was right. Jim knew that Uncle Treville appealed to him a lot more than Grandmother Dorsey's doubts should have permitted. It seemed to him that Uncle Trev was leading a pretty free life, and after all Loudy Jack might be the exception among his followers. The others might be better than her prejudice would grant.

Grandmother was grave again. She was either angry or sad and he couldn't tell just which one it was.

"This Loudy Jack starts for the Holston settlements day after tomorrow and you shall leave with him. At least you'll have John Tendergrass for company."

"John Tendergrass!" exclaimed Jim in spite of himself. "He isn't quite my idea of a borderer."

"That same John Tendergrass in my judgment is twice the man Timms is or ever will be. I have been considering Tendergrass since I met him this evening and the more I consider the less respect I have for myself for underrating him. I've written him and sent Moses at the gallop with the letter. I've asked him to come see me tomorrow."

With a tinge of contempt Jim remembered the creaky voice and the shambling gait. He was even driven to making a slight defence of Loudy Jack, who at least looked like a woodsman. "Loudy Jack isn't so bad. Maybe you've been underrating him too."

"Maybe I have, James, but as far as the Holston settlements you will travel in Tendergrass' care if I can arrange it, even if that Loud fellow must show you the way. We'll outfit you in the morning and I will give you a horse."

With that she closed the subject and began again to talk of land, only in a different way. How to judge it and what to look for in the soil. She made it so interesting that Jim listened harder than duty required but he was conscious of the way she kept looking at him in the candlelight.

It was hard to sleep with Kaintuckee arranged for, when only the night before he'd been still a schoolboy. Except for Grandmother and a few friends, he thought he had nothing to regret leaving behind, not realizing that he was as stupefied with freedom as any man with drink. He gloated, naturally, over Mary Raeburn. By God, he'd shown her at the ball that he wasn't to be trifled with! And when she'd hear that he was going away to the indian country she'd have to admit that he was a lot more dashing fellow than the militiamen and the others who just hung around Baltimore. On that consoling thought, his closing eyes drew a curtain.

He was up early in the morning, but early as he was Grandmother Dorsey was waiting inside and Loudy Jack outside, still talking unabatedly whenever he could get anyone to listen. Grandmother called Loudy in for consultation about the necessary gear (all of which Happy Return could supply from its own resources). Timms was quite airy, saying that outfits like his own could only be obtained upon the frontier itself. Whereupon Grandmother grew tart, and, after cutting a few sound timbers from his wilderness of words, chased him out again. Jim was astonished at the wisdom she showed in the selections and he said so, only to receive a rebuke almost as sharp as she had given Loudy.

"James, your grandfather fought indians, real, wild, hostile indians—not the tavern brand which are the most I credit

Timms with having seen. Being a good wife, which means being a good listener, I have learned quite a lot, especially when your grandfather was on his third bottle of claret. If your uncle, when you arrive, thinks you need buckskins and a smearing of grease then let him give you both of them himself. Meanwhile you'll have linsey shirts and good stout breeches, with a hat instead of a murdered coon which gets its revenge by making you too hot in summer and letting sun and rain into your face for lack of a brim. Out with you, and shoot that rifle of yours to your heart's content. And tell me after a year on the frontier whether or not I'm right. Then, damme, I'll listen to you."

Jim obediently went out to shoot at a mark, so as to learn the allowance he must make for windage and such like technicalities, until John Tendergrass appeared with the message that Grandmother Dorsey wanted to see them at the big house.

"Reckon I'm going with you," he remarked briefly. Then to Jim, "talked to your Grandmother and she and I came to an agreement 'bout certain things. Do my best for you as far as the Holston, but I'm going to stop there and look things over first."

Loudy Jack was listening with pushing curiosity. "Reckon that's all you'll do," he jeered contemptuously. "Not comin' with us to Kaintuckee then, 'spite of all your big talk?"

Tendergrass looked at him from under his brows. "I got a wife an' two younguns to think of. Can't set out to carry them to Kaintuckee less'n I know what it's like."

"How you goin' to know what Kaintuckee's like if you sit on your hunkers on the Holston?" asked Loudy Jack in so irritating a bellow that Jim expected Tendergrass to take measures with his fists. He stepped out of the way and waited.

Tendergrass kept his hands at his sides. "Reckon I can find out about it from somebody on the Holston who's been there." There was no change to his creaky tone but he turned his face partly away.

"Well, I know about it!"

"Seems to me all you've said was that you'd heared about it. Owe it to my wife to get forward step by step an' not push on in regardless."

35

"Wouldn't think you were ever the kind to push," said Loudy with a knowing wink at Jim. "Seems to me pushin' folks always get somewheres."

"Sometimes into a swamp," replied Tendergrass calmly and from then on paid no attention to Timms.

Grandmother Dorsey was waiting for them at the house.

"Timms," she said, and Loudy Jack grinned ingratiatingly, "you brought with you a riding horse and a packhorse. I'm giving you a fresh riding horse in exchange for that broken-down one of yours. You've over-ridden him until he's nearly foundered, but I'll waste another on you. Tendergrass, there's one for you too. We'd best see if they suit."

Loudy Jack looked as if he'd like to have a lot to say. From his expression Jim knew that it was not the gift that mattered. He had adjusted his agile ego into feeling that such tribute was regularly due him. What rankled was the slur on his horsemanship. Grandmother Dorsey, however, had her "warface" on and he knew enough to keep quiet. She stumped ahead of them to the stables, helping herself by a long staff.

Mr. Bates, the overseer, was waiting for them. He was a silent man usually, but an evening in Loudy Jack's company had made him positively morose. At Grandmother's word he brought out two strong farm animals of the type she used for hauling tobacco down to the Patapsco for shipment overseas. After inspection both men were satisfied, Tendergrass really grateful and stammering.

She shook off his thanks. "No more than you deserve if you're going with the boy. Furthermore you can set the pace and keep Mister Timms from galloping the whole of the way, or at least as far as his horse can hold out, and then finishing the trip on foot. Now, James, I've picked one for you."

The breeding stables were separate from those of the farm. Grandmother had once told Jim, with a shrewd laugh, that when she quoted a price to a purchaser she didn't want anything cheaper around so that he could make a quick escape and avoid saying "no" directly. The long, low barns were beautifully kept up, and even now a slave with a hammer was walking along the paddock fences scrutinizing them for projecting nails which might rip a smooth coat.

Jim felt guilty. He hated to take one of Grandmother's racing thoroughbreds which she pampered like children. It was on the tip of his tongue to say so and refuse any such gift, but she walked right past the first range of sheds without stopping. "Justice!" he said to himself and was pleased, for the big, sweet-tempered hunter was his own favorite. He'd expected to have Justice anyway before Grandmother began acting so oddly. The big horse had his head out the half-door and whinnied a greeting, but Grandmother didn't stop here either. She went on to a little ell that stuck out behind from the regular sheds.

Then she spoke to Mr. Bates. "Bring her out!"

What came out was a little half-bred mare, seal brown with a white star and a white stocking on her off hind foot. A little mare who pricked her ears and danced along beside Mr. Bates nipping at his coat. Jim looked at her and at his grandmother as if he didn't believe his eyes. Why, this mare was so small that his feet would almost drag on the ground when he rode her!

Loudy Jack gave his bellowing bray. "Why ma'am, she's a toy like the kids whittle out of cherrywood with their jack-knives. Jim'll have to pull up his feet to cross a molehill. He can put her in his pocket every time she gets tired and rest her thataway as he walks along."

Grandmother Dorsey answered him only with a smile that reminded Jim of the way John Tendergrass did it—a mere wrinkling of the lips. She pointed to the mare and gave her explanation to Jim and the others.

"Her name is Cricket. I bred her for an experiment, James, and, except in size, she hasn't disappointed me. You have been raised among horses, James, not among jackasses like some others. You can't use a big horse like Justice in the wilderness. You've got to have something small and handy, with a lot of endurance, that you can wind in and out among the trees. Did I ever tell you that I visited your grandfather once or twice when he was in camp up Champlain way? That is why I speak from experience. Will you try her?"

The reason might be good—at least he couldn't think of any way to answer, but, just as he had thought, when he mounted his stirrups were much nearer the ground than he had ever ridden before. The mare moved beautifully, but he was think-

37

ing what a ridiculous, gawky sight he must make on top of her and winced at Loudy's shouted amusement.

"Ma'am, she may be all you say, but if Jim opens his legs she'll run right between 'em."

Just at that moment the mare gave a quick sideways leap and whirl. Jim was listening to Loudy, and he shot over her shoulder to land on the grass. She twitched the reins out of his hand and trotted back to the stable, head up and tail out as if she were pleased with herself.

"You told the truth, Mr. Timms," said Grandmother Dorsey with perfect composure. "If he opens his legs she'll run right out from under him. James, may I suggest that you try her again, this time keeping the knees well pressed in and forgetting how you may look. I can tell you that you look far clumsier sprawling on the ground than you do on her back."

It hurt his pride, and when he remounted he was ready for tricks. Feeling his determination she gave in almost at once and he found that she had an easy trot and a comfortable canter. He began to think that he'd been a little ungracious, since he'd heard it said that Grandmother knew more about a horse than any man in Maryland. He admitted it to her as he pulled up.

"General Washington said much the same to me when I met him at Annapolis for the races. He was good enough to include Virginia in his estimate," answered Grandmother calmly. "Now, are you satisfied with her?"

"I am," said Jim, almost meaning it completely.

"Good." She turned away towards the house and propped herself on her stick. "John Tendergrass, be over here tomorrow early, after you have said farewell to your wife and the children. I will keep an eye on them and see that nothing goes wrong. Mr. Timms, my grandson will be down and ready as soon as Tendergrass arrives. See that you leave as soon after dawn as you may. I will say my own farewells to James tonight and I will not see you start. I am an old woman given to sentiment, and you go on a long journey. I will not spoil that beginning by silly tears. So start early!"

She clumped off towards the house while Cricket whickered after her.

IV

It was time to go, for the gray was showing in the east and
the gravel of the drive was crunching under hooves. Jim wasn't
too happy in the chilly, fading darkness. He remembered
vividly Grandmother Dorsey going up the steps the night
before, cupping her hand to shield the candle flame. She had
talked with her decisive, short intonation and hadn't lectured
him long. The last thing she had said stuck in his memory:
"I've tried to raise you as a gentleman, James. It's a fine thing
to be but it takes a lot of patience."

Now she lay abed in the great, dark house, and if she was
giving him a last look through the lattice, he wasn't going to
look for her for he knew that was the way she would want it
to be. Mr. Bates was bringing up Cricket for him and testing
her girths. The butler was holding a candlestick and had clean
forgotten that the light had blown out.

The dawnwind was upsetting the maples again, and family-
minded birds were discussing their problems at the top of their
lungs. The gray was spreading now, showing a dark cluster of
servants against the lighter stone of the back wing. The saddler,
the butler's helper, the dogboy and some of the grooms were
there. Jim swung up on Cricket and leaned down to shake
hands with as many of them as came diffidently forward. John
Tendergrass was changing from a dim shadow to a rather
lumpish figure on a brown horse, and Loudy Jack came out of
the kitchen wiping his mouth on his buckskin sleeve.

"Settle yourselves in your saddles," he commanded. "We got
a long way to go an' we can't linger. Here, Tendergrass, take
this leadrope an' tow the packhorse along with you."

"Just a minute," said Tendergrass, and pushed up to Jim.
"Duck your head, boy."

He slipped the straps holding powderhorn and shotpouch
onto Jim's shoulders and thrust Jim's new rifle into his hands.
It was awkward to handle, and when the butt touched the

mare's side she would have sprung forward had not Mr. Bates kept his grip upon the bridle.

Loudy gave a contemptuous snort. "What you doin' that for, Tendergrass? An' carryin' your own rifle too! Such damn foolishness I never saw! Put 'em on the packhorse an' tote 'em thataway. The youngun will be off'n that mare 'fore he gets half a mile!"

Mr. Bates exploded with so much rancor that his voice sounded like steam bubbling the lid of a kettle. "Hush your mouth! Do you want to wake Mrs. Dorsey?"

Loudy stopped with his mouth open, then bobbed his head and led off down the drive.

Tendergrass took the leadrope, and the four horses went in a bunch between the long rows of maples whose rustling nearly drove Cricket wild. Jim tried to keep her straight but the rifle persistently tangled itself in his reins. Once when she whirled he found himself holding it by the butt while the muzzle trailed in the dirt. From Loudy's renewed roarings he realized that Tendergrass must have been an equally ludicrous sight.

When they turned out upon the main road the mare's antics became worse instead of better. She was determined to go back to her stable and she was as quick as a little blacksnake. A rabbit darting from the bushes finally sent the rifle clattering to the ground while Jim only saved himself from following it by a hasty grab at her mane. Humiliated though he was, he at last had both hands free. Then it was easy to make her behave, with his heels pressed firmly into her sides and a steady, demanding pressure on her mouth. When she gave in disgustedly, he cantered her back to where his companions were waiting.

Timms had picked up the fallen rifle and was examining it with care. " 'Tain't hurt," he said furiously, "but 'twas no fault of yours, throwin' it down like that. Why don't you listen to what I tell you an' get off that worthless horse an' pick it up? You're not fit to carry a fine piece like this."

"Maybe it's because he knows more about horses than you do," said Tendergrass in his rusty voice. "His troubles would have been only beginnin' if he'd given in to that mare. I've been livin' ten years down here in thoroughbred country an' it

40

strikes me that them that raises 'em oughter know how they should be ridden."

Loudy Jack paid no attention. He thrust Jim's rifle under the lashings of the pack which the packhorse carried and whirled upon Tendergrass. Without apology Loudy strode up to his stirrup and grabbed for the rifle which he still gripped.

"Now gimme that an' stop playing' the fool!"

Tendergrass looked down at him and his voice was rustier than ever. "Reckon I wouldn't lay hands on it if I was you," he stated flatly. "It's loaded."

Loudy jerked his arm back and stared. His face grew long, and with his mouth puckering like that of a slapped child he turned to his own horse, mounted and started off, this time taking the packhorse himself. Jim, almost as surprised as Loudy, fell in silently behind.

Maryland in late June wrapped its dust and its perfume about them. The trees were in full leaf, and the crows cawed a warning at the sight of the plodding horses. The three riders kept their silence although they occasionally changed their order of going as one or another of their mounts varied pace. During such a shift Jim found Loudy beside him. Timms spoke in a low tone and pointed. "See there," he said, "there's a dogwood that's a mite uncommon around here though there's a lot of other kinds growing. That's a red osier dogwood, 'kinnikinnick' the indins call it. They cuts off the bark an' dries it. Then they smokes it along with their tobacco as a sort of flavoring."

Jim became interested, particularly as John Tendergrass was riding along saying nothing and the way was getting boring with no one to talk to. Seeing the change in his expression, Loudy pointed again. "There's another tree you probably hain't thought much about. That's a shellbark hickory an' you'll usually find it in higher country than this. Best wood in the world for axe-helves. Put an axe-head on it an' measure off a foot on the handle. Then you got tool an' rule for building the biggest cabin in Kaintuckee. I've seen borderers do things with an axe you'd disbelieve if I told you now."

In the same low voice Loudy went on indicating tree and shrub and plant and explaining their uses. Such a one was a medicine, another made a dye, this one burned with a bright,

41

almost smokeless flame. When they were going through a ravine where the hooves were almost soundless and only their heads showed above ground level, he was the first to see an old dog-fox trotting parallel with them and the first to laugh when the fox sprang into the air at his warning hiss and turned into a red streak vanishing in the brush.

They stopped for their midday meal and Timms again took charge. He fetched wood and built a fire in half the time it would have taken Jim or John Tendergrass. His deftness with the axe was apparent. He seemed to know by instinct just where to cut and the fewest number of strokes necessary to split or shape the log. John Tendergrass, still speaking no unnecessary word, went off to see that the picketed horses did not tangle themselves in their ropes as they grazed, and Loudy Jack seized the opportunity to speak with Jim.

"Now, boy," he said with a deprecatory grin, "you mustn't go jumping to no judgments. Your Uncle Trev he told me to fetch you along safe an' to teach you a mite about the woods whilst I was a-doin' it. I didn't count on no quarrelsome, sullen fellow like this Tendergrass bein' along. I likes young folks an' I likes to show 'em how a borderer lives. But they got to trust me an' not always be doubtin' me an' squinchin' up their eyes at me.

"Now you take that rumpus back there down the road a piece. I was just a-skeered of your being thrown an' hurtin' yourself before we got well started. How would it be if I had had to tell your Uncle Trev that you done busted your arm before we made the first mile an' I had to take you back to your Grandma? Either I'd have had to wait for you to get well or your Uncle Trev might have had to start across Cumberland Gap withouten me an' he needs me bad for a trip like that."

Jim tried to be fair. There was much to be said for Timms' arguments, and he had to nod.

"Take them rifles," resumed Loudy with growing confidence. "I saw you was havin' trouble with the mare because of your'n. An' why should you carry it anyways? There ain't any indins within a hundred miles an' jest because that Tendergrass feller wants to play big hunter an' scout ain't no reason for you to risk a bad fall. When you needs a rifle I'll tell you. You don't

42

see me a-carryin' mine, do you? An' I've lived all my life on the border."

Jim agreed with him about Tendergrass' insistence. Firearms might be carried by travellers, but they were usually kept discreetly hidden or packed with the baggage. Loudy had good grounds for his complaint, and Jim hated to be conspicuous. Yet he hesitated at remonstrating with Tendergrass. The latter had cut no ridiculous figure when he had repelled Timms' attempt at snatching his weapon from him.

When they started Loudy took his place as by right alongside Jim and kept on imparting knowledge. Cricket swung along under her rider, only occasionally lifting her head to snuff the breeze or to jump at some new sound or sight. The gritty dust was on Jim's lips as he listened to Loudy telling him the thousand-and-one things which are a habit to the hunter and raw discovery to the home-bred man. Not all of it was new. Such things as how to "lead" a flying duck before you fired and how to rig a snare for cottontails were part of his own experience, but his knowledge simply served to check the truth of what Loudy was telling him. He felt a lot friendlier towards Timms when the setting sun brought not only the glint of the Potomac but John Tendergrass drifting up from their wake with the suggestion that they seek a place to harbor.

Jim recognized the neighborhood. He knew the Morgans, and their place was near; it never occurred to him not to seek their hospitality. He did not realize how dusty and homespun he looked until a Negro groom pointedly suggested that there was a tavern a mite further up the road. Then he straightened up on Cricket and sent the man scurrying to the house. The "family" happened to be away, but the butler, who was in charge in their absence, recognized his name and admitted him at once.

The dinner was difficult. Tendergrass ate noisily but governed his liquor, whereas Loudy Jack fell afoul of the wine. He swallowed it until he was belchingly confidential, discoursing upon his personal exploits and those of Uncle Trev. The butler finally passed him by with the cloth-wrapped bottle and looked scorn at young Marse Cheston. Jim laughed with stiff lips, but he was glad to leave the next morning, and wondered just what

43

sort of a tale would drift back to Baltimore about him and his travelling companions.

They crossed the Potomac by a ford near the mouth of Watts' Branch into Fairfax County, Virginia. The river was wide and Cricket distrusted the ripples in the shallows. She could not be forced into the stream until Tendergrass took her bridle and hauled her alongside his own mount while Loudy Jack pushed close against her other flank.

Splashing and plunging she struggled through the water, soaking Jim to the waist and making him look to his riding. Tendergrass clung a moment too long to her head, for near the Virginia bank his horse stumbled and his grip jerked him off into the stream. He came up still clinging to his rifle, although Loudy Jack had to offer him a stirrup to bring him to shore.

Jim calmed the panting mare and swung off to wring out his wet clothes. Tendergrass sat down on the grass, the water trickling off him, and with methodical deliberation wiped his rifle dry. He merely nodded at Jim's apology and, drawing the wet charge with a worm, inserted a new one.

Jim stared down at him with rising exasperation.

"Can't you leave that be?" he asked.

Tendergrass looked up at him without expression. "I've been teaching you a lesson, lad, which you ain't ready to learn. When you are, you'll find it's a right useful one."

He stood up and walked over beside his horse, which Loudy was holding.

"Reckon your clothes are dry?" he remarked with underlying sarcasm, and mounted, disregarding his own soaked condition.

"Let's be travelling on," he said.

As they worked southward, Jim's opinion of Tendergrass grew lower still. Loudy had been properly contrite about his behavior at the Morgans' and didn't get too drunk again. They slept at the best taverns—"ordinaries" they were called in Virginia—and Tendergrass didn't seem overly grateful. In fact he suggested less comfortable quarters but shut his mouth when Jim looked annoyed and Loudy laughed. He seemed more and more unsociable and Jim was sensitive to the grins with which the people they met greeted the sight of that ever-present rifle. Loudy talked and explained and made himself entertaining,

44

gradually recovering his self-esteem. Then an incident occurred which made Jim's old doubts come raging up once more.

They had been on the road for Culpeper and had met a hardbitten Virginian driving a team of oxen. The familiar dust grayed him and his ox-goad was held carelessly over his shoulder. Loudy Jack, prancing by on a good horse, hailed the trudging figure at once. "Feller from my own county. Hey, Jack Sanderson, how are you?"

The other scanned him up and down at leisure. "Jack Timms, ain't you?"

"That's me," said Loudy patronizingly. "How's things in old Loudon?"

The Virginian spat into the road. "Hens are roosting mighty low since you left."

Then it was that John Tendergrass laughed and guffawed and slapped his hands upon his thighs while Loudy Jack galloped ahead.

"Learnin' a little?" asked Tendergrass with a wink, and might have talked further had not Jim with youthful shame put Cricket to her rocking canter. Loudy kept quiet for a little after that, but boredom again overtook Jim and he went back to listening to Timms and not to the plodding, lumpish figure behind.

They had crossed rope ferries, the rope strung from bank to bank and squeaking loudly as the ferryman pulled it over the wheel by which the boat was dragged along. Jim had paid the toll in every case. Grandmother Dorsey had given him gold, not the depreciated Continental notes, and it never occurred to him to do otherwise. Even though the money in his purse was jingling less and less, he also paid the tavern reckonings. He regarded himself as responsible for the party and being used to wealth did not stop to ask himself where more funds were coming from. It was only when they reached Orange Court House that he thought of inquiring how many more days they would be on the road.

" 'Bout six," answered Loudy Jack. "We turns west to Charlottesville an' then goes on to Staunton in the Valley. That'll put us on what they calls the Pennsylvania Road as far as Ingles' Ferry where Byrd's Military Road begins. We follers that to the Holston. Here's the ordinary. Carry your saddlebags in an' make yourself comfortable."

Six days! For the first time Jim began counting his remaining funds, and what he found made him sleep less well than his tired body demanded.

Next morning he came out of the semi-private room he had shared with a lawyer and a planter, to hear the tail-end of an argument between Tendergrass and Loudy. Tendergrass was jutting his chin and Timms had raised his voice hotly.

"Oh for God's sake listen to the fool . . ."

Suddenly Tendergrass gave Loudy a violent push that sent him flying through the door and stalked out after him. Jim, wondering what had started now, turned to the keeper of the ordinary, a swarthy, pockmarked man who was drawing Monongahela whiskey from a jug to serve a customer, obviously a farmer from his calloused hands and work-stained linseys.

"Charge this to the tickler, eh? And that's right," said the proprietor and looked over his shoulder at Jim.

"My reckoning, sir, if you please."

The proprietor straightened up, the jug on his shoulder.

"You're Jim Cheston?" Then, seeing the answering nod, "Your reckoning's been paid."

Jim stared at him in astonishment. "Paid? Who paid it?"

The proprietor set the jug down. He and his customer seemed to grin within themselves.

"Reckon you'll find out about that outside, suh. One of your friends was offerin' money, the other was offerin' words. I'll leave you to find out which was which."

"But . . ."

"Your reckoning's paid as I said," said the proprietor and measured off his customer's drink with his fingers. "Your tickler's runnin' might low," he told the farmer. "Better buy yourself a fresh gallon or so, less'n I have to chalk up a score agin you."

Jim went out into the yard to find the horses being girthed up. John Tendergrass was adjusting the saddlebags in front of his saddle. Loudy Jack had just finished taking care of Cricket, and he led her forward with a toothy smile.

"Mount, boy, mount," he said. "Let's get out on the road."

Jim stood with the soft morning wind ruffling his hair. "Which of you paid my reckoning?" he demanded.

"Your Uncle Trev's goin' to make up for everythin'," answered Loudy Jack soothingly. "Here, take your mare."

That was enough, and Jim turned on Tendergrass who came around slowly, even sullenly.

"It was you then?"

"If I did, it's my own concern," said Tendergrass as he mounted, and he rode out of the yard, uncompromisingly erect.

"I keep tellin' you," remonstrated Loudy, holding Jim's stirrup, "your Uncle Trev's goin' to make up for everythin'. Now don't keep frettin' yourself."

Jim was alongside Tendergrass before Loudy had stopped speaking.

"Why did . . . ?" he began, and stopped, for Tendergrass was in a bristle of resentment. Jim pulled on Cricket's rein and rode quietly along. For the first time he found the dark doggedness of Grandmother Dorsey's selected man directed towards himself. Loudy trotted past them with an inviting look, but Jim made no move to follow him. He was thinking hard, and his memory brought up both the incident between Tendergrass and Loudy and also Tendergrass' remark at the ford. He had not asked for an explanation then, but he would now.

"Why did you give me the rifle to carry that first day?"

John Tendergrass jerked up his head and looked him straight in the face. What he saw seemed to reassure him. He hunched himself into his shoulders and measured the distance between them and Loudy, whose hurt feelings showed in the slouch of his seat.

" 'Tain't my part to judge," said Tendergrass slowly and with apparent irrelevance. "It's just when I see a youngster with money taken advantage of that it hurts me some. Your Uncle Trev, he may shut his eyes to all this—this payin' our ferry tolls an' our tavern reckonings—an' he may be right ready to pay you back for everythin' you've spent and make a fool out of me. But I told Miz Dorsey I'd see you safe to the Holston an' I count on doin' it withouten you payin' much more'n your share. If I'd had my say we'd have counted our money an' spent nights where we could afford it, not where we'd have like to, like we been doin'."

47

Cricket stepped ahead but Jim pulled her back again. Tendergrass was talking through his teeth. With wonderment, Jim realized that the shambling man had leather in him.

"I'm no hired servant, ridin' with you just because I told Miz Dorsey I'd go along. I want to look at land an' get land. When I fin' what I want, there I reckon to settle an' break the soil an' raise my family like they ought to be raised. Goin' to take a lot to run me off'n it once't I find it. Your grandmother, she has the right idea. Build an' give a chance to your children to build it up more."

Jim thought he had finished, but after a time he broke out again. "Yes, I paid that reckoning an' it makes up part ways towards bein' my share of the trip. Your grandmother outfitted me but she never offered me no money. She's a mighty wise lady. A man's got to make his own way."

They went along side by side although Loudy was dropping back towards them. "Now you take that feller your uncle sent," said Tendergrass, raising his voice rustily until Loudy scuttled back to his place. Then he lowered it again. "Maybe your uncle knows why he sent him but I don't. He's been tellin' you a lot about the woods. Reckon he's got a right to, any feller that makes his livin' by hunting would know more'n me—but I reckon I know somethin' more than he does about indins."

Jim gaped at him, but Tendergrass was utterly serious.

"Wonderin' a mite, ain't you? I was just a little shaver when my parents died an' I went to live with my brother. He'd settled on the Pennsylvania frontier in the Susquehanna valley. He was mighty kind to me, him an' his wife both. He didn't have much chance to show me how to git about in the woods, didn't have the time. 'Bout a month after I was there I went huntin' the cows—they strayed pretty often—an' I was on the hill, and he an' the cabin an' his wife, they were in the valley. He was plowin', an' 'cause the roots were tangled, he'd leaned his rifle against a tree an' was usin' both hands on the plow.

"I saw it an' I ain't forgotten. It was a warparty. The devils waited until he was at the far end of the furrow an' then they came boundin' out; seven or eight of them, there was, but he turned an' ran towards them so's to get to his rifle. They shot him three times an' then they skelped him in front of me. I could see him kick so I knew he wasn't dead yet when they

48

took it off. His wife was outside. She snatched up the axe an’ they killed her too—with a musket shot ’cause she was swingin’ the axe mighty free. Next they burned the cabin. I ran for the fort because I was only ten an’ the only weapon I had was a willow switch.”

His griping fingers crept out and left their imprint on Jim’s knee.

“Maybe I’m just answering you now, boy, what you asked me in the beginnin’. Why I stays with my rifle even when there’s them that laughs at me. If my brother had been able to lay hands on his’n he might have killed one of them, an’ warparties don’t like to lose a warrior. Probably he’d never have saved himself nor his wife, but a warparty that’s lost a warrior don’t go rampaging around massacreeing helpless settlers. I know that much about indins. There were nine other people killed ’fore they left an’ I saw the bodies brought in.”

He tipped his rifle forward so that Jim could see the stock. His voice was still that rusty snarl.

“When I grew up, the first thing I got was the best weapon the Lancaster gunsmiths could make me. Take a look at her. She’s got a pocket in the butt for holding patches an’ I wish they could have bored it out until I could have an extra charge of powder an’ ball. I’m not huntin’ indins but if I gets my land I aims to hold it.”

Abruptly he seemed ashamed of his emotion. He faded back into the accustomed lumpish figure.

“That’s why, when I started for the border, I began to make a habit of never gettin’ far from my rifle. It’s a good habit, a lifesavin’ habit an’ you got to git into it as quick as you can. We ain’t got too many days to the Holston, an’ the more you trains your hand to reach for her an’ your mind to keepin’ her close, the safer you’re goin’ to be.”

Jim looked at him hard. Grandmother Dorsey had been right. The shambling man had a *lot* of leather in him.

V

In a pouring rain they came to Charlottesville—a courthouse, a tavern, and a dozen houses, stolid champions against the misty challenge of the neighboring hills. Jim cuddled his rifle close under his jacket, but he doubted if he had been able to save the priming. When he looked down to see, his tricorne hat poured a tiny stream from its brim down onto Cricket's steaming neck. Instead of being annoyed he looked over at John Tendergrass who gave him a covert grin. They shared a private joke together. "The murdered coon," as Grandmother Dorsey had described Loudy's coonskin cap, was having its revenge as she had said it would. Loudy kept passing a buckskin sleeve across a soaked face and muttering to himself.

They were riding between the outermost houses and Jim was acutely conscious of the smell of travel. It was a damp, clinging odor, compounded of rain-drenched, sweaty horses, linseys, buckskins and human bodies—not overly unpleasant if there was fire, shelter, and a warming drink in immediate prospect. Discomfort became a seasoning to anticipated comfort as the two mighty chimneys, which seemed to compress the tavern building between them like a collapsed accordion, drew nearer with each stride.

Then a small boy hurtled out of a door while a cannon boomed and the muddy, rutted road in front of the tavern filled with a boiling crowd of men who fired off muskets into the air and yelled like fox-hunters with the fox in view.

The horses plunged and whirled in panic. "Get off'n 'em!" cried Tendergrass. As his feet splattered into a puddle he caught the small boy with his rifle hand.

"The British here?" he demanded, clinging to the rein of the rearing brown.

"No suh!" answered the boy, wriggling. "It's the fourth of July."

They looked at each other blankly until the cannon boomed

50

again and the boy burst into tears. "I tell you, it's the fourth of July an' they're goin' to shoot it off thirteen times if their powder holds out. Please, suh, loosen your hold on me. If you don't I'm goin' to tell my pappy on you."

The crowd outside the tavern had noticed them and there were fingers pointing. The boy squirmed loose and went tearing down the street like a dog with a bucket tied to its tail.

"Pappy! Pappy!" he yelled. "They're Tories. They don't know about the fourth of July."

A reeling farmer, undoubtedly full of Monongahela, aimed at them but his unsteady hand sent the bullet whistling overhead. Jim's stomach crawled, Loudy began to bellow their politics, and a gunlock clicked where John Tendergrass stood, his horse turned loose and galloping up the street.

"Get in behind that house there," said the rusty voice. "Reckon we can explain better from some place where we can shoot back if we has to. Hold up! Here's somebody with sense."

A tall, erect man had stepped forward and was waving his arms friendly-wise. The shooting ceased and the crowd stopped the ugly forward surge which had begun to develop and waited.

"Maybe my constituents are mistaken," called the peace-maker in a cultivated voice. "Did I hear one of you hailing that you are supporters of the thirteen United States?"

The cannon most inopportunely boomed and drowned Loudy's reply. Jim shouted their answer in a voice too shrill for his pride. "We're not Tories!"

"Steady yourself, lad," counselled John Tendergrass calmly, uncocking his rifle with the same efficient click that had been heard in the cocking of it. "They was mistook, that's all."

The peacemaker waved acknowledgment and, turning his back, explained, though they could not hear what he said. The mob, listening, changed from an ugly thing to a drunken, laughing crowd of celebrants.

"Youngster was wrong, no Tories here! Reckon they're the right sort." As the cannon boomed again they surged forward behind the erect man and Jim found himself being clapped upon the back by whoever could reach him through Cricket's frenzy.

"Your servant, sir," said the leader to John Tendergrass. "Can we do ought to atone for our over-enthusiasm?"

51

"You might send somebody to catch my horse," answered the shambling man, his lips wrinkling. "That's the first thing. The second is to tell us what all this ruckus is about it's bein' the fourth of July?"

The leader smiled a bit wryly. "It is the first anniversary of the signing of the Declaration of Independence."

"So it is!" exclaimed Tendergrass. "I should have remembered. It's a right good piece of writing though they's a mite of damn foolishness in it as well."

"I'd be glad to listen to your opinions," answered the other, but by then the congratulators had broken through the magic ring which Cricket's heels had created about Jim. Some stranger took her bridle and he was half-carried, half-dragged into the tavern. He was slapped on the back and his hand nearly crushed by friendly grips. The shakiness which had come from that miasma of hatred he had felt when the muzzles were being turned towards him began to dissolve.

"Stood right up to us with his weapon in his hand," chuckled a pockmarked fellow who carried a heavy musket, and Jim blushed.

"Reckon I'd forgot I had it," he admitted honestly, but the chuckling was approving.

Jim began to feel that these dirty, tree-felling farmers, these Albemarle militiamen, were his kind of folks. They were not so far from the frontier that they had lost the individual self-reliance that arose from the necessity of defending their lands, their families and their beliefs.

Impulsively he handed his rifle to the pockmarked man, who took it tenderly and examined it with skilled glance.

"Now there's your friend," he said. "She's a long-barrelled, powder-in-the-pan friend that's better than being ten feet high an' just as broad, 'cause she talks right decisive in your favor. Now, Henry, I'll thank you to pour out a touch of Monongahela for our traveller here." His pleasant twinkle took any sting from the banter. "He could sure use it. I've been shot at myself an' I finds it mighty strengthening afterwards."

The Monongahela went down Jim's throat and he leaned his elbows on the table, letting it warm the reaction and the fatigue out of him. It had been the mob rather than the humming bullet which had shaken him. The smiling faces that waved

52

the jug away when Henry offered it the second time were the sober men, the electors of the county who talked quietly and were interested in him. The pockmarked man, who proved to be a miller, led him on to talk. Maybe it was the whiskey and the sensed approval, but he found himself telling about where he was from and where he was going. Then he remembered where he was, and looked around for his companions.

Loudy Jack was living up to his name and was the center of a noisy crowd. Some of the laughter there as the jug passed was not kind. John Tendergrass sat at a table in the middle of the room with the man who had checked the mob and two or three others who looked as if they were respected. Jim wondered what he was thinking. That high, hysterical tone that Jim recalled using when shouting that they weren't Tories now burned his pride like a stake-fire set by the indians. Then John Tendergrass caught his eye and waved him over. He obeyed with hanging head.

He felt better when they rose to their feet to greet him. The erect man bowed gravely. "Mr. Cheston, my compliments, sir. I'd admire to hear what you think of a horse of mine which is tethered outside. Your little mare has caught my eye and Mr. Tendergrass here declares that you are grandson to the Dorseys whose name is famous among breeders of fine stock."

Jim mumbled his willingness and minded his manners by making a leg to them. They trooped outside to survey a magnificent horse at the hitchrack.

"He's by Young Fearnaught's colt out of Allycroker, a two-year-old," explained the owner. "Probably I should not ride so young an animal but his manners are perfect."

Jim forgot his troubles. These gentlemen were deferential, they put him on his mettle. There was no trace of condescension in the way they asked for his opinion. He surveyed the colt, forgetting everything but the knowledge which Grandmother Dorsey had instilled into him.

"He'll never be a racer, sir," he said at last. "I'm sorry, but he's too big to avoid clumsiness and his quarters aren't what they should be."

The owner did not seem disappointed. "I feared as much. His name is Caractacus, and like that early British king he would fail magnificently. I asked your advice, sir, because of

53

your family's fame, and listening to your judgment I realize that it is not trumpeted forth vainly. Very well, Caractacus shall not go to the races."

He moved over and surveyed Cricket carefully. "I congratulate you, sir, on most of your company. With such a mare under you and so brilliant a philosopher as your companion, you should go far."

John Tendergrass looked thoroughly uncomfortable. "Maybe I talked too much, Mr. Jefferson."

The tall man bowed to him. "Any damn foolishness in a right good piece of writing should be pointed out. That you've done for me and I am grateful for it. Now if you gentlemen will rejoin me . . ."

He included Jim and the others in his invitation but he linked arms with Tendergrass. Jim walked between a planter and a judge with his mind in a whirl. This was Thomas Jefferson, one of the authors of the Declaration of Independence, and he treated John Tendergrass as an equal.

They were seated again at the table in the middle of the room with Jefferson at the head of it as host. Jim watched him, speaking only when he was spoken to, as a young man should in the presence of his elders. Mr. Jefferson was a delegate to the Virginia House, a famous man. Everybody knew who he was and yet he didn't seem to breathe different, nor act much different from anybody else. Still it was just that little difference that made Jim realize why Mr. Jefferson handled his fame well. People came up to speak to him every now and again. When they were noisy or pushing he could be cold and short-spoken, mashing their forwardness as a hammer strikes a nail. Let a diffident, stammering fellow come up and he treated him as kindly as a neighbor.

The table was talking philosophy, and Jim, thanks to Master Blackthorne, could follow what they said; but John Tendergrass, who was sitting beside him, looked utterly blank. Then Mr. Jefferson noticed and let the others go on with their discussion while he devoted himself to the two of them. He drew Jim from polite monosyllables into eager talk and showed his courtesy by deftly including John Tendergrass.

Mr. Jefferson was very enthusiastic about Grandmother Dorsey's beliefs about Happy Return. He talked a little about

54

his own place that he was building on a hill outside of Charlottesville. He gave its name an odd pronunciation—"Montichello" he called it and then explained that he was pronouncing it in the Italian fashion—"Monticello" you'd say in English. He mentioned that he was planning to put the stables under the northwest wing, and Jim was bold enough to speak up disapprovingly, then caught himself and felt like a froward young fool. However, Mr. Jefferson didn't seem to be annoyed and looked as if he were really interested when Jim explained that the smell would be too penetrating and the horses wouldn't benefit either.

Then Mr. Jefferson began to talk about land titles and John Tendergrass set down his drink and listened intently.

Kaintuckee was a county of Virginia, said Thomas Jefferson, had been made so last year. He was interested in the west, though he admitted that he'd never been nearer the frontier than Staunton. Tendergrass snorted at this, as they planned on reaching Staunton their next day's ride. Mr. Jefferson flushed, but explained that he wanted to make the west safe for the settlers. He was studying how to plant small farmers with safe titles in a maze of land grants which confused even a lawyer like himself. There were royal grants, colonial grants, land company grants, state grants, overlapping each other until there was the devil's own mess as to who owned what. He spoke bitterly about what he called North Carolina's effrontery in claiming Virginia's territories. He thought he had the ear of Governor Patrick Henry and he was going to do his best to repulse such outrageous claims and see that Virginia and Virginians had the main say in the disposal of their own.

Jim felt uncomfortable. Mr. Jefferson had probably forgotten that he was a Marylander and didn't know that his father's lands derived from the Henderson Patent, which, at best, was a North Carolina grant. Maybe Uncle Trev would have an answer.

Then John Tendergrass interrupted, jutting out his jaw the way he had done when he and Loudy had disputed over the reckoning at the ordinary.

"It's a mighty good plan for the future," he remarked, "but what concerns me is the land right now. You say there ain't no certainty as to who owns it?"

"Unfortunately that's true," said Mr. Jefferson, "but . . ."

Tendergrass wasn't too deferential in his reply. "I advances step by step and 'fore I takes my family out there with Boone an' them fellers, I reckons to know who owns my cabin an' my cornfield. Lawyers was foaled of the devil, excusin' present company, an' I don't aim to work for another man."

"Another man?"

"Yes, sir. You got a brain an' I got hands. My hands are goin' to cut down the trees an' fight the indins an' set my hills of corn. Your brains can take it all from me when there ain't no more indins, when I done added a leanto to my cabin an' when my children are thinkin' about doin' a little better than their pappy an' bringing in horses an' building in brick."

Mr. Jefferson's cheekbones were touched with red. "I'll do my best for you. Virginia will do her best for you."

"Can't ask any man to do better'n his best," agreed Tendergrass and shut up like a clam. Jim tried desperately to think of a way to sift the unpleasantness out of the conversation. Mr. Jefferson had gone out of his way to be nice to them and he seemed so kindly and gentle that Jim didn't like to see him rebuffed. He was about to speak when he noticed that a couple of men, shaven and clean and in good clothes, were standing over them, shifting from foot to foot.

Jefferson apparently became conscious of them about the same instant. His bearing lost its diffidence. "Well," he asked coldly. "What have you done with my seeds?"

"Planted 'em," answered the bolder of the two. "We're goin' to need a mite more money to cultivate 'em proper."

Mr. Jefferson reached into his coat, at which the young men's faces brightened, only to gloom over again when he brought out a notebook instead of a pocketbook.

"When did you plant them?" The voice was as chilling as the rain which Jim had been facing all day.

"Well . . ." The bold one got no encouragement from his companion. He faced Jefferson in a sort of desperate defiance. "Just now," he admitted.

The whole table had noticed and was silent. It was the more impressive since the rest of the room was full of buzzing and yelling. Jefferson kept looking at his book, turning over the pages towards a table of accounts.

"Get out!" he said, stiff-lipped. He halted any argument by stabbing a forefinger at two separate entries. "These seeds should have been planted a month ago. I am trying to develop the products of this county by distributing the means of doing it. I trusted you and paid you. It seems to me that you've lost track of the trust and reckoned on the pay."

The pair beat a hasty retreat into the crowd. Mr. Jefferson faced the table and his guests again, but his anger, as he strove to control it, was so apparent that even the judge and the planter kept silent. Then Tendergrass spoke up calmly.

"You're interested in seeds, sir? Well, I'm interested in 'em myself. Wherever I go I takes along some of the vegetables I likes to cultivate and tries to match 'em with the soil. If you feels like it, I'll get 'em out of my pack an' you're welcome to whatever I can spare. You've dealt kindly with me."

Jefferson looked at him sharply, then the red left his cheekbones and he smiled.

"I should be most happy to see them," he said.

A few hours later, Jim went to bed. The judge and the planter had left earlier but Jefferson and John Tendergrass were still head to head over the tiny piles of seeds. Mr. Jefferson's notebook had received some new entries and the discussion was apparently as technically interesting as it had been from the beginning. Loudy Jack was already asleep on the floor, wrapped in somebody else's blankets, his snoring and his gurgling keeping Jim awake for some time. He slept at last, to be aroused by a steady shaking.

"He seems right well informed," said the rusty voice. "That is, about seeds an' plantin'. It's near dawn now an' we'll ride. At least we'll get as far west as he's been."

The dawn overtook them as they started. First the dark, and then the birds chirping the outpouring of light. Jim, tired and irritable, watched, over the complaining undernote of Loudy's headache, John Tendergrass plodding thoughtfully along on his brown horse.

Jim spoke to him diffidently. "Mr. Jefferson helped us a lot," he ventured.

"He's a nice man," agreed John Tendergrass heartily and then relapsed into silence.

Jim put Cricket beside him. "I begin to wonder if my father's grant in Kaintuckee is worth much."

"It ain't. That is, if what he said is true an' I ain't got no reason to doubt him."

If the land was worthless what excuse was there to go on to Kaintuckee?

Jim had set his heart upon the road and the road had taken him to its rough bosom. The four feet plodding under him, the creak of leather and the jingle of the bit, that was part of it. The heron that rose heavily from yonder pond was another, and the deertracks in the muddy patch summed it up. He could not keep the disappointment from his voice.

"What are you goin' to do, John? Go back to Maryland?"

"I should," answered Tendergrass, thereby, had he known it, draining the last happiness from Jim's heart.

"Sho'," said Miz Dorsey's chosen man after a moment. "Anybody can listen to a lawyer an' stop when he says stop. That's a lawyer's business. Reckon if we'd listened too close to 'em we'd still be squabbling over the land titles at Jamestown or Plymouth. Just draw rein an' think. At Charlottesville they faces east, towards the cities an' the Tidewater. You crosses one fold of the mountains like we are doin' an' you comes to Staunton. There they faces west, it's true, but they ain't the frontier. They're kind of betwixt an' between. One more fold of the mountains an' you loses track of Mr. Jefferson. Not that he won't come stealin' after you—him an' the rest of the lawyers—but . . ."

He stood up in his stirrups and waved at the hunch-backed glory of the Blue Ridge lying along the skyline.

"See that? Mr. Jefferson's a grand man but he's talkin' one thing an' thinkin' another. Maybe he's goin' to put all those small farmers on safe titles but he's mostly considerin' Virginia. Let a Virginia land company come along, not a North Carolina one, an' Kaintuckee's goin' to belong to them. Seems to me Kaintuckee ought to belong to them that settles it. I advances step by step, as I've said, an' I sees them mountains. I'm thinkin', jes' thinkin', mind you, that when I've put a couple of 'em behind me, I'm goin' to make my stand and run my risks with the lawyers."

58

Jim was awed by the long, blue-clad range towards which they were riding.

"They look mighty high," he said doubtfully.

"Yes," said Tendergrass, "but somebody's got to climb over 'em."

VI

The Blue Ridge was crossed and had begun to recede on their left as they made the turn at Staunton and climbed gradually out of the Shenandoah Valley. The laurel and the mountain ash were growing bold against the precariously held trace of the Pennsylvania Road. Jim could see where the long-bodied, tarpaulin-covered Conestoga wagons had scraped the bushes with their sides and had had need of their four-horse teams at every creekbed and gulley. Jim's Maryland hills were far tenderer than the slow rise and thrust of green and gray which marched daily on either side of them.

The elation of his adventure took a sterner savor the day they climbed out of a ford across a summer-shrunken river, the horses glistening to their bellies and grunting with the effort.

"Headwaters of the James," remarked Loudy Jack. "If we pushes a bit we can sleep tonight at Big Lick on the Roanoke." He leaned forward in his saddle and pointed ahead. "There you are, Jim."

There was a cluster of cabins, each with its cornfield and its pasture enclosed by worm fences. In the center was a square and solid building with its top story projecting above the lower. Heavy shutters were in place on the windows and an equally heavy door stood half open.

"Your first blockhouse," said Loudy. "They builds 'em that-away so's the indins can't get close enough to set a fire without bein' shot from above."

Perhaps it was then that Jim crossed his own mental mountain and made his first separation from Maryland. The line of the divide was not immediately apparent, but it was pushing itself into notice. There had been ordinaries with sanded floors, the sand sometimes worked into fanciful designs, with tables where whole turkeys or geese, quarters of beef or lamb were waiting to be cut into, with Negro boys to pass the plates and brush away the flies, with a horse lot outside and a bell hanging by the door to be rung for proprietor or servant. After Charlottesville, it is true, John Tendergrass had insisted that they use simpler quarters, but even these had some luxuries. However, about the time they passed the blockhouse they entered a region where there was no choice. Jim found he must sleep in a one-room shack, stinking of liquor and ancient meals, where he must roll himself in his blanket on the stained floor with the chance of being trodden upon by a drunken man. He must tend his own horse and get used to pork, bacon, and hominy, for nothing else was offered.

Loudy was growing bolder now. Belted buckskins or belted linseys with leggings and coonskin caps were common. At Big Lick Loudy took his rifle out of the pack with an unspoken air of triumph. He grew patronizing again, showing off his axe-man's skill, and on one occasion stepped into the woods and came back with a couple of squirrels, mangled by the heavy bullets, but which were a welcome aid to make the last of their cornbread and their strong Bohea tea more palatable. Jim was inclined to resent his airs and his reassumption of leadership, but Tendergrass was placid and soothing.

"Now, lad," he remarked as they rode stirrup to stirrup, "don't get upset. 'Nother couple of days an' we'll be on the Holston. Accordin' to my reckoning this here Loudy Jack is a right triflin' feller, but your uncle don't seem to agree else he wouldn't have sent him for you. Tryin' a mite reluctantly to be fair, I got to admit that he's been a help the last few days. Them squirrels set easy on my stomach. Mebbe you better begin bein' nice to him."

"That no-'count fice . . ." exclaimed Jim hotly, and Tendergrass touched him restrainingly.

"You're goin' to have to live with him, remember that. I'm just ridin' the road with you."

"But I'll be seeing you!" cried Jim. He had grown sincerely fond of Tendergrass and, though he did not admit it even to himself, had drawn reassurance from his stolid presence.

"Sure hope so."

Jim went on gloomily, knowing in his own heart that Loudy would have the last say and not doubting what that say would be.

"Going to stay on the Holston?" asked Jim finally, more to keep hope alive than for any other reason. Tendergrass smiled bitterly.

"Don't you listen when I tells you that I advances step by step? Pull up the mare a minute an' get down."

Wondering, Jim dismounted. Loudy called a question, but Tendergrass waved him on. He knelt down and scooped up a handful of dirt. The red earth stained his hand.

"Take it. Now feel it, smell it, taste it. Don't taste sour, does it? That's good soil but I'm lookin' for better. What I've seen has been encouragin', what I've heared along the way is better still. I don't think I've wasted my time comin' this far. How much further I go depends on this and on nothin' else much but this." He brushed the last grains off against his breeches. "Reckon you can work out your own answer."

It wasn't too hard a sum to work out. Jim hoped that the Holston could do better than match this soil. Then Loudy dropped back with a worried expression and told them that they had best put the horses to a trot to make Ingles' Ferry before sundown.

Seeing Loudy worried, with the silent woods and the silent mountains growing sullen as their color faded, was a new experience for Jim and he let Cricket out while he looked nervously to his priming. However, it was waste anxiety, for half an hour's alternate trot and walk brought them to a substantial ordinary planted upon the shore of a sluggish stream.

"New River," said Loudy, leading up impatiently towards the house.

John Tendergrass stopped his horse. There was a confused roar of excited voices from the ordinary, but Tendergrass was watching the ferryboat which was just lowering its apron on their own bank. Jim followed his glance, but so far as he could tell there was nothing extraordinary in the tall young man who was heaving the rope over the pulleys nor in the peddler and two packhorses who constituted the load.

61

Finally he realized that Tendergrass was watching not the boat but the river itself. The brown horse was again in motion before it dawned on Jim that this river was behaving mighty oddly. By God, its flow was northwest!

A week ago he would neither have noticed the fact nor drawn from it its significance. The piled-up, forested mountains he had been seeing and this river that flowed into the Ohio, not into the Atlantic, cumulated in his mind to give an effect that was strong and unaccustomed. It was the same momentary hesitation which troops experience when first in contact with the enemy and sailors first putting to sea in wartime. As the ferryboat's apron grated on the shore, Jim knew that he was on the border and that neither Grandmother Dorsey nor Master Blackthorne nor any of the comforting supports of the past could directly avail him now.

Then Cricket with pricking ears minced towards the house and Jim became alive to the row that was issuing from it.

His companions had dismounted and he followed suit just in time to check a panicky rush on the mare's part. Two men crashed through the doorway, locked fiercely in each other's arms, to fall to the ground and squirm together cursing and yelling. A crowd poured out after them reminiscent of the mob at Charlottesville, save that these fellows gathered close about the grapple on the ground, shouting oaths and encouragement, laughing and cock-crowing. Through the legs of the crowd he could see the battlers locked with each other and he grew physically sick at the sight. He had witnessed fights among the sailors and the stevedores in Baltimore but this was so inconceivably bestial that he retched. Neither man used a weapon, neither man showed even an inkling of fair play; they fought with teeth and gouging thumbs, their knees jerking at their opponent's groin. They whirled over and over until one screamed in pain and the other, growling like a dog, swung on top, his jaws locked about the under man's nose. Fingers reached down towards bleeding eyeballs while the frenzied bucking and outcry of the tortured victim rose to a shrill pitch. There was no pity and no mercy in the crowd.

But a tall old man was pushing through it carrying a steaming kettle. "Make way!" he shouted and if the voice quavered from age there was no quaver in the command. The ring opened for him. He stood over the battlers, gauged his distance and poured the kettle-full over them.

There was a double howl, the voice of the loser mounting to a height that brought the acid bile to Jim's throat. The old man, reinforced now by a stalwart younger one upon his right hand, was rapping out commands, fierce and unafraid, in the grip of righteous anger.

"The next time it'll be on the full boil! You drunken sons-of-bitches,' I sell you the good Monongahela as a man's drink and you turn to boar pigs on me! I'll not have my ordinary a sty for your wallowing. Get out! Get out! The whole of ye! If you'd be as bold before the Shawanoes or the Delawares as you are before each other we'd not have had our trouble at Draper's Meadows."

The tall young man from the ferryboat hobbled through the dissolving crowd and took his place by the old man's left hand. Yet even he and the other formidable flanker seemed small before the old man's wrath. He would have been as fiercely masterful if he had been alone.

"Aaron's friends, drag him off. Steve's friends, throw him off my property since he seems the better able to walk of the two. I'll not have him walk on his feet from my ordinary if he thinks he can brawl and bluster here. Tell them that if I see them again on my land I'll break my staff over them."

The old man tottered but caught himself on that very weapon. The sons beside him reached forward and then snatched their hands back lest he should see and his pride be hurt. The crowd dispersed with the injured brawlers, leaving only three or four who had quietly grouped themselves behind the grim old proprietor as an unneeded reserve. John Tendergrass and Jim, with Loudy and the peddler behind them, were left in front of that aged, shrunken face that showed no fear.

"Begone!" he ordered, but the son with the crippled feet spoke up in a queer, measured accent.

"These be not concerned," he said. "I carried the peddler over on the ferry and the others rode up as I landed."

"Then be you welcome!" cried the old man heartily and with his eyes indicated the door. He seemed too spent to do more.

Jim still flinched from the too vivid memory of the fight, and his queasiness must have shown in his expression, for the son with the crippled feet and the measured sentences brought a sweet-smelling, aromatic liquid in a flask and offered it to John Tendergrass.

"No whiskey, I think," he suggested. "Rub him some with this————," he spoke a deep guttural word and then smiled— " 'Witch-hazel' I think 'tis called among the white men." Instantly he caught himself with a tiny frown. "Witch-hazel, we call it."

Jim remembered Charlottesville and was carried away in a torrent of shame. Nineteen—and yet he had to be revived every time they reached an emergency. He said as much bitterly.

"You see more'n we do an' it hits you harder," said Tendergrass, so gently that the crippled son smiled again and again used a deep guttural word. He threw up his hand as both of them scowled self-consciously.

"You don't understand. I have felt the same towards my own indian foster-father when I was a prisoner off there." He waved his arm vaguely towards the west. Then he turned to Jim with a flash of teeth. "I was only a child and I stumbled into a campfire. You see what it did to my feet. It was my foster-father who gave me comfort just as your friend here gives you. He took me from the squaws and cured me, rubbing through many hours when he might have been hunting or sleeping. When your friend spoke, I remembered his tone."

There was a low call from the other side of the room and he obeyed it with the same quick step as a fox puts his pads down. The old proprietor was sitting in a ponderous armchair before the fire and trailing his staff in the coals. The dinner was set forth, hominy and bacon, but this time with the addition of venison and wild turkey. There were no portions except what each guest wanted and, save for the hominy, no side dishes. A Negro brought in the food and was alert with the plates. Jim had glimpses of the women who had cooked the meal, but they stayed within the kitchen leanto and did not enter the common room.

When the men had eaten they lay back against the walls and smoked or chewed while Jim let his glance rove about. Casual at first, it came alive as his eyes reported to his mind the plugged gaps that appeared evenly spaced in the heavy logs next the shuttered windows. The fire, though held low, was hot, and the warmth of July made him sweat under his linseys, but the windows were shuttered and those gaps with the plugs in them would admit no air. Then their meaning came to him. They were loopholes, and he straightened up against the logs only to meet the kindly glance of the old man.

"Ever heared the tale of Draper's Meadows, boy?" asked the patriarch. He was sitting so near to Jim that his voice came clearly above the general conversation of the room.

" 'Tis why I keep my house as my fortress. It's just a few miles away, and 'twas there that I lived with my dear wife an' my three children. The Shawanoes came down on me whilst I was out hunting to bring in something tasty for my friend, Colonel Powell, who was sittin' writin' when I left, with his sword before him. When I came back from that hunting I found my wee babe dead next the cabin . . ."

Involuntarily Jim's glance shifted to the face of John Tendergrass, twisted and set in pain. The old man was quick as a panther; he addressed Tendergrass with a change of inflection.

"It has happened to others—God save us all. I'll not linger upon it. Colonel Powell had met them, as we see'd, for there was two dead warriors there in the ruins beside him with his broken sword stuck in the skull of one of them. My wife and my boys they carried off."

A queer memory came to Jim. One night (and he suspected the *usquebaugh* of being the root of it) Master Blackthorne had sung in his cracked voice some of the ballads of the Scottish border.

"I have taken the lance and Willy has taken the spear," . . . he couldn't remember the rest, except that Willy's marrow had gushed from his leg and that the reivers had gotten away with the cattle. Only these reivers weren't content with cattle. He started guiltily back to the present, but old Mr. Ingles had gone off into the past and was poking the fire, unheeding.

"My wife, she came back," he resumed at length, but only three of them heard him—Jim, John Tendergrass, and the crippled son who rested against the wall beside them. "My son George is dead—that we heared. His little sister, born while my woman was a prisoner, she kissed in her birch cradle and left to the mercy of the squaws. That I know, for she is a great woman an' she did not spare herself the story. Forty days wanderin' in the wilderness she was, with nobody along with her, save an old crazy Dutch woman who once tried to kill her 'cause of the wilderness. I've read my Bible an' I've always had a sneakin' sympathy over them that disobeyed Moses. They wandered forty years an' the wilderness can be right tryin'. I know. I didn't set on my hunkers when they took my own from me. I went a-seekin'. Yet when she was home an' my heart warm because of it she bore me other children. A good woman, a great woman. I tell you I've wandered in that wilderness an' I know."

Mr. Ingles kept on poking at the fire. It was just about out and the tallow candles were giving the light and the smell. He gestured towards his crippled son.

"Thomas was prisoner amongst 'em for a long time an' I've always been grateful to him that he come back with me when I got to him. The baby we never heard of."

His voice rose and he glared upon inoffensive Jim and John Tendergrass as if they had been at fault. "Want to know why these indins are so sly an' clever an' fierce? It's 'cause they've carried off, generation by generation, the best blood on the frontier an' mixed it with their own. My baby girl . . ." he shut his grim mouth until it was a solid, ruthless line. Then he jerked his head with irritation. "I grow old and tell my troubles. I want no pity."

He hauled himself around in his chair and addressed John Tendergrass. "I beg your pardon, sir. This ain't by no means a usual evenin' in this ordinary what with them swine brawling an' now me a-whining. You looks like an understandin' man an' I hopes you'll bear with us. If you feels like using 'em, there's a store next door that I keep an' a ferry before you that I set up, but I am damned, sir, if I want your patronage for either of them unwillingly."

He poked the fire again and the last spark of it died out. "I await your time of uprisin'," he said dreamily. "My boys will see you across the river."

Jim went to sleep with that high, assured, though quavery, voice running through a restless night and insistently pushing

66

out of his brain the cultivated accents of his friend, Mr. Jefferson. Mr. Jefferson was already one mountain behind him.

VII

From the New River to the Holston was no more than a step when one was well mounted and the weather remained clear. A day's riding took them there and another day carried them down the wide valley with the river as its backbone, a far-wandering river which eventually joined its flow, like that of the New, with the realm-draining Ohio. The smells of the valley were mountain smells and the mists of the morning had a thick persistence that spoke of the Alleghanies, rough and broad and bloodstained, brooding over the soft alluvial bottoms. The ordinaries were loopholed, as were the larger cabins, while even in the smaller ones it was a morning rite to peek through the chinks between the logs of the loft to see that the unbarring of the door did not give entrance to a warparty. There were occasional forts, formed of well-hewn logs with rifle platforms and flanking blockhouses. It was all buckskin and linsey now until the broadcloth of a parson or the rare buff-and-blue of a militia officer drew an extra glance.

On the second day the border grew overly real. They were riding through a deep thicket which paralleled the river when Cricket threw up her head and jumped sideways with ears pricked.

"What's she a-scared of now?" began Loudy Jack. "Rabbit in them bushes or a branch waving? She gets upsot easier . . ."

Beyond the thicket the water splashed and John Tendergrass brought his rifle up.

"Something," he snapped abruptly.

Jim swung his own rifle around in tingling excitement and Loudy dropped the packhorse's lead.

The splashing ceased and a voice came from the thicket.

"Mite slow, ain't ye," it asked. "Now if I was an indin I'd have had my choice of ye."

It was reassuring, if sarcastic. Jim kept the spot covered, he'd heard that some indians spoke English.

"It's just me," soothed the voice as if it had read his thoughts. "Take your fingers off'n that trigger. There's no sense to ye ridin' as open an' careless as this even when you're in the settlements. I couldn't hear ye because of the water but I saw your dust. Been right dry around here an' your horses stirs it up. Now if you'll calm yourselves, reckon I'll come out."

A further crackling and the bushes whipped aside before the shoulders of a raw-boned gelding. The rider was short, stout and very masculine in appearance. There was nothing unusual in the shouldered rifle, the tomahawk and butcher knife thrust through the leather belt, the long, dirty coat over buckskin breeches; but what caught Jim's unbelieving glance and made him look a second time at the lined, wild face was the petticoat which poked out betrayingly where it had been tucked into the top of the breeches.

"Ann Bailey they calls me," said the jarring voice. "'Mad Ann Bailey' some of them calls me, but not when I'm looking at them. I'm ridin' post from the Clinch River to Arthur Campbell at Royal Oak. 'Colonel,' they've taken to calling him now, but it hain't made him none better, not as I could see. If I'd been a Delaware he'd have killed me 'fore I'd got acrost the ford. Reckon you're ridin' his way?"

"We sure are," said Loudy Jack, huffily.

The woman looked him up and down, turning her horse in beside them and insensibly urging them on. "Then I better ride with ye. Goddlemighty ye needs a pilot! You couldn't see the ford, an' all you could think of doin' was lumpin' together till you couldn't be missed."

She eyed Loudy with such disfavor that his underlip came up in that familiar, childlike pout. She jerked her head at Tendergrass but still addressed Timms. "This 'un looks like he's ready to fight but don't know quite how. Little 'un there on the mare looks like he's willin' to learn but you look like you're ready to do neither, 'spite of them buckskins."

She scorned Loudy's scowl and put her raw-boned mount to a single-foot, dispensing comment over her shoulder in jerky remarks, but turning her head slowly from side to side to take account of woods and trails.

"Can't trust nothin' too far, not even this deep in the settlements . . . Holston's got its mind on the Cherokees, who ain't too peaceful but who don't raid this far north . . . Over on the Clinch, now, we've got right smart to worry over . . . There we got the Cherokees *an'* the Shawanoes *an'* the Wyandots *an'* the Delawares *an'* a bobtail of other tribes to look through the chinks for . . . Shawanoes is up an' hittin' the warpost mighty hard with their hatchets, likewise the settlers out in Kaintuckee . . . Tried to rush Boonesborough an' made folks at Harrodsburg an' St. Asaph's wonder whether the turkeys gobbling outside the stockade was real or just the fellers who scalped the last hunter who went out lookin' for a mess of meat . . . Clinch valley lies to the westward of this, that's why you can go traipsin' along withouten any risk." She didn't say much more except "Howdy" to the settlers they met along the way, the majority of whom seemed to know her and respect her.

That casual remark of hers kept rolling about in Jim's mind. "Tried to rush Boonesborough." Mr. Ingles and his lame son had managed between them to add to his maturity. There had been much left unsaid at Ingles' Ferry that a sensitivity to the atmosphere of the place could piece out. The indians stopped being a word and walked out of the stories. They were real and pervading. Even the unspoken reserve of Thomas Ingles, the former prisoner, had made the impression more vivid. They couldn't be ghouls and devils altogether—apparently he had experienced kindness during his captivity. There must be a reason to make so reserved a man speak with so much understanding of an indian foster father. Thomas Ingles' own father had betrayed an odd gratitude for the fact that his son had been willing to come home with him. Was there an unreckoned factor, a love of the forests and of the free barbaric life which drew the brother of the murdered children to itself? John Tendergrass had seen the blood-debt paid; would he be stout enough to bring his family here? Would the borderers themselves stay in Kaintuckee?

He followed the thought and on an impulse called to Mad Ann Bailey.

"Is Daniel Boone still at Boonesborough?"

"Surely. They got his girl and the two Callaway girls back,

if that's what you're drivin' at, an' killed a couple of indins too. That Shawanoe Hanging Maw was right smart of a fool to grab the three of 'em in broad daylight, an' with no more than a scatterin' of warriors with him. Reckon he couldn't resist the temptation when their canoe drifted square under the bank where he was a-lyin'."

John Tendergrass looked again at Jim. He must have sensed the motive behind Jim's question.

"Boone's right lucky, ain't he?" he asked softly. "Settling in indin country an' keepin' the hair on his family's heads."

Mad Ann gave a sound so explosive that Jim thought for an instant that it was her horse that had snorted. "If you're allowing in your ignorance that Dan'l ain't had his troubles, how about that son of his that Big Jim, the Shawanoe, caught near Martin's Station? Big Jim was tol'able handy with a knife, an' he didn't let the memory that Dan'l had filled his belly more'n once when he was hungry stand in his way. There was a nigger who hid in the woods an' got free but he was close enough to hear. First the boy kept remindin', then he began to beg that Big Jim finish him. Big Jim took his time about it. Dan'l came scoutin' back next day an' found where he'd had his fun. There was another killed beside Dan'l's boy an' I reckon he had some trouble tellin' which was which. Live out along the border long enough and about the fourth pull on the jug you begins to count your dead an' not your acres."

There was a tight little pause and she grumbled to herself. "Whyfor should he send his family back? He's making his stand there, ain't he?"

Without warning she rode aside into the woods, beckoning them urgently to follow. She was as rigid as a bird-dog. Even her horse caught her alertness and blew his nostrils. Then she relaxed a trifle.

"We're near to Arthur's, so I reckon it's all right but I'll have me a look."

"What's the matter?" asked Loudy and she glared at him.

"I'm sayin' you're damned lucky to have me for a pilot. Lucky beyond your deservings. Didn't you see that buzzard drop? Maybe he's just restin' or maybe there's somethin' dead off there. I aims to find what it is. By God, if you was on the

70

Clinch you'd ride safe 'cause no warrior in his senses would ever figure that you was aught but bait to draw him into an ambush. Stay here!"

She was gone like a she-wolf into the brush, dropping the rein before the raw-boned horse, which began placidly to crop the grass. In twenty minutes she was back again, reappearing with nothing more than a tiny rustle of leaves.

"Cow done dropped a dead calf," she remarked as she caught the bridle. "Reckon it's one of Arthur's an' he may feel upset over it." She looked at Loudy Jack and expelled her breath in a very audible "huh!" With that explanatory scorn puffing out from the almost masculine face, it dawned upon Jim that Loudy Jack was as incongruous upon the Holston as he had been in Maryland.

In no time at all they came out upon broad fields with solid fences that enclosed a dwelling so different from the eternal succesion of cabins that Jim gasped. It was not that it was pretentious, but its clapboarded sides, its wide porches took him home to Maryland. There he would have put it down as the residence of a small but substantial planter; here it was a mansion.

"Royal Oak," said Mad Ann. "Arthur's a-settin' there on his porch not anticipatin' the sorrow I'm bringin' him."

Colonel Arthur Campbell, red-haired with a salt sprinkle of gray, thrust a powerful and inquiring jaw towards them as they rode up. He wore broadcloth with moccasins as footgear, a not inappropriate foundation for the man who had held this frontier of Virginia by the strong hand against raiding indians. He surveyed them inclusively before centering his attention on the woman.

"Tidings, Ann?" he asked in a quick, excitable voice.

"Bad news," said she, and grinned in his face. "Reckon to break it quick. Your brindle cow's lost a calf an' the buzzards is at it."

The red-haired Colonel swore explosively and fully. "What else?"

"One damn idjit killed near Maiden Springs through girdling trees withouten a guard along with him. Left his rifle home an' reckoned that there warn't no indins within a hun-

71

dred miles. Delawares, three of 'em by the sign, lifted his hair an' no trouble to him."

"Tahgahjute?" rapped out Campbell in quick alarm, the indian gutturals, though unintelligible, rousing a responsive thrill in Jim.

"Logan?" Mad Ann shook her head vigorously. " 'Twan't him. He'd have done a cleaner job. Just three young bucks on their first warpath. Know that because they done killed a turkey 'bout five miles on their backtrail an' hadn't stopped to bury the feathers. When did Logan the Mingo ever forget anythin' like that? Why—" she wheeled round and pointed to Loudy Jack, "this feller might have done the same."

John Tendergrass bowed his head forward onto his horse's mane and the red-head bowed itself equally towards the porch rail in stifled amusement.

" 'Light down and eat with us," said Colonel Campbell hospitably, his features now under control; but Loudy with a fiery face mumbled that it was still early and they had to ride on.

"Surely," said Mad Ann in a high screech, "but I hope ye ain't goin' far. Gallop your horses, boys, an' you'll be harder to hit."

She turned from them and was going up the steps as they pounded away, for Loudy seemed bent on following her advice.

They went behind him down the valley where the road began to lose its firm identity and surrender itself to the thickets. There were old axe marks on felled trees and newer axe marks on sturdy saplings, withering in the dust, which revealed where later wagoners had been forced to clear the encroaching growth if they would carry wheels where wheels had gone before. The cabins and clearings brought no further ambitious anomalies such as Royal Oak. Jim asked Loudy how much farther it was to Uncle Trev's place and got the brief reply that another three hours should fetch them there. Beyond that he would say nothing, though Jim made a half-hearted attempt to draw him out. It was half-hearted indeed, for every anxiety that he had nursed upon the journey was coming to a head.

What did he know of Uncle Trev? Grandmother Dorsey might not have condemned him personally but she had certainly condemned his works. If Loudy Jack was the product of Uncle Trev's judgment and industry in gathering the right sort of people about him, then Uncle Trev was no bright prospect with whom to spend a year—maybe Uncle Oliver down on the Pamunkey might have been preferable after all.

Every step that Cricket took brought him nearer to a separation, the more painful because he had begun to put a proper value on what he was being separated from. John Tendergrass represented Grandmother Dorsey and the security with which he had so blithely parted ten days ago. More than that, Tendergrass had grown not only upon him but in general stature as well. Jim could understand some of this growth. Freed of responsibility for his tavern and his farm, out where he could dream dreams and grapple with the future, the shambling man had the inner strength to expand with the traversed mountains. With each mile of the journey he had cast off the defeat of his ten-year-long halt.

Jim felt mighty small and cursed his own cockiness. He had cast himself like bread upon the waters and these waters were unknown and bitter. The Bible said that bread cast like that would return sevenfold. Well, he might return like that or he might get soaked and sink, soggy and useless, to the bottom.

"Round the next turn," spoke up Loudy, and gave an "I'll get even with you" look at John Tendergrass. The latter, not so calm, fumbled in his pouch and drew forth a letter, at least a piece of paper, set with sealing-wax. He did not speak to Jim nor did Jim venture to speak to him, but Tendergrass' hand reached out and took the lad's knee in a grip that left the print of all five fingers impressed in the flesh. The bruise was a pleasant one and Jim did not wince. He kept his face straight to the front and mentally said his own farewell.

In spite of himself he could not repress his open curiosity as they emerged from the clump of liveoak which sentinelled the turn. Uncle Trev was a trader in land and had made land his life's work. Surely it would show in cleared fields and growing crops. He mentally estimated Colonel Campbell's Royal Oak and compared it with what a man could do who hadn't occupied the greater part of his time in fighting indians. Then he checked Cricket in her canter.

Before him was the familiar forested plain broken only in

one spot where three cabins—not houses—squatted in a clearing barely big enough for them and for a small pasture where a half-dozen rough horses grazed.

"That's it," yelled Loudy and thundered on down the road with the packhorse galloping behind him. Jim sat and stared until the rusty voice spoke in his ear.

"Reckon we'd better be gettin' after him," it said. "Seems we've fetched to the Holston."

Just a few strides on Cricket, and Jim was in the space between the cabins where Loudy was already dismounting. A squat, powerful man had come out of the door and was helping with the packhorse. Jim stared at him openly. He looked strong enough to lift a bull. His complexion was swarthy and exuded grease. His clothing stank of it, his face fairly ran it, and the big jaw was like a hog's jowl. That was Jim's first impression, and he knew that John Tendergrass shared it by the smothered grunt that sounded beside him.

Then the squat man came towards them to help, and when Jim saw the tender, broken-witted countenance, smiling like a friendly puppy, he answered the smile almost as quickly as Cricket and the brown horse, obeying their instinct, reached questing muzzles towards the kindly hands.

"That's Greasy Pete," called Loudy, beating the dust from his clothes. "He ain't all there."

Greasy Pete showed no sign of resentment as he took the reins. "I skin for your Uncle," he said in an accent that Jim did not recognize. The clear blue eyes, unclouded by intelligence, joined in the smile upon the thick lips.

"You're a nice boy," he stated without reserve. "I like you."

"And I like you," said Jim instinctively and would have blushed had he not heard John Tendergrass say almost the same thing. "An' I likes you too, Greasy Pete. Beggin' your pardon but I'm not gettin' off. I'm ridin' on."

Out of the largest cabin came an enormous gray-haired negress, exclaiming loudly as she waddled in a burst of speed to the embarrassed Jim.

"Marse Jim!" she cried. "My baby! I was house servant to old Marse Cheston an' I knows you when I sees you. You're the spittin' image of your father." In one enveloping sweep she took him in her arms and crooned over him, then shot a command over her bulky shoulder to a slatternly negro girl who was standing in the yard with her mouth wide.

"Worthless!" she commanded. "Tell Marse Trev that Marse Jim is here."

Disengaging himself gently, Jim looked where she looked. His Uncle Trev had not needed any further summons. Taller than even Jim's memory had admitted, clean of face and of linen, his uncle strode forward and put out his hand. His hunting shirt was spotless linsey, his breeches spotless buckskin, the leather of his belt was the dark brown of well-kept saddlery.

Jim met firm pressure with firm pressure and his heart leaped with the unloading of the burden of dread. Uncle Trev's complexion under his bronze was clear, there were no tell-tale veins prominent on his beaky nose. John Tendergrass swung down from the brown horse and broke in on them as they stood measuring each other.

"You're Treville Cheston?" he inquired without impertinence and, Jim thought, with considerable relief.

"I am, sir," answered Uncle Trev in an assured, commanding voice.

Loudy Jack was clutching at his arm. "Here's the boy. I done brought him safe in spite of this feller."

Uncle Trev frowned. "Hush, Jack. Who is this?"

"John Tendergrass," answered the shambling man. "You got ink and a goosequill in the house?"

"Possibly so," admitted Treville Cheston. Rising annoyance was turning the bronze of his cheeks to copper.

"Then will you fetch 'em? I've got somethin' here that requires an answer."

He held out the folded sheet of paper and Uncle Trev, with a puzzled sweep of his eyes from the out-thrust lip of Loudy Jack to Tendergrass' immobile countenance, opened it.

One glance and he gave an exclamation. "A receipt! From Treville Cheston to Mrs. William Dorsey for James Cheston travelling in the care of John Tendergrass."

"Just that. Will you sign it? I've made delivery."

Uncle Trev signalled the colored woman. "Juno, fetch the pen."

There was an unexpected objection. "Marse Trev, I don't know where it's got to. You had it the last time I seed it."

Treville Cheston turned on his heel and went into the cabin. While they waited they could hear Timms questioning Greasy Pete.

"Where's the others?" he asked as if he were surprised. "Out huntin'?"

Greasy Pete's expression clouded over. He swept his hand towards the little group. "You, me, Juno, the girl," he paused and when he finished the accent was stronger than ever. "Is all."

"What the hell do you mean, 'is all'? Talk English, can't you, you damned Dutchman."

Greasy Pete made that sweeping gesture again. "Is all," he repeated and this time with a finality that proved he had no more to say.

Uncle Trev came out again with the paper in his hand. He walked straight to John Tendergrass.

"It is signed." His tone was completely unfriendly. "I cannot deny the rites of hospitality as practiced upon the border though I may say that I do not care for your manner. Will you eat with us?"

John Tendergrass was back on the brown horse. The paper was safely bestowed in his pouch. "No," he answered, and the rusty tone predominated. "Reckon now I can pick and choose for my own self."

For the first time in their acquaintance he touched his hat to Jim.

"You'll do to cross the mountains with. Couldn't find no better than you."

He and the brown horse plodded out of the yard, the long rifle across his saddle.

"An insolent scoundrel!" exclaimed Uncle Trev.

VIII

Loudy Jack was full of grievance and Treville Cheston's angry comment on the departing John Tendergrass gave just the tilt to pour it out. "He's every bit what you say, Trev, and I'd have had it out with him long ago 'ceptin' I was afeared that the boy here . . ."

"Excepting that you were 'afeared,' " interrupted Jim, unable to contain himself.

His uncle spoke sternly. "Jack Timms is my friend, James."

It was a pontifical, arrogant statement and Jim was stung. "John Tendergrass is mine, sir," he said between his teeth.

Uncle Trev's brows drew down. "Then he is a bad friend who will teach you defiance of your own kinsman. Go into the house and await me there."

White-faced with anger, Jim barely managed to control himself. He obeyed, to find Juno bustling consolingly after him.

"Now, Marse Jim, let them thunderclouds pass from off'n your looks. That Timms man runs kind of stunted and puny in my mind. Marse Trev is good an' mad right now, but it'll pass quick unless you goes on defyin' him right out. I knows he's got a lot of worries that you ain't heared about yet. You set yourself down an' I'll fetch you a pitcher an' a basin so's you can wash that there dust off. No gentleman can think real comfortable if he ain't clean."

Greasy Pete carried in the saddlebags and Juno bore down on him.

"Gimme them," she cried, "an' don't you go near a chair."

Pete showed hurt. "I knows I sits broad but I only broke the one."

" 'Tain't that," said Juno, relenting. "It's them filthy buckskins. Last time you set yourself down I was a week rubbin' the grease into the wood so's it wouldn't show."

She took the saddlebags and carried them off by a doorway that led through a partition in the rear of the room. Pete smiled shyly at Jim and made a comprehensive gesture at the walls and the furnishings. "Pretty, ain't it?" Then, without waiting for a reply, he walked out. Jim took time to look about him and was surprised at what he saw.

The walls were no more than the usual chinked logs, but they were lined with shelves upon which stood silver plates, pitchers and goblets, alternating with a few pieces of glassware that did not match. Bear and deerskins, cured with the hair on, covered the floor. While the table was a rough thing hewn

77

from puncheons, the chairs were the same dainty, well-designed pieces that Jim had heard admired at Grandmother Dorsey's. "Imported from England," he thought in surprise and his surprise deepened as he saw the books carefully ranked in one corner, the great punchbowl on a small, varnished sideboard and the muslin curtains at the windows. He was prepared for the rifles resting on pegs in a row like an armory, prepared also for the deep fireplace with the logstick from which the kettle could be suspended. He was not prepared for the twin vases that crowned the mantel, nor for the hand-drawn map, a yard square, tacked to the wall behind them.

Juno caught him at it. "Here's your pitcher an' your basin. The water's hot an' I brung you a towel." There was a catch in her breath as he thanked her and began to wash himself. "I does my best, Marse Jim."

"It's a mighty good best," said Jim and meant it. Except for Ingles' ordinary, he had seen no such neatness along the border.

"I thanks you, suh." He looked up at the tears in her voice. "What's the matter, Juno?"

The old negress wiped her eyes on her dress, exposing a mass of red petticoat. "Don't you pay no 'tention to me. It's jest that I was raised as a house-servant an' I has my pride. Lord, Marse Jim, the houses I've come to keepin' for Marse Trev. Them chairs had mates an' we had a table, real mahogany, but we had to leave that when we left York State an' Marse Trev bought land down in Pennsylvania. That glass was real handsome once, but it don't keep when it's hauled in wagons or toted by packhorses. Seems to me every time we moves we has to leave somethin' an' we never gets anythin' to make up what we loses." A world of longing showed in her round, furrowed face. "Some day I hopes Marse Trev settles down in a real house an' I can keep it right."

She whisked away the towel as Jim finished drying himself.

"I ain't complainin'. Marse Trev's been mighty good to me an' he's a big man out here—only he's got feet what carries him all over a-huntin' for land an' he ain't never satisfied when he gets it."

"That will be enough, Juno," said Treville Cheston's deep voice behind them. He did not sound annoyed, but took down a long cherrywood pipe from over the mantel and filled it with tobacco.

"I beg your pardon, James." He reached for another and offered it to his nephew. "Do you smoke?"

"On occasion, sir," said Jim guardedly.

"Shall we consider this an occasion, then? I assume it has a right to be. It has been ten years since we have seen each other."

The two Chestons sat and covertly studied each other under the curling smoke. The strong cast of Uncle Trev's face did not disguise its amiability, although Jim sensed care and trouble underneath.

"I fear that I was not too courteous to your companion—this man Tendergrass. I trust that you will not feel too bitterly towards me. Had I considered I would have realized that it was your Grandmother who sent him with you and that you had no choice."

Just in time Jim remembered Juno's warning, but he must have betrayed his thoughts, for his Uncle frowned.

"I sent Timms for you with a purpose. I cannot blame you that neither your Grandmother nor yourself could realize it. Timms has a solid foundation of woodlore and he is willing to impart that knowledge to those who are sympathetic and ready to appreciate his teaching." (Here Jim involuntarily harked back to Loudy's hurt, insinuating voice after their first halt along the trail.) "I had hoped that you would have arrived here with a grounding of instruction which I must now impart to you myself."

Jim tried to be respectful. "I'm sorry to cause you inconvenience, sir."

"It is most certainly inconvenient, coming at this time. I am busied with preparations for my journey to Kaintuckee and I find my nephew the least ready of those who are to accompany me."

There was no reply ready on Jim's tongue and he studied the cracks in the floor. Treville Cheston puffed at his pipe.

"Perhaps I am being unfair," he said at last. "I am unaccustomed to young men and I may judge you too harshly. If you will stop to consider I am sure you will realize that Jack

Timms several times saved you from the consequences of Tendergrass' brawling temperament."

Jim glanced up with so much astonishment that his uncle unexpectedly twitched his lips.

"Perhaps I have heard only the one side of the story, yet Timms does not lie. You may have drawn a wrong impression. Will you tell me about your journey?"

Jim, encouraged, gave a brief report, watching his uncle's reactions as he did so. Too wise to dwell upon the minor matters which had caused the chief irritation he mentioned the original quarrel over the carrying of the rifles only in passing. If he drew a correct conclusion, his Uncle's sympathies were entirely with Loudy until Jim came to the argument over the reckoning at Orange Court House. Then the listener set down his pipe while his fingers clenched over the stem.

"Timms had money! I gave him enough for both of you! You say he paid nothing?"

"Nothing, sir, while he was with me. He kept saying that you would pay for everything."

"And that I will!" The anger that Jim had felt in his uncle was now diverted after a new quarry. "I knew that Jack was unscrupulous where money was involved, particularly when the money was to be obtained from someone else besides me. When we were in Pennsylvania he took my guests who visited me upon the frontier out to hunt and charged them for it, as I found out afterwards. He a hunter! He a woodsman! A blind child would be a better guide in deep forest!"

Jim was bewildered. Five minutes ago Loudy Jack had been extolled as an expert, now he was condemned without measure. Uncle Trev sat looking at his pipe; then he refilled the bowl and laughed.

"Ah, he's a rogue! Probably the first ordinary at which he stopped on his way north took the most of his money and the rest followed with each ordinary *in sequitur*. He would use his wits to bring you back, especially as he knew I stood ready to pay."

Juno was setting platters upon the table, and the clatter gave Jim an opportunity to collect himself after these bewildering changes. There was a puzzle here that he could not fathom. Why did his uncle dismiss as amusing the bare-faced cheating of his deputy? Uncle Trev, still chuckling, told him to go on.

When he came to the account of their meeting with Thomas Jefferson, he was halted and asked to repeat the conversation at the Charlottesville ordinary. His uncle's eyes were alight with interest and he leaned forward in eager consideration.

"So that's his plan! At least it's good politics whatever its practicability. He'll be the next Governor of Virginia, James, and he'll do his best to carry it through. Yes, yes, that conversation is the deciding factor in sending me up the Wilderness Road. It means that Virginia will try to hold the West and we can deal with Virginia for our land titles. The Henderson Patent probably will be vacated, to leave room for new owners to take up the abandoned properties. We will go there and each make our claim, you, myself and my men . . ." He stopped and the animation went out of his manner. "I had forgotten that the most of them have lef'," he continued slowly. Jim expected an explanation but Uncle Trev did not offer one. "No matter. We must content ourselves with what we can get. If we are early enough we are in a strong position when Jefferson's acts pass. We will be original settlers, do you see, and furthermore we can buy up the claims of others who are discouraged and turn back. There's money in it."

He sprang to his feet and paced rapidly up and down the room, Juno avoiding him deftly as she brought in platters of steaming venison and hominy. He talked as if he were thinking aloud and only partly addressing Jim.

"Tom Jefferson may plan one thing but he must deal with the House of Delegates and with the Tidewater planters who have an affinity for speculation. He must modify it! He must! He will take the half loaf to save the rest. What a chance!"

Jim watched him and considered both his manner and his words. He seemed to be in agreement with John Tendergrass as to what would happen, but his attitude was utterly different. Tendergrass had talked about making a stand in Kaintuckee and building up a property; Uncle Trev apparently had no such idea but merely looked to the financial profit. Then Juno announced that dinner was ready and his uncle came to himself and offered Jim a chair.

It was an almost pathetically grandiose table for the simple meal. Candles burned in silver candlesticks, there was linen and plate and even a chipped bowl of flowers as a centerpiece. Uncle Trev called for Madeira and, sharing it with Jim, drank in moderation. It was a wonderful, old wine, in wineglasses which did not match and were nicked at the edges from much washing.

Jim heard with increasing bewilderment his uncle explain to him amusingly the difficulty of bringing in such wine over the rough roads. "Colonel Campbell shares with me in this bacchanal enterprise," remarked Uncle Trev and was interested to hear that Jim had met the Colonel. From the subject of wine Uncle Trev slipped easily into others, reminiscences of his own days on the border, of hunts, of being lost in the woods, of people he had met.

Listening in polite puzzlement at first, Jim yielded to the fascination of the man, yielded the more easily since in spite of their unfortunate beginning his uncle was clearly showing his interest in his nephew. He was sorry when the meal was over and they took their wine to the chairs by the fireplace while Juno cleared away the dishes.

When they were alone, Uncle Trev sipped his last glass of Madeira slowly while his thoughts were obviously on another matter. The big shoulders sagged and the deep forehead was wrinkling under the sandy, gray-splashed hair. Then the cherrywood pipe was filled again and he stood to light it at a candle.

"I have talked a lot, it seems to me," said Treville Cheston, "but I am unaccustomed to the company of a kinsman." He bowed from the waist. "Our interests are the same, since you are my heir after your father."

Jim muttered his thanks. Whatever he thought of his uncle's speculations and his uncle's policy was partially disarmed by that bald statement. He knew that the older man thought to pay him the highest compliment in his power. He could not sense the need that existed in his uncle's mind for someone to talk to whose upbringing was the same as his own.

"I see no reason," continued his uncle after a moment, "why I should not tell you about my affairs."

He twiddled the stem of the wineglass in his hands. "Your

grandmother, I have no doubt, has condemned me. She has a right to. I sold Balcombe and I know that it grieved my brother when I did so. Yet a man must have his life as he chooses to make it, not as others will make it for him. I could not have stayed with my acres and my strongbox. Was it not one of the old Douglas lords who declared that he 'would rather hear the lark sing than the mouse squeak'? I had to see the new countries, the raw forests and the running streams.

"Lad, your face is not yet schooled enough to hide your doubts of my motives, but what I am saying is true. It is not only the small men who open up the wilderness, we speculators too have our place. It was Judge Henderson's money and trouble that sent Daniel Boone to cut the Wilderness Road—though I am willing to admit that there were others like Harrod and Ben Logan who went in of themselves. Henderson may have lost his money and his trouble, but Boone has stayed and the Wilderness Road remains. Yes, we have our place. What has the government done except dole out powder reluctantly and send militia commissions?"

His pipe had gone out but he drew upon it strongly. He set it down and held up the glass. Jim drew a breath. Treville Cheston, he realized, was justifying his life and his policy not only to Jim but through him to Grandmother Dorsey and to his brother, Jim's father. Then his uncle gave a little, bitter smile which showed that he had followed Jim's train of thought.

"Perhaps, James, you think I am growing most eloquent as counsel for the defense. It may strengthen my case if I confess to you that I have failed, failed almost utterly, and that you come to me when my affairs, about which I talked so largely earlier, are near their nadir. I have bought lands but never stayed to see them developed. I have sold out to other speculators, my dreams unfulfilled, and all because of myself."

He was still holding the glass and staring at the Madeira in it. With a quick, decisive gesture, he threw the last of the wine into the ashes on the hearth. "*That* I can resist," he said, "but land speculation I cannot."

Jim tried to say a word of consolation, groping through his vocabulary for an appropriate phrase. His uncle smiled wryly.

"Don't try, James. You are too young to console the sorrows of experience. Do as do the judges in the lawcourts and take the whole matter 'under advisement.'

"Wherever I went I acquired friends—or so I considered them. Six of them were in my employ. They did the things that I was too busy to do for myself, built my cabins, herded my stock, drove my wagons and hunted game for my table. In return I housed them, fed them, and not only paid them well but saw that they shared in my ventures. Also, by God, I protected them with my own money when my ventures went badly, as nearly all my ventures have done, James. I have had just enough success to lead me on when actually through the years my funds were slowly dwindling. Two days ago these followers of mine left me, except for Timms who has just arrived and for Pete who has the virtue of loyalty. No doubt you have noticed that Pete is not mentally sound—which probably accounts for it."

"Loudy Jack admires you," ventured Jim for lack of anything better.

Uncle Trev nodded but with a line above his eyes. "I don't know how he'll behave when he finds out just how badly off I am financially. The others were shrewder, and to be honest I don't know what Jack would do if he didn't have me to support him. By the way, James, you'll oblige me by not calling him 'Loudy.' He is sensitive about it, though I never saw a nickname better bestowed."

He patted his nephew's shoulder, then spoke slowly.

"Why am I going to Kaintuckee? Because my lands near here have failed me disastrously. I paid too much for poor property. I am selling them now and putting what I get for them in my saddlebags to carry up the Wilderness Road. It'll be a month or so before I can be ready and in the meantime you can consider another matter—whether or not you'll come with me. I can send you back to your grandmother without going to debtor's prison and meanwhile you've seen the border. One glimpse is enough to last a lot of people for a lifetime."

Jim felt a surge of liking overcome his early distrust. Before he could answer, Treville Cheston shook his head with a smile.

"I still say, take it under advisement. I've been near to flat-

84

tering you, James, and flattery is easy medicine to take, only it does you no good once you get it down. I should know, I've been having regular doses of it for the past ten years."

His shrewd glance read Jim's expression. "You've heard of it, no doubt. It's my second vice and I'm not sure which is the worse. From now on I'm going to try to believe a little less in what I hear. Now let's to bed. Juno has been complaining that we are nearly out of venison, and with no hunters to do it for me I suppose I'll have to hunt it for myself."

He led Jim through the partition to where built-in bunks, deep in quilts, invited their company. He was silent and introspective until Jim tumbled into bed.

"I warn myself against flattery," he remarked. "It is as insidious as a taste for Monongahela carried to an extreme. Now I'll 'outen' the candle, as Pete says, and I will have words with Timms tomorrow about that money."

Next morning before sunup, they ate mush and milk and, taking their rifles, went out to where Greasy Pete and Loudy Jack were waiting with the horses. Cricket whickered a greeting and Jim went over to her. As he tested girth and bridle, Loudy Jack sidled up to him.

" 'Member what I said before?" he asked in a carrying tone clearly intended for Treville Cheston. "Now you'll see some hunting." Jim shot a quick glance. Uncle Trev was smiling.

Ashamed for his uncle, Jim mounted angrily. Cricket threw back her head and rolled an eye at him. He released the curb which he had drawn too tightly and patted her neck. Then his anger evaporated. For the first time he had begun to understand Treville Cheston. Failure and defeat had aroused a need for bolstering that was ready to accept any prop, even flattery from a cheat.

Jim let Cricket walk out. He hated to admit it even to himself but he had begun to pity his uncle.

IX

Possibly Uncle Trev was determined to prove that on one point at least he was right, for he again mentioned Loudy's prowess as an instructor, telling Jim to go with him while he himself handled the hounds on the deer drive. The hounds had bayed Jim's arrival and he had noticed them leaping in their pen. Loudy discoursed upon their cleverness as they rode towards a narrow ridge running between two knobs which was a favorite crossing for their quarry. They were wise and well-trained dogs, and their function was to drive the deer to the ambush where Jim and Loudy lay side by side with a clear view of the run, a faint passage daintily scarred by pointed hooves.

Jim looked forward to the sport. At first when the priming spat he peered eagerly through the smoke to see whether or not his aim had been true. He held his fire when does or fawns ran past, but Loudy's rifle cracked without mercy. Loudy was shooting for meat, and deer without regard to age or sex represented only that. All in a whisper, Timms exclaimed jubilantly when he hit or cursed when he missed, until Jim felt a sick sense of massacre.

His rifle muzzle tilted upwards as a puzzled fawn, its mother knocked into a brown and white heap, nuzzled her to the click of Loudy's ramrod and then sprang aside into the bushes only to be cut down by Loudy's buckshot. Jim began to miss and miss regularly in spite of the muttered instructions, more and more angry, of his mentor. If he held high he could let the young does and their little ones take law of him and of the forest. When the hounds came up the trail and the gunfire ceased, he drew no pleasure from Loudy's boasting over the numbers of their kill.

The hound voices and the cessation of the reports were a signal to Greasy Pete. He and his packhorses broke through the laurel as Loudy gloated:

"Watauga settlers must have been drivin' 'em into the hills an' right into our arms. Never had such a day as this. With a man beside me instead of a crazy youngun like you we'd have got more."

Jim had partly finished reloading, the powder was rammed down and he was reaching for a bullet. Once he would have writhed impotently under the lash of Loudy's scorn; now without conscious volition he spat the bullet into the barrel and checked his priming with a hand that shook from rage. Loudy saw his eyes and the slack jaw fell open. Then Greasy Pete's soft crooning brought Jim to himself.

"Poor children! Poor children!" the skinner was saying as his knife made incision and sweeping cut. "Saint Nicholas needs you to play with the little girls and the little boys. Maybe you are hurted but not from me."

Jim wiped his damp palms on the grass and got control of his voice.

"How about the wounded ones?" he asked. Loudy cleared his throat nervously.

"I'll see to them," he said hastily. "You stay here with Pete."

Whistling to the hounds he vanished into the timber with a wary glance over his shoulder. Jim, still rather appalled at his own fierce reaction, felt the relief of wry amusement. Loudy was afraid of him!

Greasy Pete's kindly remark showed that he too had seen. "Maybe you better not go with Jack alone until we get to Boonesborough over," he said, and Jim, puzzling out the warning, was inclined to agree. Maybe he hadn't better be alone with Loudy until they got over to Boonesborough. It might be safer for both of them. Then he looked at Pete with surprise. Possibly the skinner's mind was affected but his powers of observation were not.

"Thank you, Pete," he said awkwardly but the only answer was the diffident, uncertain smile and a sort of generally pleased expression like that of a praised hound. There was no more to be said and Jim turned to helping with the skinning.

Jim talked that night to Uncle Trev. It was strange to sit opposite that dignified figure, quick to renew the forest-stained linseys, and discuss matters with the luxury of Madeira to soothe them. Uncle Trev was interested in his opinions of the hunt.

"As you say," he summed up, "you have no feeling up to a point towards the deer any more than towards the calf slaughtered to make you your veal, but I confess I share your disgust when that point is passed. Sometimes I hold my own fire—and yet why should I? Venison is our food and the deer our enemies. Wait until you have planted an early garden and have those clever noses and sharp hooves spoil your labor. You may feel differently after that." He refilled his glass, and came to the subject that Jim dreaded. "Did you learn anything from Jack Timms today?"

Jim considered his answer. The border-change was working on him. He met his uncle's glance squarely. "Reckon I can't learn from him, sir."

Uncle Trev's temper rose. "I would appreciate it if you would modify your attitude."

"Sir, the man's a scoundrel!"

"James, I'll not tolerate such language!"

Jim did not quail before his wrath. He had seen anger more formidable at Ingles' Ferry and he stood up without hesitation.

"You have condemned him yourself, sir, and to me directly. I have travelled with him and I too have formed an opinion. Of my own free will I've come here, but now I'll tell you that if you ram that man's company down my throat I'll ride back to Maryland and I'll go alone."

For a moment Uncle Trev seemed ready to continue the quarrel. Then he turned away and walked to the window. Jim, having issued his ultimatum, waited quietly for the result. Regardless of how much the other might bluster, Jim was resolved not to subordinate himself to Loudy Jack.

Uncle Trev abruptly left the window.

"Sit down, kinsman," he said, smiling. "Let us agree to disagree. Perhaps it is better that you hunt with me in future."

Jim had outfaced his uncle because in a sense he represented that family opinion of which the latter was so conscious. Both of them subtly acknowledged the fact. Confronted with a flat refusal to be bullied, Treville Cheston had no alternative but to let Jim go or to accept him approximately as an equal.

From the incident arose a new relationship between them. There was more respect on both sides and a dawning affection. They hunted together, and inexperienced Jim began partly to believe Loudy's description of his uncle's abilities. From him he learned to put his heavy bullet through a squirrel where it crouched along a limb, learned the lore of tracking in which logic and experience share equally, and looked forward to their evening talks when, reserving his own opinions, he listened fascinated to an educated man's experience and reactions to frontier life.

One night his uncle in one of his moods of introspection made an admission that surprised Jim.

"I have never been on the true border," he remarked. "The Holston is as near to it as I have ever come, and I have been here less than a half year. Always there have been settlements to screen me from the indians just as the Clinch partially screens us. That is why our hunts always take us towards the Watauga.

"Keep that in mind, my lad, before you decide to take the Wilderness Road in my company. There is no shame to you if you decide not to go. It might be the part of wisdom."

"There's no wisdom in the young." Jim was half joking, half sincere.

Uncle Trev laughed. "You have the inclination, I see, but I have not decided for you. July is more than half gone. My holiday with you is over and I must see to the selling of my lands. Let us say the last of August or early September. We shall examine your father's grants and see whether or not I should take up lands of my own. With luck we should be back here in the late fall; if not we must resign ourselves to spending the winter at Boonesborough or at Harrodsburg. That is another factor for our calculations, James."

Jim mulled this over and then asked a question. "What makes these Kaintuckee settlers go so far beyond the safe limits?"

"Some, of course, go for adventure, but the majority, I think, for freedom as well as gain. Good land is expensive and easily exhausted. The poor man can never get his farm more cheaply than by risking perils others will not face, and the man whose farm is worn out must become a tenant or seek another."

"The border seems a bloody country."

"It is and more so today than ever. There is always an undeclared war raging, with its steady drip of blood. When a great conflict breaks out the drip becomes a stream, for the indians are armed and encouraged by the warring sides. Burgoyne has taken Ticonderoga and the raids we hear of clear down here are the ripples of his advance. If the King ever defeats us the indian war will still go on. It has been easy to start—it will be less easy to stop."

He covered a yawn with his palm. "Tomorrow you shall fend for yourself with no more caution from me than that you stick to the main trace and go not into the forest alone."

Next day Jim was left with Cricket's back and the Holston to range along. The mare was company in herself. She gave her rider her full confidence and occasionally would stick her nose back towards his knee and whicker in a low tone until he patted her neck. With her powerful young body under him he could go fifteen miles in either direction and fetch back easily to Uncle Trev's ceremonious dinner.

At first there were unfriendly looks from those he met or passed. Did he want to water his mare? The devil himself was welcome to spring or trough by the code of the frontier. Jim took this small favor with a smile and courteous thanks. Next time he rode by there might be an answering smile, and the third time, perhaps, a hand on Cricket's shoulder and a brief discussion of the weather, the hunting or the crops. If the men did not say much they were deft on sounding him out, and what he had mentioned to one soon seemed to be a part of the universal knowledge of the settlement.

This comparatively rapid thawing puzzled Jim until the day Cricket cast a shoe near the tavern and blacksmith shop kept by one Sim Nottaway, an uncleanly man with a shrewd eye. The tavern was near enough to Uncle Trev's to provide an occasional jug of Monongahela whenever the household had need of it, but Treville Cheston had spoken disparagingly of the proprietor ever since, on drawing a cork, he had discovered the corpse of a woodmouse. Jim was too wise to ride Cricket on three legs and led her to the smithy with the shoe in his hand.

"Lucky you found it," remarked Nottaway, setting skilfully to work. "Lose a shoe and lose a horse we say. Well, we advances step by step and tacks it back on."

Jim stiffened like a pointer dog. That phrase was too individual not to carry a message for him. The blacksmith pared down the hoof.

"Feller named Tendergrass had his liquor and fed his horse here a while back. You're Jim Cheston?"

"Yes."

"I recognized you by the mare. She's better known than you are. Lads are right plentiful but mares like that is some scarcer. Tendergrass he said to tell you that he was ridin' back to Maryland. Said he'd found out what he wanted."

Jim tried to puzzle out the meaning. "Was that all?" he asked.

" 'Fraid it was," said Sim Nottaway. "He did let on that he thought a heap of you. Couple of times you've rode by I reckoned I'd hail you but I kind of wanted to see first how you'd act. No high and mightiness about you, son, like there is about some others that I ain't mentioning."

"That's all he said?" repeated Jim rather forlornly.

"If you can't figure it out I can't either. I've got to admit I've done some wonderin' myself but then it ain't none of my business. Reckon them nails will hold. I charges a shilling."

Jim paid him and rode home, for once provoked at Tendergrass' taciturnity. He thought it meant that Tendergrass would be back, but he could not be sure and the possible double meaning made him mope for a day or so afterwards.

Meanwhile, being a perfectly normal young man of nineteen, he had looked at the Holston girls. He had seen too many swinging appetizers to his fancy, real handsome ones in spite of the daily toil, to believe that the average frontier woman had eleven children and one tooth. Yet if he tried to strike up even a speaking acquaintance he found them stand-offish. He hadn't understood. Was he so bad looking that they walked away after ten words or treated him as if he had the smallpox?

He got his answer eventually from a man whom he noticed at a cabin washing himself next the trough, using a leather bucket so the water would not be fouled for the stock. Adam Dobson had seemed nothing better than another of the dirty, weary settlers whom one met when the sun was going down and the long shadows from the mountains were eating up the valley. It was only when he took his head out of the bucket, blinked his eyes rapidly, saw Jim and gave a wide grin that he became a person in his own right.

" 'Light down," he invited. "Take your share of the soap. It's right strong with lye but it takes lye to get the dirt out of a huntin' shirt an' my face must be better tanned than the leather." He surveyed Jim with a humorous expression. "You can use it. If you don't think so, pick yourself out a nice still bit in the next creek an' have a look."

Jim laughed and shared the soap. It stung him until he stamped with pain but Dobson with a commiserating mutter poured on fresh water until Jim could see again. When the tears stopped flowing he found himself surrounded by a covey of grave children, the oldest about nine, while two women, one with a baby nippling at her breast, smiled at him from the cabin door.

"There now," soothed Dobson, "familiarity breeds respect in this case. Ain't never anybody had contempt for lye soap once they've tried it. This is my wife an' this here's my sister-in-law. The children sort of confuse us in a nice way. We know which belongs to which but they are liable to swop houses dependin' on what we serve at meals. Will you take cornbread and bacon with us?"

Jim had stayed overtime on occasion before, when he had miscalculated how long he would need to get back. Juno had grumbled but Uncle Trev had made no complaint. He decided to risk it.

"I'd be mighty glad," he answered and surrendered himself to a hospitality which fed and cared for his mare as well as him.

Contrary to the usual frontier custom the women ate with them, and for the first time Jim found that he was welcomed naturally in a settler's cabin. It was not just Dobson who did the talking; the women were perfectly willing to interject remarks and address Jim directly. Halfway through the meal, Dobson turned to him.

"We're getting to know you, Jim, all of us along the Holston. Your uncle is a well-meaning man but those he called his friends were not, especially with women. It's fortunate they left when they did. People were coming to the end of their

92

patience and were thinking about taking steps. Perhaps that accounts for their speedy departure."

The change in him, even to the manner of speech, was so abrupt that Jim forgot to defend Treville Cheston and merely gaped.

Dobson chuckled. "Don't look so astonished, lad. I went for one year to the college of William and Mary while my brother sweated to send me there, but I had no ambition to be a lawyer nor a physician and I ran away to come back here—only we lived on the Watauga then. We are not all uneducated boors on the frontier."

Jim stuttered a disclaimer but they were amused rather than annoyed at his embarrassment.

"Ever hear of Lulbegrud Creek?" asked Dobson. "Daniel Boone discovered it in Kaintuckee."

"Don't know that I ever have," answered Jim, puzzling out the meaning. Was it some indian word with an appropriate application?

Adam Dobson chuckled again infectiously. "Have you ever read Swift's *Gulliver's Travels*? I thought not. It's the greatest satire on the human race that ever any man put down on paper. Boone fetched a copy with him on a long hunt and thus Dean Swift named the creek. Reckon I've shot you through with a new idea."

He changed the subject at once and began to talk of his brother, a paragon of all virtues according to him. The sister-in-law was listening with an intent face, though an over-clouded one. Jim soon understood the reason. Moses Dobson was in Kaintuckee now, had ridden there with the Virginia militia who had gone under Colonel Bowman to succor the settlements.

"They were picked from the whole valley," said Dobson. "We felt one of us was enough and as he is the better woodsman I stayed home to take care of things."

Jim wondered why Uncle Trev hadn't mentioned it. Surely if they themselves were going to Kaintuckee the fact was important. As Dobson went on talking and the full extent of the bad news emerged, he decided that his uncle might have been concealing it from him. The indians had been bold beyond

93

belief, far bolder than even Mad Ann Bailey had said. Raids and massacres had cleared out the scattered cabins and the minor settlements. McClelland's was abandoned, Hinkston's was abandoned, even Ben Logan was near to giving up at St. Asaph's. Boonesborough and Harrodsburg had both been attacked, and Boone himself had been badly wounded. Logan had ridden for help, ten days alone in the mountains, and the Holston had rallied to him. The warriors had drawn off, though for how long no man could tell.

Jim left with an invitation to return. He told Treville Cheston what he had heard. He spoke at first with a lingering resentment at being deceived, and then with astonishment, for obviously the other's surprised expression was not counterfeit. After Jim had finished his tale, his uncle sat still in his chair.

"I had not known," said the bitter voice after a pause. "I have not called upon Colonel Campbell, who is my chief source of news."

"But surely, sir, the settlers knew since so many went with Bowman. Surely you were consulted."

Uncle Trev flushed. "Must I tell you, James? Must I trail my shame before you? I may astonish you with my tricks of woodcraft, but not the border hunters. When the warriors are out I am left to sit at my hearth with the women and children. Likewise I am hated. How much of it is for my own sake as a landlord and how much for my deputies' sake I do not know. They are hard men along the Holston but also Christian men, else I would have been shot down as I rode long before. This Dobson can be a valued friend, I advise you to see more of him. Not altogether selfishly, lad, but because he can make you understand these people, something I have never been able to do."

He stood up with his hands slowly clenching themselves at his side. "Now care for your horse, care for the hounds, do what you will, but leave me to myself."

In misplaced loyalty Jim did not go back to Adam Dobson's.

The hot, dry August drew to an end and there began a bustle of preparation. Jim was included, though his uncle had as yet not made up his mind. Packsaddles were brought out and checked carefully, horses were reshod by Sim Nottaway, while

94

the packs themselves were made up. Uncle Trev mentioned that they would start in three days, and the words released several skeins of individual thought which promptly though imperceptibly began to twine themselves into an inharmonious whole.

The preparations of course took precedence. Four riding horses, three packhorses (Jim was omitted as a packhorse leader owing to his inexperience), extra moccasins, ammunition, cornmeal, sides of bacon, tea, flints, armorer's tools, salt, iron for horseshoes, blankets, horseshoe nails, shirts, socks, axes and even a spyglass went into the equipment, each article debated as to quality and quantity between Uncle Trev and Loudy Jack. A tiny anvil for repairing gunlocks was reluctantly laid aside, but leather, an awl, a sailmaker's needle and stout thread were added. Last of all, Uncle Trev laid out a jug of Monongahela.

"No more Madeira when we are on the road," he remarked to Jim with a smile. "Here is solace for the wet and the weary. Next to the flint and steel this shall be our comfort when the tea runs low. We shall ride the first day to Sapling Grove, 'tis no more than eighteen miles, and there halt until we are sure that nothing is forgotten."

He hammered home the corncob which plugged the jug. "Never start on a long journey without making the first stage a short one," he remarked. "Then what you have forgotten can be bought if you are at a settlement, or sent back for if you are not. A dull axe and a forgotten whetstone can cause trouble in plenty later on."

Old Juno had been hovering about them and Uncle Trev took money from his pouch. "You'll stay here," he said and poured a goodly stack of coins into her hand. "We'll be back for Christmas or not until next spring, depending upon how long we must stay to scout the country. You'll not be afraid?"

"No sir," she said. "It's only for you gentlemen that I'se afraid."

Her master laughed. "You help me, Juno, more than I can say. It's good for a man to have someone who'll fear for him when he is away."

The door opened and Loudy Jack came in without knocking. Jim had been trying on a pair of unaccustomed moccasins which Uncle Trev had advised him to substitute for shoes. As he looked up he was struck by Loudy's expression. It was a mixture of boldness and nervousness and it gave him a fore-warning of what was to come.

"I wants my pay and a settlement for my lands," said Loudy almost in a shout, as if he were whooping to his courage to stay with him.

Uncle Trev frowned. "For a spree, Jack? You are entitled to both and you shall have them, but why drink them away at Sim Nottaway's when we are so near to our start?"

Loudy's tongue wetted his lips. "I ain't a-goin'."

There was a dead silence; then Uncle Trev spoke deliber-ately. "You mean you are quitting me now?" he asked.

"Your risk is your own to take if you sees fit. I don't see fit. I'm a-quittin'."

Jim was about to speak his mind, but Uncle Trev silenced him with a wave of his hand.

"Juno, fetch me the saddlebags from under my bed. You shall have every penny of it, Timms, and on the instant. I had thought . . ."

With a strong effort he recovered himself, and when Juno brought him the saddlebags he counted out the money into Loudy's outstretched hand.

"As to the lands, the settlement for them is here. I explained your share in their valuation when I talked to you and Pete last night. Are you satisfied?"

"Yes," said Loudy ungraciously and turned to go as if he were glad to escape.

Uncle Trev said nothing. As Loudy started to leave he can-noned off the chest of Adam Dobson who was entering.

"Better stay," advised Dobson and spun Loudy back into the center of the room. "I got a bone to pick here an' I aims to find who it is I got to pick it with."

Dobson held a paper in his hand and he proffered it to Uncle Trev.

"Your man Greasy Pete brought this to me two hours ago. I acquit him of any knowledge in the matter. It is a demand for the final payment upon my lands."

Uncle Trev glanced at it and nodded. "It is, sir. I wrote it yesterday myself."

"Knowing that I had paid it in full?"

Uncle Trev started and his cheeks paled. "I had no such knowledge," he said steadily.

Dobson did not flinch. "I thought not." He too kept his voice down. "I have heard much evil of you but never that you would tell an untruth. Perhaps the matter has not been reported to you. Yesterday I rode here to find no one present saving your agent, Timms. I delivered the money to him on his promise to inform you and took no receipt since he said he could not write."

"He cannot write," answered Uncle Trev instantly. "Well, Jack?"

Timms was his own man now with money in his pouch, and the knowledge emboldened him. "I don't know nothin' about it."

Uncle Trev did not have to make a decision, for old Juno stepped forward with a swirl of cotton skirts and a flash of red petticoats. Her dark face was full of indignation.

"Don't you lissen to him, Marse Trev. I knows I'se a slave an' I'se got no right to mix in white folks' business but I see'd it all. I was a-freshenin' up the beds back there an' I saw this gentleman give the money to Marse Jack an' I heared what they said. I knows I can be whipped, but as my good Lord sees me, he's lyin'."

Treville Cheston set a hand for an instant upon her shoulder before he picked up the pen and wrote out the receipt. Then Adam Dobson was gone and Uncle Trev was looking upon Loudy Jack with a brooding expression. Loudy was licking his lips again and his head was turning towards the door. Treville Cheston spoke only after a long interval.

"You cheated my guests and I was amused, you cheated my nephew and I excused it, but now you try to cheat me of my honor. I shall do nothing about this attempted fraud if you return the money—for you're riding with me to Kaintuckee."

Loudy slunk out and Jim had the good sense to follow him after an interval, for his uncle was sitting with his face in his hands. Once outside Jim had some meditating to do on his own account. Should he go to Kaintuckee in such a company? Then he felt a pluck upon his linsey sleeve.

"You go for ride with me?" asked Greasy Pete humbly.

Jim looked back at the closed door. There were two hours before the time for dinner and he could do a lot worse than soothe himself in the kindly company of the skinner.

"Surely," he said and saddled Cricket.

When they started Pete took a definite direction and did not ask for Jim's suggestions. Jim was content, for he wanted a chance to consider what he had heard in the cabin. What mates upon the trail! Uncle Trev he could trust, but his respect for Uncle Trev's ability as a woodsman had suffered some diminution. Still it was only Uncle Trev himself who had deprecated it. But Loudy—and Loudy supposedly the second man in skill!

Then he happened to glance at Greasy Pete, who sagged forward on his horse and kept wiping his hands on the animal's mane.

At first Jim came near to laughing until he saw that the skinner was in a pitiable state of terror. Drops of sweat ran down his cheeks and his eyeballs showed so prominently that Jim thought he was ill.

"What ails you, Pete?" he asked concernedly.

"The Conjure Woman! I got to see her before I go the mountains over."

"Who is she?"

The answer, being in Pennsylvania Dutch, was perfectly unintelligible, but Pete at that moment turned his horse into a narrow path that led aside from the main trail. Jim followed him until the path ended in a clearing amidst a grove of hickories with a ruinous looking cabin perched on a hillock above it. Pete dismounted, but his hands trembled so that Jim had to tie his horse as well as his own. Affected by the skinner's fear, he looked to his rifle as Pete stumbled towards the cabin.

When Jim topped the rise he saw an old woman throw down a wooden hoe and hobble towards them from a scrap of a garden which lay behind the house. He examined her apprehensively but she seemed no different to him from a dozen grannies he had met—until she drew close. Then he felt a shock, for out of the mass of wrinkles peered a pair of fiercely bright eyes, with such an air of assurance in them that he bowed to her involuntarily.

To his surprise she caught her breath and studied him with a steady gaze that he found disconcerting.

"Are ye here to see the Conjure Woman?" she asked and her voice in spite of the tremors of age was sharp and clear.

He shook his head. "Not I, madame. My friend here . . ." He indicated poor Pete, who was bent almost double with terror.

"In with ye! In with ye!" she directed, and bending their heads under the low lintel they came into the cabin.

She took her seat on a three-legged stool which she drew to the far side of a heavy table, scarred and stained from years of use. Jim looked about him. The interior was as rough as any he had seen. The pallet bed in the corner was covered by a worn quilt and the pegs in the wall from which hung her few extra articles of clothing were concealed by a piece of cloth hanging from a deerhide thong. Though the dirt floor was muddied in one corner and the roof above it showed a glimpse of sky, the hearth was swept and even the kettle was scoured.

"Ye've a question?" she asked of Pete. Too shaken to speak he thrust his hand into his pouch and drew out a couple of gold pieces which he signed to Jim to give her. Jim laid them upon the table. Leaving them where they were, though her eyes brightened, the old woman went over to the hearth. She put several pinches of material upon it, taking them from a tiny chest, most incongruous to the place, a chest which looked to Jim as if it had come from overseas in some sailor's seabag. These she kindled with a coal from the banked fire and muttered over them. The smoke rose and tinged the cabin while still she knelt and muttered.

Jim's nose began identifying the ingredients. Tobacco, yes, and that's kinnikinnick—I learned to recognize the smell at Ingles' Ferry—the lame man smoked it, but what's the other? Then he knew it. Balsam! But where did she get balsam this far south?

The Conjure Woman helped herself up by holding to the stones of the hearth and came back to the table. From the little chest she had taken a handful of something which Jim could not make out, and she sat down, her hand still clenched, in front of Pete.

99

"Ask it," she commanded.

Greasy Pete spoke again in Dutch and Jim involuntarily smiled. If she could make out what he said he was prepared to say that there was more of the genuinely supernatural in her than he suspected. She raised her head and looked straight at him and he could have sworn that her lips twitched too, but the fierce eyes commanded silence. Then she dropped her glance to Pete, who had noticed nothing.

"Shawanoe devils and Cherokee devils and Delaware devils, I command, also the devils of this place," she said. "Would you have me call upon others who are strange to the Holston? Speak now in the language of the Holston and I'll answer ye."

Twice Pete called upon his English and twice he failed. The third time he spoke so low that Jim, who guessed what he was saying, could not be sure until she repeated it.

"You ride to Kaintuckee," she said and kept her glance down. "You've told me your company and you ask me will the journey be prosperous. See, I put no words into your mouth that you have not said. Is it not so?"

Pete managed to nod. Crooning again in a sort of wail that gradually rose higher and higher, she opened her hand to show the dry bones of some bird. Three times she tossed them into the air to let them fall upon the table. She examined their pattern until the third time, when she made them into a little pile. Her tone when the crooning stopped wiped the amusement from Jim's face. It was as if she spoke to them from far off but with such intensity that the meaning must be clear. In such a voice might a drowning man cry to a passing ship.

"Danger and death! Danger and death! Four dead men ride from the Holston. Kaintuckee ye shall not see!"

She rolled her eyes upwards, and Jim, while the gooseflesh pricked him, caught Greasy Pete under the armpits before he could slide to the floor.

"You've frightened my poor friend nigh to dying . . ." he exclaimed furiously. Again he was struck silent by her look.

"The warning is to you also, young gentleman. Lay him outside and come you back to speak with me."

Jim hauled Greasy Pete to the door and set him down on a grassy bank, muttering words of comfort which fell on unheed-

100

ing ears. Then he strode back into the cabin, furious with himself for being impressed by an old woman tossing bird-bones and talking in threats. The Conjure Woman was smiling and the gold still lay upon the table.

"Sit ye down, young gentleman, and assuage yourself of your rage. You may have your friend's gold back if you will; meanwhile hark to me."

"Madame!" he began again, and she changed personalities before his eyes. A wise, tired, aged face was before him.

"'Madame!'" she said. "Aye, 'twas that, and you bowed to me! You have the air about you too. Sir, I'll not keep you long but if you be a true gentleman you'll take the other stool."

Jim groped for it and sat down. His rage had evaporated.

"I'm English," she said, "from the North Country. I came over the seas as an indentured servant, a young girl, right frighted by what I met. I married me a man, a good man an' a good husband and by him I had three sons. They be all dead now and without childer of their own. Therefore I was left by my lee lone when my youngest fell at Point Pleasant three years ago. Who was there to till the ground for me? Where was I to go? You've seen my garden. Nay, young gentleman, needn't to nod. I saw you look an' look again when I came towards you an' look yet more when I had you within my poor house. My mother and my grandmother were wise women. Never a one but came to them for herbs or for childbed. My great-granny they burned for a witch when Cromwell was black upon the land. I kept them to mind when I saw that I would starve, an' since then I have been the Conjure Woman. Will you blame me, now?"

"God!" said Jim as her pathetic predicament became clear. He reached for the money which Uncle Trev had pressed upon him.

"Aye, God," she said and he knew better than to offer it to her. "D'ye think He'll remember me in my pain an' forget the Witch of Endor? Starvation and want is not a happy death—which is why I prey upon these poor fools. Yet I do not prey too hard. I heals an' I helps an' maybe I helped you and you not knowin'."

He could do no more than to thrust Greasy Pete's coins towards her. This time she took them and smiled.

101

"Have a care, my bonny young gentleman. There is reason in my warning. You'll go upon the Wilderness Road with danger and death upon your right hand and upon your left. You'll go with Treville Cheston—there's no witchcraft to my knowing. Greasy Pete has been here before an' I'd heared of you. A good man is Treville Cheston—he's sent me a haunch of venison more than once—but no Long Hunter. The Shawanoes are desperate bold an' I do not think that you'll fetch through. If you are caught, then most like there'll be four of you dead. 'Tis so I warned you an' I'd stop you if I could, but go if you must, young gentleman, an' may an old broken granny's blessing go with you."

Jim, blessed for the second time by a woman, got out of the house. He helped Greasy Pete upon his horse and led it by the bridle until the skinner recovered himself. They were almost back to the cabins when Pete straightened up and rode alongside. His hand still trembled and the sweat still coursed its droplets down his cheeks, but he had regained the gentle, quiet speech to which Jim was accustomed.

"Your uncle was kind to me, right kind to me when everybody else thought I was tetched. If he rides the mountains over, I'll ride too despitin' the hex she put on us. I'm afeared, awful afeared, but I'll ride with that kind man."

It was the decisive factor for Jim when Uncle Trev in serious conversation again urged him either to go home to Maryland or to stay upon the Holston, Jim told him in a tone that silenced argument: "Reckon I'll ride to Kaintuckee too."

X

Hooves upon the road again, jingle of bit and creak of leather —an old tune that still has power to stir the depths. To hear it in its proper setting there must be an accompaniment provided by the other senses: the smell of earth and crushed grass as the horseshoes bite into it, of iron and greasy wood from the rifle, of man and animal mingled; the sight of the rock-fronted mountains which uplift the trail and the heart as well, of the forest, half-brother to the ocean, rippling its leaves to the breeze with the red and yellow of the autumn turn floating in it like rare and colorful fishes; the feel of the muscular play of the horse beneath the saddle and the hard support of the stirrups, tangible through the soft-tanned sole of the moccasin. And if to these be added the very taste of adventure, the lips slightly dry and the tongue stealing out to wet them, then the road leads not only to its physical goal but also to the storage-wells of memory which make the minds of the very old turn eagerly from their daily shadow-existence back to the realities of their youth.

Four men with seven horses rode the Holston trail to Sapling Grove, then turned westward towards the valley's walls and to the sentry at the gate—the blockhouse at Moccasin Gap. One sleep amidst familiar surroundings, an ordinary archetypal of border ordinaries; then by a mere change of direction they dropped into the forest like a stone into a pool, leaving upon its surface only a thread of fading dust and the faint sound of their passing. This second night they must sleep with nothing but their own vigilance and skill to watch and preserve them, save for the off-chance of their meeting other travellers or hunters who might or might not be able to aid or advise. This was Boone's Wilderness Road.

The bearing of each of them changed as they rode. Treville Cheston was a Roman on horseback, rigid and controlled save that his eyes moved in scanning the trail; Jim leaned forward, unconsciously stroking the stock of his rifle; Loudy Jack kept staring and shifting, his hurt-child look prominent as he meditated upon his hard fate, making a new excuse for himself with each mile; while Greasy Pete, his tallowed cheeks pale to sallowness, thrust out his jaw and defied Fear to make him turn back.

The news at the blockhouse was bad. There had been talk of reoccupying Martin's Station, that further outpost in the Powell Valley at the foot of Cumberland Gap, but nothing had come of it. A scouting party had seen indian sign, footprints and a dropped feather, which showed that even as late as a fortnight before there had been a visitation from warriors to the deserted cabins.

103

"No sense in tempting fate that close unless you're one of them born fools who have made a stand in Kaintuckee. Not goin' to be many on the Road, 'ceptin' those a-comin' back an' knowin' better now." Their informant spat tobacco juice and slapped the peeled logs of the blockhouse, built that same year in case Kaintuckee should fall and the war come closer to the Holston. "This old bullet-stopper bids you welcome. She's thick an' she's solid. She'll give you good cover 'gainst the Shawanoes. Hark to her now an' don't go traipsin' off into the brush." He spat again and looked at Loudy with a grin. "I can see one of ye who's a-listenin' right close to good advice."

Uncle Trev regarded Loudy from under his brows. The night was coming down and the mountains seemed to crush down with it. "I thank you," he said, "but we'll camp tonight in Moccasin Gap."

The borderer stopped the monotonous movement of his jaws and stared at him. "Camp in the Gap tonight! Man, your horses are fagged, the sun's nigh ready to set an' you'll leave here to sleep under an ash on a mountainside!" He laughed softly but unpleasantly. "Well, you might be doin' us a favor unbeknownst to yourself. If there is any indins up there, and I ain't prepared to say that there ain't, you'll maybe save us a raid. With four fresh scalps an' them horses, 'pears to me they'd be mighty pleased an' go back to their lodges without a-botherin' us. Have it your own way."

Uncle Trev only nodded and gathered his reins, the others following, even Loudy Jack, for there was a decisiveness, a Rubicon-attitude about their leader which forbade questioning. Four miles deeper in the Gap they made their camp beside a little creek hardly deep enough to wet their feet, but cool and flowing. There they tethered their horses and built their fire against a breastwork of logs to reflect the heat, for while it was early in September the mountains offered chill foretaste of the fall. Jim and Pete gave each horse a chance to roll and fed them a small ration of corn, Loudy Jack cut wood, and Uncle Trev did the cooking with an ear alert for the sound of the axe. Once when it ceased overlong, he took his rifle and went off into the forest, only to reappear almost instantly as the sound began again. Jim, a trifle big-eyed, grinned at himself as he realized that it was not the peril of indians which

104

had set Uncle Trev to searching but the possibility that Loudy might be sneaking back to the settlements. Poor, blustering, frightened Loudy was the tonic Jim needed for his own courage. It was only human for him to bolster himself with the contrast.

Jim was assigned the first watch and Pete the middle, while Uncle Trev took the last, which would end with the dawn, usually the most dangerous time for indian attacks. Loudy would sleep in, and the risk of an inexperienced watchman was accepted lest he should leave them in the lurch. There was little talking before they went to their blankets, for already they were tired. Jim sat at the edge of the firelight, cross-legged, with his buttocks on soft moss and his rifle in his lap. The horses stamped and twitched tails while he listened to the night sounds. The wind was swishing softly in the bushes and a whippoorwill began the haunting, whistling song that made him think of graveyards and ghosts and other unpleasant subjects. There was a rustle behind him that made him swing around, finger on trigger and thumb bringing the hammer back, but it was only Uncle Trev, who slipped from his blankets and came silently beside him. His uncle spoke in a whisper.

"If I had stopped at the blockhouse I would not have gone on," he said. "If aught happens you will not think the worst of me?"

"No sir," said Jim, feeling more at home with his uncle than ever before. If Treville Cheston too was oppressed by the night and the strangeness, it gave them a bond. The older man seemed to feel it as well, for a slight smile crossed his serious expression. Then a distant, high-pitched scream which seemed to reverberate from the hills would have fetched Jim to his feet had not his uncle pressed him down.

"Painter," came the explanatory mutter. "Had you not heard it before?"

Jim knew he would not care to hear it again, particularly in the darkness of the indian country, but the panther twice more at intervals gave that eerie squall, terribly reminiscent of a woman in mortal terror. It was good to have the strong, reassuring figure squatting beside him, but his pride felt injury. Uncle Trev was giving up his own sleep to watch with him. He said as much and was rewarded by a deep chuckle.

"I'll go back to my blankets then. But, nephew," the serious note was back again, "remember it is not for money but for land that we are going to Kaintuckee."

Jim, with eyes and ears intent on the forest while the stars wheeled by, kept considering those words even as his active mind and senses kept guard. His thoughts were spaced out, interrupted by the small alerts which brought finger to trigger —the gleam of eyes which stared at him and the fire and then vanished; a fox, he judged, to be confirmed later by hearing it bark, high and yappy; the beat of an owl's wings overhead. At first Uncle Trev's remark seemed unnecessary, a mere restatement of a known fact, but later he began to capture its true meaning. His uncle was justifying himself, clumsily perhaps, but sincerely. He was following his old dream, his old consuming dissipation, but he was true to it and not plunging his followers into danger for mere avarice. Did he mean that this time he would carry out his scheme of development and not merely buy and sell?

Jim threw more wood on the fire and considered his own position. He was sure that Grandmother Dorsey wouldn't have approved of this trip. She would have preferred, like Grandfather Dorsey, that Major under Lord Amherst, to do it more in order with more men, competent guides and some semblance of the military art. Yet here he was in these uncultured mountains aiding and abetting Uncle Trev in his passion and his fault. Furthermore he was enjoying it, even the heartstopping thrills. Was it perhaps that he too shared that landhunger, unappeasable because it was spiced with adventure, which had brought Uncle Trev to the brink of poverty? Grandmother would have been firm about all this, he thought wryly as he shook Greasy Pete awake for the next watch.

There came times later when he caught himself wishing that Grandmother had been a lot firmer. The journey grew harder and harder; their ride to the Holston had been a joyous parade as compared with the Wilderness Road. Once over the low Gap they reached and crossed Clinch River well below the settlements, where they had to swim their horses and spoiled a portion of their cornmeal by careless packing. The Road, marked by blazes on the trees and by old cuttings, then began a sinuous twisting, here following a river upstream or down until it flew off on a tangent and stumbled higher along a creek to a divide in a mountain wall. The Alleghanies were unveiling their heights, not in one splendid sweep seen skytopping from a plain, but in a series of rugged buttresses each higher than the next, enfolded in laurel and rhododendron, which wound themselves like cypress roots across the compass direction of west.

Once they got off the Road through missing a blaze and clawed and cursed their way through a swampy bottom until they were fetched up short by an unscalable ridge. Getting back was even worse, for the horses stampeded, probably scenting a bear, and a packmare broke a leg. They shot her and went into conference over the disposal of her load, for even with its redistribution there was more than they could carry, and where every article was a necessity there was small room for choice. Some of their bacon, salt and ammunition, extra horseshoe iron and a hammer were buried under a liveoak next to a lightning-riven pine which might mark it, and they went on, that much shorter in their margin of safety.

Past Little Flat Lick, through Kane's Gap at Powell Mountain, down another creek to Wallin's Ridge, another climb and descent with grunting horses and muscles straining from holding back, then into Powell Valley and another river to swim. Here they reshod some of the animals, for the stony ground wore the iron thin, and Greasy Pete killed, in camp, a rattlesnake, which was showing an unwelcome desire to share his blankets. The Cumberland Range, seen ahead, aroused in Jim a momentary flare of interest, for fifty miles southward was the gateway to Kaintuckee, Cumberland Gap.

Martin's Station, temporarily abandoned owing to the indian peril, gave them shelter in its empty cabins with the old ashes still on the hearths and discarded articles of clothing making mustiness of the bare interiors. There Uncle Trev shot a hog, fast turning from tame to wild but still habit-bound to its broken pen, and they feasted upon pork, shameless of the grease which stained their fingers and their mouths and made them brothers in appearance to Greasy Pete. Three days' hard rain with a big wind kept them stormbound, and they blessed that unfortunate hog which kept them from dipping too deeply into their supplies. Jim looked for indian sign, hoping fear-

107

somely to find some, but the downpour had wiped it out and the dripping woods were not inviting. Then on again, past a second abandoned stand eight miles below the Station and even more forlorn, for the roofs had begun to cave in and the damp was spawning toadstools and fungus in the wreckage. Another camp succeeded, where Jim, who had walked beside Cricket part of the way to spare her, suffered a slight attack of "scald feet," an inflammation produced by wet socks improperly dried inside the wet moccasins and a definite danger in wilderness travel. He did not suffer the full effect, the boil-like agony that made even the hardiest borderers temporary cripples, for he could ride and take the weight off them.

At last they came to Cumberland Gap.

There was more color to the trees now and the white palisades of the naked cliffs made Jim think of the Cumberlands as a gigantic new-felled log lying in a bed of flowers, with the Gap itself like an axe-cut gashing the middle of it. Possibly the comparison occurred to him from the axe-swinging which they had to do often as they struggled up its flanks. The storm had brought down trees across the Road which had to be cleared before they could get by. Chop until one's hands were blistered, cut a sapling lever, thrust the severed trunk aside, lead the horses through and then look apprehensively ahead for the next inanimate nuisance which might lie just around the bend of the trail. He hardly realized that they were on the divide until Uncle Trev pulled up and pointed.

"Kaintuckee," he said.

It didn't look very extraordinary to tired Jim. Mountains still rolled their scornful shoulders on either side of a valley which seemed just like the dozen other valleys they had threaded, even to the inevitable creek draining its middle.

He should have thrilled, should have exclaimed, but he was dog-tired, his blisters irked him and his feet still hurt. What came to his lips was a wholly inconsequential expression of relief.

"Thank God it's downhill."

XI

Laurel and holly gave place to the great trees, oak, elm, pine and chestnut. As they descended further they came first to canebrakes and then to the creek. It was a well-known landmark, for the sulphur in the water gave it a distinctive yellow tinge and its name as well, Yellow Creek. The Road too was easy to follow. It was as much as eight feet wide, the remnant of the ancient Warriors' Path, the wartrail of the tribes. A wagoner would have found it a nightmare, with its sinkholes, its twisted roots and trappy rocks, its whipping branches overhead; but to a mounted man it was almost a bridle path after the slippery, winding, treacherous stretches in the deeper mountains.

The canebrake was a nuisance, however. The horses loved the fodder and swallowed it so greedily that they came near to choking. Then the exasperated party must stop to help one beast while the others did their best with sly lunges to sicken themselves as well. The men grew impatient, and snapped not only at the horses but at each other, until Uncle Trev wisely camped beside a spring where the water was not flavored with the sulphur. It was still early and they hunted in hopes of getting a deer, but brought in only a half dozen squirrels for stew, after an undue expenditure of ammunition.

They posted no sentries now. No watchman could keep awake after the gruelling toil of the trail. Their eyelids kept coming down like the quick curtain after a bad play. Fatigue was becoming cumulative. Every night they were tired, chafed and wet with sweat when they came to their halting-place.

Inevitably there followed the tasks of the night. The horses had to be unsaddled, watered and fed. Fire must be made, food cooked, moccasins and socks dried, and the wear and tear of the day's travel repaired. The rocky ground was hard on horseshoes and they might have to set up a smithy when every movement started a new ache. Jim's feet continued to give

109

trouble, though they were annointed with a decoction of oak bark and hardened by rubbing on salt, a tear-drawing process. Uncle Trev consoled him by saying that the worst part of the trip was over and went to sleep while he was saying it with the leg of a squirrel in his hand.

The mornings were as bad as the nights. To have slept on the hard ground and to crawl from blankets into the dew and the dawnwind, once friendly but now a searching chill which announced the presence of every damp spot in linsey shirt or breeches; to saddle again the worn horses, too ready to stumble—all that was hard. What was worse was the realization, increased by the mental and physical strain, that today would be another monotonous, slogging period of dragging hours with no more to anticipate than another camp as wretched as the last. And this day it rained again!

Cumberland Ford was their objective, fortunately a short ride but with the prospect of swimming their horses when they got there. The icy dip would be sure to wipe out the precious dry spots in their clothing which the beating rain and the frequent crossings of small streams had left. The discomfort of a wet seat, added to wet feet, with a saddle and stirrup contributing their punishment, is the last straw to a horseman and gives rise to a boundless exasperation. Jim, riding behind Uncle Trev, fortunately did not center his ill-feeling on his relative but upon William Augustus, Duke of Cumberland, the victor of Culloden, after whom the mountains, the Gap, and this triply damned river and ford were all named. Why in the devil should the wigged, redfaced, stiff bag of suet scatter his God-abandoned title over every obstacle in the Wilderness Road?

He warmed himself with consoling rage, while each time Cricket set a foot forward, each time the hard leather chafed him, each time a sinkhole made them dismount to lead past and his feet sank over his moccasins in mud, his body told him that it was ready to quit and lie down beside the trail. Of course when they reached it the river was running bank high and the ford was impassable.

They were looking at the flood when Uncle Trev whirled his horse with a warning shout, snatched at Jim's bridle and bolted for the woods. Jim, nearly losing his seat from the unexpectedness of it, caught one swift glimpse of a mounted figure on the far bank and hammered his heels into Cricket's flank. Then through the crashing of bushes and the confusion of plunging horses came a mellow hail:

"Quit your runnin'! We're white too!"

To pull up and disregard the panic on the other faces was easier for Jim in the realization that his own expression must have shown the same fear. They came back to the bank in haste, being unnecessarily rough with the innocent horses to conceal their shame. Then hail answered hail and the crossing was discussed.

The far party had a canoe. They were planning to ferry over and to swim their stock. Uncle Trev answered in a bellow that they'd be glad to help and the man on the far bank waved his arm in thanks. The canoe put out, four men in it, while the stream became studded with swimming horses, breasting, straining and snorting against the current, with an occasional cow shaking a horned head. The canoe led them like a bell-mare and, when they had put foot in the shallows, dropped back to aid the stragglers. The herd came out of the water panting and squealing, and was gathered in a compact clump, not too hard to do since the animals were bony and ragged of coat from hard travel and underfeeding. Jim, turning back the strays, was elated at their numbers. If there were this many of them there must be a powerful lot of people to meet here on the Wilderness Road!

Two men in buckskins leaped from the canoe while the paddlers took it back. Fires were built and the herd tethered. The sun was breaking through, and spirits revived. There was occasional joking even while, throughout the afternoon, nearly fifty persons, men, women and children with their gear, were ferried across with the hardfaced rearguard nursing their rifles. More fires added to the feeling of well-being, and the smell of cornbread, bacon, venison and bear was added to the steam of drying clothes.

Uncle Trev was talking with the leader down by the river-bank. Jim, watching them with the feeling that he had seen the newcomer before, decided that it was Adam Dobson's brother if the resemblance could be trusted. His uncle broke away with a grave expression and came towards him. His

111

linseys were no longer neat. The sweatstains under the arm-pits showed dark against the drying cloth and the weal which a lashing branch had left upon his face gave him an oddly sinister expression. He spoke to Jim as to an equal.

"Ten men from Bowman's force escorting twelve or fifteen families. They are quitting their stands and going home. It may be the beginning of a retreat from Kaintuckee."

He looked at his nephew as if he expected him to give him both consolation and advice. Jim swallowed and said nothing; then he recalled Mad Ann Bailey with her head over her shoulder, discoursing on the frontier.

"Is Boone among them?" he asked.

Treville Cheston smacked his hands together. "You have it! No, Boone is not among them. So long as the leaders remain the hardy ones will stay. These departures will cheapen land values! What a speculation!"

Unconscious that he had displayed the worst symptom of his land fever, Uncle Trev clapped Jim upon the back and sent him off to the fires. The red sunset, promise of good weather, was fading, and the flames were thrusting themselves into prominence. He looked at the wan, drawn faces, marked as much as his own by the Road. Then a girl a year or so younger than he held out a pewter plate, heaped and smoking.

"Might as well eat," she said.

He took the plate with a word of thanks and found that room was made for him at the fire. While he ate he answered the questions that were asked by right among travellers: the state of the trail ahead, the weather they had encountered, news of others' passing. He was not long in speaking, for most of these refugees had been over the trail before in his own direction and knew the landmarks, though a few had entered Kaintuckee by way of flatboats on the Ohio and thence overland from Limestone Creek. In turn they volunteered the same sort of information as to what he must encounter, and rather to his surprise were encouraging about the remaining difficulties.

" 'Tain't bad now," said the first girl. "It's what you've got to face when you get there. Being forted up all the time is kind of wearin' on the temper."

"Seemed to be particular hard on yours, 'Becca," commented another who might have been her older sister. "You sure treated Lige Bonham as though he wore on you like a millstone a-hittin' the grain.''

There was a drum-roll of laughter and the girl called 'Becca turned her head. "Lige looked at me calf-eyed once too often," she remarked in general. "Sittin' around inside the fort you gets to fallin' over people an' when one of them puts himself under your feet like a hound puppy, comes a time when you just kicks out without noticin'." She faced Jim directly. "When you gets to Boonesborough you might be kind enough to tell him that 'Becca Dunlop don't feel mad at him no more! Might even be glad to have him here, though you needn't tell him that."

"He will, he will, an' you won't be sorry when he does it either," remarked the sister.

"Maybe that's why she told him," put in a third, who was mending a packstrap. "Here, lad, throw over them moccasins of your'n an' I'll put a patch on 'em for you. Be more patch than moccasin before I'm done I reckon."

Jim was embarrassed but nobody else seemed to be in the least; so he took off his footgear reluctantly and handed them over. 'Becca's eyes twinkled.

"Nice, well brought up young man," she commented. "Don't like to stand barefoot in front of us women. We loses most of our manners on the trail. For instance now I ain't commentin' on the appearance of your hunting shirt, nor yet your breeches, but I might let on that you're sportin' a stubble beard with what's left of your face that's peekin' out above it speckled like a trout's back."

Jim ran his hand hastily over his face and the fireside laughed.

"Looks less like a trout than a mole after that. The mud-specks have smeared. Next time you rides through a rainstorm, raise your face and take off your hat. 'Bout the only way you'll get a wash less'n you fall into a creek." This was from a young rifleman who was sitting on a moss-covered rock.

The wits turned upon him instantly. "Tom, you sure speak true about that mole. Looks like you been a-burrowing all the way from Boonesborough. Why your nose is all wore down."

Jim felt warmly amazed, both at the resolute cheerfulness with which these people shrugged off hardship and defeat and

113

at the way they made him part of their gathering. This was far different from the Holston, where save at Adam Dobson's cabin the women had been unfriendly. The difference lay in his being where he was, on the Wilderness Road, as travel-soiled and strained as they were. He did not guess the truth—that their humor was their only weapon against the sting of their total and admitted rout.

It was pleasant to sit with them while his moccasins were being mended. The contrast between this and the overly glum and serious camps of his own party became more vivid to him and he wished he could stay longer; but the talk soon died away, for they were as tired as he was. Then the moccasins were handed back and he said goodnight.

"Wish you well," said 'Becca, spreading her blankets. "Don't you forget now to tell Lige Bonham what I said. He's tall, light-haired and . . ."

"Just old enough to be troubled with whiskers," cut in the sister. "Likewise he's kind of squint-eyed . . ."

"He is not an' you knows it!"

"It's what you told him when you was sayin' goodbye. He dropped your pack into the mud an' you sure made mention of his looks." They were still squabbling in a sisterly exchange when Jim walked towards his own fire.

Uncle Trev was having a look at the weather. "Good tomorrow, I think. That sunset was promising. Well, Dobson has given us the canoe and it will be a great help when we swim the river. He says it won't fall for a day yet and there is no sense in our waiting until the ford is usable."

He was not often so communicative and the others regarded him in surprise, except for Loudy Jack, who sat sullenly with his chin on his hand. Treville Cheston towered over him and spoke suddenly.

"Timms, get your horse and your outfit. You're going back with Dobson's party in the morning and it would be as well if you slept at their fire tonight."

Loudy's head came up with a jerk. His loose mouth gaped open.

"What's that you're sayin'?"

"I'm telling you that you are going back with Dobson, back to the settlements, back where you ought to be. We'll give you enough supplies to reach to where we buried our stuff after we lost the black packmare. Dig it up. It'll carry you the rest of the way."

Loudy had scrambled to his feet and was hastily gathering his gear. "Sure I'll go, just like anybody with sense ought to."

They watched Uncle Trev measure out the food and ammunition while Loudy saddled his horse. Neither Jim nor Greasy Pete made any effort to help him. When all was ready and Loudy was about to lead the animal over to where the Dobson horses were tethered, his blustering boldness came back.

"I wants my pay," he said.

Uncle Trev did not answer. For an instant Jim thought he was going to knock Loudy down, so grim was his expression; then he laughed without mirth.

"Always the same Jack, blustering, cowardly and shameless. Yet I encouraged you to turn yourself into what you are." He reached into his pouch and paid over some coins. "This is conscience money, and given you only to take you out of my sight forever. I would not stop to count it if I were you, nor ask for more."

He fairly spat out the last words and Loudy stepped back a pace, then led his horse away. When he had gone Uncle Trev turned to Jim and Greasy Pete.

"Gentlemen," he said, "I have ridded us of our encumbrance. Now you two who came willingly have a right to express your opinions. Our company is cut from four to three and God knows it was small enough to begin with."

"We haven't lost much," commented Jim.

"More than you think, nephew. To an indian scouting at a distance Timms was a man. To us who know him he was not, but the indian would not know what we know. Just that one extra in our numbers might stave off an attack."

"We've come this far," said Jim. "They say the rest of the Road is easier. It seems a pity to quit."

Pete looked up. "You go, I come too," muttered the thick lips below the haunted eyes.

Treville Cheston flung up his hands in a gesture of thanks and acquiescence and sat down beside the fire.

The unaccustomed stir in the morning roused Jim even earlier than usual. There was no delay in getting ready for the start, no joking nor horseplay. The day's journey had to be faced and the sooner they got to it the better. The three scrambled into the canoe with their gear; Jim was cautioned to sit squarely in the center as he was unaccustomed to the tipsy bark boat. Dobson and some of his men came down from their own preparations to drive the horses into the water. Loudy Jack sat on horseback on the bank above and commented to two or three more who rested for a moment beside him. He was his own self again, confident and loud-mouthed. Dobson shook hands and the canoe shoved off. Above the shouts of the herders and the splashing of the horses, Loudy's voice came clearly in its old timbre.

"Well, I piloted them safe this far. Now let's see how they'll do fendin' for themselves."

"Sit still," growled Uncle Trev to Jim and the paddles dipped.

They came safely to shore, their horses following. By the time they had saddled, the last of Dobson's party had left the clearing with a backward wave.

"Eight miles to Big Flat Lick," said Uncle Trev in a level voice. "We'd best get as far as we can tonight, for the Road gets rougher beyond it."

The steady pound of travel began again, but with a change to it. The mountains began to sink from great cresting seas to long rollers. The peaks lost their bite, became worn molars, more easily passable. Beyond the Lick, where the Road left the Warriors' Path and turned to axecut once more, it led with more directness across the barriers and they burned sparking rhododendron in their fires. At Raccoon Spring they saw brown backs moving into the brush, tearing suddenly forward with a thunder of hooves and crackling of branches as their horses snorted.

"Buffalo!" exclaimed Uncle Trev and reached too late for his rifle. Jim's dreams were coming true, the haunting names of places and things were becoming realities. This was the wilderness of Kaintuckee and he was a tired unit of it.

Yet it was hard for his spirits to revive, even when Uncle Trev dismounted in some of the bottoms they encountered and tested the soil, alight with eagerness and expatiating on its richness. Never for an instant did the strain of the journey

116

cease. The forest was too encompassing, too contained and sufficient and lonely to give any sense of bounty or pleasure save on the rare occasions when one of them, almost too tired to hunt, brought in a turkey or a rabbit to vary the monotony of cornbread and bacon. Even these last were running low, for the rains had held them back beyond their expectations.

They were still moving across the uplands when they came to the Hazel Patch. It was another signpost and marker, these few acres of hazel bushes growing closely together. Here suddenly the Road divided, one branch turning down Hazel Patch Creek while the other trended northwards. Hazel Patch was famous, the only crossroads in Kaintuckee. Go left into Skaggs' Trace and eventually you would reach St. Asaph's and Harrodsburg, keep to the Road itself and you would come to Boonesborough. There were no other settlements, no other human oases sending out their foot-beaten lifelines to link up with the slender, marshy, rocky, pitted surface of Boone's Road. They camped there in hopes that they might intercept another party coming down either trail and hear news or even the consolation of a rough voice giving them a hail in passing, as a relief from the animal cries to which their ears were accustomed.

There was nothing and no one. The wind in the trees, the soft rustle of the canebrakes and their own few words were the street-sounds of the Hazel Patch.

They climbed to saddle again and ploughed northward through the underbrush. Jim would have given his future prospects of a fortune for two days, even one, of uninterrupted rest. To lie down in safety with clean clothes, soft and soothing to his skin, and then to sleep without alert, without the dawn's summons to riding, became an obsession. Rattling through the canebrakes, he would try to visualize it, and would on occasion doze to the vision until the dull chafing of his damp linseys or the perversity of a packhorse would bring him awake to the reality of the Road.

Rockcastle River, named from a huge, square rock which frowned over the forest like a baron's hold—once, he remembered, it had been a name of romance; now it was no more than another place where he must plunge almost to his knees, though not dismounting, into icy water, and count the hours until nightfall and a fire to dry him.

Big Hill, you'd see from Big Hill. They had told him that at Cumberland Ford, and the memory braced him to ride further. He might be having a mighty rough time but those girls had gone through it, those who'd come out by the Road. He wasn't going to give in where they hadn't, and so he strengthened himself from pride, not realizing that his own party, well-equipped though it was, had suffered more than was necessary owing to the inexperience of their leader. At least the country was more open and Uncle Trev less taciturn, talking beside the fire with the good soil trickling through his fingers, though Jim could not find enthusiasm to respond. "Big Hill" was fixed in his mind and to Big Hill they came, where the mountains lay down and the little hills below them skipped at the beginning of the rolling plateau of Kaintuckee.

Forty years' wandering in the widerness and then the Promised Land, Jim thought, as he looked down on the Bluegrass country. He didn't need Uncle Trev's low exclamation to make him appreciate it. It took him home to Maryland, seeing the roll and descent of it. Well-watered, with the limestone in the slopes showing clearly, it was a stockbreeders' paradise. Uncle Trev yelled high and clear, and with a simultaneous impulse they pelted down the long descent to its flat opulence. Then Jim looked at the soil with eyes like John Tendergrass', and felt it, tasted it, and smelled it, while Uncle Trev, on fire, asked him to look and feel and tell him when he'd seen better.

For two days they luxuriated through the smiling land. For the time the forest seemed set upon rewarding them. They shot a deer and two turkeys while the trees drew back to give place to cane and natural meadow where their horses fed like starved things, for September was only half gone and the grass still tender. When the clouds came up and they went into camp in a drizzle, they did so uncomplainingly, for Uncle Trev announced that Boonesborough was only fifteen miles away and they'd reach it on the morrow.

A big outcrop of rock gave them shelter. In its lee was a grassy hollow, ringed by timber, the road going in and out of it like the string to a bead. It had obviously been used as a camping place before, for the tiny spring had been hollowed out and lined with clay to form a basin at which the horses could be watered, and there were old dried droppings and trees which bore axemarks. The turkeys which they had shot were at Pete's saddlebow, fat, tender birds asking to be eaten. The three men made a jolly camp, even Pete as he cooked losing his hunted, despairing look and singing in his own tongue. The drying moccasins, drawn back from the blaze so the heat would not scorch them and stuffed with grass to prevent their curling, made a companionable row; the horses were tethered in the trail itself under the trees where the drizzle hardly penetrated. Jim heaped up deadwood for the blaze and Uncle Trev smoked contentedly as he sewed a rip in his hunting shirt.

They ate, sprinkling the birds with the last of the salt, and when they were through, Treville Cheston measured out a drink for each from the last of their Monongahela. He pledged them with his stately formality, smiling equally upon his nephew and upon the honest, cloud-witted Dutchman.

"Gentlemen, your servant. The Road has purged me of many things and given me better knowledge of true friendship. Should I journey again I'd seek no better companions." He drank and laughed. "No, I'll not alarm you. I have no intention of journeying further. This soil and this land are what a man seeks for his life long, and a fool I'd be to leave it. Here I'll stay in Kaintuckee and speculate no more."

He fell silent after that, and when Jim crawled between his blankets he saw his uncle still sitting by the fire and trickling the rich earth between his fingers.

XII

Jim awoke from a sudden slumber shot through with increasing discomfort. He came to consciousness slowly, with the clinging wet of his blankets informing him that he was lying in a puddle. A jutting horn of the outcrop had funneled the night's drizzle down near his head and the water had seeped under him while he slept. Had he not been so tired he might have awakened before, but, as it was, the dawn felt near though it was still black dark. He grunted angrily and tried to find a dry spot, only to stop and raise himself on one arm as he heard a horse give a whistling snort. That in itself was no uncommon sound. They had a haunch of venison hung in a nearby tree, and some night prowler—panther, fox, or wolf— might have sniffed it and come to investigate. Two factors brought him out of his blankets, his soaked bedding and the remembrance that once before a horse had broken its tether and had caused them an hour's delay before they could catch it again. Afterwards they had found nearby wolftracks which gave them the explanation.

His kneebones cracked audibly as he reached his feet and a chafed spot between his thighs sent him an arrow of protest. A swift glance showed him no visible cause for alarm, and his mind registered that only one horse was snorting though the others were now stirring in their pickets. He picked up his rifle, checked the priming and noted that it had fortunately been on the dry side of him. John Tendergrass had taught him not to forget and the lesson had become a natural reflex. The fire was low but it gave him light enough to see Uncle Trev sit up and Greasy Pete stir in his huddled heap.

"Something at the horses?" asked Treville Cheston. "Go see and I'll throw wood on the fire."

Jim strode across the little hollow, rifle over arm and heard the thud and crackle of a log being tossed into the embers. He was nearing the woods now and he could see the light reflected in the eyes of the nearest horse as it tossed its head uneasily. The snort came for the third time and he recognized it.

"Cricket!" he exclaimed in exasperation. It wasn't the first false alarm she had caused. The greater sensitivity of her thoroughbred blood had made her restless on occasion when the other animals had remained quiet, and there were times when he considered her a nuisance.

He looked back and could see Uncle Trev stirring the fire; it blazed up cheerfully as if competing with the first streak of dawn which showed overhead. Pete was on his elbow, watching, and rubbing sleep from his eyes. With soothing words Jim passed the horses and came to Cricket, the outside one on the picket line. He had faithfully carried a halter for her instead

120

of tethering her by a rope around her neck and she was braced back against it, front legs planted and body tilted backwards as if she was about to sit down. Her ears were pricked and her nostrils crackled. He followed her direction, but the dripping woods were silent except that one bird remarked "Whee-oo" in a soft, disgusted whistle which just matched Jim's mood. The mare's picket pin was loose in the ground and he untethered her, scolding her under his breath and vowing that the next time she made a fool of herself he'd throw away that halter and tie her so tightly by the neck that she'd choke herself and be damned to her. But the mare did not plunge back, did not yield to his steadying pats; she kept looking in that same direction, prick-eared and tense.

"See anything?" called Uncle Trev, tall and dark against the firelight.

Jim had his mouth open to answer, and his tongue was rolling the first syllable of his reply when the bushes to the north blazed. Reports thundered flatly against the rock echoes, while above them came a screaming panther-cry, the more ghastly because of the human note of it. Jim saw Uncle Trev fall like a wheatsack partly filled, sideways into the fire, the sparks flying, and the bushes took to their feet and became whirling forms, nearly naked, coppery in the glare of the disturbed fire. Some leaped, others squatted so low that their buttocks balanced their heads as they sprang in with upraised tomahawks.

Two red flashes snapped towards Jim, a horse screamed, and another scream blended with it as a tomahawk came down over Pete's blankets. Jim caught a glimpse of a warrior, bounding towards him, his face a twisted, yelling mask painted vermilion. Instinctively he thrust his rifle forward, pulling the trigger without taking aim. There was no report, for he had forgotten to cock his weapon, but the indian dove into the bushes like a snake. There was a cutting, hacking cluster about each of his companions and another indian sprang towards him. He knew his friends were dead and he would be dead too if he lingered.

The horses had gone mad and Cricket was plunging wildly, but Jim flung himself onto her back, still clutching his rifle, and the two of them tore up the trail. There were other yells

121

behind him, culminating in two long-drawn whoops, but no further shots.

He did not have time to comprehend the meaning of this or to wonder if there would be pursuit. He was too busy keeping his seat as the mare galloped frenziedly. Fortunately the cleared road beckoned to her terror and she kept to it while the bushes snapped and flogged them both. All those years of riding stiffened Jim's knees and kept his balance though his mind was numb with horror. It was instinct rather than clear thought that made him jerk back upon the rope, and finally, when the wild gallop broke, steer her into a clump of bushes which by their resistance slowed her enough to let him jump off and check her.

He stood next to the panting, sweating mare, the rifle still clenched in his hand and his heart pounding. He listened, cursing the heaving of her chest and of his own which prevented him from hearing clearly. Then he backed her from the thicket and looped the rope so as to form a rough bridle, while the tears ran down his face. Not unmanly tears, for the frontier had steadied him, though it had not as yet steeled him against violent disaster. But he knew without self-deception that he was alone without remedy in the new, lovely, grim land of Kaintuckee.

He cleared his eyes with his sleeve and saw to his rifle, though his nerves sent tremors through his body until he twice spilled the powder from the horn as he strove to reprime. The forest and the meadows presented their everlasting sameness, only now he looked at them with a mental difference. Before they might have threatened as he had known them, breathing of loneliness, starvation, cold, and the thousand obstacles of the journey. Now they stretched smiling in the full dawn, red, yellow, green with autumn, loveliest of seasons; but underneath the skin of them was a lurking corruption. Never again would he look at the forest with nothing but a forester's eyes. Now he would see them with the borderer's intent examination—that leafy oak might have a rifleman among its branches, that thicket might hold an ambush. John Tendergrass—Jim blessed him for the long-barrelled borderer's friend still clutched by his side—had "known indins"; now Jim Cheston had had his first lesson.

The mare was ready to go again and he had the chance to consider. They might be after him and using the captured horses, but he knew Cricket could outrun them. Where was he? A glance at the sun beginning to creep up over the horizon, and he saw that he was on the advance trail, that much nearer to Boonesborough. Thank God Cricket's wild race had not taken him down the backtrack. Fifteen miles Uncle Trev had said (he wouldn't dwell on that name, it brought too vividly the tall form falling and the shower of sparks), and he must have covered two or three miles before he'd got the mare stopped. He took an apprehensive glance over his shoulder and turned to mount.

There was a stir and a shadow beside him. His rifle was twitched from his hands and an arm took the halter. A voice, a strong voice that ran all its words together, spoke beside him.

"Well-with-thee, lad? Well-with-thee?"

A face looked down into Jim's, a blue-eyed, big-nosed, long-jawed face.

"I'm a friend, lad, a scout from Ben Logan's stand at St. Asaph's. I'm Simon Butler."

Jim clutched at the man's arm before he could convince himself that Butler was real. Tall, spare, brown-haired and young; the battered buckskins made him look even thinner than he was, for he wore them closer cut than was usual.

"We got caught," said Jim unsteadily.

"Judged you might have been. Saw your fire last night an' was workin' up to it. Goddlemighty, who was you signallin' with a bonfire like that?"

Butler shoved Jim's rifle back to him without waiting for a reply. "Sorry to take your weapon, but since I was goin' to introduce myself right sudden I thought it'd be better if you didn't have no chance to shoot me. Think any of the others got clear?"

"No," answered Jim with a shudder. "I know right well they were both killed."

The scout stared at him. "Only three of you an' you build a fire like that!" Then, instantly, as if aware that he had been involuntarily offensive: "Still, I reckon that's your concern. Man cooks his vittles an' builds his fire to suit himself, an' no-

123

body else. Even Captain Boone got caught 'bout a mile from here couple of years back. Now, lad, are you hurt?"

Though arms and face were lividly wealed from the branches, Jim could not find any other injury. He gave his name and Butler nodded.

"We'd best get goin'." His hands gently felt the mare. "She don't seem harmed either. Nice little thing, halter an' all, too." The last was gravely humorous. Halters apparently were about on a par with buckled shoes and kneebreeches hereabouts.

With a direct, searching glance that swept the woods, he started off so silently that Jim, had he not seen him move, would have been left behind. Jim followed with Cricket's lead in his hand. After a few strides Butler swung southward into a game trail which cut the Road, and struck an easy dogtrot with which Jim found it hard to keep pace.

Fortunately when he had crawled out to see about the horses Jim had slipped on his moccasins. To travel barefooted would have been unbearable, since Butler abruptly switched direction and left the trail for a rocky ridge, well screened with brush and trees so they would not be silhouetted. From this he angled downwards into a stream where he waded, Jim and the mare behind him, for a full half mile. Another rocky patch let them leave the water and dive into a canebrake, so tall that it towered above their heads.

Butler showed no signs of fatigue, but Jim was gasping and wet with perspiration when the leader stopped with a frown.

"Reckon you better get on the mare if you can't move no quieter than that. You tromples worse'n she does."

"I'm doing my best," snapped Jim in a shaky burst of anger.

"Doin' your best ain't enough. What counts is what you've *got* to do. An' you got to move a lot quieter. Get on the mare."

Butler did not raise his voice, but the nose beaked down over the thinning lips and his eyes showed an unyielding impatience. Jim mounted and the scout gave a slight smile.

"You're right reasonable after all. Hark to what I'm sayin'. Bowman's men are still at Boonesborough an' the Shawanoes have mostly gone north, but they's still a parcel of them lurkin' aroun' to do what deviltry they can. Might be that same parcel what caught you, but we can't be sure. There might be more. We'll work towards Boonesborough today an' sleep tonight in

124

the woods. I'd try to get in with you tonight 'cepting that you look like you're ready to fall off that horse. Here, chew on this." He drew from a pouch a strip of dried venison which looked like leather and tasted worse. When Jim was tearing at it Butler gave him a final caution.

"We been talkin' too much. There's many a man opened his mouth to ask for a chaw of terbaccer or to cuss a bug what's got into his ear an' let an indin know where he is. Keep that in mind an' think twice, no, four times, by God, before you says anything."

The rest of the day was never clear in Jim's memory. The shock of the massacre had numbed him, but what remained with him, indelibly impressed, was the way Simon Butler led him. Such assured, practiced going among trees and bushes was a revelation. Butler would ghost softly along, his glance scanning the ground for "sign," every few strides raising his head to make that searching sweep of forest and sky. When he stopped he was a tree, rigid, immovable, his brown buckskins like a barky trunk. When he moved he was a shadow among shadows, never casting his own outside the concealment of others. Even the mare's going was quieter, for he took her where her hooves would make the minimum of sound. All this was accomplished apparently not by conscious thought, but by a sort of instinct which gave warning when a stick was dry enough to snap or the dead leaves dry enough to rustle more loudly than the breeze.

Jim was lost before they had travelled an hour, save that the sun told him that they were trending first westward and then northward. Streams existed only to be followed up or down so the running water would wash away the trail; hard or rocky patches existed for the same erasure. Twice at least, Butler had him dismount and sit beside Cricket, his hand next to her nostrils to choke off a snort or a whinny, while the scout backtracked a mile or so to give a reception to any warrior who might follow them. Each time he reappeared, Jim and the mare jumped in unison, for he would come upwind so she could not scent him and the first they would see would be his long face, always with an increasing twinkle in the blue eyes. As he had said, he did not speak, giving his directions by sign alone, but Jim felt that he and Cricket, a pair of innocents, afforded Butler a mighty inner amusement. He began to like the big-nosed, quiet borderer in spite of himself, for Butler's twinkles showed neither scorn nor contempt, and Jim knew that his own inexperience must have been a trial, whatever the spirit in which it was met.

As the sun sank the mare began to stumble. Jim did not dare dismount to rest her, but once he signalled Butler with a look and pointed at her. Butler nodded in return, but kept on until they reached a ravine, a cut in the hills, high banked upon one side but with a steadily declining edge upon the other. Up this he began to move with utmost care, scrutinizing the higher bank with great attention. At last he halted and, pushing aside a screen of grapevines, revealed the entrance to a cave, a common enough feature in limestone country. It wasn't much of a cave, hardly more than a deep niche, but it seemed to satisfy him, for he gestured to Jim to get off.

"Goin' to den you up here," he said, in a voice that could not have been audible more than ten feet. " 'Tain't too cold yet an' though you ain't got no blanket, if we cover you up with leaves reckon you'll make out all right even without a fire. We've travelled nigh on to twenty miles today an' only made about ten of 'em good. Boonesborough lies about four miles thataway, but you an' the mare ain't up to makin' it, since that's goin' to be the worst stretch. Sun's down now."

Jim was too tired to make any objection even if Butler had seemed more amenable to argument. He rubbed down Cricket with a handful of grass, saw Butler tether her with care under a chestnut tree (they had all drunk deep at the last stream), and crawled wearily into his shelter, dragging his rifle behind him.

His companion handed him some more of the jerked venison. "Here's your supper. Now chew it lying down an' I'll shovel these leaves over you. Got your moccasins off? We'll dry 'em out tomorrow inside the stockade. Can't build much of a fire tonight. Lie still now an' don't get to dreamin' 'bout b'ars. Some b'ar probably used this once—sure he did, here's an old hair of his caught in this crack—but he ain't a-comin' back. If he does I'll run him off."

Jim swallowed the last of the food and, too late, flushing a dull red, he looked up at the scout.

"What'll you have to eat? I hogged it all."

"Belt soup, Jim. I'll just haul it a mite tighter. Don't you fret. I'll feed good tomorrow. Now I'll have a look round."

He melted into the forest and the twilight, to reappear after a few minutes carrying a burden of sticks. In the gathering darkness Jim watched through the vines his quick preparations for the night. Selecting another chestnut tree that commanded a view of the ravine, he drew his tomahawk and dug a hole under it about the size of his head. Into this he put the sticks, laying them carefully for a fire. Then he sat down, back against the tree and legs spread about his diminutive fireplace. His rolled blanket came off his shoulder to be draped around him, while the rifle rested against his arm, the barrel so placed as to provide an opening for the smoke. Jim, too interested for immediate sleep, heard the faint clicking of flint and steel under the covering; then Butler leaned back, and to Jim's nose came a faint whiff of smoke. Whatever wood had been selected gave off little, and as Jim himself pillowed head on arm he would hardly have known that the blending shadow against the tree trunk was an armed, experienced borderer.

Exhaustion sent Jim into deep slumber. If occasionally he twitched and groaned in his sleep, his subconscious mind sent him the reassuring, heart-warming message that sitting between him and danger was his self-reliant companion, Simon Butler.

He was wakened by a hand pressed gently across his mouth and a quiet whisper.

"When I put you in a b'ar's den I didn't mean for you to start your winter sleep. There's the sun again, only this time it's goin' up, not down. We'd best go."

When Jim had donned moccasins and put bullet pouch and powder horn over his shoulders, Butler was leading up the mare. At sight of her dishevelled master she commenced a welcoming whinny which was choked off instantly by a quick grasp of her nostrils.

"Can't-have-that, can't-have-that," exclaimed Butler in his running-together style. "She's more cheerful than most women this hour of the morning but t'ain't no time for talk. Get on her, Jim, an' today you rides real careful. If I hisses like a snake,

127

slide off an' kneel down beside her. And, Jim, check your primin'."

There being no breakfast they started at once. If Butler had been cautious before, now he was doubly so. This time he apparently made no particular effort to hide his trail, but instead watched the line of advance with unceasing vigilance. When a squirrel chattered or a flight of birds rose from the trees, he would halt in his tracks, big nose upraised as Jim had seen a buck do when he sniffed the wind for the scent of enemies. They were traversing low hills and there was the gleam of a river on their left. Then Butler halted again with expanded nostrils, turned his head to twinkle at Jim, and went on without explanation. A rapid traverse of a rocky shoulder, a patch of hickory, and the ground began to slope downwards while the trees thinned out. They were nearly back to the Road now, and Jim could see a blaze on an oak off to the right. Then faint and clear came a thudding sound. He almost snatched at Butler's shoulder before he recognized the noise—an axe was being used down there. He pressed Cricket's flanks but Butler spun aside to the shelter of a tree and gave an urgent warning hiss. Jim slid off the mare, jerking her back, and threw his rifle forward in imitation of his companion.

They stood thus frozen. Even Cricket pricked her ears and held her head rigidly forward; then Butler straightened up with a low chuckle. "Boonesborough," he said, in a low tone. "We're safe now."

Jim didn't understand, but he came up alongside the scout, who had shouldered his rifle and was stepping off calmly down the Road, giving Jim sidelong glances and obviously bubbling again with inward amusement. The axeblows echoed more clearly now and the woods opened out. There was a valley ahead of them with a river running through it. In the middle, perched on a high cutbank, was a group of cabins, the gaps between them fenced by a palisade.

"Smelled the woodsmoke a while back," chuckled Butler, "an' you heared the axes your own self. That's Boone's stand."

Two men in buckskin noiselessly entered the Road from the far side. The foremost was a smallish, peaceful figure under a battered slouch hat. Each had his right hand raised in greeting while rifles were cradled in the left.

Butler's shoulders shook. "Front one's Dan'l hisself," he remarked, his voice unsteady with mirth. "He's been watchin' you ever since I ducked behind that tree. Didn't you see him?"

XIII

Daniel Boone, viewed at close quarters, was not as small as Jim had thought at first. It was the contrast he offered to Butler and the lanky young six-footer who stood humbly back but grinned pleasantly at Jim, that made the couple of inches' lack of height the more noticeable. Boone smiled too but with a certain gravity, like a church elder greeting a new member of the congregation. Jim felt, however, that he was being appraised with the same inward amusement that Butler had shown.

This faded out perceptibly as Butler told Jim's story in a minimum of words. It was replaced by an honest, steady sympathy, as if these tidings, tragic though they might be, were no novelty.

"You were coming out to join us?" said Boone in a voice utterly different from what Jim had conceived. It was not high nor authoritative but almost a drawl. It bore an undernote of approbation which Jim was able to catalogue. A man coming out was in a different category from one who had quit. He was a reinforcement, the value of which remained to be seen, but still another settler for the river bottoms. Had Jim known that when Bowman and his companions went back to the Holston, Boonesborough's riflemen would barely be sufficient in numbers to protect the corn harvesters a hundred yards from the stockade, he might have understood still better. Right now the sight of the wooden walls after the shifting, danger-laden trail gave him a sense of security.

Boone and Butler were consulting together without excitement and without raising their tones. The habit of the woods which Butler had explained clung to them. When they asked Jim questions they were few and succinct, not wordy and windy

129

like those the lawyer had asked back in Maryland when he had examined Jim at the time of the lawsuit. Back there some countryman had brought action against Grandmother Dorsey for a foot crushed when a tobacco hogshead had struck him, as it was rolling downhill faster than the checking ropes could control. The fellow had been drunk then and the lawyer had been drunk in the court, until the judge had had to caution him, and he had tried to prove that Jim and the other witnesses had all been drunk too at the time the accident happened. It had been an afternoon of yelling and table-pounding, and the facts hadn't come out anywhere near as clearly as they did right now.

Jim spoke freely, even mentioning the saddlebags of money which Uncle Trev had carried with him. He knew that his uncle was dead and Greasy Pete with him, but he still felt that he owed them a pressing debt. He did not want them to be gnawed and worried by beasts but to rest as peacefully under the earth as they might in their mangled bodies.

Jim was not greedy for the money. He was still hypnotized by having been brought up in wealth. There was more where it came from, with Grandmother Dorsey and Happy Return behind him. He thought the gold might spur these men to take the backtrail, in order that the last friendly act might be performed for his companions. Instead he found three pairs of eyes regarding him with grave pity.

"Indins know gold and notes," said Daniel Boone. "It's right likely they took that along with the horses an' the guns an' everythin' else they might conceive they had a use for. Don't reckon we'd find anythin' but—them."

Butler's long arm touched Jim's shoulder as the youth stood ashamed of his own thoughts.

"He's young, Dan'l, an' gently reared. He ain't used to it," he said as if he were apologizing for himself as well as Jim. Boone set his rifle butt upon the ground and leaned upon the weapon, meditating. The reddish cheekbones grew more prominent, the blue eyes piercing. Their color matched those of Butler, and Jim errantly wondered if these frontiersmen were a type or if the life bleached the pupils.

Then Boone made his decision. "We'll try an' give 'em burial. I knows the place. Fifteen men we'll send, an' if the indins are

still aroun', which I doubts, we'll flusterate their intentions since they won't be expectin' more than five or six of us. We can do it both ways today. You'll ride with us to pick up the gold?"

The clubbed hair, pulled back, made the face and its expression clear. Jim met the steady glance. Butler had released him and was standing to one side.

"I'd like to ride with you, but not just because of the gold."

He had met the test successfully and he sensed a feeling of approbation. Butler spoke up.

"He's mighty tired an' so is the mare. They've had a right tryin' journey. I've kind of adopted them both. Maybe, Jim, you'll let me ride instead?"

Boone smiled. "If you trust the one of us, you'd better trust the two. Simon Butler is well known to me. We can find you another horse or we'll account for what we find."

This time it was Jim who laid his hand on Butler's buckskinned sleeve. "I owe him a lot and I have heard your name, Captain Boone. I want to make the ride but I fear I'll only hamper you, like I did him. I leave it to your judgment."

"That bein' so, we'll let Simon go."

They struck hands and Daniel Boone led the way down into the valley where Otter Creek poured its flow into the river which was named after the land, the Kaintuckee.

As Jim had glimpsed, Boonesborough lay on a little upland, its cabins forming a more-or-less intentional oblong. Butler mentioned that the cabins had doors both on the inside of the stockade and others opening to the outside. "That's 'cause of the weather," he said gravely. "Durin' indin weather we uses the inside doors; t'other's for when it ain't raining Shawanoes. Lets you step out into your cornpatch might easy an' likewise has the advantage of bein' close an' handy just in case somebody does take a shot at you."

The palisade which closed the gaps between houses was not militarily shaped and made brotherly, but just such timber as tired men might plant as an almost unbearable chore after grubbing and stumping the fields. The tops had been pointed with axe blows, but the body of it swayed and reeled with each upright log. There were more or less inadvertent loopholes where the fitting together was worse than usual, and a few

131

regularly made ones. At the diagonal corners were blockhouses. The whole defence seemed unfinished and jerry-built, the sort of structure which a scoundrelly contractor further east might have foisted off on the state of Virginia.

Sprawling out from it were fields, stump-laden and ragged with weeds, but high with corn ready for the shucking. There were fences of hewn logs, fallen in places, and overgrown with vines. There were even occasional cabins scattered outside the gates, but they had an air of their own, a strumpet-look of abandonment, with the mud chinking coming out of the chimneys and the doors off their hinges. Jim could recognize the symptoms spread before him. Once these cabins had been occupied, once the clearings had burst their way into the forest. Then had come the blight of indian war, and what was left was only the hard core, men and fortified houses, who resisted in the hope of spreading again should their resistance be successful.

The fields were busy with people and brawling with laughter. Corn was being shucked to an accompaniment of rough jokes and a drinking of whiskey, despite the damping effect of the silent, vigilant guards who patrolled the outskirts near the forest. With Boone's benign return—and Jim knew that he had made thorough investigation before he walked so carelessly down the slope—there was a stir of interest and a fire of remarks directed at himself. The yellow ears stopped their fall into the bark baskets and the women who were carrying them laughed and listened.

"Now that's a nice mare," came the first comment, which Jim had learned to expect. "Is he wet-nursin' her all the way to Kaintuckee or is she wet-nursin' him? On my soul, a halter! Ain't see'd one since I left North Carolina."

"Tidewater's come to Kaintuckee an' just for the stroll. Bareheaded . . ." (for Jim had lost his hat in his wild ride).

"Why didn't you stop for it, friend? Kind of a shame to throw that hat away—an' it all hung around with gold lace."

A heavy-set, middle-aged man who managed to keep an air of distinction in spite of a torn and dripping homespun shirt ran his glance over the mare and made a business-like proposal. " 'Fore you get much further, keep in mind that I've got a stallion that she'd nick with fine." Jim passed through the open

132

gate with the feeling that clean-limbed, dainty Cricket meant a lot more to Kaintuckee than did Jim Cheston, the scion of the Dorseys.

Boone had turned off into the fields, Butler with him, and Jim was left with the tall young fellow about his own age who had made the fourth of their party.

"Don't you mind them," he said comfortingly. "They ain't heard about your trouble yet. Know anybody here?"

A general miserableness settled over Jim, who could only shake his head.

"That's easily remedied then. I'm Lige Bonham an' you can stay with us—me, my mother an' my sister—till you decides on what you'll do. Simon usually stays when he's here."

"I'm grateful, mighty grateful, but maybe I'll be too much bother. The ordinary . . ."

"You're a mite too far back in the woods for ordinaries an' you ain't a mite of bother."

The name had been troubling Jim. Now he recognized it and managed a smile.

" 'Lige Bonham'—and you're tall and light-haired. A girl called 'Becca Dunlop was asking kindly for you at Cumberland Ford."

Lige nearly dropped Cricket's leadrope. " 'Becca Dunlop! An' she asked kindly about me! Sure you ain't mistook in the name or in the girl?"

"No. She said for me to tell you that she wasn't mad at you any more."

"Now that's a relief, ain't it? Just like a woman thinkin' 'bout her own feelin's first an' forgettin' mine! Never thought, did she, that I might be just as mad at her? She called me a squint-eyed, ham-handed, good-for-nothin' when . . ."

"You dropped her pack into the mud. I heard about that, too. But she also remarked that she'd like to have you with her."

Lige drew the back of his hand slowly across his mouth. "Women! Ain't that just what I finished saying? I asked her to stay here an' marry up with me an' she like to threw the kettle at me. Now she gets half way back to the settlements an' she changes her mind . . ."

A girl came up to them with quick, light steps. Her brown

133

face was flushed and damp with running and her greenish eyes snapped.

"Lige Bonham, what you mean standin' here with this poor lad pouring out your own useless life to him when you know he ain't eaten since God knows when an' been chased by indins into the bargain? Take care of his horse while I get the pot on. Simon just told us an' Maw sent me in. Simon, too, he ain't fed either, an' he's fixing to ride with Captain Boone just as soon as they finish hammerin' some sense into Colonel Callaway. Tom Roper said for me to take that venison he's been savin' an' to tell Jim Cheston here that he's right sorry he made a mock of him. Didn't know he'd been caught, Tom says. Now get with the mare."

"That's my sister, Liza," introduced Lige in guilty haste. "Your women troubles is just beginnin' but for God's sake don't tell her what you just told me."

"What was that?" snapped Liza with the light of curiosity dawning in her eyes, but Lige led Cricket away without answering. Liza gave his retreating back a scorching glance. "Poor creature, he reckons to plague me, but I'll have it out of him before nightfall. Now, Jim, best come along of me 'cause Simon will be in before many minutes an' he's bound to be sharp set."

She was yellow-haired like her brother, and she walked with a long easy stride which became her, although Jim, accustomed to more social graces, thought it unbecoming. Her dress was plain homespun and her sleeves were rolled up to her elbows to reveal a skin so creamy white that the tan of her hands made her look as if she were wearing gloves.

The Bonham cabin lay on the far side of the stockade and he got a view of the settlement as he sidestepped an occasional stump. A well with a well-sweep, a rickety stable indicated more by smell than appearance, cone-shaped stacks of firewood, and the rows of cabins made up the metropolis of Kaintuckee. Still there was a busyness about it that comforted him, so long accustomed to forest silences. There was a steady stream of laden women, young boys and girls, who were bringing in the corn and depositing it in the cabins or in roughly constructed cribs. Small children made themselves happily grubby in the dust while a cornhusk doll was being dressed in the same sort

134

of homespun that Liza wore, by a patient and understanding mother, aged about six. Best reminder of home, when Liza thrust open the door, was the wren which fussed about the gourd with the hole in it that hung under the eaves.

An experienced builder had dovetailed the logs neatly and cut a window facing inside the stockade, the light from which saved Jim from taking a header over the stump which defiantly obstructed the dirt floor. It was crowded enough already, and he wondered at the carelessness which had left the stump as a trap for unwary feet. In one corner was a fireplace, built in the familiar "daubin' chimney," a ladder-like construction of wood, daubed with clay, stiffened by grass. Pothooks and a pot hung from the wooden logstick while the face of it was festooned with drying "herbs," wild onions, and a turkey-wing hearth brush. A table and an axe-hewn bed, shelves and a sort of combination sideboard and storage bin, made up the rest of the furniture, excluding a scattering of three-legged stools. The outside wall was windowless, with only the familiar, plugged loopholes and a doubly barred door to break the plain sweep of the chinked logs.

"Take a stool," invited Liza. "No, not that one. I should have warned you. Lige built that an' he can't get it square yet. He cuts it down ever' so often but he usually does it when he's been at the Monongahela an' he ain't got it to satisfy him. Pretty soon he'll have it right down to the ground. Always know when Lige has been drinkin' 'cause he takes the axe an' moves on that stool."

She had raked aside the ashes, and took the bellows to blow the coals which they had shielded.

"It'll blaze up in a minute an' I'll put some wood on. Then you take off your moccasins an' dry yourself while I goes over to Tom Roper's an' fetches that venison."

Jim obeyed her, and was glad to feel the heat on his feet where the pains were beginning again from the irritation caused by the damp. In her absence he could not help but take further stock, from the ladder which led to the loft overhead, to the water barrel in the corner. Save for the pewter dishes which were racked in the sideboard, everything was most cunningly made of wood, artistic joinery pegged where nails were necessary. In point of luxury the cabin lay halfway between that of the Conjure Woman and the civilized refinements of Uncle Trev's Holston home. That set him to thinking of Juno. He didn't know whether he was in fact Uncle Trev's legal heir, but at any rate he would accept the responsibility for the poor, faithful, old thing. Maybe if he could get her to Grandmother Dorsey she would—then he recalled with a shock that Grandmother Dorsey was a mighty long ways off, that he had no money, for his money-pouch was still in his blankets at the scene of the massacre, and that his total possessions consisted of Cricket, a halter, a rifle, and the clothes he stood up in.

Liza interrupted his reflections by bustling back and setting hominy and venison to cooking. As she cut strip after strip from the deer's haunch and set it to broil he began to remonstrate, but she stopped him.

"Simon's goin' to need plenty, besides you. I've put a dab of bear fat in the hominy. Makes it better eatin' an' takes the place of butter which we ain't got." She looked into the pot and pursed her lips. "Not enough for the two of you. Reckon I'd better pound some more."

Then Jim learned the whyfor of that mysterious stump. The center of it had been adzed out, charred, and then scraped clean and smooth. Into this she poured corn, added boiling water from the kettle which had just begun to steam, and set a cloth over the top. Then she set out the plates, keeping an eye both on her cookery and the steeping mass.

"Hardly goin' to be ready in time," she remarked reluctantly and then she caught Jim's expression. "Ain't you never seen hominy made before?" she asked in surprise.

"Eaten it plenty, but don't know that I ever have," he admitted.

"Where you from?"

"Maryland."

"Lord, thought you might have been a Yankee an' eat beans done day an' night, likewise them kind of things what looks like scorpions."

"Lobsters?" asked Jim, smiling genuinely for the first time since the massacre.

"That what they call 'em?" She whipped off the cover, and, taking a wooden pestle, began to pound furiously. "Steam loosens the husks," she explained. "Now I knocks 'em clear off. Who did your cookin'? Slaves?"

"Yes."

"We got a few out here. They come in handy on occasion, I reckon. Callaway's got some, and there's a scattering of others, but the middlin' of us does our own work."

He came over and relieved her of her task.

"I'm obliged to you. Them venison strips is bound to burn, less'n they're tended. And here's Simon . . ."

Simon Butler came in cheerfully. "All set to go, Jim. Colonel Callaway he got reasonable after a bit an' gave me the loan of a horse. Likewise he helped us beat down some of the others by pointing out that we was nigh through with the huskin' an'— we've always tried to bury our dead. We got plenty willin' to ride too, more than enough."

Liza hustled him to a stool. "Then start eatin', only kind of hold back on the salt. We ain't got too much. Jim, let me get to that poundin' task an' you eat too. I'll hurry as much as I can."

Butler began to eat voraciously, and Jim, his courtesy overcome by hunger pangs, joined him while Liza resumed the pestle.

"Is Colonel Callaway in command?" he asked after he had swallowed a bowlful of hominy and a couple of strips of venison. Butler rolled his eyes at him and chewed vigorously before he could answer, while Liza gave a deep chuckle.

"Jim, ain't nobody in command, if you're thinkin' like a soldier," explained Butler. "This here's Kaintuckee where most everybody has a title an' everybody, without no 'most' to it, does as they pleases. Now Dan'l's a Captain in the militia but I reckon if he stood out there in the fort an' yelled 'Handle your firelocks,' most people would put it down to too much Monongahela an' go on about their business. What he does say is, 'I'm goin' down the road a piece, to bury some fellers what got caught comin' in to help us,' an' them that says they'll come trails along with him. T'others just sit."

Liza had stopped her pounding, and her deep, laughing voice took up the tale. "The Boones always outthink most people. His brother's named 'Squire.' Dan'l says 'tis after his own father, but I suspects that most everybody believes he made it up.

137

Kind of handy out here if you christens your son 'Colonel' or 'Judge' so he don't have to wait any time to take one of them names as a how-de-do."

She had dipped out the crushed corn into a wooden tray and, stepping outside the door, tossed it into the air, the falling motion ridding it of the remnant of the husks.

Jim was almost satiated but Butler was eating as if he were starving, and Jim marvelled at the amount of food the scout stowed inside himself. Liza was back and making a fresh pot of hominy when Butler looked up and grinned.

"Kind of wonderin', ain't you? When God showers down His benefits, 'specially well-cooked ones, I takes advantage of 'em, 'cause there's plenty times in the woods when benefits ain't available. Thank you, Liza, I think I can get aroun' a leetle more hominy." He drawled it out as the full bowl plunked in front of him.

Lige thrust his head in the door. "Got your horse saddled an' mine too, worse luck. We calls him a horse 'cause he's got four legs an' a tail, no horns an' he don't give milk, otherwise we can't be sure! I'm goin' too."

Butler gulped the last of his meal, the spoon rattling against the side of the bowl.

"Horse an' rider worth about the same," he remarked, rising and taking up his rifle. "Liza, I'm beholden to you an' I hopes I left you some salt." Light and quick as ever, he put his hand on Jim's shoulder. "We'll do our best for you," he said and was gone.

There was a stir outside, hooves and loud calling; then the settlement subsided into its normal calm with the children's voices the highest note.

Jim was fumbling for his moccasins with a vague idea of going out, but Liza in that deep tone which he had found so soothing made a remark apparently directed at the cabin walls.

"People what have been nigh massacreed an' coursin' the woods at night needs more sleep than most, an' I say they deserves it. There's a cornshuck mattress on that bed an' you won't have Lige to share it with you an' kick like a mule. Now if I was such a feller an' wanted to be right sensible, I'd clean myself an' fall into it. I've got the kettle boilin' an' I'll step

138

outdoors. While you're sleepin' I'll try an' wash them linseys of yours—they're ripe an' ready for pluckin'.' "

"I'd liked to have thanked them who rode out," said Jim, with a bitterness caused both by fatigue and an undeserved sense of his own inadequacy.

"They're bein' naught but neighborly. They take the thanks for granted. Sleep, lad, sleep, 'tis your best remedy."

He could not resist the advice, though his tired mind tried to rebel at it. She did not wait to argue, but poured first cold water and then the hot kettleful into a wooden tub. Lye soap she laid out and also a ragged cloth to serve him as a towel. Then she picked up a basket and swung it to her shoulder.

"They need me at the huskin'. Leave your clothes on the floor," she said and went out, closing the door after her.

The sight of the steaming tub brought him to a full surrender. Let his worries wait until tomorrow. Meanwhile he would strip off the linseys, stiffened by dirt and sweat, and scrub his body clean. The clogged pores, the red rash on his skin rejoiced at the feel of the water. When he had finished he lurched out onto the dirt floor and dried himself as best he could, his objective that cornshuck mattress under the blankets. The safety of the four walls, the security of the palisade took him and sent him off into a slumber that restored him, blankly sleeping, to his normal self. The Wilderness Road and the sodden half-rest of its camps, the exhausted numbness of last night spent in the bear's den, took their proper place as memories, not as living, agonizing realities. He was Jim Cheston again when he stirred and grunted and found himself in the cabin, and beside him a strange woman of fifty-odd with a care-lined face.

"Back, are you?" she asked pleasantly. "You haven't done too bad, lad. I'm Miz' Bonham and my children have cared for you, I hope none too badly. They're good younguns, though I could wish that either of my two daughters who are married now down on the Yadkin in North Carolina or my oldest boy who's with Morgan's Riflemen could have been here instead. I did not care for you myself for the corn had to be husked an' Liza would have been a sore hindrance with a young man in the house who bore news down the Road. How d'you feel?"

"Better, ma'am, much better," said Jim, and started to

139

struggle out from under the blankets until he realized that he was stark naked. Then he subsided and blushed while she laughed with that same deep note that he had found so attractive in her daughter's voice—possibly because it carried a reminder of Grandmother Dorsey's own tones.

"Lie still, Jim, lie still. Liza's got your clothes washed an' they're nigh on to drying. The boys ain't back yet but there's a few who'd like to see you, waitin' outside. They don't mean no harm, just that you carries news an' news is something we don't often hear. Can I let 'em in? If you keeps that blanket pulled up aroun' you I reckon you won't scarify nobody an' anyways they don't scarify easy."

She took his silence for consent and admitted a dozen or so men, some of whom were slightly the worse for whiskey, accompanied by half their number of women, probably her own gossips whom she honored with this early reception of the news. Liza came in quietly with them and smiled at Jim before she did the honors with such hospitality as the house afforded.

There was no particular attempt at introductions. One heavy-set man, his burly body hiding behind a projecting chin, was Colonel Callaway. Jim recognized him as the one so set on breeding Cricket; the rest were only names. They sat on the stools and the table and the floor or lounged against the walls while the Colonel asked him questions and got him to talking of his own accord.

He had not much of novelty to tell them. They had heard of Burgoyne and they were excited over a rumor that Washington had won a great victory over General Howe, but when he said that the latest reports had mentioned nothing of it, they accepted the correction with calmness. Had he but known it, he could have held them spellbound with the account of his talk with Thomas Jefferson, for land was what had brought them here and land titles were their meat and drink; but Thomas Jefferson was quite a number of mountains behind now and Jim never thought to mention him. When at last he began to describe his journey there was a stir of interest. This came home to them and they leaned forward and broke in both with question and comment.

With such an audience he felt free to talk. Once or twice he stole looks at Liza who smiled back at him encouragingly. He told them of their daily journeys, his resentment at the occasional disparaging remark as to Treville Cheston's woodcraft overcome by their knowledge of places along the way and their appreciation of the grinding effects of the continuous travel. When he came to that last camp, the comments ceased as he spoke of the rifles that spat from the thickets.

"We made a mistake about the fire. That I've been told already," he said looking at one frontiersman with a cowlick and a loud voice who apparently had been assiduous at the jug. "No use telling me again. We didn't have a watch posted . . ."

"Nobody does," interrupted Colonel Callaway with authority. "It's always easy to say after things happen that there ought to have been a watch, but those that say have never been over the Road. Tell us, lad, how came you to escape?"

Jim found nothing to complain about in Callaway's attitude, though he thought him a trifle overbearing. He had dreaded the question but he answered it honestly. He told of his experience with the pursuing warrior, of his failure to cock his rifle, and how the man had dived into the bushes. He had expected scorn and braced himself for it, but instead there was a burst of laughter.

"Don't that beat all?" cried the cowlicked man. "Reckon there's one Shawanoe who'll be thankful to you that you don't tell the squaws about it!"

Colonel Callaway twisted his grim lips amusedly. "You just pulled the trigger without cocking?"

"Yes, sir."

"He ain't the first that's forgot!" roared another and slapped his knee.

Colonel Callaway hushed him with an upraised hand. "Lad, all he saw was your rifle pointing at him. He did not hear the click of the lock which would have told him either that it was empty or had misfired. When everyone else has fired the man with a loaded rifle is king. I do not wonder he turned aside."

There was more guffawing, yet not the kind that Jim had heard from Loudy Jack. He had told a real wilderness joke without intention and his listeners appreciated it to the full. It made no difference to them that he was the butt of his own story. Not one of them but had had some similar absurdity happen to him.

"Then I met Simon Butler . . ." Jim resumed, only to be interrupted by a lounging figure who turned his head politely to spit tobacco juice outside. "I'm on the gate," he drawled. "The boys is just in sight. Looks like most of 'em is there."

The last words brought the women to their feet, tight-lipped, and the gathering broke up. Mrs. Bonham put a hand to her mouth, then smiled wearily as Liza ran out.

"No use our worryin', Jim. Some may have dropped behind."

Nevertheless she waited, hardly moving while the shouts and the hooves sounded again within the stockade, her hand betraying her by that repeated gesture. Her son was among the riders, Jim recalled, but there was nothing to be said.

Then Liza threw open the door and stood to one side while Daniel Boone, Simon Butler and Lige Bonham filed in one by one. Mrs. Bonham's face lighted but she made no comment while Simon Butler spoke up in haste.

"All's well," he reassured them. "Three of the boys is followin' up the trail of the Shawanoes. Lige here was some inconvenient but we'll blame it on his horse an' let it pass. The two of 'em kept hangin' back, but we saw Lige a-kickin' at its flanks so we reckon it was the horse, an' not Lige what was doin' the hangin'."

Boone glanced at Jim, and Liza intercepted the look. "Maw, if you an' me an' Lige goes to look at the evenin' star I reckon we'd be thanked."

Lige stared, laughed, and left, the women following him. Boone and Butler came over beside the bed. Jim had sat up, the quilts exposing his nakedness, and their lips twitched.

"Hid your clothes out on you, did they?" asked Simon. "Reckon they was right sensible."

He nudged the other, who reached into his pouch and brought out a greasy cloth. Boone's face was very steady.

"They were dead, Jim. Just as well you didn't see 'em. Shawanoes are a mite on the unkind side as I have cause to know. We buried 'em, buried 'em deep."

He took a long breath, rather astonishing for one of his bronze austerity.

"Like we thought, they'd carried most everythin' away, Jim. What they hadn't they'd either scattered or burned in the fire. Simon's got part of it."

142

Butler reached into a pouch and drew out a horseshoe, the spyglass, and a battered copy of the Bible with most of the pages missing.

"Reckon they tore 'em out for gunwads," he said, offering the book with averted head. Jim knew it for the one which Grandmother Dorsey had slipped into his pack. He stared at the damp-faded ink of the inscription, familiar once but now strange within its peeled cover. Boone coughed gently. He was unwrapping the greasy rag.

"Your trustees, Simon an' me, brought what we could find."

In his hand were three gold pieces. "The pair we found in the brush, the third in the fire. There warn't no more."

Jim let them lie on the blanket. He looked up at the serious, responsible faces bent over his own.

"I know there were no more. Gentlemen, I'd stake my life on it. Will you take them and ask the men who rode with you to drink my health?"

Butler and Boone looked at each other.

"I reckon they'd be right obliged," said Boone after a pause, "but one'll do for that."

He handed a coin to Butler, who tried to speak, thought the better of it, and went out with that ghostlike lightness which Jim associated with him. Boone drew up a stool.

"Jim," said he quietly, "that was a right nice thing for you to do, whether or not you could afford it. I ain't a-goin' to ask you now—don't hold with bein' curious 'bout other folks' affairs—but what are you plannin' to make of things now that you're in Kaintuckee?"

His big hand covered Jim's and he stood up.

"You're young, lad, and proud, both of which is right, yet 'fore you sets your mind I'd be real glad if you'd come an' talk it over with your friend Daniel Boone."

And even softer on his feet than Simon Butler he passed through the door.

XIV

The sun rose as usual in the morning, but for the first time in more than two weeks Jim was able to appreciate it. Even Lige's kicking around in the bed had not been able to rob him of the restorative rest which let him at last consider Kaintuckee clear of the fog of nervous exhaustion. He was conscious of Lige rolling from under the blankets, and met him with a grin as he came back after stirring up the fire.

"Must be aroun' five of the clock, we've been slugabeds," said Lige. "Women have been stirrin' in the loft for some time. Sky looks good an' the weather's promisin'."

Jim was interested, the weather so much affected their daily work that it was more than a topic of conversation.

"Your clothes are here," Lige continued, "but best not take off your huntin' shirt, your breeches is some distressin' from the rear."

"You-all up at last?" called Liza from the loft. "Tell Jim I'll make him some proper breeches an' leggings today if I can. If I can't I'll do 'em tomorrow. Lige, you might consider makin' him a fur cap, he ain't got nothin' for to cover his head. Now get to poundin' hominy an' sing out when you're decent."

Jim, scrambling into his clothes, felt embarrassed at this torrent of aid.

"I feel more and more that I'm taking advantage of you," he began, but Lige, pounding corn, only grunted.

"We're just bein' neighborly," he answered, and Jim realized that "being neighborly" covered a multitude of charities, small and great. Being now dressed he asked what he could do.

"Yell up to the loft," said Lige between strokes of the mortar. "Not that they ain't heared you, but it makes 'em feel better. If you feels like it you can tote some more firewood. Simon Butler says that a man's part is to pound hominy, cut wood an' bring in game, which seems right sensible to me."

Liza and her mother had descended the ladder soon enough to hear him. "Simon ain't married," Liza snapped, "an' at best all he does is overlook the fields. If it warn't for his bein' a scout in the militia an' bein' the best hunter almost in Kaintuckee, he'd be no better'n these Monongahela hounds what stands aroun' sayin' how they're reckonin' to start work tomorrow an' thinkin' up excuses for to use when tomorrow comes."

Lige threw down the pestle and even Jim was stung by the taunt.

"Liza, you can't say nothin' 'gainst Simon, why he . . ."

"Woman's got a right to speak her mind even in Kaintuckee," answered the sister composedly. She looked into the stump-mortar and was scornful.

"Never stopped to soak it proper, did you? Threw in a mite of lukewarm water an' kind of trusted that the Lord would loosen the husks for you, didn't you? I now says everythin' that 'Becca Dunlop said an' means it. Which one of you's goin' to fetch that wood that Jim was talking so eager about a while back?"

The two young men made tracks out of the cabin and condoled each other by the shrunken woodpile.

"Don't you pay no 'tention to her," said Lige consolingly. "She's got the best heart in the world towards Simon Butler but she ain't his woman an' she never will be—lucky for Simon. Gather yourself an armful, Jim, an' I'll do the same. Reckon we got to go woodcuttin' today or tomorrow. Damme if she ain't got me talkin' just like them folks she was a-blaming of. Only thing on my mind is that we've got to finish getting in that corn. Holston men are planning to go home in a day or so an' them extra hands makes easy work."

They came back into the cabin to find Liza pouring freshly boiled water over the corn which Lige had merely bruised, while the mother sliced bacon with a butcher knife.

"Stop your bickerin'," she said. "Gate must be open by now an' the others passin' out into the cornpatches. Lige Bonham, keep to mind that you ain't no paid scout an' don't go sneakin' off with your rifle 'stead of husking corn like you should."

"Where is Simon, by the by?" asked Liza, now beginning to pound.

145

"He slept over at the Watkins'. Said he reckoned our bed would be right crowded though he knows well enough it'll sleep three."

"Wanted to get away from you," commented the unrelenting sister. "Simon's a growed man an' sent out as a scout. Don't do him no good havin' a youngun like you traipsin' aroun' after him, bustin' down the bushes but thinkin' he's Jim Ray over to Harrodsburg."

Jim remembered guiltily what a handicap he himself must have been to Simon Butler if Lige, whom he already recognized as a far better woodsman, could be so maligned even by sisterly malice.

"Who is Jim Ray?" he asked, to keep the peace.

"Right smart of a lad," replied Lige ungrudgingly. "Seventeen an' he fed the settlement with the indins about it. Used to ride out, kill game an' gallop for the stockade with the carcass 'crost his saddle. Others who tried it didn't fare so well, at least they never come back to tell."

Liza winnowed the corn while Mrs. Bonham clucked at the lateness of the hour and Jim mulled matters over.

"Have you seen indians?" he asked at last. There was a general silence. Liza, who was pouring the cleaned grains into the pot, stopped as if she had been stung, then joined in the chuckle which went about the Bonhams'.

"Reckon we all have," she remarked. "They've been prevalent around here for too long."

Lige got in a jibe. "Liza saw one in particular. He was behind a stump out there in the clearing an' he stuck his head up. She let drive at him, but considerin' that I dug the bullet out'n the stump after the indins had left don't reckon she did him no harm."

"Scared him, though," said Liza composedly, ladling hominy onto the plates. "This ain't got no bear fat in it an' mighty little salt. Not much salt in the whole settlement. Looks like we're goin' to have to get some somewheres."

There was more interest in the salt shortage on which the conversation settled than in Liza Bonham's near miss of an indian besieger. Jim, devouring the frontier "hawg an' hominy," considered matters. He blushed for his manhood. This sharp-tongued but goodlooking girl, mighty goodlooking he had to admit, had "scared an indin" just as he had, only she had cocked and fired with intent to kill while he had done no more than point a rifle and squeeze a trigger in blind panic.

He returned to the subject when he and Lige were in their cornpatch. There he was some help, for he had husked before at Happy Return. Stripping and throwing the yellow-orange ears into the basket while Lige's shoulders swung rhythmically next him gave him a chance to talk occasionally.

"Did Liza really shoot at that indian?" he asked.

"Surely. So did we all. Didn't have so many men we could afford to do without the women. Maw loaded for me."

That news he had heard along the Holston, "Boonesborough attacked, Daniel Boone wounded," roused the imagination of the new defender of the station. He glanced apprehensively at the woods. To his further embarrassment, Lige noticed the glance.

"We got riflemen out there, Simon an' Dan'l among them," remarked Lige. "I don't think there's any danger though. Dan'l says the warriors what caught you were the same what's been hangin' around here. Probably followed the Road before they went home hopin' for just what happened, a careless party comin' into their hands. No cause for worry." Then as he saw Jim's concentration on his work, he changed the subject with natural tact.

"Liza's done pretty well, considerin'. Last fall, 'fore the indins got so bold, we'd built on Red River, a fork of the Kaintuckee. Paw was failin' fast—he died in the spring—an' it made it right strenuous for Maw an' the two of us. Maw had taken Paw into Boonesborough for to see a doctor. There was a rumor of one havin' come there but it warn't true an' we ain't seen none yet. Anyway I was out huntin' an' Liza was alone. We had meat in the cabin an' a painter smelled it. Must have been starvin' or powerful bold 'cause he stuck his head in the door. Never heared of one doin' that before or since, but anyway there he was. Liza fetched him a lick with the axe an' he busted out 'cross country. When I come home there was Liza in the loft, still clutchin' the axe, an' askin' me if I hadn't had enough yet. Reckon she thought I was the painter."

When Liza came to fetch the basket Jim had another look at her, a look that was more appreciative and respectful than

147

before. Even the clumsy homespun could not conceal the lithe easiness of her movements. She walked as if she were ready to spring into a dance, so light on her feet that she might have delighted good Queen Bess in a morris or a galliard.

"The two of you ain't doin' so bad," she thrust at them. "Ain't more'n a row or so behind Maw. I'm cuttin' them buckskins for you, Jim. 'Fore long you won't be afeared to stoop."

"Now ain't she contrary?" commented Lige when she had gone. "She likes you, Jim. She'd cut the buckskins an' make the breeches for anybody who'd run into a mite of trouble, but when she starts discoursin' on men in general an' lazy men in particular she's careful how she scatters her fire."

There were mocking shouts as swifter workers finished their patches, in many cases coming over to lend a hand to the more belated. Jim noticed Daniel Boone come out of the forest, speak to several, and then set himself at a row like any farmer. A young man strolled up to Lige and hailed him cheerfully.

"Restin' yourself as usual? Howdy, Jim, reckon you don't know me but I found out who you was when you come in. Name's Nick Watkins."

He had one of those faces which seem to drip downward from the broad forehead to the pointed chin, big-lipped, big-eared, the sort that lends itself to being either sardonic or merry. His was the latter as the twinkling eyes and the upward quirk of his mouth gave evidence. Addressing himself to Jim, he began to husk ahead of them.

"Ever noticed how Lige approaches an ear? He comes up to it hopeful-like, sayin' to himself, 'Now mebbe I got a real kindly one here that'll shuck itself 'fore I have to put my hand to it.' Ears never are so obliging but Lige never stops hopin'."

"Picked your time just about right," retorted Lige. "Liza'll be along any minute now. Just saw her drawin' water at the spring."

Nick Watkins tried to pass off the remark by anathematizing the smallness of the well inside the stockade.

"Careful, Nick," said Lige relentlessly. "Goin' to talk yourself into a job of work. Everybody's been cussin' that well but you're the first to volunteer to do anythin' about it. You will be doin' somethin' about it too if Liza hears you. An' here she comes so it's mighty fortunate I had time to warn you."

148

Nick turned in haste to husking, but not before Jim had caught his look at Liza, which was sufficiently betraying to make Jim grin.

She arrived with an empty basket in one hand, and in the other the wreck of a hat which she handed to Jim.

"Here's your head-coverin'. Put it on, it's still hot enough in this field to make you want it."

"Ain't there nothin' better than that?" asked Lige. "That belonged to Paw and it's near wore out." He talked as if the gift from its poorness belittled the giver.

"We takes shame to ourselves but it's all we got," said Liza as if she shared his feelings.

Jim, too, was ashamed, but from a different reason. They had to all intents reclothed him and he had nothing to offer in return. He almost said so but fortunately expressed himself a little differently.

"You're doing so much for me, and I'm doing nothing for you."

"Husking corn, ain't you?" said Lige. "We all has a run of bad luck once't in awhile. When we has ours, mebbe you'd do the same or better."

That night Jim sat in a corner, considering his situation, while Liza and her mother sewed at the new leggings. Lige was mending a gunlock under the supervision of Simon Butler. Jim had offered to help, but they had understood his preoccupation and had done no more than hand him some flints which he was to "pick" sharp to produce a better spark. He kept at the task in a desultory fashion while he reviewed his future course.

He could go back with Bowman's men, who had postponed their departure for a day, which gave him another twenty-four hours free. They'd be willing to let him ride with them, and once upon the Holston he could pick up Juno and head north for Happy Return. If he needed more money he could undoubtedly borrow it from Colonel Campbell, who had been Uncle Trev's friend if not his intimate. But to go back like a whipped puppy, to go crying to Grandmother with his troubles, didn't seem right. People out here got along and without much help either. He had enough, he hoped, to buy ammunition, an axe, blankets and whatever else in reason he would need. Maybe he could hunt, and with game and deerskins provide a stake for

149

the winter. The thought of selling Cricket never crossed his mind. She was his grandmother's gift and furthermore he had become fond of her. At last he stood up, his resolve taken.

"Do you suppose I could see Captain Boone tonight?"

"Surely," said Butler encouragingly. "I just come from him. His cabin's right across the way. Ain't no journey an' no danger, long's you don't fall into the well."

"Dan'l's a sound man," said Mrs. Bonham.

"Remember to keep that huntin' frock on," reminded Liza with a flashing smile. "These leggin's ain't finished yet."

He reached Boone's after barking his shin on a stump and was welcomed heartily. While the eldest daughter had married off, there were several big-eyed, self-contained youngsters to stare at him until their mother herded them into the loft. Boone himself was shaping an axe-helve with his hunting knife, and Jim found time to marvel at the dainty finish of it, almost as if it had been turned on a lathe. Boone asked him to sit down and listened silently to Jim's project.

"Axe, blankets an' all are easy to have. Got a pair of blankets here made out of buffalo wool that you can buy reasonable." He had amended his last words as he saw that Jim would not accept them as a gift. Jim was feeling too much like an alehouse sponger to take advantage of his hosts. "My daughter, Jemima, her that's married to Flanders Callaway, has buffalo wool socks that I reckon she could spare. That'll help some an' the rest we can figger out, 'ceptin' a saddle. Reckon we'll have to make that, but I'll show you how. As for your makin' a livin' by huntin' though, I ain't so sure. Game's gettin' a mite scarce an' a hunter's got to have a gift for it. Not that I'm a-sayin' that you might not have it," he added hastily. Boone was not given to snap-judgments.

"I doubt it," admitted Jim. The experience of accompanying Simon Butler in indian-haunted woods had made him humble.

" 'Fraid that's so. However, we needs men an' if you'll make yourself handy over at the Bonhams' for instance, reckon they'll winter you. 'Tain't goin' to be too pleasant," he warned, appraising Jim, who squirmed slightly. "Might be better if you did go back to Maryland. Indins kept us from properly culti-

150

vatin' our crops an' towards spring eatin' may be right monotonous an' some unaccustomed too."

Jim, feeling completely inadequate, burst out, "I know I won't be much good even as a handyman, but I'd like to try. I'm not afraid."

"Know you ain't afeared, lad," reassured Boone with a slight smile. "Me an' Lige'll take you out tomorrow an' get a witness on just how handy you are."

"Reckon I'd better plan on going back then," continued Jim gloomily. "Still I'd like to look at my father's lands before I go."

Boone's interest sharpened at once. "You got land here? Where is it?"

Jim told him. By great good fortune he had memorized the boundaries, for any notations he had made had perished along with Uncle Trev. Boone obviously found them adequate. "One I knows well, but I'm afeared it's pretty nigh worthless. Mostly hill an' swamp. T'other, though, might have some value but I'm afeared it's shingled."

"Shingled?"

"Ain't heared of that? Well, now, I'll tell you. You claims under the Henderson Patent. 'Nother feller runs his lines so they overlap yours like the shingles on a roof. Sure he conflicts with you, but the question is, does his claim stand up better'n yours does if it comes into court? Your'n is shingled twice, so far as I know, but the part back from the river ain't disputed."

"You mean I'll have to take it before the courts?"

"Reckon most of us will have to. I hates lawyers. The two we got over to Harrodsburg never agree. They always ends up with the best part of things once they've had their fee, an' you got to fee 'em even if they loses the case for you. Say it's to pay 'em for their work. Like to know who's to pay us for ours."

This time Jim remembered Mr. Jefferson's remarks and spoke of them while Boone listened with almost excited attention.

"More confusion!" he exclaimed. "Sounds reasonable but it puts us who've been here an' made our stand equal to them who comes later an' just buys up claims. Seems to me we have a right to own more because of what we've put in."

He recovered his gravity. "Well, that's to be seen. We'll have a look at that better land of yours tomorrow. Indins has gone north an' we can see a mite how you handles a rifle. Tell Lige he might come along if he wants to."

Lige, of course, wanted to, as Jim found on his return. As they were not to start until afternoon, he propitiated his mother by setting out with Jim and a couple of axes to clear the land before they left. There was a clump of trees out by the end of the cornpatch that he was anxious to fell, with an eye also to cutting them later into lengths which could be split into rails, the residue being used for firewood. He went to work on one and posted Jim before another.

Jim had felled saplings before, but this was the first time he had faced a full grown hickory. He examined it unhopefully, selected a spot and set his blade aswing, grunting with each stroke. By the end of five minutes he had chewed a ragged gap in its side, with a few miscellaneous scars to show where strokes had missed. His arms tingled as far as the shoulders, and blisters were beginning to appear on his hands even though they were already calloused. He kept at it, sometimes stopping and examining his axe-edge, wondering if it needed sharpening. Then he heard a warning call from Lige and the crash of a tree.

Lige strolled over to where Jim was vigorously chopping. There was a pause while Jim, not turning his head, made several strokes, then a low whistle.

"Tried usin' your teeth?" asked Lige softly. "Might make better progress an' not gnaw it so much. Don't work so hard, pick your spot with your eye an' come down with your axe on an angle so it'll cut deep. Here, let me show."

He was kindliness itself as he taught Jim the technique, but Jim felt miserably incompetent when the hickory fell at last and Lige set him to clearing out the hampering brush while he began on another. Then Boone and Butler materialized in their quiet way behind them and the young men picked up their rifles.

"Ready?" asked Boone as he smiled gravely at the scarred trunk of Jim's tree. "Simon's goin' to give us cover as we walks. Want to pick up a mess of squirrels an' don't want the shootin' to bring down any lingerin' warriors."

He took the direction of the river, Butler vanishing ahead of them and off to one side. The fort and the clearings dropped behind and they were in the forest aisles almost at once. Jim gritted his teeth as they progressed. Uncle Trev had given him good teaching but it was not adequate for Kaintuckee. Uncle Trev had been a journeyman; these hunters, including Lige, were masters. Jim felt as if unseen sticks thrust themselves under his feet to be broken, as if bushes swooped down so he might brush their branches far too audibly. Lige kept turning his head, little jerks which might express warning or exasperation, but Boone betrayed nothing. As Butler had done, Boone watched the ground for sign, except that he swept his eyes upward more frequently, until Jim remembered the game they were after. At least he could shoot, he thought, he'd measure up on that. Uncle Trev had said he shot better than any of them.

Boone stopped and pointed towards a branch. A gray squirrel was nestling along it, looking down at them with beady eyes. The others stood aside and Jim put himself on his mettle. The heavy rifle came up carefully and was steadied in a rigid line while he aimed. The flint clicked, the priming spurted and with the crack of the charge the squirrel was hurled sideways and rattled down through the remaining leaves. Jim, concealing his pride, stepped forward, but Boone checked him.

"Reload your rifle, lad. Notice you keeps it with you which is a good idee but here's another just as good. Squirrel's harmless, ain't like to charge ye, but a bear now, or a buck, might be different. You can stun 'em or knock 'em down an' find 'em full of fight when you gets to 'em an' you with an empty gun. Not to say that there might be an indin who's heard you fire."

As Jim obediently reloaded, Lige brought back the squirrel. The heavy bullet had hit it squarely, as Jim was proud to see. He had hoped for a compliment, but nobody said anything and they moved off again, Boone in the lead.

This time it was Lige for the shot. He threw his rifle up, lingered on his aim for an instant and fired. Jim ran forward and picked up the squirrel. With a sinking heart he noted that it had been hit fairly in the head so that the body was undamaged. Without a word he handed it to Lige who gave him a friendly grin but kept his ramrod clicking. Jim's confidence evaporated. Of course it might have been a lucky shot, but the humorous expressions showed that it was not.

It was now Boone's chance but the next squirrel was tardy in putting in an appearance. Jim glanced covertly at the heavy-calibre rifle in the brown hands and wondered what would be left of the squirrel even if Lige's feat were repeated. At last Boone came to a halt and glanced up. It took a pointing finger before Jim made out the beady eyes showing from a clump of leaves. Boone seemed only to look at his quarry and the rifle followed the look. At the booming report and the puff of smoke, the squirrel whirled up into the air and came down. Lige nudged him and the two went to pick it up together while Boone with a twinkle reloaded. The little animal looked as natural as life, save for its limpness and the drop of bright blood which quivered at its nostrils.

"Barked it," explained Lige in a whisper. "I can do it too, but for me it's mostly good fortune. He shot under its head at the branch it was lyin' on an' the shock of the bullet killed it. Dan'l don't miss often, not with old 'Tick-Licker,' which is what he names his piece."

They worked on through the woods, with the presence of the river occasionally making itself known through the trees by the glint of the sun on its surface. More squirrels joined their bag. Jim had three shots, hitting twice and missing once. The others did not miss, and Boone repeated his feat continuously while Lige joined him in one successful barking. Then their pace increased and they ceased to shoot. Jim was much subdued. It looked like even if they accepted him as a handyman he would be a mighty unhandy one. Off to their right sounded a gobble, and instantly Boone was behind a tree, while Lige, almost throwing Jim to the ground, took shelter with him behind a fallen log, peering intently towards the sound.

Another much fainter gobble came down on the wind and Boone relaxed. "First one was a turkey," he remarked. "Second was Simon tellin' us that all's well. A turkey would come in handy right now, if you feels like movin' forward."

Lige consoled Jim in a whisper. "Speakin' honest I couldn't tell the difference either. It might have been an indin. A turkey's gobble is a favorite signal of theirs. You ain't doin' so bad. Don't fret yourself. We makes our livin' thisaway. Now be ready for a shot."

They got three of the great bronze birds in four shots, for Butler had joined them. Two fell heavily and one fluttered away to be killed with a blow from a ramrod. Jim thought he saw the twigs fly just as his own turkey took to wing, so he could fairly well attribute the hits. Only he was wrong, for Lige was gloating and Simon grinningly cast down.

"Branch hit my sight just as I loosed off," he excused himself.

"We knows, we knows," said Lige pityingly. "Last time it was a big mud-dauber wasp that stung you. Goddlemighty, Simon, I beats you so seldom that I can afford to crow."

Another half mile and Boone called Jim. "This here's your land, lad. I surveyed it an' I know. Marker's that blighted beech there. Think we'll find my initials on it if we look."

They did look, and the initials, cut deep, were plain to see. It took them some time to view the claim. There was good bottom land down by the river and a tiny rill ran through it, rising from a spring in a limestone hill.

"This is the part that's shingled," explained Boone. "The hill ain't."

Jim could see why. It was one of those rugged limestone outcrops such as he had become used to. It was covered with bushes and the soil was clearly uncultivable.

"Funny, ain't it, how they never shingles bad ground?" remarked Butler. "Feller that first marks it out may make mistakes, but not the one that follows."

Down by the stream was a ruined cabin, the roof falling in and the rank growth strong in what had once been a cornpatch.

"Whose was that?" asked Jim as they took the back road.

There was an uncomfortable silence, broken at last by Lige who seemed in duty bound to answer.

" 'Twas Levi Watkins' stand, father of Nick whom you've met. Settled there 'bout the time we did over on the Red River an' gave it up for the same reason that we gave up ours— indins."

Jim gave a brief "oh" which was noncommittal and apparently was comment enough. They travelled in silence for a time, keeping to a more direct route than that by which they had come.

"Gentlemen, you've had time to judge," he finally broke out. "You've seen me. I'm no good with my rifle an' worse with an axe. Seems to me I'd be right useless."

Lige clapped him on the shoulder. "Seen worse, a lot worse,

155

come to Kaintuckee an' do mighty well. You can stay with us an' earn your keep. Maw was sayin' last night that she considered you a right up-an'-comin' young man."

Jim, warming, nevertheless looked at Daniel Boone. The great borderer considered gravely.

"Reckon I'd stay," he said.

Boone's words were all that Jim needed to make his decision. Grandmother Dorsey had commanded him a year's absence from Baltimore. She had not contemplated Treville Cheston's death, but he would avail himself of it. He would write her that he was staying. She could not complain, since he was attending to his father's business. It was about time he stood on his own feet.

XV

When Bowman's men rode out, one of them carrying letters from Jim to Grandmother Dorsey and to Juno, Boonesborough reverted to type. It was no regularly maintained fortress with soldiers to do the watching and the scouting, but a farming village where the farmers by turns performed such duties for themselves. Jim enrolled himself in the Kentucky militia, signing a blotted muster book where a good proportion of the names were indicated by marks. Education was not at a premium, whereas a good eye along the sights was. Private Cheston found himself entitled to a few shillings in the depreciated Virginia currency, usually never paid, and an occasional issue of powder. In return for which he was expected to clothe, feed and equip himself and be subject to all the various pains and penalties which a courtmartial might mete out for a dereliction of duty. Of course the clothes were no trouble. When the call came the militiamen answered to it in buckskins, linseys, or their shirt sleeves, as they saw fit. Major William Bailey Smith was reported to have carried a scarlet uniform clear across the Wilderness Road. Admitting that it was his old British one and therefore not quite indicative of his side in the Rebellion, still Jim understood from those who had seen it that it was mighty smart. Then young Major George Rogers Clark had a uniform too, buff and blue, but the reports were less certain about this. Some said he had it and some said he hadn't, but whichever was true he was an upstanding fellow and "tarrifyin'" to those uncertain-of-purpose militiamen who decided to go home after joining him.

Now quitting an expedition was quite usual if militiamen lost confidence in the leader, or decided there were too many indians, or just got uppity over something. If there were enough of them to go openly they left, or if there were not, one might just slip away in the woods. Nobody probably would say anything about it. After all it was one's own concern, and the border might gossip but otherwise attended strictly to its own business. There wouldn't be any courtmartial or any such nonsense. As to hanging or shooting a man for desertion, Kaintuckee had never heard tell of such a thing and would have considered it plain murder. So if Clark was "tarrifyin'" it must be with his tongue and his fists.

He lived up to the notice when Jim saw him. Jim was stacking wood when he and Boone and Colonel Callaway passed. Tall as Simon Butler but bigger still in chest and shoulders, black eyes hooded by red eyebrows, his glance merely passed over Jim, but the latter felt that he had been noted and considered merely in that flick of a look. Not that Clark was dressed up either. Linseys and a black hat were good enough for him but, by God, thought Jim, if he'd just buckle on a sword now he wouldn't need anything else to stand up beside one of General Washington's own brigadiers.

Lige was bubbling over with excitement at supper.

"Somethin' big on, somethin' really stirrin' in the bushes. Nobody sayin' much, not even Simon, but there's a story goin' round that they's men bein' picked out."

"An' you're hopin' to make one of 'em," sniffed Liza, but there was a shade of anxiety in her tone.

Mrs. Bonham compressed her lips. "Elijah Bonham, you've got other fish to fry. I'm lookin' for to marry Tom Roper 'fore long an' you're goin' to have to scratch gravel for Liza here. Can't have Tom supportin' the two of you as well as me an' his own chillun. Scout here you may, but go traipsin' off with Major Clark you may not, an' I lays it onto you as a task."

Jim was the only one that looked surprised. Liza and Lige merely looked at each other and then at their mother.

"Thought so," said Liza. "Tom was mighty obliging with that venison when Jim here rode in."

"Been expectin' it," affirmed Lige. "Tom's a good man an' he's got nobody to bring up them six younguns."

"Reckon you three can get along?" asked Mrs. Bonham. "I'll be just over the way."

Her offspring laughed together. "Surely," replied Lige, and Liza contributed, "After all we've only got one youngun to look out for, an' you'll have six."

Even Mrs. Bonham joined in the hilarity at Jim's abashed expression.

"They're devils, Jim, an' don't you pay no attention to them. God knows if I had I'd been worrited into my grave by now." Her expression became stern and she considered him and Liza. "Just as I layed it on Lige I lay it on you two. If Lige or somebody else ain't here don't the two of you ever stay a night alone in this cabin. One of you come over an' sleep with us. There's enough gossip an' scandalmongerin' goin' on in this settlement without you addin' to it. Mind you, now."

Jim's ears tingled and Liza looked down at her plate. Lige roared happily, "Mind what Maw says. No bundling! To make it surer still we'll have Nick Watkins come over them nights when I'm away. He an' Jim'll set up an' watch each other, one with the axe, t'other with the butcher knife, each ready to grab the first one that sets foot on the ladder."

Liza jumped up and Mrs. Bonham suppressed both of them sharply.

"You'll not quarrel now! I'll not have it! And Lige, you'll not be talkin' in that fashion even if you think you're not bein' overheard. I tell you there's too many ill-thinkers who licks their chops and waits for a chance to talk when the winter comes an' there ain't nothin' else to distract their minds."

Liza came back to her usual practicality, though she avoided speaking directly to Jim.

"Lige'll be too busy makin' ready for the merrymakin' to

158

talk even a mite. I'll see that he's too tired to do more'n' flop into bed of nights."

"I'll help all I can," said Jim, though he was feeling awkward. Liza wasn't like the Baltimore girls, of course. None of them would have deigned to smoke a pipe, which Liza did occasionally. On the other hand he couldn't quite see Mary Raeburn taking on a panther with only an axe as a weapon. But then (and his excuse was for Liza), if it was back in Baltimore there'd be a lot of young men who'd be ready to do the job for her and leave her to admire.

She was looking at him now, sober-faced, but her green eyes betrayed her.

"Surely you'll help," she remarked. "Now you're bein' neighborly an' we welcomes you. If you don't sink the axe into your foot, or try to pound hominy with the corn still on the cobs, or swallow that tobacco you was tryin' to chew like you did yesterday, you'll be right much of an aid."

Jim managed to take it with proper humor, but inside him was a welling annoyance. He had read correctly what lay behind her teasing. Lord, she was being motherly towards him!

Motherly her attitude continued, as he fell more or less smoothly into a settler's life. It was hard, ceaseless toil—nearly as bad as the Road except that the cabin provided its humble comforts. They were clearing ground, tearing out the weeds and saplings which indian attacks had permitted to choke the fields, rebuilding fences, milking cows, collecting what extra fodder they could to get the stock through the winter; they were building, repairing, gathering nuts and berries, and tanning the hides of the deer which Lige brought in, a dirty job and one that Jim particularly hated. The most they'd let him do in the woods outside of these tasks was to go out occasionally with a party for firewood or small game. Cricket had become a reluctant packhorse with a penchant for heading between the trunks of two trees, wide enough for her but too narrow for her burden. Then Jim would have to repack her while the other men laughed. Jim was exasperated when she repeated this trick twice in an afternoon, but Boone's son-in-law, Flanders Callaway, dropped him a word of advice.

"Don't get so het up. She's the best horse in the settlement,

159

not even excluding my uncle's stallion that he's pesterin' you about. 'Tain't just her looks either, nor her breedin', it's because from what you told us she smelled them indins that attacked you. That's some valuable, more than you know. Looks to me as if she spoiled the ambush. They couldn't get around you. Ask Simon Butler 'bout them two dogs he had what'd guard him at night. He was awful cut up when he lost 'em. You might grow to feel the same towards the mare."

Jim took the words to heart. Naturally clever, he was picking up tricks of woodcraft, both by precept and observation, and had noticed that most of them were designed to spare the workman as much as was possible. He could get a tree down now in about double the time it took Callaway, for example, but it came down where he wanted it instead of lodging stubbornly in the branches of another. He was going to show Liza Bonham as soon as possible that he could earn his keep.

Lige he didn't see so much except when he came home, for Lige was hunting every day to bring home the game which meant the difference between rude luxury and a bare living. Yet it was Lige who brought Jim up all standing with a casual remark as they went out to look for oak bark to use in tanning.

"There ain't goin' to be much to be cheerful about this winter, particular with us. Time we has our merrymakin' we'll have used a couple months' supplies. Better store up your enjoyment just like a squirrel does nuts so's you can thrive on it when things turns agin you. Likewise keep a-practicing your shooting. Come spring an' we'll have indins. Now there's an oak just made for us."

There was no whining nor complaint in his tone, merely an acceptance of presented facts. Nobody had talked much about the indian visitation of the past year, but the constant presence of the rifles, of the hovering scouts and of the night guard upon the stockade, was a very real reminder. The first time Jim took his turn at this latter duty (Nick Watkins was his companion at the northern of the two gates), he kept in mind that this period since his arrival had been peaceful, a sort of interregnum between the horrors that had been and the horrors which might come. The clearing was shadowy and the stumps persisted in standing up as warriors, each one wearing the semblance of that vermilion-painted mask bounding towards him. More than

160

once he clutched his rifle ready to thrust it through the loophole, so certain was he that the next moment would bring the
panther-yell. Then he would squint sideways at Nick, a deeper
darkness at another loophole, and steady himself, hoping that
his nervousness had gone unnoticed. He thought it had until
the dawn brought a stir from the cabins and Nick left his post,
unshaven and yawning.

"Never heared your lock click once which is right good restraining," he remarked with a grin. "First time I was on watch
an owl called 'Who?' an' I shouts back, 'It's me you bastard' an'
fires. Ain't lived that down yet an' reckons I'll be hearin' of it
the rest of my born days."

He couldn't dislike Nick, although he kept for him a couple
of reservations, one admitted, the other present though denied.
Nick's father had shingled his own father's lands. It might be
a good time to mention it now and get that poison out of his
heart. The second and innermost was Nick's courting of Liza.
There was no earthly reason why he should object. Liza was no
more than a frontier girl, older than most before they got married, and certainly if Lige approved of Nick he should too. But
he couldn't. Had he so much as admitted the existence of this
concealed jealousy, he would have been ashamed; yet it was
there and it put a brusqueness into his tone when, the day
guard having relieved them and the gates opened, he asked a
question.

"Planning to go back to your old stand when the troubles
are over?"

"Uh," grunted Nick, "so's you're a-bitin' on that, are ye?"

"Reckon I got a right too. The land's my father's."

"Who ain't here."

"But I am," snapped Jim, and, setting down his rifle, glared
at his companion.

"So I sees, which don't stop me from goin' where I wants to
or settlin' there either."

Jim's fists clenched. A little crowd had begun to form about
them, collected by the raised voices.

"Don't give a damn where you go or where you settle so long
as it isn't on our land."

There might have been a fight, for Nick, too, was setting

161

down his rifle, had not two women exchanged very audible question and answer.

"Who's a-roosterin' who?"

"No more'n a couple of cockerels tryin' out their spurs. Talkin' 'bout land, but I reckons Liza Bonham's at the root of it."

Not even Mr. Ingles' kettle of water brought about a quicker separation of the would-be combatants. Both young men hastily picked up their rifles and went on about their business, followed by a buzz of talk and laughter. The story would be about the settlement before an hour was up, and Jim, angry to the core, stalked into the Bonham cabin and sought Lige.

Simon Butler and he were finishing the last preparations for a trip after a bee tree which Simon had spotted. They had collected the axe and the kettle, the latter for the honey they hoped to bring home. Both straightened up when they saw Jim's expression, and Simon rapped out, "What's riled you, boy?"

Jim hesitated. "I think Lige should hear of it first."

"Surely," said Butler heartily and effaced himself.

Jim hesitated, for the easy humor was gone from Lige's eyes and a stern self-reliance replaced it.

"Spit it out if it'll ease you. Who's been sayin' what about who, 'cause that's what I judge it is?"

When the matter was clear, he shook his head. "Picked out the trail mighty quick, didn't they? Mite quicker than I thought they would. Yet I knowed they'd do it. They had to make you a lovin' feller towards somebody aroun' here or their milk an' mush wouldn't have sot right. We been expectin' it. Man can't have a private argument with a friend withouten the women mixin' in an' usually addin' a few pine branches so as to see the sparks fly."

"I'm sorry it happened, but damme if I regret saying what I did to Nick Watkins. It's only what the thing was made into by the others."

"Of course, of course. That part I'd pay no 'tention to. I'll tell Maw an' Liza'll hear of it by herself. There's them who take care that she does. Wouldn't worry yourself none. It happens to everybody an' while it's right annoyin' there most usually ain't no bones broke over it. Why there's them that keeps whisperin' that Dan'l Boone's a Tory, 'cause some of his

162

relatives is an' he was a Royal Captain in Lord Dunmore's War."

He picked up the kettle, then halted.

"Hope you ain't goin' to fight Nick. 'Twouldn't be right."

"And why not?" cried Jim with rearoused belligerence. If there was nobody else to take it out on, Nick Watkins would be his target.

"If you stops an' thinks, that's just what you two are, a couple of cockerels. It's your paw's land, ain't it? An' Nick's paw is the one who settled on it. Seems to me the fight ought to be between the two of them an' not between the two of you."

He threw up his hand to forestall another outburst. "Nick's my friend an' so are you. Tell you somethin' else. When George Rogers Clark was here he brought the news that the Henderson grants has been disallowed by Virginia and by Congress too."

Jim sank upon a stool. "Why didn't you tell me?"

"Reckoned to break it to you easy. Old Man Watkins has filed on your land, so I supposes he has the better claim to it now."

So his father's lands were definitely gone and his journeying had been for nothing. Treville Cheston had foreseen it, John Tendergrass had foreseen it, but Jim had cherished the thought that they might be wrong, that he could save the property.

Being young, the worst was hard to comprehend. It was difficult to realize that a legal decision had made the toils and dangers he had encountered mere wasted effort, as in fact they were. Stripped now of his lands as well as of his gear, he stared up at Lige, who returned his look with something like pity. The very thought of pity stung Jim like a hornet.

"Then by God I'll claim my own!"

"Surely," purred Lige, "I was hopin' you'd say that."

"But I'm under legal age!" Jim exclaimed.

"Surely," said Lige again. "So am I, but I claims mine just the same. It might hold up in court. After all this is Kaintuckee! Some day we'll have our own say."

He and the kettle went out to join Butler.

Confused by his own vehemence, Jim waited for what he expected over the scene with Watkins—a torrent of reproaches or a frozen coldness from Mrs. Bonham and Liza. Instead when Mrs. Bonham came in her only remark was "Take it out in

163

clearing brush," and she handed him the second axe with a tight smile. Liza wasn't around and he didn't like to linger; so he obeyed orders and felt better when he was sweating and chopping under the sun, which was still hot though October had come. Dreading to meet her, he put in a harder day than usual, broken only by Nick Watkins who came with a wry grin.

" 'Feared we've both been fools, Jim. Lige stopped an' talked to me 'fore he left, Simon Butler too. No use your cryin' over spilt milk an' I reckons you had a right to stick up for your paw."

Jim met his handclasp and managed a smile. " 'A couple of cockerels.' First the women called us that and then Lige said the same to me. Reckon they're about right."

" 'Tain't them I'm worryin' about. It's Liza. Goddlemighty, what's she goin' to call us?"

Jim reconsidered. He couldn't hate Nick Watkins. Not when both of them shared a mutual lively apprehension.

Yet it was misplaced, as he found when he dragged wearily in from the field that night. Liza only looked at him and pointed to the kettle.

"Wash yourself," she said. "You've brought in most of the soil. Been fightin' again?"

Like a small boy he could only shake his head.

"Made up with Nick?"

"Yes," he stammered, avoiding her glance.

"I've been made out to be the woman of every man here at one time or another," she remarked, not bitterly but with a certain resignation. "I don't fit 'cause I'm eighteen, risin' nineteen, an' I ain't married up yet. That's a mite uncommon."

"You're an uncommon girl!" Jim said spontaneously. He could not bear the pain which looked out from her eyes. Furthermore he meant what he said.

"Thankee," she answered. "Now if you'll take the whetstone an' put a new edge onto the axe, I'll feed you. Maw's gone over to Tom Roper's an' I'll foller just as soon as Lige gets back."

After he had eaten she lighted her pipe and sat down on the stool opposite.

"Tell me 'bout your grandmaw an' them girls back in Baltimore. Most usual I ain't got much time to listen but I sure

164

enjoys them tales. People dressed up in purple an' fine linen ain't so common out here."

She puffed smoke as he cast around for where to begin. "Now in Baltimore . . ." he commenced.

"The women don't smoke pipes," she finished for him.

"I didn't say that," he stammered in confusion.

"But you looked it, lad. Well, since it seems to bother you I'll get rid of mine," and she tossed it into the fireplace.

"Don't aim to make myself better," she continued with a trace of fierceness. "Reckon them Baltimore girls misses right smart of consolation if they don't use tobacco. Still if it makes you even a mite uncomfortable . . ." Before he could say anything else she was curious again.

"They reads too, don't they? Now I can spell out the Bible an' I can write. Maw taught me them things. I don't hold with people like Simon Butler who can't do either an' reckons it a waste of time to learn. I've heared what they reads about, too. Books what goes on about love till you're sick an' tired. They goes on about other things as well."

She meditated while Jim wondered what books she had been hearing about. After a time she spoke out, still thoughtful.

"In Tidewater now, it appears to me that the more petted your women gets the more they craves man-chasin' to satisfy 'em against bein' what they'd like to be. An' they don't really want to be that."

Her arms were wrapped around her knees. Eyes on the fire, her brown face in repose was beautiful; strong, firm-jawed, yet clear with health and as yet unlined by work and childbearing. The light glinted on her hair. Then she shook her head.

"Better hark back to your grandmaw."

He told her more of Happy Return, and when Lige swung in he had to go on, for Lige was as fascinated as she.

"Simon'll be along in a minute," he said, chewing and listening. "He got a deer an' he's hoppusin' it in."

Jim understood the word, though it would have puzzled him a month before. To "hoppus" meant to carry in the cleaned carcass slung over the hunter's shoulders. He went back to his story.

"Grandmother's always helping lame dogs over stiles. When I wrote her about Juno in that letter I sent back with Bowman's men, I knew then that she'd take her in. Never had to think of it twice. She's got one servant that's been with her a long time. She bought him in Baltimore, but the man who sold him said he was the worst calf and poultry thief he'd ever seen and he was selling him for fear of worse happening. Yet he's been true ever since."

He smiled reminiscently, his eyes too were on the fire.

"Simon the butler," he said. "Understand there's a warrant still out for him in Virginia."

The next instant he was seized and thrown down, the breath knocked from him while arms of maniacal strength tore at his throat. Horrified, he stared up at glaring eyes and a twisted face while the life was being choked out of him. Dimly he heard a scream from Liza and an oath from Lige. He could no more have defended himself than he could have battered down the cabin with his fist. The weight on him became heavier as Lige mixed in, but the hands did not relax. Far away through the roaring in his ears came Liza's voice. "Give me room an' I'll fetch him a whack with the poker." Then the weights rolled off him, the hands relaxed, and he lay gasping and exhausted but free.

Liza was pouring water on his face and Lige was propping him up, while Simon Butler towered over them, his face still contorted.

"God's sake what ails you?" snarled Lige to the tall man.

Jim was able to sit up, though his throat felt as if it had been wrung like a chicken's. The marks of those fingers would show black the next morning.

"You heard what he said," Butler's tone was savage. "So he told you, did he, that there's a warrant out for me in Virginia? Did he tell you too what for?"

"So that's it!" said Liza in a changed voice. Then he heard her speak further, explaining, but he was too busy trying to collect his wits to realize fully what was going on. He even threw up his arm defensively when Butler, his expression changing to one of agonized anxiety, picked him up like a child and set him on a stool. Through the torrent of repentance, Jim made out that it had been a complete misunderstanding. Butler

166

was sweating and shaking, patting and feeling Jim to be sure that there was nothing seriously wrong. Then Liza's solid common sense soaked up the hysteria.

"Simon, let loose of Jim or this time I'll really take the poker to you."

She fetched out the jug and poured whiskey for Jim and Butler, who needed it equally.

" 'Simon the butler,' that's what he said an' you comin' through the door an' not hearin' clearly thought he was talkin' about you. Looks like you ain't let a cat but a catamount out of the bag, Simon Butler."

Jim understood at last. "I won't talk," he gasped, though every word was an effort.

"None of us'll talk," said Liza, and Lige chimed in with an affirmation.

Butler was fast returning to his normal self. He had weighed them and apparently found none wanting.

"Got in a fight with a feller once an' beat him bad. Think he died so I headed out for the frontier."

"You don't know whether or not he died?" asked Liza sharply.

"Didn't stop to ask an' mebbe put the rope aroun' my neck. He didn't come to, though I worked over him good."

"We can't go inquiring," Lige contributed. "Might set it off again—the hue an' cry, I mean."

"True, Lige, an' if you asked about Simon Butler reckon there'd be none to tell you anyway. My real name's Simon Kenton." The name meant nothing to them; it did not then carry with it the fame it was to hold later when, the victim of Simon's assault having been proved alive, Simon resumed the Kenton, and became the "Cuttahotha" who by his warnings, forest skill and brilliant courage was to save so many border lives.

Jim Cheston could not read the future, but he could hold out his hand in pledge to a man who might possibly be a murderer but who was also his friend.

"Be sure we'll all forget it," he croaked.

XVI

Maw Bonham and Tom Roper were getting married; the wedding day had come at last, and Jim was relieved that it had. Even in Kaintuckee a wedding caused preparations which the women considered commensurate with the importance of the event, but which Jim felt were a trifle exaggerated. The whole settlement, with the sole exception of old Mrs. Wickham who was bedridden with the "miseries," would attend with a sharp thirst and a hearty appetite.

Lige was worn out with hunting, while Liza and her mother were in such a bustle and scurry that even their tempers bustled and scurried too. Jim found it best to keep at the corn-patch and the nut-gathering during the daytime, and in the evenings he occasionally sought relief by dropping in on Daniel Boone. Under Boone's supervision he had built himself a saddletree. Actually the supervisor had done wonders with an axe while Jim had watched and learned. The deerskin for the covering had been provided by Lige, and Cricket's halter had been changed into a bridle by the addition of a leather bit and reins. A good portion of Jim's money had gone to complete his outfit, as Boone had advised. Now almost penniless but yet a substantial citizen (did he not own a horse and a rifle?), he was finding his level in Boonesborough.

It wasn't an easy level to find and it caused him as many mental readjustments as he had had to make during the whole time of his journeying and his sojourn on the Holston. It was a shock to his natural sense of social stability to find that one of his closest friends was possibly an escaped murderer and that the man he most admired was suspected of Toryism. Not that fine people couldn't be Tories—he'd learned that in Maryland by seeing who stood by the King—but to be a Tory in Kaintuckee which Hamilton, the Governor of Detroit, had sent the indians to attack seemed grotesque. Yet Colonel Callaway had obliquely confirmed Lige's story. Though he had allied himself to the Boones through the marriage of his nephew, Flanders, to Daniel's daughter, Jemima, he had his own opinions and some of those opinions were diametrically opposite to those of Daniel Boone. He had talked to Jim more than once—after all he was mighty anxious to breed Cricket to his stallion—and Jim, courteous but non-committal, had heard certain criticisms of Boone's tactics against the indians particularly galling to Jim, who had heard much of Boone and little of Callaway. Vigorous, stubborn, yet very intelligent and possessing more than the usual frontier amount of education, Callaway was Jim's best link with the past. He was cordial, too, and willing to explain the causes of things that had baffled the newcomer. Walking over to the Ropers' cabin where the guests were gathering, he laughed pleasantly at Jim's glowing tribute to the kindness which he had encountered.

"Yes," he said, "they are good people. There are some here who are better on the frontier than in Tidewater and others who would be better off in jail, but the most of them are God-fearing farmers. You'll keep in mind, though, that your way has been made smooth. You've had the good fortune to see the best of us, for in trouble you came and trouble brings out the best of the border. Now they are growing accustomed to you and I fear you may see some of the worst of us this winter. It will be a starving winter, though, and most hell-raising comes from overfeeding. That may help you keep your ideals. We'd best stand outside. The cabin's overcrowded now."

The wedding ceremony, heard in snatches through the open door, was merely the appetizer for the merrymaking. The bride wore no finery except a lace shawl, yellowed from age; the groom was in linseys but freshly shaven. The listeners were respectful, but there was a sigh of relief, from the younger throats at least, when a general stir and loud congratulations proclaimed that Tom Roper had a wife. Liza came out dry-eyed and set Jim flying back and forth with pots of hominy and wooden platters of venison.

There followed a feast where men and women stuffed themselves and even the babies greased their round faces with cracked marrow-bones. Lige and Jim did the heavy fetching and carrying and kept the fires going in both cabins, but the bride, Liza, and a few friends did the dishing up and the cook-

169

ing. The males ate first and the women took the second sitting. It had amused Jim until he discovered the reasons for it. It was still the age of the patriarchs. To be the "head of the family" was a meaningful phrase, and furthermore it made for chatter and relaxation among the wives and sisters when, the meal prepared, they could sit unhampered at table. Also it let the men get quicker to the whiskey.

Jim lay down against the cabin wall, legs stretched out before him, and rested from his labors. He was next to Daniel Boone in a line of whittlers. It was as natural as breathing for a Kentuckian to select a piece of wood and go to work on it with his hunting knife. Jim even tried it himself, though his hands grew still as Boone answered a question in his soft voice.

"Indins? Now there's a subject that don't get stale. Most people feels that indins is altogether hellions an' yet I don't hold with 'em."

"Would have thought ye would," said his far neighbor, cutting a big slice from his stick. "Seems to me you lost a son to 'em back on the Wilderness Road."

Boone did not take offense. "What some does don't condemn 'em all, though I'm the first to admit that scalpings an' torturin' don't sit right. Still if it warn't for their everlastin' fightin', against us and 'mongst themselves, they wouldn't live so bad."

"How so?"

"Huntin', now there's a good life. The squaws makes patches of corn an' punkins an' squash an' tobacco, too, so the meat don't sicken on ye."

The other chuckled. "Never liked farmin', did ye, Dan'l?"

"Don't say's I do. But there's more to indins than just huntin' an' makin' war. They're good to their children an' kind to each other. Not much thievin' an' brawlin' in their villages either, the old men can come down pretty hard."

"Notice you don't mention the squaws," interposed a third lounger. "Kindness like you've been talkin' about seems to stop at them."

"That ain't so," replied Boone with more energy in his voice. "There's rough men amongst 'em, I'll admit, but there's rough men amongst us too. Yet an indin can have a good squaw just

170

as a white man can have a good wife an' treat 'em the same way. I tell you indins is good people in lots of ways."

"Less I see of 'em better I like it. Reckon I might feel kindly towards 'em if I was back in Tidewater now an' just hearing about 'em. Couple years back I was in Norfolk an' I got talkin' about indins. Feller there in the tavern said to quit talkin' about 'em, they bored him. Told him they bored me too, but they kind of edge themselves into the conversation out here."

"They bored me too," announced a big fellow who was sitting crosslegged and smoking a corncob. "Right here." He pulled up his sleeve and showed the blue scar of a bullet hole on his lower arm.

There was a grim chuckle and Boone's neighbor kindled his tobacco with flint and steel.

"Huntin's a good life, as Dan'l says. Wonder if that's why some of our fellers what gets took turns indin an' don't come back."

Jim was listening intently, his memory going back to Ingles' Ferry and to the lame son who had been a captive.

There was a short silence and the crosslegged man spoke harshly.

"Sometimes they comes back with a warparty like Simon Girty an' some others."

"Not all of 'em do," answered Boone, who had let the conversation flow on without comment. "Warrior don't have to join a warparty 'less'n he wants to. 'Course if the whole tribe's out he'd better go or they'll make a squaw out'n him. But then there's always bickerin' goin' on between the tribes an' he can get his exercise thataway." Boone laid aside the peg he had whittled into shape and picked up another piece of wood.

"They don't live so different from us. They eats like hogs when there's plenty an' they starves when there ain't, an' I can't see that we does much different. They're free to do what they wants an' there ain't no land nor taxes nor nothin' much to bother about. If it warn't for all the fightin', like I've said, they'd have a right peaceful time."

For an instant Jim thought that he was joking but a side glance at the reposeful face showed that Boone meant what he said.

171

The crosslegged man spoke with a hint of malice. "Reckon you an' Simon Butler'd make pretty good indins, 'spite of your not likin' to fight."

Boone's knife stopped with a curl of wood showing before the blade. "Mebbe so," he said, but he looked straight at the speaker with a dark glance. "Still I've been took twice an' I ain't gone over to 'em yet. Don't see no use in hating, though. Leave that to your Tidewater people what's never seen an indin or to them what's had greater injuries than mine. I've fought agin 'em, an' I'll fight agin 'em when they interferes with me, but otherwise I ain't molestin' 'em."

"Don't hate the British either, do ye?" asked his opponent, the malice in his tone deepening with the insinuation.

"I do not!" said Boone and he shoved the knife home in his sheath. "Some of my people is with 'em as you doubtless have heared, but that don't make me a Tory either."

His expression had changed, the peace had gone out of it and left it watchful and somehow more formidable even than Simon Butler's wild rage.

"Don't mean no harm," muttered the crosslegged man. "I was just a-baiting of you, Dan'l."

Jim doubted if the apology were genuine but he would have apologized as quickly had he even less justly aroused Boone's wrath. The others obviously felt as he did, for after a decent interval of whittling the neighbor asked in a neutral voice:

"Don't you ever hate anybody, Dan'l?"

"Hate wastes too much time."

"Not even Hamilton, the scalp-buyer?"

Boone had been subsiding into quietude but this last question brought him back to alertness.

"Aye," he admitted. "I might hate him. He loosed the indins on us."

The women came out, and from indoors came the preliminary scraping of a fiddle. The gathering roused itself for the dancing. Lige came along the line with a jug of Monongahela and a cup from which they drank in turn. The young people began pairing off while the fiddle, having tuned, struck into a jig. Jim went for Liza, but too late—Nick Watkins was already there.

"Save me a dance," grinned Jim and Nick laughed with a tinge of triumph.

"Better be spry or there ain't goin' to be none left. Bucks is a-pawin' the ground an' the does is a-lookin' coy. Get inside 'cause here we go."

London, Colonel Callaway's Negro, was sawing with his bow, and the dancing began, wild jigs and reels which yet retained an ingrained dignity of their own. The old dances were slow in dying, and the quick-stroked fiddle might be lute and viol and hautboy combined into one. The tunes took Jim's foot and made him tap out the time.

He danced with girls whom he had hardly met besides those he had grown to know, found shouting, flushed men bounding along with him, and released himself to real enjoyment and happiness, unclouded by the bloody past. At last, sweating, joyous and pleasantly fatigued, he went out into the gently nipping November evening and found Lige, who poured for him from the jug.

"You does right well," complimented Lige, handing him the cup.

"Too well, by God," said another, and Jim spun round to encounter a flushed young man whose aroma was mingled perspiration and whiskey. Gabe Venable was his name, but Jim could not guess the reason for his sudden belligerency.

"He jumps an' he slides right well," continued Venable, drawing closer. "Mebbe a little better than us who lives out here."

"Shut your mouth," said Lige. "You're drunk an' lookin' for a quarrel."

"An' you shut yours, Lige Bonham. It's Jim Cheston I'm talkin' to. Him an' his Tidewater hoppin'—an' squinchin' too close to the girls."

Jim was on uncertain ground. He hesitated. For all he knew he might have made enemies by some inadvertent violation of frontier etiquette.

"I assure you that they were merely partners in the dance. I treated them no differently from my partners at home."

"That may be, but you dance too damn well for me."

There were two or three hostile faces backing up the flushed one. Jim still sought peace though his muscles were tensing.

"I don't look for trouble."

"You drunken fool," put in Lige harshly to Venable, "he didn't do nothing wrong an' you knows it. You're puttin' this on him just because the girls are nice to him."

There was a murmur of approbation and Jim saw that he had supporters as well as his opponent. His doubts fled and he stiffened against Venable like a housedog who, finding himself on his own ground, turns ready to defend his rights.

Venable was just drunk enough to be mean. He was resolved to push the quarrel. "If we respects you with Liza Bonham mebbe you'll leave us alone and our girls, too."

The jug fell to the ground on its side with a gurgle of spilling liquor until someone thriftily set it upright again. Lige spoke in a tone of ice. "What he leaves I'll take, Gabe Venable. Rely on that."

Jim was hustled behind a woodpile and stripped to the waist. Nick Watkins had joined Lige and the two whispered advice which Jim did not hear. Then he faced the other half-naked figure in the light of the rising moon which shadowed the stockade. Venable looked gigantic in the shimmering moontide and his hands were clenched to spring. Jim's throat was still sore from Simon Butler's grip, though it was a week past that that grip had been applied. He stood on the defensive, with the memory of the fight at Ingles' ordinary clogging his mind. He had to be prepared for any sort of tactics and he would not be spared if he lost.

Venable sprang at him and they battered each other with their fists. Jim could not stave off the rush and the other closed enough to get a wrestling grip. They strained together, panting, but Venable twisted his leg behind Jim's and they fell to the ground, Venable on top. Instinctively Jim shut his eyes to protect them and grappled. His hand caught Venable under the chin and forced his head back. Then his rage and fear of mutilation exploded in him and he rammed his fist into the other's belly.

They writhed over and over, wrestling and striking, but Jim had Venable by the throat with one hand and with the free one was hitting short-arm jolts which kept crashing Venable's head against the logs of the woodpile.

"You got him, boy," shrieked Lige into his ear, and in blind

174

fury Jim exerted the full power of his muscles, hardened by those long weeks of toil on the Road and in the cornpatch. A return blow cut his lip but he got his knee into the prostrate man's stomach and knocked the wind out of him. Still blind and deaf he kept hammering Venable's head onto the ground, until a grip beyond his resistance drew him off and hurled him to one side.

" 'Tain't advisable to kill him," said Simon Butler. "Did you know that he's been past speakin' this last minute or so?"

Jim lurched panting into the arms of his supporters. At first he was so filled with the passion of fight that the words penetrated only disjointedly. Then he recognized the buckskin chest upon which he leaned and the rather awed looks with which his seconds swam into view.

"If he wants more . . ." he ground out, emotionally exhausted but still combative.

"He don't want no more." The long nose and the keen eyes which he had seen as both friend and enemy were bringing him back to sanity. "You come near to makin' the same mistake I did. He ain't dead, but he's goin' to keep this fight in mind for a spell. Lad, I don't know what riled you, but you come so near to killin' him that Lige an' me were debatin' about your horse an' a quick ride to Maryland where Virginia writs don't run."

Jim came completely into focus, his chest still heaving. A group which included some of his own backers was working over Venable's prostrate figure, pouring water over it and whiskey into it. Then Venable got up, though he needed an arm about him to hold him erect.

"How is he?" asked Jim.

The answer was reassuring. Venable's red and white spotted countenance was still unfriendly but it was obviously coming back to normal, as near normal as possible with one eye rapidly closing and an ear that was puffing out.

"Hop as you want, hop as you want," he gasped. "I ain't a-arguin' with you no more. By God you've sure hopped all over me."

He limped away and Jim was led over to the Bonham cabin. Liza was there on some errand and she met him with a hawk look.

175

"You've been at the whiskey," she accused. "Get into bed an' sleep it off."

Jim's split lip cracked in a smile. "I've tucked in somebody else but I aim to do some more dancing before I tuck myself in."

The firelight came on his face and hers changed with the sight of it.

"Brawling!" she said bitterly, and then to his three friends, "Couldn't you keep him out of it?"

"It had to be," stammered Simon Butler. "The boys was bound to try him out."

She had dipped a rag in water and was wiping the blood from Jim's mouth.

"That's a man's answer," she snapped. "Can't tell what a man is, can you, until one of you's rolled him in the dirt an' chewed his ear? No, I ain't goin' to ask what it was about. Not as if I don't know. You mix whiskey and a dance an' there's only one answer to account for a busted arm or a black eye or even a split lip like we're considerin' at this moment."

She tossed the rag back on the table while Jim announced that he felt fine. He said it hastily, but not quickly enough to divert her brooding wrath from the faithful three who were shuffling their feet on the earthen floor.

"There'll be more fights tonight. You knows it an' I knows it. Don't let me catch any of you all crawlin' aroun' in the mornin' less'n you've got a Goddlemighty quick an' sure explanation that don't deal with women. Jim's settled the matter concernin' me. Judge so since he remarked that he'd tucked the other feller in. Don't sparkle your eyes at me, Lige Bonham, know 'twas what you all would call a good fight. I don't want to hear about it. Now git. I'll be over 'fore long, soon's I persuade this fool Jim that he ain't goin' to shake a foot no more tonight."

They were halfway out the door and she was facing Jim with her hands on her hips when a rifle cracked from the direction of the palisade.

"That ain't celebratin'!" exclaimed Simon sharply. "There ain't enough powder!"

A sentry's long shout sent them scrambling for their rifles.

176

Nick was sprinting in the direction of his cabin to arm himself while Simon and Lige ran towards the gate. As Jim snatched up his gun, Liza handed him shot pouch and powder horn. "I'll load for you," she said calmly and ran beside him into the moonlight where the sounds of merriment had been replaced by shouting and the crying of children. There was a dark stream of men pouring towards the loopholes while Boone's quick, incisive voice told off guards for those parts of the defenses from which the alarm had not come. Indians might make a feigned attack on one side and pour over an unguarded flank. Then the sentry's voice raised itself again.

"Don't look like indins. Can't see yet, but they got pack-horses an' they're headin' straight for the gate. No, by God, they're white."

Jim was too stiff from his injuries to travel fast, and furthermore the loopholes were occupied by the time he reached them. He could see nothing and could only listen to the parleying which went on over the palisade between Callaway and the newcomers. The word went around.

"Party from the settlements. Pushed through tonight since they were close enough to get here on a long traverse. They're openin' the gate."

The bars came down and the slab doors opened into their halves. Through the entrance came five men, three women, and a straggle of children. The men were on foot, the women and the children rode, though there were three children to one horse, clinging to each other in a solemn line on the animal's back. The gates were slammed shut behind them, and the sentries resumed their staring through the loopholes while the settlers gathered around.

Callaway was questioning in a booming tone when another broke through, a rusty voice that sent a thrill through Jim.

"Is Dan'l Boone here?" it asked and Liza looked at Jim in wonderment, for she felt him stiffen.

"That's my name, friend," came a soft, familiar answer.

"Well," resumed the rusty voice, "the soil's right an' if you're here reckon I'm set to stay."

"John Tendergrass!" shouted Jim and shoved through the crowd.

"I hears you, boy." Jim was still elbowing through the parting ranks but already the moonlight showed the shambling man, leaning on his rifle.

John Tendergrass spoke quietly but every word was audible to Jim.

"That settles it," he said. "I've been advancin' step by step but here I takes my stand."

XVII

Boonesborough felt good. Here were five more rifles and three families who had come on out to take up land in spite of what must be said about Kaintuckee back in the settlements. Sure, there would be more mouths to feed, but then maybe the hominy could be stretched further too. John Tendergrass' popularity was enhanced when he announced that he had brought a packhorse load of cornmeal along with other things. A hundred and fifty pounds of meal, carefully nursed, would go a long way.

Boone, Callaway, Tom Roper, and some of the other leaders held a conference. Then Roper came over to Jim and Lige.

"If it's agreeable to your wishes we'll put Tendergrass an' his'n in with you all. You got a fair emptiness in your cabin. Less'n of course you think it might dispute your rights to it."

" 'Tain't our'n," replied Lige promptly. "Our'n is over on the Red. Far as I know it belongs to Sime Knowles who went back to Virginia last year. Don't know who owned it afore him."

The cabins in the settlement had been built by the original arrivals, and there had been so many changes that except for Boone's and a few others' their original ownership had been so fogged that necessity had made them community property.

"You ain't got no objection then?" asked Roper.

"Not at all, not at all. Feller seems to be a friend of Jim's an' he's welcome to share it with us, particular now that maw's married you."

Tendergrass, his angular wife, his two young children and

178

the still younger baby moved in with no more delay than was necessary for the unloading of the packhorses. Tendergrass and Jim were diffident but Liza and Lige took it as a matter of course.

"Can't live outside the stockade durin' indin troubles an' we got plenty of them," announced Liza. "Furthermore we ain't real crowded. Countin' the baby we're only eight and most of 'em sleeps twelve, which I'm willin' to admit is some close quarters. Nice baby, too."

"We calls him Culpeper," announced John Tendergrass proudly. "He was born there on the way out."

Jim chuckled involuntarily. "Culpeper Tendergrass" would be a mouth-filling name when the smelly red mite wrapped in a wolfskin got old enough to carry it proper. Wonder what they'd make of it later? "Cully" or "Pep" most likely.

"We're celebratin' a weddin'," explained Lige as the settlers flowed away and the fiddle struck up again. "Come over an' have a cup of cheer."

"Don't know's I won't," exclaimed John Tendergrass eagerly. "Got a letter here, though, for Jim. It's from your grandmother. She's well."

He took out a skin pouch and from it produced the letter. "Let you read that whiles I wets my throat. It was a right long walk."

"You walked from the Holston!" exclaimed Jim involuntarily.

"Walked most of the way from Maryland. My wife was on the horse your grandmother gave me, an' my packhorses were loaded. I'm admittin' it was a right smart stroll."

Jim looked at the feet whose torn moccasins were stuffed with rags. There was a trace of red on the earth floor where Tendergrass had stood. The shambling man was lean and his eyes were sunk back in their sockets, but he seemed quite cheerful in spite of it. Even to Jim's nostrils, hardened now to close contact with toiling men, he smelled a trifle strong.

"Yes, reckon I could do with a dose of painkiller," continued Tendergrass. "Molly, I'll bring you some."

He and Lige departed side by side. Mrs. Tendergrass was up in the loft settling the children and Liza had filled the kettle and was stirring up the fire.

179

"Best read what your grandmaw has to say," she suggested and threw on a log so the fire would blaze up. " 'Culpeper Tendergrass,' the names people will bestow on their childer! Best thank the Lord, though, he wasn't born at Orange. 'Orange Tendergrass' would've been nigh on to too much."

Jim laughed but kept looking at Grandmother's flowing handwriting. His affection for her kept running the words together at first. It took a brush of his hand across his eyes before he could make sense of what she had to say.

She had a lot to say. She had had a letter from him on the Holston but had not as yet heard of Treville Cheston's death. Most of her news was the trivialities which he loved to hear. His friends were well and she had almost had to restrain Henry McKim from taking a rifle and going out to fight indians too. Jim, remembering his one encounter with the warriors, skipped over this, his own unheroic role too vivid to be forgotten. Anne Turnbull had been firm about it, remarked Grandmother, and Henry was in the militia where he should be until Anne married him. After that he could do what he wanted, or so Grandmother rather cynically commented. Mary Raeburn (here Jim read eagerly) hadn't seemed much impressed by Jim's departure . . .

He put down the letter for a moment, deeply annoyed, then he gave a quiet chuckle which made Liza turn her head and smile in sympathy before she poured the boiling water into the tub. Jim followed her movements with an appreciation which shocked him as he realized it. The compactness of her body called to him and made him forget all about Mary Raeburn's rounded prettiness. He could not resume reading at once but must stare at her until the red began rising in her face and she snapped at him to be quick, as she was going to stir round the younguns and later Miz Tendergrass in the tub.

"Lord," thought Jim, "is she the one I really want?"

His eyes followed the rest of the news mechanically. The servants were well and the horses. The new filly "Happy Medium" was shaping up fine. Grandmother thought she would be a great sprinter. Angustus had lamed the red colt and had been relegated back to being a stable hand.

Then the last paragraphs took his attention and held it. The writing was a trifle shaky and hard to read. Grandmother had

had to restrain herself emotionally as she wrote. Tidings of his father had come at last from an exchanged officer. Captain Cheston's leg was off but he was doing well, as well as anybody could who was in the hulks anchored in New York harbor, old ships converted into floating prisons whose unsanitary conditions had already made them notorious as hell-holes. He would have been exchanged among the first, since his injuries made him unfit to fight further, but he had had a difference with a Captain McNeil on General Howe's staff and McNeil had acquired a grudge. He had something to do with the prisoners and the exchanges; so Jim's father's name was far down on the list. Captain Cheston had had rough treatment . . .

Jim clenched his fists and leaped to his feet. "The bastards! The dirty lobsterbacks!" He cursed in a monotone, every oath and obscenity that he had heard came to his lips. Then Liza had him by the shoulders and was looking him straight in the face.

"What have they done to ye, Jim? What have they done to ye, lad?"

"My father . . ."

"Dead?"

"No, but like to be done to death."

Her arms were about his neck and her head pressed against the side of his own. Her hair was in his nose and he could feel the wet of tears on his cheek. Hardly knowing what he was doing he pulled her over to him and kissed her, her hard young breasts firm against him.

"Reckon I'm interrupting," said a rusty voice and John Tendergrass stood in the doorway with a cup of Monongahela in his hand.

Liza fairly bounced away from Jim, but the very act made him tingle with the quick strength of it. She was really red now and it took a moment for her to reply.

"Showin' him sympathy," she said. "Mebbe you thinks too much sympathy but I reckon he needs it. Get in there an' do what you can your own self. The water's on the boil an' I reckons you an' your family can stand some boilin'. I'm goin' over to see Maw bedded."

She brushed past Tendergrass who stood aside forbiddingly. When she was gone he looked down at Jim.

181

"Didn't think it of you, boy. Takin' advantage of her or was she takin' advantage of you?"

"If you think there's anything wrong . . ." exclaimed Jim, and the red haze of his recent battle was flooding his mind again.

John Tendergrass pointed to the letter, the last sheet of which was still clutched in Jim's hand.

"Keep a-readin'," he said. "Your grandmother told me what was in it. You and I have got to have words together."

Jim subsided reluctantly and ran his eyes over the rest of Grandmother's letter. Captain Cheston had not met entirely with enemies, though they wore the scarlet or the blue of George III. There was an army doctor, O'Connor, who had been more than kind. O'Connor had taken his health in charge and was bringing him to a speedy recovery. There was a Lieutenant Bayliss of the Royal Navy who commanded the hulk in which he was confined and who had not only defied McNeil but who had put Captain Cheston into decent quarters and had him to his table. There was hope that a speedier exchange might be arranged after all, said Grandmother's informant, for the matter was becoming notorious.

Her last paragraph, however, sent Jim back into a sullen mood.

"I am still firm, James, against your serving in the army until your father has returned," she wrote. "Should Burgoyne continue to advance the King may triumph. If so, your father is a rebel in arms and must abide the consequences. I need not tell you that I am convinced of the justice of our cause, but if we are to be defeated I would not have a plea for pardon marred by having you also regularly enrolled in the Continental Army. When he is exchanged, if you and he together decide that there is yet hope for our rebellion, I will withdraw my objection."

Jim cursed in renewed exasperation until he saw the words below the signature.

"*Postscriptum.* If you go to Kaintuckee we may be casuists. Herkimer has shown St. Leger at Oriskany that militia, if it realizes it cannot run, will fight like devils against the indians and the French" (the word had been lined out and "Tories" written in above). "The battle has like to ruined Burgoyne's

182

plan. If the frontier forts hold, Washington will not have to send troops from his army to protect his rear. Therefore if in Kaintuckee you happen to encounter either indians or British remember that a straight sight and a holding of the breath while one squeezes the trigger may help these newly united states as much as drawing the same aim upon one of George's regulars."

John Tendergrass had taken the cup into the loft. Now he descended, carrying a naked little girl under his arm.

"Stop your squallin'," he chided her. "You'll have a bath or I'll know the reason why."

He plopped her into the tub and stirred her around while the lye soap brought renewed howls.

"Read it?" he asked over the commotion.

Jim nodded.

"Seen any indins?"

"Yes," replied Jim.

"Heared you did."

Jim was puzzled. Grandmother Dorsey did not know; how then did Tendergrass? The Holston! Of course, he must have heard there. He said as much but Tendergrass only partly agreed.

"Got it confirmed there, of course, but I knew it before." He scrubbed vigorously. "Hush your cryin'. Know it hurts if it gets in your eyes but if you squinches 'em shut 'twon't be so bad."

The conversation now was being conducted in a half-shout above the lamentations.

"Juno was right much of a help when Culpeper was born."

"Juno!"

"Surely. I was hurryin' to get to the ordinary because my woman was beginnin' to feel her pains when I passes two big wagons loaded with goods an' a black woman settin' big as life on top of one load. 'Marse Tendergrass!' she screeches an' I stops, though I was right reluctant to. 'I'se Juno,' she says, 'I belongs to Marse Jim Cheston. I recognizes you an' that brown horse. I got news for you, but I reckons I'd better git back to Culpeper with you 'cause looks to me like you could make right good use of me now.' 'Fore I could git a word out she was tellin' the wagoners to turn round an' she traipses back with me an'

183

helps until the child is born. She didn't tell me the news right off. I was some agitated."

He hauled the little girl out and began to dry her with a cloth which he had found.

"When it was all over she told me that she'd heared from you, showed me the letter in fact, so's I knew about your uncle's getting killed. She was a-cryin', but she could talk clear. Don't know as if I haven't a lot of respect for her. She'd taken the money your uncle left an' packed everythin' an' hired the wagons an' she was bound up for your grandmother's. Kept a-askin' me too if she'd done right. 'Spite of what you'd writ her it looked like she thought she'd ought to have stayed down on the Holston until you got back."

He slapped the child gently on her round stern and sent her up the ladder.

"Reckon I'd better boil another kettle," he remarked. "I've likewise got to find my boy, Amasa, who's probably pestering Daniel Boone right now. When that's done, you'd best go back to this here merrymakin'. Miz Tendergrass needs to get herself clean too. Sorry to hear about your uncle and Pete but I ain't so sorry you sent Loudy back. Juno, she says that he was a-rollicking aroun' the Holston tellin' everybody that it was your uncle's fault."

"Damn him!" exclaimed Jim.

"Felt much the same," replied John Tendergrass, looking at his knuckles. "I just happened to encounter him in an ordinary 'fore we turned off onto the Road. Don't know if he'll ever chew his vittles in comfort again. He's missin' some teeth. Reckon I lost my temper."

He came over to sit down and Jim saw that his feet still left that red trace.

"Better take care of yourself too," said Jim. "Take them moccasins off an' I'll put on some bear's grease. That'll help."

He leaned down to remove them, but noticed Tendergrass regarding him with a queer expression.

"Liza's pretty good with yarbs," Jim babbled. "She keeps a lot of 'em dryin' by the hearth. She's told me how to use 'em too. There's wintergreen, hoarhound and burdock for colds, boneset for chills, sage for sore throats and—what we want right now—smartweed for sore feet."

The moccasins off, he was unwinding the rag bandages when he felt John Tendergrass' hand on his shoulder.

"How long you been here, Jim?"

Without looking up, Jim made a rapid mental calculation. "Seven weeks. Why?"

"You've got used to Kaintuckee people right quick," the rusty voice commented. "You've begun to talk like 'em and you knows about herbs an' all. Ain't you forgettin' Maryland kind of soon?"

"Reckon it's because I like 'em," answered Jim, still not looking up. He had a feeling that something more was coming.

"That's as good excuse as any," remarked Tendergrass.

The bandages were off and Jim drew in his breath sharply. The bruised, cut, battered feet must have been exquisitely painful to walk on.

"We got a last jug of whiskey here," Jim exclaimed and bustled around, fetching Tendergrass another drink while he poured the dried smartweed into a jar, moistening it with water from the kettle which was beginning to sing.

"How did you walk on these?" he asked, uncomfortably returning to his own formal enunciation.

"What you got to do you does," answered Tendergrass, unconsciously quoting Simon Butler's own philosophy. "We didn't have much wet an' I managed to keep from getting scald feet. Them you can't walk on."

Jim had poured the mess into a second wooden tub; he filled it with water and set Tendergrass' injured members into the soothing bath. He reached down the depleted pot of bear's grease, a seasoning and a medicine as well, ready to anoint when the time came. He knew that Tendergrass had more on his mind than just criticizing the way Jim talked.

Yet Tendergrass hemmed and hawed. Jim could hear him gulping down the whiskey.

"Reckon I'm an interferin' fool," at last said the rusty voice. "Yet I'm obliged to your grandmother an' fond of you, lad. Appears to me you've got right smart to remember."

"What?" asked Jim, perfectly aware of the probable reply.

Tendergrass did not disappoint him.

"There was that girl, Liza I think they calls her, who you was a-huggin' and a-kissin' of when I come in. Think that was right?"

Jim rocked back on his haunches. "What business was that of yours?"

"None, as you say," replied Tendergrass instantly, but his tone carried with it not reproval nor admonishment, but, as Jim recognized with astonishment, real regret.

"The Bonhams took you in, Jim, I've heared that over at the merrymakin'. She's a right fine girl, I've heared that too from Daniel Boone, no less. What you plannin' to make of her, Jim? You can't marry her an' take her home to your grandmother! 'T'wouldn't be fair to her an' Happy Return."

"Why not?" snapped Jim, and this time he looked straight at Tendergrass. Whether or not his sharp question sprang from perversity or his real feelings he did not know. Only he was determined not to be put down.

The shambling man was very serious. "Because, Jim, she won't fit. I don't say that your grandmother wouldn't take her. She's got idees an' pride as well. Who you takes for a wife she'll take too an' do her damnedest to make fit. But you can't do it. The other women will think she ain't got no breedin', no right to be a Cheston. They'll make life hell for her an' you knows it if you'll only stop and think."

Jim appreciated the motive that made Tendergrass speak as he did. Whether he loved Liza or didn't love her, he did not himself know. That yielding, that fierce embrace was so new on his lips that for the life of him he could not have said if his feelings were sincere. Only Liza had stopped treating him motherly.

"Do you love her, lad?" asked Tendergrass persistently, but Jim was spared. The pet blacksnake, which served to keep down the rats in the cabin, glided softly across the floor to drink from the tub. "Hamilton" they called him, after the scalpbuyer up in Detroit, for he took his toll and demanded to be fed.

"Goddlemighty," roared Tendergrass, hoisting his feet out of the tub.

"It's only Hamilton," said Jim wearily and was saved the reply.

186

XVIII

Jim knew John Tendergrass wouldn't talk. Indeed his occasional outbursts of loquacity were always a surprise to Jim when they occurred. Mrs. Tendergrass might have overheard from the loft. Probably she had, for there was small chance of keeping a secret in the confined space of a cabin. It was not that she was much of a talker, being an angular, good-hearted mother and an obedient wife who kept her tongue for her family; but she must have dropped a hint. To expect a woman not to talk about a titillating love affair is to meet a hydra without a head or a cloudburst without rain. She might only have betrayed an over-interest, but whichever it was, Liza's pride was aroused and Jim was treated to a solid course of being ignored. Not even the motherliness remained, save that she saw to it that his gear was in order just as she did her own brother's.

Except for Liza's studied indifference and Jim's puzzled gloom, the other inhabitants of the Bonham-Tendergrass cabin contrived to remain fairly cheerful. With November the Border expected the cessation of indian attacks. The warriors usually did some intensive hunting about that time and then holed in for the winter. Spring and the rising sap would bring the councils and the formation of the warbands. Therefore Lige took Tendergrass and Jim both with him, and they sought game over a twenty-mile radius, penetrating even across the Kaintuckee.

Jim got his buffalo, likewise a bear, and might have put on a few airs had he not been in Lige's company. Lige was on his mettle, for the wedding merriment had consumed a dangerous quantity of their stores, and while Tendergrass' packload would keep them from want, he was determined that the Bonhams would make their full contribution. Simon Butler had gone back to St. Asaph's, but Jim felt Lige was a good substitute. Even Boone had remarked on the quantities of meat they brought in.

The sheer effort of the hunting kept Jim from quarreling with Liza. He was too tired when they came home after a night or so in the woods to do more than eat and rest and warm his chapped hands at the fire. Before he could get up the energy to challenge her changed attitude he would have to heave himself up and go out to chop more firewood, or to care for Cricket, who was fast beginning to look like a little woolly bear, her seal-brown turning almost black as her winter coat came in.

Not that Liza was idle either. By tacit consent Mrs. Tendergrass cared for the children and did the cooking while Liza occupied her time in jerking or smoking the meat which the men fetched. Her face grew a trifle thinner and her green eyes more crackly, but once or twice Jim caught her looking at him and could not fathom her expression.

December brought the first snows, and Jim at last found a chance to speak with her alone. He had packed in a load of wood and was stacking it on the woodpile when he saw her coming back from the spring carrying two buckets of water suspended from a yoke across her shoulders.

"Give me a minute," he said, "then I'll tote that in for you."

"No need. It balances right." She was looking thoughtfully at the snow which lay in patches where the shade from the buildings had kept off the cold sun. "Wished that was salt. We're nigh to being altogether out."

"Maybe somebody's got some he can spare. We've got a little money."

"Heared you had," replied Liza with a trace of unjust sarcasm in her tone. "Heared you had an awful lot back in Maryland, but even if 'twas here there ain't nobody that's got salt to buy."

"Don't put on about a lot of silliness, Liza," snapped Jim. "I said our money, didn't I? What's John Tendergrass been telling you?"

"Nothin' that I didn't know before from what you told me your own self. Only them tales seemed just that—tales out'n a book. It's some different when there's those about who looks down their noses at me just because of what property you've got. God knows I don't want it."

Jim felt himself distinctly out of charity with the shambling man. Liza apparently realized it, for when she spoke again her voice was softer.

"Don't you go tromplin' on your friend Tendergrass. He don't mean nothin' by it. It's just that . . ."

She stopped and he put out his hands towards her, jostling one of the buckets.

"Don't spill it," she warned him sternly. "I toted that water all the way from the spring an' I don't reckon on breaking my shoulders fetchin' more. Keep them tales as tales an' keep me out of 'em."

Her chin was up as she went on to the house, and he finished piling his wood in rising anger, so intense that he bungled the job and brought down half the stack. In a spate of exasperation he kicked a log and sent it squarely into the shins of John Tendergrass as he came in with another load.

"Hope you're gettin' a mite of enjoyment out of it," remarked Tendergrass, rubbing his shin. "Knows I ain't."

Jim forgot Liza's caution. "You've been talking, I hear," he began angrily.

"She say I had?" asked Tendergrass with a keen glance.

"No," admitted Jim after a pause. "Only that you've been looking . . ."

Tendergrass fortunately kept his face straight. "Can't help looking nor my looks either. Wouldn't have been born with 'em if I'd had the say. Now, Jim, you keep this in mind. I've spoke my piece an' I ain't speaking no more, neither to you nor to anybody else, by God. Furthermore you heared me when I did an' it's up to you to form your own judgments on it. You're nigh on to twenty an' you're old enough to kill your own snakes withouten any help. Git back to pilin' wood. It'll occupy your time an' settle your stomach."

Even an amateur physician could have diagnosed that Jim's stomach had nothing to do with his complaint. He was teetering on the edge of falling in love and was therefore rather pompous and subject to fits of brooding, notably when Nick Watkins was unostentatiously showing off before Liza. Even Lige lost some of his normal cheerfulness. He ironically complained to Tendergrass that they spoiled his hunting. "Let me draw a bead on a buck with one of 'em along and first thing you know they fetches out a groan or a puff what blows the beast clear across the Ohio. Wish Liza'd make up her mind or git rid of the two of 'em."

He must have spoken to her about it, for he came in one night with a very flushed face and Liza followed him with a forbidding look. After that he did not interfere, apparently having learned his lesson.

Liza was impartial in distributing her rebuffs. She was ungracious to Nick when he brought her a new pair of moccasins, remarking that he must have sewed them in the dark, but she was even fiercer to Jim when he bowed to her as she came down the ladder in the dawn.

"If you're doin' that so's you can see better, remember I don't care for it. If you're doin' it for to show off, then I don't care for it either."

"I was trying to pay honor to you," exclaimed Jim, red and ruffled, while Lige and John Tendergrass bolted for the outdoors with shoulders shaking.

"Honor me! All you do is make me an' yourself ridiculous. Folks'll think you're full of whiskey or tryin' to weed corn."

She was thoroughly annoyed, lips compressed and firm chin high. Jim found even that angry little mouth too disturbing to resist. He kissed her and then rocked on his feet from the force of her return slap.

"You'll not do that again!" She stood away from him, quivering.

"Hark you, James Cheston. Your honor's an easy word when you follows it with a kiss which you know I don't want. You've put ideas into my head, ideas I don't cherish. It's entertainin' for a girl to hear tell of Tidewater an' the grand manners there, makes a girl long for a lovely dress an' the bowin' an' attention that goes with it. But it ain't true, not in Kaintuckee! I ain't one of your racin' fillies to be imported into Maryland for to improve the breed."

"You hush!" exclaimed Jim, both angry and shocked, but she did not heed him.

"I suits this here country an' it suits me. Reckon some day we'll import our own manners or make them for ourselves. Right now this 'honor' you're talkin' about shows up best when a man helps a girl with her tasks an' makes 'em easier for her. If you'd keep them hands of your'n off'n me an' put 'em to

190

poundin' the mornin' hominy instead, you'd be honorin' me the way I likes it."

Jim quailed before her. There was nothing of the virago in her stern, level-toned rebuke. She deflated him and made him ashamed. It was a mood which held, but with unfortunate consequences, for Jim let his humiliation carry him into resentment and a desire to make her feel that she had treated him badly.

The opportunity came soon. Late in the month a visitor came in from Harrodsburg. His errand was to borrow salt, an unavailing one for there was no salt to lend, but he brought great news. Even the failure of his mission did not dampen his spirits, for after a consolatory swig at a jug he wiped his sleeve across his mouth and remarked quietly:

"Burgoyne's been took."

There was a general exclamation, but Boone asked, with habitual caution, "How d'ye know?"

"Bowman's back from the Holston. No, he ain't brought no force with him, but he says it's definite. He says Burgoyne capit— . . ." The unfamiliar word was too much for him and he tried again. "Burgoyne capitaliated at Saratoga in York State, seventeenth October. Gave up his gun, he an' his men, an' was took prisoner."

There were yells, and rifles cracked into the air. The news was soon all over the settlement, traced by the rejoicing shots and the cheerful outcry. The jug passed from hand to hand and other jugs appeared, but Jim noticed that there were a few who let the jug go by and took off their caps in thankfulness. As for himself, he was too elated to drink. The grim danger of a treason trial which had hung over his father was temporarily lifted. The rebellion would go on. Of course there was still Howe, but Washington was facing him and Grandmother had enormous confidence in General Washington.

He said as much to John Tendergrass, but got a sobering reply.

" 'Tain't only Howe. There's Hamilton as well an' he's the feller we'd best be thinkin' of."

"Snake or governor?"

"Little of both, I reckon."

London was hurrying across the clearing carrying his fiddle.

"Merrymaking's gettin' its sleeves rolled up to begin," observed Tendergrass. "You aimin' to dance or fight tonight or take a mixture of the two?"

Jim laughed rather grimly. "I'll take what comes." He turned to the other with a quick appealing look. "Do you suppose I could do some good about my father if I went back to Maryland now?"

"How'd you get there? There's snow in the mountains."

"There's those that pass through even in winter. I'd wait for somebody going to the Holston and go with him. A partner's always welcome on the Road. We'd get through."

The shambling man chuckled dryly. "Border's doin' a lot for you, Jim. You wouldn't have talked like that a few months back. Stay here an' get your growth. You can't help your grandmother as I sees it."

The fiddle was striking up and the crowd was whooping towards the sound of it. Jim looked at the gaunt walls, the huddled cabins, the frozen ground dotted with cattle droppings; he breathed in the crisp air pleasantly flavored with woodsmoke but tainted with the odors of close living, and then he grinned.

"It suits me, but I'm damned if I can tell you why."

Grandmother Dorsey had answered the question for him before he started, but he was finding the answer for himself. "Beads and buckskins," she had said, and, as Jim stood watching, the young face grown stronger, the wind-reddened skin and the considering eyes showed that they had agreed with him. But for how long? This could be an interlude before his love of books and of the ordered life at Happy Return stole him back from the novelty of the wilderness, or it might be the beginning of the dominance of the same strain which had set Treville Cheston to roving. He could not know himself until he found himself.

Lige hurried past. "Comin', you two?" and they followed him.

Boonesborough settled down to eat, drink, dance and, of course, fight. The women might have their pleasure marred by the thought that while the food was low there was plenty of whiskey, but they knew better than to complain. The men would have their way even if they made animals of themselves. However, there was a bedrock of Hardshells who would keep matters from getting completely beyond bounds. Kaintuckee didn't have much religion but what there was of it was taken seriously. Then, of course, there were women who wandered around defending morals and getting pleasure out of it. They could manage to put the wrong impression on whatever they saw. In spite of these deterrents there were quiet corners and those who would make use of them.

Jim mostly left the jug alone. He had the good sense to realize that he couldn't spite Liza by getting drunk and he was wary of quarrels, not realizing that his treatment of Gabe Venable had exempted him from bullying. The rougher youngsters were not anxious to tangle with him, and the older men, even though there were a few wild ones whom liquor inflamed, would leave him alone by the pack-instinct which keeps the old dogs from attacking the pups. He kept watching Liza both from the sidewalls of the cabin and during the dances, when he might touch her or spin her but never get into close contact. The more he watched, the more his sullenness grew. He was done with her and her high-and-mightiness. If he couldn't have her he'd find somebody else that he could; while, underneath and unrecognized, boiled stronger and stronger his determination to make her sorry for treating him as she had.

This undercurrent sent him outside and made him mingle with a group who were giggling and shifting in the darkness under the eaves. Gabe Venable was there and others whom he recognized, and when he pushed in among them they hailed him with laughter.

"Here's the Squire," said Venable, and the three girls tittered. One of them had her arm around a lad, the other two were drawn back against the logs while the men clustered about them. Jim had seen does draw back the same way when the hounds cornered them. Only these does were willingly cornered.

"When he sees us, the Squire's goin' to run," announced Ilcy Corwell. "He don't pay no 'tention to women."

" 'Ceptin' one," said the other girl.

"Hush, child," exclaimed Gabe sarcastically. "Don't rouse him. I did an' I ain't aimin' to do it again."

"More's the loss to us." It was Ilcy again. "Must say Liza's a mite selfish keepin' Jim to herself the way she does. Has she seen you a-wanderin', Jim?"

"I go where I please," said Jim in a tone of general challenge. Nobody took him up; instead there were guffaws.

"Can't start no fight here, Jim," commented a voice in the background. "Us men ain't got no part in this here wolf hunt."

"Don't pay no mind to me, either," said Ilcy. "You've got to allow us bein' jealous."

She left her stance by the wall and took his arm. "You've partnered me in a dance once before, Jim, only you wasn't lookin' at me. Will you do it again, only this time kind of take a glance my way once in a while?"

A clear hunting yell sounded and a youngster skittered around the corner before either Jim or Ilcy could resent it.

"That's kind of mean teasin'!" exclaimed Ilcy with a shade of tears and Jim's determination was fixed.

"I'd be happy to dance with you." He took her arm and led her towards the doorway.

"And look at me whilst we're doin' it?" she whispered up at him.

"I promise that."

He wasn't too loyal about keeping his word for he was stealing side glances at Liza to see how she took it. As far as she was concerned he might have spared himself the effort, for she was talking to Nick Watkins and apparently had not so much as noticed his entrance. He was too inexperienced to interpret the unaccustomed vivacity with which she applied herself to Nick, to the latter's dazed joy.

"Turn your eyes thisaway. You promised," whispered Ilcy as she whirled past him. "Liza ain't the only one what can dance."

It was true. In fact Ilcy was a better dancer than Liza. Liza danced with a certain reserve, Ilcy danced because she had a passion for it. She loved the excuse to flirt in time with music. She was a small girl but with a strong physical appeal, big-bosomed, and with lashes she knew how to use. She could hardly be called pretty, but Jim forgot the too short nose and the too long jaw in the vivacity of her expression. He began to look down at her and enjoy it. His pride and his manhood were

194

both stirred by her obvious liking for him. At least that is the way he put it to himself, though the rampaging gossips were nudging and muttering, seeing other motives than he did.

He danced with her as often as he could, paying more and more perfunctory attention to Liza, and he was waiting for Ilcy when she came out from the women's sitting after the meal. His attitude must have been noticeable, for Lige came over to him, started to say something and then walked away. Jim didn't care. Ilcy might be flaunting her triumph but it never occurred to him that she was.

She could tease and tease pleasantly in a soft, drawly voice. She asked him how he liked the callouses on his hands and told him that he had broadened out a lot since he had come to Boonesborough.

"Broadened in more ways than one," she said. "When you first come you was a Tidewater gentleman an' us no more'n a bunch of squaws. Hope we've improved on acquaintance, know you have."

She talked in the familiar Kaintuckee way, often dropping the pronouns, but her hand was soft in his and her tone made the slurring speech another attraction. There were torches now in the clearing, bursts of drunken laughter, and the shifting of figures outlined in the glare. The light took her face and softened it until only the appeal and the drooping lids remained. London had struck up again and there was more dancing, but their desire was for something more. She frowned at the rackety noise and he frowned with her.

"Can't talk through this," she remarked softly and used her lashes. Jim nodded and they went off into the shadows.

"You've been looking at me, Jim." Her voice was very soft. "Reckon you're a noticin' sort of feller after all."

Jim tried a feeble joke. "Being on the border has taught me to look a lot closer than I used to."

"An' you likes what you sees?"

For answer he pulled her to him. She kissed him hard and thrust up against him so her whole young body was in contact with his. He held her closer still and kissed her again without restraint. She pulled her head back with half-closed eyes, then her lids flew open and she pushed him away, looking over his shoulder.

Jim broke apart from her and followed her glance. Regarding them were two pursed-lipped women.

"It's a cryin' disgrace," said the first.

"Ought to be ashamed of themselves," chimed in the other.

Ilcy had been too open in her pursuit. It was hard to be subtle in Boonesborough.

XIX

Jim kept on seeing Ilcy. The stockade was so small that he could hardly have avoided her even if he had wanted. Winter was outside the palisades just as the warriors had been earlier. The snow flurries had drifted the woods to make hunting more difficult, the deer were yarded, and there was nothing to be done in the fields. Dark skies blended with dark forest, and the only cheerful note was the ringing of the axes as more firewood was cut. It was a sound pleasant to hear but Jim had small opportunity to listen. Most of the day he was providing the music, his axe-helve stinging his hands through the fur mittens while John Tendergrass silently packed in the cut lengths.

That silence irked Jim. He had no need to ask from whence it arose. Already he had had proof of the news-collecting and news-spreading abilities concentrated within the group of cabins. John Tendergrass had either observed or been informed, probably both, of his and Ilcy's activities and matched the winter in the coldness of his disapproval. He made no remonstrance and minded his own business so strictly that Jim could not find any basis for complaint, but at the same time he made Jim feel much as Loudy Jack must have felt. Even Loudy had had his ego to fall back on, whereas Jim had a subconscious pain from the remembrance of how friendly he and Tendergrass had once been with each other.

Lige knew also, but Lige treated it more charitably. He had even cracked a few feeble jokes which had gone utterly flat, and then had taken refuge in hunting stories which went even flatter—for there is a certain sameness about hunting stories and he had told most of his before.

196

Liza hadn't said a word. She went on about the household tasks, only now he could pound hominy or not pound hominy as it suited him and there was neither praise nor reproof from her. She had gone back to smoking a pipe, filling and lighting it with a finality that headed off any remonstrance.

On the other hand Ilcy was available. She made a practice of being in the vicinity when Jim came home from work evenings. Either she was bringing in water from the spring or boiling oak-galls in a kettle outside her cabin to make a tan for leather. She would look up and call to him, and of course he would have to see what she had on her mind. It wouldn't be much, just a greeting or an observation about the weather to start with, but soon they would be talking and then it wasn't too hard to steal a kiss or so. Ilcy was throwing herself at him without much skill but with an abundance of enthusiasm.

If there was visiting back and forth between cabins Jim would be pretty sure to find Ilcy waiting for him wherever he went. Sometimes she didn't appear and then he would gloom for a day until she made up with him by the gate. Insensibly his companionship changed. Lige stopped going out with him, and so did Nick Watkins; instead he was thrown into the company of Gabe Venable and some of the brasher young sprouts whom he liked less. There were other girls, too, who made up to him, and it amused him to show off his formal manners to see Ilcy pout. If there were quizzical looks or even unfriendly ones from watching oldsters, he was having too good a time to pay much attention, and thus he lost a part of his popularity and indeed, without realizing it, came to the verge of an unpopularity which might have had serious consequences.

He got no further with Ilcy than kissing and cuddling. Winter had clamped down a morality stronger even than the Hardshells could preserve by their best efforts. The woods were cold and there were not only sentries at the gates but a perpetual patrolling outside them whenever they were open. The cabins were packed to the eaves with people, and even married couples had to have general cooperation from the other occupants before they could engage in the natural processes which might result in another towhead to crowd the quarters even further. When the indian peril should be lessened and the settlers

197

spread out from the three little forts which were the only safe islands in this winter of 1777, then the standards of morality might drop with the removal of restraint. At present Jim was luckier than he knew, for the disapproval was kept in bounds by the lack of an overt act to stir it to action.

Ilcy's parents were, as Jim soon heard, "right triflin' folks." Indeed, as Lige remarked one night with an outthrust jaw, " 'Bout the only reason why they haven't gone back is that Old Man Corwell is too bone lazy to make the trip." Jim, having seen Old Man Corwell, was privately inclined to agree, but he fired up in Ilcy's defense. She hadn't picked her parents, had she?

"Poor girl," drawled Lige, his long body sprawling loosely on the stool, but his legs gathering under him. "Reckon her paw just wore out 'fore he got round to her."

Mrs. Roper was in the room. She looked at her son and then at Jim, both of them tensing and about to fly at each other.

"That's enough for the two of ye. That's tomahawk talk. I've got some news for you. Boone's goin' to take thirty men over to the Blue Licks to boil out salt, Tom was tellin' me before I came over. Seems Dan'l has been right taken with John Tendergrass here, so he's to be one of 'em if he'll go."

While still angry, the young men nevertheless were interested. These were tidings indeed. Nearly half of Boonesborough's men to set out on a winter expedition—a relief from monotony and petty bickering.

John Tendergrass with ready wisdom took the cue from her. "Reckon I'd be willin' to go all right, if I can be a help. What do we do?"

Mrs. Roper explained to him, in so doing soothing down the ruffled feathers on the two gamecocks. "Plenty of salt springs over there. Buffalo an' deer use 'em so the hunting will be good. Boone'll take the big kettles, fill 'em full of water an' boil it off, leavin' the salt. When he gets enough he'll send it back on packhorses. Lord knows we needs it. Vittles haven't tasted good since fall, we've had to be so sparing."

"How long will it take?" asked Jim.

"Couple of months, I reckon, but they thinks to relieve the first party with another one when the work's half done. Give most everybody a change of scenery and improve some tempers, I trusts."

Lige grinned rather shamefacedly. "Reckon Jim an' me can keep peace."

"Wouldn't trust you to. You're goin' as well as Tendergrass."

"Both of us?" asked Jim, brightening.

"Just Lige," she answered briefly. "Simon Butler's staying at St. Asaph's this winter, so Lige is goin' in his place as scout."

John Tendergrass was watching the disappointment cloud Jim's expression. "Mebbe the lad here could go in place of me. He needs a change worse'n I do," he offered with his old thoughtfulness.

Mrs. Roper compressed her lips. "He wasn't asked."

There was an awkward silence; then Jim got quietly to his feet, nodded to them all and walked out. Once in the covering darkness he let his disappointment have full play. He knew better than to plead or remonstrate. Boone had selected his men and he wasn't among them. He forgot the many reasons which might have swayed Boone, his own inexperience as contrasted with Lige's, Tendergrass' age and steadiness of character. He was still a boy, was he, unfit to do a man's work? Then he stopped short as bitterness flooded him. Was his playing around with Ilcy the factor which had swayed Boone, or had he perhaps been swayed by the Bonhams, who were good friends of his?

He chose to nurse that grievance and rather defiantly carried it to Ilcy. He was rewarded by an over-sympathetic understanding. Ilcy was all in favor of the second hypothesis. The Bonhams were pretty much stuckup and they didn't relish Liza's not having married. Now with Jim living right in the cabin with her, they might be pushing Liza forward.

"It can't be that," exclaimed Jim, and Ilcy was quick to catch the changed inflection in his voice.

" 'Course you wouldn't think it," she said. "Probably it ain't occurred to Liza either, she's right hardy and minded for her own way. Still, there's some that thinks that Miz Roper would like to see her well provided for now that Lige is gettin' to the marryin' age himself."

He did not answer, but the doubt had been well sown in his grievance and it did not need much cultivation. He rehearsed to himself what he had heard said, that Liza was well above the usual marrying age and still holding off. Perhaps Nick Watkins was her last hope and she was keeping Nick dangling until she could find whether or not he himself would be available. The thought soured him, but underneath his resentment was a deeper hurt that she should have deceived him so. He tried kissing Ilcy some more as a remedy, but she could not give him the fierce quality of Liza's one embrace.

As a matter of fact he was getting tired of Ilcy. If Liza had given him the least encouragement he would have turned back to her with even more eagerness, but she too had her pride and he had hurt her almost beyond forgiveness. His feeble attempts at a reconciliation—feeble because his own pride would not let him admit that he had been in the wrong—were not enough to pierce her indifference. If anything, they merely produced a certain snappishness to which he was too ready to reply.

Meanwhile the news of the salt-boiling trip had been confirmed and Lige was too happy to let anything disturb him. To be selected as a scout was no small honor, a compliment both to his woodcraft and to his character. If Mrs. Roper occasionally wondered aloud who was going to take care of the fields when spring came, Lige was full of hollow promises and reminded her that he got extra pay for his new duties. Liza gave him sisterly abuse for turning himself into a mere "timber beast," too proud to dig with a hoe, but actually she was proud of him. Jim overheard her one night scorning off Lige's pangs of conscience.

"It's your wife when you fetches one home that I'm concerned about. 'Tain't so easy those first few years before you raise a brood of younguns to help grub the fields. You'll be off earnin' Continental shinplasters for fighting indins while she sets the hills by herself. Ask Miz Boone if that ain't so."

"If I brings me home a wife, she'll have you to help her."

"Thankee, Lige, for handin' me a hoe an' pointing out where to dig alongside her. Mebbe I'd better get married up my own self an' have another lazy man to support—only this time one of my own."

"You reckonin' to do so?" asked Lige with lively curiosity, but Jim did not hear her reply.

The conversation shook him. He wasn't considering marrying Liza, or Ilcy either for that matter. He hadn't thought of marriage at all, particularly out here on the frontier. When marriage came to him it would be a decorous mating with a selection from the Tidewater belles, but he wasn't even ready for that. He liked the border life and he was having a lot of new experiences. He felt a lot more of a man now that he had met Ilcy. It was a real pleasant and flattering feeling to have a girl tell you what a fine fellow you were, yes, and bring your maleness alive in doing it. Still Liza's having thoughts of getting married was an unexpected flaw in the gem of his enjoyment. If she was, then he was pretty sure her thoughts wouldn't be concerned with him. Certainly there was no love in their brisk bickering. Who else, then? Nick Watkins? If she was keeping Nick dangling as Ilcy had insinuated, then the one for whom she was keeping him dangling couldn't be himself— not the way she treated him. Was it perhaps Simon Butler—or Kenton—whom she was after? He had a distinct revulsion in his feelings towards the scout. Possibly if he had had someone in whom he could confide he would have realized that he was jealous, but John Tendergrass was treating him with reserve and there was no one else to talk to—except Ilcy, and she was beginning to bore him.

Came the day when Lige burst in, recovered himself, and with as much dignity as his eagerness would allow announced that they were leaving in the morning. The calm stream of preparations flowed into a final rapids of last-minute hurry. Mrs. Tendergrass anxiously checked the last of her husband's gear while Liza did the same for Lige. Blankets, extra moccasins, mittens, socks, food, cooking utensils were brought out and made up into packs. The men examined their rifles and moulded bullets. Jim by now was familiar enough with the bustle, but this time he felt utterly out of it. He was one of the home guard and the fact that Nick Watkins too was to stay behind did not console him. There was to be a celebration—a sendoff—for those who were to go and the whole settlement was invited. In fact it was an axiom for the whole settlement to attend anything from a wedding to a funeral. The monotony of the life made any community project an excuse for a jubilation and everyone had contributed. Colonel Callaway's house was the rendezvous, and any aching heads among the salt-

201

boilers would be taken care of by the cold air of tomorrow's trail.

Again there was pounding of hominy and smoke of cooking fires. Liza's sharp tongue sent Jim bolting off into the woods for small game. He spent a wet, snow-laden morning searching for rabbit burrows, poking in them with his ramrod and killing the terrified occupants with smart blows as they scurried out of their refuges. He had good luck, but it brought to a boil his unjust resentment at not being among those chosen. Lige and John Tendergrass were fully accepted, he wasn't. By God he'd arrived before John and yet his assignment was to kill bunnies while Tendergrass faced the winter trails. He forgot the night at Charlottesville when Tendergrass had sat in the seat of the mighty as an invited guest, forgot Ingles' Ferry and the soft-voiced son who had been a captive and had sensed the protective affection of the older man. Ilcy had done her work too well when she flattered him. Wet and angry, with a dozen small carcasses in his belt, he reentered the stockade to find her waiting for him under the lee of the gate.

"You been huntin'?" she asked slipping her hand under his arm.

"No, I've been massacring rabbits."

His voice was louder than he had expected and he saw Nick Watkins, who was the sentry, turn his head towards them, then jerk it straight again as he met Jim's eyes. Ilcy hurried him towards the cabins.

"Oh Jim, they don't treat you right. You ought to be the one to go."

"I wasn't asked," he replied bitterly, quoting Mrs. Roper's words which had rankled in his brain ever since he had heard them.

"I know, I know. There's them that don't give credit to them what deserves it."

They were out of sight of the usual busy group in the cleared space of the stockade. She had led him behind a sheltering woodpile and her lips came up to his. For once his did not meet hers.

"Maybe they're right," said he in the voice of a sullen child.

"They're not, I tell you." Her arms slipped round his neck. "You're the finest feller here in Boonesborough. There's one that wants you, Jim, wants you bad and who's tryin' to keep me away who wants you mostest."

She was kissing him now and straining against him, regardless of his wet hunting frock. His ill-mood and his grievances were submerged in her surrender and his arms in turn went about her while his mouth met hers.

"You're what I wants, Jim. To have a man like you to love me. Can't you feel me givin' in to you? I don't care what folks think or what they say."

They blended together in a passionate embrace. There were voices on the other side of the woodpile. Somebody was asking someone else if there was enough hickory-nut butter to go around. Jim swore and Ilcy looked at him under her lashes.

"The north blockhouse," she whispered rapidly. "I'll be waitin' for you after the merriment starts. In the upper story, Jim. We can pull up the ladder. There won't be hardly nobody patrollin' tonight an' they won't bother to come up, 'specially if there ain't no ladder."

She sprang away and he could hear the snow creaking softly under her moccasins as she fled around the corner of the cabin.

Jim fetched home his rabbits and sat silent before the fire while the steam rose from his wet clothes. He was too keyed up to think, answering in monosyllables what few remarks were directed his way. The cabin was full of activity, with Mrs. Tendergrass seeing that the children were bundled up and that the new baby was well wrapped in the wooden trough which served as a crib. Jim heard Liza say something about watching Culpeper until Mrs. Tendergrass had eaten; then there was a procession out the door, Lige and John Tendergrass carrying kettles and Mrs. Tendergrass herding her children. Nick Watkins had come in and had been pressed into service as bearer of the demijohn. The snow was falling softly, but it was everybody's opinion that it would stop before long. It whitened their shoulders as they left.

Jim stood up as Liza came over to him.

"I'm mindin' the baby like I said," she remarked. "Surely you ain't goin' out like that?"

"What's wrong?"

"Wrong!" She laughed more naturally than he had heard her for weeks. "You got rabbit blood all over you. Shuck your

203

clothes an' climb under the blankets till I can wipe 'em off."

He looked down and saw that she was right. Not only was he stained, but bits of fur adhered to his buckskins.

"I can do it," he replied huffily.

"You can do it badly. Strip 'em off an' I'll step outside. Holler when you're ready."

Her sudden friendliness puzzled him in spite of his impatience. He waited until she had left, then reluctantly took off frock, breeches and leggings and pulled the blankets up to his chin.

"Don't see why you should go to all this trouble, but here they are," he called, still wondering. Liza had never gone to so much trouble before over his appearance.

She came in promptly, took the clothes, and went over by the fire, where she dipped a handful of buffalo wool into the kettle and began to scrub. He watched her where she sat, her head on one side and a grim little twitch to her mouth.

"I've been observin'," she remarked after a short silence. "Ain't nobody around here with a reputation as hard as mine unless it's Ilcy. Point is, mine's been inflicted on me. Ilcy, she's asked for it."

She picked up her pipe and lit it at the fire while Jim watched her in speechless indignation.

"You're innocent, innocent like a woolly lamb, only you thinks you're a ragin' lion. You're goin' out with Ilcy, ain't you? Needn't pretend you're not. I saw you both at the gate an' I knows Ilcy."

Jim sat up in bed, the blankets falling from his shoulders.

"What concern of yours is that?"

"I'm making it mine, whatever's the rights an' wrongs to it." She bundled the clothes into her arms and her jaw muscles tensed. "Hark you now. I could have had men that Ilcy Corwell would have given more than her virginity for, aye, had 'em if I'd crooked a finger—married 'em, boy, not bundled with 'em. Why I do this for you I don't know. 'Tain't that I love you—I got too much sense for that—but I'm damned if I see Ilcy liftin' your scalp withouten my raisin' a finger."

Jim, too angry to care what he said, was ready to hurt her.

"You're jealous, that's the reason for it."

He might as soon have slapped her across the mouth, that straight firm mouth in the white face below the blazing eyes.

"Jealous, am I? Ain't you flatterin' yourself a mite? What have I got to be jealous about with Simon Butler a-chasin' me not to speak of Nick Watkins? Both of 'em are better men than you. They can provide and all you've got to offer is John Tendergrass and his word that your grandmaw has plenty of land an' money that she's willin' to share with you. Cut yourself down to size, Jim Cheston."

In a fury he started to climb out of the bed, but she rapped out with a white-hot intensity that checked him:

"You do an' I'll scream for help. If I does you'll have to kill Lige an' Tom Roper an' mebbe Nick Watkins too. Boone an' them is liable to set you afoot on the Wilderness Road with a rifle an' one charge. Now you talk sense!"

Jim knew she meant it and pulled the blankets up slowly, his mouth agape. She threw the bundle of clothes into the corner and sat down on the stool.

"I ain't a-goin' to see you act like a young stallion in breeding season. You've made me think about things back in Tidewater and by God I'll make you do the same."

Suddenly there were tears running down her face, glistening in the firelight.

"I knows I'm a fool," she half-muttered, but then spoke out strongly again.

"Boone's takin' out the saltboilers tomorrow. You're goin' to be one of 'em. Dan'l don't know it, no more'n Lige and John Tendergrass, but you're goin' to be one of 'em. I'll see to that."

XX

Boone and his saltboilers marched at dawn, marched, that is, in as much order as any body of Kentucky militia, which was only to keep in single file, spaced by the packhorses. There was no semblance of parade formation, no thought of keeping step, but the scouts were out in front, the column closed up, and the rifles were ready for immediate use. Neither was there

205

any cheering crowd at the gate to see them off, merely the anxious-eyed women, the envious gate-guard, and the usual irrepressible small boys who tumbled and yelled in the snow but did not leave the stockade. That precaution was ingrained in them—outside was no place for anyone save armed men.

Jim was in the line, towing along an excited Cricket whose one ambition seemed to be to root or roll in the drifts. He kept his head down and did not look at Ilcy as he passed. Liza had cowed him, and he recalled only too well Lige's wooden expression and John Tendergrass' lip-wrinkling when they had returned the night before. Tom Roper had allowed that he would do his best with the hunting for both households, and Daniel Boone had stopped in to say in his soft voice that Jim would replace an individual who, with a full load of Monongahela on board, had managed to sink an axe into his foot while doing last-minute chores for his family.

Liza had been quite placid. She had seen to it that a rather mangy bearskin had been added to his blankets, had reminded him to put extra gunflints in his pouch, and when he left had kissed him competently but without too much warmth.

"Take care of yourself," she had said. "Grease your feet of nights an' you won't get 'em scald." Then she had laughed unexpectedly in her deep, bubbling way. "Now ain't that an elegant thing to say? Still I'd sooner you felt kindly towards me as you rubs it in than feel unkind towards me an' everybody else when you comes to peel off wet moccasins an' buffler wool socks an' find your skin coming with 'em."

He had muttered ungracious thanks but she had refused to take offense. She had put a hand on his shoulder and looked him squarely in the face.

"Mebbe you'll hate me always after this, but I'm countin' on your learnin' a few things when you're in camp. Gossip an' tales ain't confined to women only."

Her eyes and her voice had softened. "Take care of yourself," she had repeated as if the words had been forced from her. Then she had turned away and started to reassure Mrs. Tendergrass.

"Dan'l will bring them safe home, don't you fret. Indins ain't about in the woods in winter, they sticks right close to their villages."

206

The saltboilers wound their way into the forest and struck northerly to the shuffle of the snow. Cricket's enthusiasm wore off and she fell in beside Jim, occasionally nudging him with her nose in hopes of a tidbit. He could see John Tendergrass shambling ahead of him leading another horse, his rifle in the crook of his arm. Sometimes when they turned to avoid a tangle of trees or a deeper drift, others came into clearer view, linseys and buckskins and buffalo coats, shoulders hunching slightly forward and weather-tanned faces tilted downwards against the wind. The gouge they made in the snow was narrow, for each walked as nearly as he could in the others' traces. They moved with a swinging stride but with occasional jerky halts as the trail-breakers in the lead changed places. When they came to the little prairies that interspersed the forests they speeded up imperceptibly, until Jim was glad of the months of hard labor which had strengthened his muscles. But even then he felt his tendons cramp with the steady pace.

They stopped occasionally to breathe the horses, and Jim, squatting beside the trail, fell into conversation with Levi Mason who was next behind him, a scarred, muscular man with patches of gray hair showing under his cap.

"How you doin', lad?" he asked, and Jim, out of courtesy, managed a friendly reply.

"I sure know I'm walking. My legs keep nudging me with the news."

Mason chuckled. " 'Tisn't too easy, I'll allow, but wait until you goes out on a summer scout 'gainst the indins when you got to really travel. Then you'll wonder if your legs ain't bein' burned at the stake."

"This plowing through snow is what tires me. Why don't we use snowshoes?"

"Now that's a right good question. I hunted once up in York State where they do, but then that's different country. Ever tried to lead a horse with them things on?"

The column was getting under way again and Jim had no chance to answer. He was beginning to grow more accustomed to the pace and his thoughts went back to what had happened last night. The labor of travelling was imprisoning his emotions, and he found himself unable to keep his feelings on their plane of injured pride. Instead there presented itself insistently

207

the glint of tears on Liza Bonham's cheeks. Maybe he ought to be thinking of Ilcy Corwell, but Liza's tears kept washing the image away. What was it Liza had said? "I knows I'm a fool." Why? Because she had interfered with him, humiliated him and got into a right royal rage at him? That was no answer and he knew it. She'd stopped being motherly for certain. Then slowly he began to admit to himself that it might be because she was more than fond of him.

He was so wrapped in this new thought that he rammed into the quarters of the horse ahead, which had halted without his noticing. Fortunately the animal did not kick and he jerked Cricket out of range and rested on his rifle. A voice sounded behind him.

"Then likewise as you sees we usual has a lot of bare spots where the snow's been blown off an' you'd be takin' 'em on an' off all the time."

It was Levi Mason still talking about the snowshoes and resuming the conversation precisely where it had ended an hour before. John Tendergrass called, "We got a river to cross," and Jim had no more time for wondering whether fondness meant love.

The crossing was made with a certain amount of jollity. While the axes flashed and the rafts were constructed they could see the almost smokeless gleam of a small fire on the far bank. Lige stood beside it indicating that here was the place to ford. They broke the skim ice and poled over, while the horses floundered through water that was nearly up to their withers. For frontiersmen they were noisy. There were hoots of joy when a horse tried to climb up on one raft and spilled its cursing occupants into the stream.

"Think it's Jordan water? You sure made a good job of the baptism," was Lige's only comment, though accompanied by a broad grin, as Jim splashed ashore leading Cricket who, of course, was the culprit. The rifles and the gear had been saved. There was no harm done which the heat from the fire could not cure. Jim, in the steam of his drying clothes, grinned back. Lige had his good points when everything was considered. It was the first crack in the barrier which his own injured pride and stubbornness had erected, stone by stone.

They travelled northward, still in the same holiday mood

but with Lige and Flanders Callaway and Daniel Boone fanned out ahead of them alert for danger. They camped under half-faced shelters, and Jim for the first time realized that the winter forest lost much of its formidableness when coped with by experience. When a pole was laid horizontally between two forked sticks and others were sloped back from it to the ground, with the interstices filled with brush and the snow scooped out underneath so as to make room for beds of boughs, it was nearly as comfortable as a cabin—and a lot less odorous. The fires that burned in front of backlogs of green timber were spaced so as to warm the men who squatted between them, little fires soon burning down to hot coals, not bonfires which scorched one side and froze the other. He commented on the pleasantness to Levi Mason, and Mason spat thoughtfully.

"Surely, surely. We got plenty men and plenty vittles, though we'll have to start huntin' once't we get to the Licks. It's a mite different though if you're tryin' it alone and the game's scarce or you get sick or hurt. Still there's some who's wintered well thataway—Dan'l for one an' me for another, when I was a Long Hunter. Goddlemighty, lad, there's them that's starved in summer if they'd lost their weapons. 'Tain't all skill, there's some luck to it even for the best of us."

Jim stared out at the gaunt trunks and the snow-laden branches, then drew closer to the comforting fire. He wiggled his toes within his dry socks and his dry moccasins and re-membered the torture of scald feet. The trees seemed to move a step closer with the memory. The wilderness was one thing to the healthy, well-fed borderer, quite another to one who was neither healthy nor fed. Then he chuckled deep inside himself. Liza had been right. He could think of her and think of her with affection when there was no physical torture to center his mind upon himself.

The Blue Licks were an amazement. Never had Jim seen so many gametrails. Deer and buffalo needed salt and the springs provided it. Therefore they came in their herds, pawed away the snow and licked up the mineral-impregnated earth. The springs themselves bubbled blue with an ocean tang that made Jim nostalgic for the Chesapeake. More wonderful still were the swampy bottoms which surrounded them, for projecting from their surfaces were bones, enormous white bones which brought the men to the swampside to gape at their size.

"Curious, ain't they?" remarked Lige, who had been here before. "Right smart of an animal to have ribs like them there. Make a buffalo look like a mouse. I'd enjoy to have had a shot at one," he finished, his hunter's eagerness expressing the feeling of every Kentuckian present. "Must have been dead a long time though. Mebbe there's some like them still a-roamin' west of the Mississippi. Reckon I'll go see some day."

Tall, loose-jointed, leaning on the long rifle, he typified the pioneers from whom would spring the mountain men, the plainsmen and the cowboys when the slow westward roll of Americans would burst out from the forests onto the grass and sage which a later age would also call the frontier.

Neither he nor Jim imagined it as they hauled a mighty rib to solid ground.

"Must be from before Noah," hazarded Jim, as he scraped the mud from a mammoth's relic.

" 'Fraid you may be right at that. Meantime if we sticks one end in the ground it's goin' to be right handy for dryin' socks."

The work began promptly. The huge salt kettles were set to boil and would be kept boiling day and night. "One hundred and twenty gallons of water to make a gallon of salt"—so said a later pioneer. Only the absolute necessity for the white grains, which not only seasoned meat but cured meat as well, could justify the enormous labor.

Jim found that the tasks of Boonesborough and those of the Licks were much the same. When he wasn't cutting wood he was out cutting cane from the brakes to feed the horses.

"Never knew what was meant by the eternal fires until I came here," he grunted to John Tendergrass after two weeks' steady chopping.

"Good practice 'case some indin scalps you an' you comes to judgment. Don't know that you haven't come a bit nearer to 'em since you started foolin' around with that Ilcy."

Not so long ago Jim would have been furiously resentful. Now he met Tendergrass' eyes and wiped the sweat from under his cap. He had heard a few things said indirectly around the supper fires—the men were too busy to talk much during the

210

rest of the day. Ilcy apparently had made her intentions all too clear and male wisdom was warning a callow innocent.

"I heard that," remarked Lige who was in from a scout and was condescending to stretch his muscles with an axe. With a few strokes he trimmed the branches from a felled tree.

"Her paw'll head for the settlements come spring, mark my words," he remarked presently. "Whole family's shiftless an' the neighbors ain't helpin' him no more. Don't do no good to help 'cause he's never ready to help back again. He's bein' told so right often. Reckon he'll take the warnin'."

He attacked his fallen tree and hacked it into lengths. Kentuckians had a habit of speaking at intervals interspersed with work. The remarks would wait, the work wouldn't.

"Ilcy's out to catch somebody," he finally continued. "She tried for me an' I reckon I was nigh to bein' skinned an' packed home. Her best hope's to have a youngun an' go squallin' to Boone an' Callaway an' them for help in marryin' up. Her paw wouldn't say 'Boo' to a goose."

Tendergrass made a smothered sound between a laugh and a snort. "That's right apt. Howsomever this wood's waitin' to be toted in."

That evening Jim was sitting on a log trying to whittle a spoon out of a stick while a half-dozen loungers gave him advice. His earnestness produced a low chuckle from Daniel Boone.

"Jim's in such a hurry when he gets to whittlin' that he never quite knows what's a-comin' out. Now that, I'd say, is a mighty good paddle for a canoe 'ceptin' it's a mite small."

"Ever seen him cut a tree, Dan'l?" asked Levi Mason. "He goes after it like a painter in a deeryard, battin' at it with his paws an' tryin' to do the mostest damage he can in the shortest time. 'Bout half way through he has to set on his hunkers an' pant, then he wipes his whiskers an' goes at it harder'n ever."

"One tree's still in the air a-fallin' when Jim's taken his first lick at the next," chimed in another. "I'm still a-wonderin' why I can cut two to his one. Don't seem right somehow when he's workin' so hard."

Boone's eyes were twinkling but his expression remained placid. "If we reckons to keep the fires burnin', Jim'll have to

211

go huntin' with Lige. He can take his mare an' tote the game in. She's pretty nigh as much in the way as he is in camp. Did you hear yesterday how she got loose an' into the saltbag? Licked up three days' boilin' before Ben Todd drove her off. Get the two of 'em off together an' we can let Lige do the worryin' for the rest of us."

Even Jim had to join in the laugh, but he knew that Boone's suggestion was the equivalent of an order. Daniel might preface a remark with "If you think it's a good idea" or "If you has time," as a salve to Kentucky independence, but he was obeyed. It was not only his force of character and his reputation for wisdom which gave him his leadership, but the tacit approval of everyone else in camp. Probably Boone was right in hinting that Jim was not up to standard as a woodchopper, but actually Lige had been complaining that the area near the Licks had been hunted out and that he needed a companion with another horse if he were not to waste time packing in the meat. In a way it was a compliment that Jim was now regarded as being sufficiently skilled to accompany a scout even in the humbler capacity.

He took up his new assignment when Lige went out again. Lige might be humorously patronizing in camp, but in the woods he was a wise and comforting companion. The work was not easy and their night bivouacs fairly sketchy, but Jim thrived upon it. He learned to sleep upright against a tree in the same fashion that Simon Butler had slept that first night they had been together; he learned the cussedness of the laden branch which, unwarily touched, dumped snow over him and spoiled an hour's cautious approach to a quarry; and above everything how to read "sign." He developed the characteristic border walk, the downcast, scanning eyes interrupted by the sweeping horizon-glance. Most important, he was schooled in the dreaded warnings, the "indin sign"—a dropped feather, a moccasin track toeing inwards, the ashes of a dead fire—and was thankful that they had seen none of them.

He had shot buffalo and had learned the trick of twisting the great head to one side and thrusting the horns into the earth so the huge carcass could be levered up for easy skinning. Therefore when Lige came in one day in early February and reported a herd feeding at the edge of the canebrakes, he reached for his rifle with no more than a normal tingling of anticipation. They tethered the horses near the edge of the woods and soft-footed towards the thinning verge while Lige scowled anxiously up at the sky.

"Snow's a-comin'," he whispered. "When we gets 'em we'll make for that windfall next the creek 'bout a mile southerly. 'Member it?"

"Surely," answered Jim. He remembered the great tangle of interlaced trees which one of the fierce windstorms that occasionally swept Kaintuckee had left to mark its passage. It would break the force of the storm and give them shelter for themselves and the horses.

The buffalo were still grazing near the edge, the brown bodies showing up now and then even if the rustle and tear of the canes had not been abundant indication of their presence. The sky grew darker as they watched and Lige swore under his breath.

"Better take one rather'n none. Next time that cow shows her shoulder I'll shoot." He glanced sideways at Jim and relented. "No, you shoot—but don't you miss."

Jim brought his rifle to his shoulder and the hammer clicked back. The first snowflakes were pattering on his face and he squinted his lids as he waited. The cow thrust her head out so near that he could see her small eyes greedily seeking her fodder. The wind was rising into a low wail and the cow raised her nose and sniffed it. She stood rigid and just as rigidly Jim watched for her shoulder to show. Far off a tree snapped with a loud report as the rising wind found its weakness, and the cow whirled towards them and started to run.

"Climb!" roared Lige. "Here comes the herd!" The frozen ground was thudding to hooves and the cane crackled like the musketry of a battle. Jim fired and the cow went to her knees, but the buffalo were thundering down upon them. Lige was already swinging from the low branch of an oak, and Jim, still clinging to his rifle, sprang behind a maple. A young tree went down with a crash as a panicky bull rammed into it, and Jim swarmed up into his refuge, praying that it would hold. Another buffalo blundered against it and the shock nearly tore him from his perch. But he clung, like a seaman to a topmast in a gale, until the thunder died and Lige called him anxiously.

213

He slid to the ground, feeling his knees jerk nervously, but Lige had him by the shoulder.

"The horses! They're headin' right for 'em. Come on!"

They ran panting along the path the buffalo had plowed while the snow whistled down with ever increasing speed. Then, with a brief cry, long-legged Lige, who was in the lead, brought his rifle to his shoulder.

"Pore thing! Pore thing!" he exclaimed and the sharp report put an end to the sufferings of his horse, which was down, disembowelled and reddening the snow.

"Cricket?" gasped Jim as he caught up.

"Don't see her, reckon she busted loose. Sure did. See she took the branch she was tied to with her. Well, we'd better take out after her 'fore the snow wipes out her trail."

Fortunately for the little mare she had not been in the direct path of the herd, which had swerved a trifle as it ran. It was an outlier who had cannoned into Lige's horse and had finished him in blind panic. Cricket's trail turned off from the buffalo and went down into a hollow and then across a windswept open space.

"It's her all right," said Lige. "See her tracks. Lord knows how far she'll run. Git a-goin' 'fore the storm wipes 'em out. If we gets separated, 'member I'll meet you at that windfall."

He struck into the long border lope and soon left Jim behind. Jim had known that it would be so. Running was a border virtue that was cultivated from boyhood. The distances covered were amazing. (In little more than six months from this time Adam Helmer was to carry the news of a raid in the Mohawk Valley of York State twenty-six miles, and the most of it at top speed with indians on his heels.) Simon Butler had stated in Jim's hearing and not as a boast that he could outrun any indian, given a fair start. There was more to it than strong legs and lung power, both of which Jim had. It was the additional knowledge of how to select a route through timber and over hills, how to place the feet to avoid a sprained ankle— each decision made instantaneously at top speed.

Jim fell into the same lope, doing his best but saving himself as much as he could. Unless the snow wiped out the trail Lige would come up to Cricket long before he did; the mare was friendly with Lige and would be easily caught. Right now he was more concerned with keeping track of his companion. Already the snow and Lige's lead had taken him from sight and Jim ran with his eyes on Cricket's deeper prints. They were beginning to swerve and grow more erratic as the panic left her.

He had covered well over a mile and his burning lungs demanded a momentary respite. He fell into a walk, drawing deep breaths, and the snow quietly and efficiently filled Lige's traces and shallowed those of the mare. He was not alarmed, for his whole anxiety was concentrated on the possibility of losing her. A man can have more than a considerable affection for an animal, and he had it for Cricket. Then the wind blew and the snow whirled and he began to lope again.

The trail was getting really faint now. Once or twice he had to stop and backtrack until he picked it up. He began to watch the country ahead of him, as Lige had taught him, treating the mare as if she were a deer. If one was trailing and the tracks died out, then one had to match the vanishing traces with one's knowledge of the animal to figure which way it would go. Twice he was right, seeing almost obliterated tracks when he had cast forward over what looked like untrodden drifts. He was wet with sweat and for the first time a little uncertain. There was no sign of Lige, neither sight nor trace of him.

He came to a deep patch of woods and a rocky gully. There was one hoofprint where a shrub, with some dead leaves still clinging, had shielded it. The storm was howling around him and the snow was matting on the front of his hunting frock. The flakes beat at him as he stopped to listen but there was no sound except the wind's rising wail. The print seemed to point at the gully, and into it he went, missing another gully which ran almost at right angles, its mouth concealed by brush and the snow-curtain. His was the logical gully, by his reasoning, and it ended in a patch of brush into which he plunged. Half an hour's floundering in the thick undergrowth, and the storm's treachery brought him to a halt with his backtrack wiped out.

"Can't have come this way," he said aloud, both for the comfort of his own voice and to reason with himself, for the wind and the driving flakes were taking him to themselves. Gradually they were insinuating their presence underneath his buckskins and chilling his sweating body.

"She must have turned off into that patch of woods," he said again, this time quite loudly, and sought his footprints. A few steps and the snow was drifted smooth. He tried to find the mouth of the gully—he thought he knew quite well where it was. A quarter of a mile over there and he'd be in it and out of the wind; but a quarter of a mile brought him head on into a wall of rock that he didn't remember having seen before. He followed that, convinced that it was nothing but the continuation of one side of his sought-for gully, but it faded off into a tangle of fallen trees.

He stood looking at them with panic surging up like tide in a cloven rock. The gale and the snow were piercing through him as his body cooled, and he shivered, a shiver which had both a physical and a mental origin. This tree tangle certainly wasn't the gully and he looked back the twenty feet which the storm had left him as his limit of vision, along the rock wall which he had followed. If he retraced his steps he'd come to— what? The gully? How did he know? If he worked through the gully he would be next to the grove. But the grove—which way did that lie from the windfall which was their rendezvous? Cricket's trail from the buffalo stampede had been a little south of west. He had registered that automatically. Therefore he would travel a little north of east to reach where she had been tethered, and from that the windfall was a mile south. Even while his mind tried to grapple with the confusion of directions his rising panic clamored that he was lost, good and lost—for which way was north? He knew the wind had shifted at least once—he'd noticed that soon after Lige had left him. Then the uncertainty and the wind and the cold and the snow united in the long storm wail—"You're lost, lost, lost, and this is the wilderness of Kaintuckee and men have starved in it and wandered until they dropped in it and you can't find Lige nor the Licks nor Boone . . ."

Boone! Who was it had said in that soft voice, "Don't know that I ever was lost but I do recall bein' bewildered for three days"? The vivid memory, a strong, saving influence, picked up his courage. Once the opening was made in the crust of panic, there was room for other memories. "If you're lost, remember 'tain't you that's lost, it's the camp or the settlement or the creek or whatever 'tis you're lookin' for."

216

He looked down at his snow-matted buckskins and drew the hatchet from its place. Even if Lige could find him or he could get back to the Licks, Cricket was gone. Still he would camp. "Camp," that was the word. He would camp now and let his problem wait until the storm blew over. His eyes scanned the fallen timber and a hole gaped at him invitingly. The branches of the dead trees had interlocked and earth had drifted up behind them. It was a snug shelter if a man had a fire.

He reloaded his rifle slowly and methodically, remembering the many cautionings he had received. It did him good to blame himself for having forgotten to reload. It steadied him as he cautiously poked the muzzle into the darkness to stir up any animal which might have availed itself of the natural refuge. Even the action was helpful in recalling Simon Butler's doing the same when he had first seen one of the worthies of Kaintuckee in action.

There was no result to his probing, and he used his hatchet to cut wood; he brought out his flint and steel and after much coaxing managed a blaze. He was dead tired but he could eat the dried venison in his pouch and wonder where Lige was, probably now worrying and stamping about the windfall. He didn't worry about Lige. Lige could take care of himself as Butler's ablest pupil.

His blankets were with Cricket's pack. Now that he thought of it, they were probably trampled and shredded under the feet of the buffalo. Still there was an abundance of dead leaves and the tangle above him was so thick that no snow came in. The earthen banks reflected back the heat of the fire. Fed and warmed, he dried his clothes, pulled out the extra moccasins from another pouch, greased his nearly frozen feet, tingling as the blood flowed into them, and burst out into silent laughter. Some men carried locket or locks of hair to remind them of their beloved. He didn't know whether she loved him or he loved her, but Liza Bonham gave him more comfort every time he followed her advice than any locket or lock of hair could afford. Then he went to sleep to dream good dreams.

There was a sound in his ears that made him fly awake, snatching for his rifle. A high, quivering sound, yet with a familiarity which checked the hammer thumb as it started to

217

pull back. It was broad daylight and in front of his shelter Cricket was standing, neighing a welcome, with Lige beside her.

Lige was humble. "Sorry, Jim, I found her but I was a mite bewildered afterwards. Seems she travelled in a circle an' I was right surprised when I saw the windfall. Reckon you turned back earlier."

Jim stared about him, recognizing the snow-laden landmarks. He too must have circled, for his tree tangle was the windfall of their rendezvous.

XXI

The loss of the other packhorse was serious enough, but more serious still was the loss of their blankets. The storm had cleared, and now fortune turned a little in their favor, for the wolves and the foxes had barely had time to get in their work on the body of the buffalo cow that Jim had shot. The meat they cut from it was more than a load for Cricket. They started back for the Licks, while Lige philosophically shrugged off Jim's sympathy.

"Just so long as it wasn't one of us, as it well might have been. If we'd been fools enough to go into the cane after 'em probably we'd have been killed. Never can tell what'll start 'em off."

"What did start them? That tree snapping?"

Lige gave him a slow smile. "Surely. I wouldn't have been takin' out after the horses so quick an' free unless I'd heared it. Just might have been an indin or so comin' down wind on 'em though I don't think no indin would be fool enough for that. You lives an' learns or you learns an' you lives, don't know which is truer in Kaintuckee."

They were a fair distance from camp and the loose snow made travelling difficult; so it was midafternoon before they approached the Licks. The cold was severe and Jim was working his fingers inside his mittens and tramping close on Lige's heels, with thoughts of a warming fire, when his companion put out his hand and stopped, head on one side. After a moment he went on, but Jim could feel him hesitate.

"What's wrong?" he asked in the breath of a whisper.

"Don't know," came the equally low reply. "Don't hear no axes, which is mighty strange. Mebbe they knocked off early but I sure can't think why."

Lige's puzzlement communicated itself to Jim. He thrust the mittens into his belt and shoved a finger through the trigger-guard of his rifle. They were entering the final belt of timber which surrounded the Licks, and the evidences of woodchopping were plain. More hesitant than ever, Lige pointed downwards and Jim could read the message in the gesture. No fresh tracks and the old tracks drifted by yesterday's storm. Certainly no choppers had been out in this direction at least today. Then Lige gave a low sound of mirth and straightened up.

"Just as well I thought of it or they'd have bust their sides laughin' at us creepin' into camp. The relief party from Boonesborough was due in about now. Probable they've arrived a mite early an' our bunch is gettin' ready to go home. Hope they waited for us. Give us some company on the way back."

Jim laughed with nervous relief and thankfully pulled his mittens on again. The fire loomed more gloriously still to his imagination. Lige strode out with sturdy deliberation, making a certain amount of unnecessary noise to reassure any listening sentry. He read Jim's understanding grin and said in his normal voice:

"Now we might be a herd of buffalo tramplin' an' crashin' the brush but we sure ain't a warparty. Even John Tendergrass'd know that, though he ain't as quick on the trigger as some. I'll give 'em a hoot for good measure."

He raised the long, mellow border shout, then stopped dead in his tracks. There was no answer to the hail, no sound of voices, no stir of activity. They took cover like rabbits at the shadow of a hawk while Cricket flung back her head and sniffed the air.

"Nobody there," whispered Lige in a rasp, peering through the brush. "Goddlemighty what's happened?"

Jim could see him questing with sight, smell, and hearing; then Lige went out into the clearing, crouching low, only to straighten up after a brief examination and beckon Jim to join him.

"They've gone," he said unnecessarily. "Lock, stock an' barrel. Horses an' men too. Yonder's their trail leadin' north-west an' don't ask me why when Boonesborough lies southerly. Let's see if they've left us any word. I know Flanders Calla-way's out a-scouting as well as us an' Dan'l said the day we left that he was goin' too. They'd sure leave us word where they're headin'."

Jim joined him in a quick search of the clearing. He knew what to look for—a carved message in the bark, a couple of blazes in line on the trees, a sapling cut down and left to point direction. There was none on his side for sure, and Lige's rapid inspection told him that there was none on the other side either. There was only the narrow gouge in the snow leading in that unexplainable direction. A low call brought him to his com-panion's side. Lige was pointing to where the great kettles lay on their sides, the salt spilled out uselessly into the swamp.

"Trouble, real trouble whatever 'tis. Question is, what is it?"

"Indians?" asked Jim automatically.

"Can't be. No sign of a fight. There was nigh on to thirty of 'em an' they'd make it hot for anythin' 'ceptin' a big war-party, an' big warparties don't come in winter. Even if one did there'd still be a fight an' we could tell."

"What do the tracks say?" asked Jim, with sublime faith in Lige's forest skill.

"Nothing," was the instant response. "We've been camped here for a month an' the ground's too cut up to read sign. We knows they took out for somewheres but that's the sum of it."

Jim tried to speculate but got nowhere. If the saltboilers had changed camp to a new lick they would certainly have taken along the kettles; if they had fled from a sudden danger whatever it might be, there would be some evidence of a hasty departure; but except for the overturned kettles there was none. Lige was standing in deep thought and cast a doubting glance at Jim, who read what was on his mind.

"Seems we ought to follow the trail," he offered. "Will I be a hindrance to you?"

It cost him a lot to say it, but Lige was too disturbed to spare his feelings.

220

" 'Fraid you would be. I got to travel fast to catch up an' I don't think you could keep pace unless you rode the mare . . ."

"Take her yourself," offered Jim instantly, starting to cut the pack lashings. Lige stopped him impatiently.

"You knows right well the only time I ever tried to ride her she threw me on my head. Likewise if I got to do some crawlin', I'm goin' to look right conspicuous with her a-breathin' down my neck. Tell you what—you ride for Boonesborough an' the relief party. After yesterday I ain't a-worryin' about your being able to take care of yourself in the woods. Give 'em word what we've seen."

He cut off several chunks of the buffalo meat and thrust them into a pouch. There was a deep crease in his forehead but his manner was calm and steadying. Only once as they separated did his anxiety break out in words.

"Can't be nothin' real wrong. They got Dan'l with 'em, or should have. They couldn't have been took—not with Dan'l."

He thrust out his hand and gave Jim a hard grip. "Don't try an' travel nights; if you've got to swim a river, raft over. Hope we ain't throwin' a scare into everybody withouten good reason, but by God I thinks this is good reason."

Then he was gone into the forest at that ground-eating lope.

Watching him until he blended with the trees, Jim fought the feeling of desolation which crept over him. To stand in the deserted camp next the swamp with the great bones thrusting eerily from its surface was a trial to his imaginative mind. Had he lingered he might have been over-oppressed by the sense of unknown tragedy and of his own aloneness. Lige had said that he was capable of facing the wilderness, but Lige was under a misapprehension about yesterday. Slowly he took out his knife and cut meat following Lige's example. The rest he left for the wolves who would not now be cheated. Then he mounted Cricket and struck southwards.

He could not travel long in the remaining daylight, but at least the mare's motion, the necessity for keeping direction and of guiding her through the tangle, made an alteration in his spirits. His thoughts took a healthier turn, though not a cheerful one. In spite of Lige's reassurances Jim was not so certain that the basic cause of the mystery had not to do with indians. Perhaps the reason for the flight of the saltboilers was a warning brought in by Boone or Flanders Callaway of the approach of a band. If so, Lige might be in great danger—might possibly be following directly in the traces of the indian pursuers; or he himself might be riding, for all he knew, straight towards the Shawanoes.

The winter sun had dipped and the cold came marching through the bare trees. He pulled up the mare, realizing that he would have to camp. Had he depended only upon Uncle Trev's tuition he would merely have sought a sheltered spot, scooped out the snow, built a fire, and waited for dawn, but the border had taken him subtly to itself. Perhaps he was a feeble woodsman in his own esteem, but Boone himself might have approved of what he did. He plowed off at right angles to his course, then circled back and sought a brushy hollow where he and the mare would be hidden and he would have a view of his own trail. If he were being followed he would have warning. Then he looped the mare's reins about his wrist, fed her the last of his cornmeal, and settled down to pass the night as he could. Raw, half-frozen buffalo meat was an unpleasant diet, but he dared light no fire; he could have not even the blanket-shielded one of a hunter's camp, for he had no blanket. Nor could he move about for fear of betraying his hiding-place.

It was a dreadful night. The cold clawed at him like an animal. He could not even doze for fear he might never awaken. Such bitter weather was beyond his experience. He worked his fingers and his toes to keep them from freezing and huddled close to Cricket, for the warmth of her body would help. When at last the gray came to replace the darkness he lurched to his feet. For half a mile he had to lead the mare before he could mount her.

This day was overcast and threatening, as if there were more snow on the way. The raw cold did not slacken. Fortunately his sense of direction did not desert him and he made what time he could. His face had stopped hurting, which he knew was a danger sign, and he rubbed it with snow until the circulation started again and tears of pain ran down his cheeks. The spring had gone out of Cricket but she forged ahead gallantly, though she was gaunting up from the effort. When he could, he staggered along beside her to rest her. He looked out from his

222

stubble of beard, watching, always watching tree and brush and gully for a warning sign.

It was nearing the next night when he had it. He was crossing an open patch, Cricket plodding with her head down, when he saw a bulge to a tree that was not natural. No tree trunk would swell out to one side like that. He fell rather than slid from the mare's back and scrambled on all fours like a startled bear towards a swale of ground. In the intensity of his effort he was deaf, and he was in the swale of his rifle poking over the top before he registered the voice that was calling to him.

"Don't shoot! Don't shoot! I'm a scout from Boonesborough."

Jim sat back weakly and waved his hand. The newcomer ran towards him while another man ran towards Cricket to catch her. She needed no catching, but stood where she had stopped, though she had raised her head. The first man came up to Jim and halted with an exclamation. "Jim! Didn't know ye. I'm Nick Watkins! Good God, Jim, what's happened?"

For perhaps a minute Jim could not answer while involuntary tears of relief trickled into the stubble on his cheeks. Nick and the other man, who Jim now saw was Tom Roper, did not seem to think any the worse of him, for they were chafing his hands, rubbing snow on his face, and their arms were around his shoulders. Nick kept talking quietly.

"Didn't recognize you, boy, nor the mare either. You've neither had it easy judgin' from your looks. We're scoutin' ahead of the second batch of saltboilers. Think you can tell us now?"

Jim recovered himself. "Lige sent me. They've gone, all of 'em." He wondered why he was croaking instead of speaking full out. "Don't know why. Trail leads northwesterly."

"Northwesterly!" He could see the two look at each other and then back at him.

"It's what I said." He tried to get himself upright, irritated at their doubting. "I tell you we couldn't guess why."

"Indins?" asked Roper with the consuming anxiety of Kaintuckee.

Jim was feeling stronger. He brushed off the kindly hands and told them the story. Obviously they were as puzzled as he.

223

Tom Roper was a lieutenant in the militia and as such in charge of the relief party. His decision was made quickly.

"We'll camp here and stop the others when they come up. If it's indins after all we'd best make for home as quick's we can. There's only eight men at the fort."

Jim cried out in unbelieving rage. "And leave them? Damn you for a coward. I'll go back!"

Tom Roper did not even flush. He met Jim's anger steadily.

"Stop an' think, lad. There was thirty or thereabouts with Dan'l. There's fewer than that with me. Whatever's wrong he's got men enough to handle it, or if he can't we should hear from him. Meantime there's all them women an' children withouten enough men to proper defend one side of the stockade, let alone all four. We'll send forward a party, I promises you, but the women an' the younguns is what we got to consider first."

"Tom's right, Jim," chimed in Nick gravely. "I'll go myself, but you ain't goin' with us. You've had about all you can well handle."

Jim subsided. He was not going to argue about going back with the scouts it was proposed to send, but they'd have a hard time leaving him. An hour later he wasn't so sure. The rest of the party had arrived and had gone into camp. As the fire thawed him the pains of hell took hold of him. His frozen face and his frozen feet clamored in agony until he writhed in his blankets and pitying men held him down while they ministered to him as well as they could. The sedative of the border was whiskey and they made him drink of it and rubbed his limbs with it until he dropped off into an uneasy sleep.

At some time he awoke. When it was he did not know, except that the firelight was clear and he could hear a familiar voice arguing above him.

"If I talks to him mebbe he'll stop ravin'. He's been yellin' about me, ain't he? Well mebbe if he knows I'm here . . ."

Jim tried to raise himself on his elbow. "Lige!" he exclaimed.

Lige dropped on one knee. If it hadn't been for the voice Jim would hardly have known him, bearded, exhausted and frost-burned.

"It's me all right. Me an' Flanders Callaway just got in. Glad to see you, boy. That was right smart of a trip you made from what they tell me."

He had travelled further and done the whole terrible distance on foot, but it was not in Lige Bonham to brag.

"You find anything?" asked Jim eagerly.

Lige turned his head away, but Jim reached out a hand, wincing as he did so, and caught his knee.

"Tell me. I've got a right to know."

"Reckon he has at that," said Tom Roper's disembodied voice.

Lige patted Jim's shoulder, but his hard, governed tones showed his emotion.

"Knew soon after I'd left you, indins. They caught them, 'spite of Dan'l. First I began noticin' tracks of moccasins some different made than ours, then I sees this." He held up a short heavy bow and a beaded quiver full of arrows. "Shawanoe work. Some indin threw it away when he got him a Kaintuckee rifle. There was more, but I reckon this clinches the nail."

Jim fell back into his blankets. Boone, John Tendergrass, Levi Mason—the friends he had made in Boonesborough and at the Licks—taken. He had heard tales enough of indian mercy to give up hope, and he hid his face in his arm. Then Lige was shaking him. Lige knew what was racking him.

"They don't kill 'em all. I tell you they don't. 'Tain't as if they'd fought, then they'd most have been killed. Didn't see no bodies along the trail either, nobody'd been tomahawked in the first five miles at least."

Another of those disembodied voices brought Jim's fears into the open.

"Probably savin' 'em for the first camp so's they could torture them in comfort."

There was the smack of a blow and a snarl. "If you got to think it, don't talk about it."

Lige pulled the cover over Jim. His lean, fierce, matured face was close to that of his friend.

"I'll go find out, Jim. I'll do my best an' so will Flanders. It's him what knocked that fool down. Now you got to go home an' let Liza take care of you. You've done well, right well, for a feller only six months in Kaintuckee. You let us do the rest."

That reassurance stayed with Jim through the near-delirium of the retreat to Boonesborough. He made it on Cricket's back, held in place by a man on either side. The memory of it came to him later in snatches . . . being on a raft with snow again falling and the straining arms of a brawny fellow thrusting with a pole . . . the pain that spun down on him in zigzag flashes seen against the red of his closed lids when they cut off two of his toes for fear of gangrene . . . the familiar, rousing sight of the open gates in the stockade and the sound of wailing as the news of the disaster spread. Then another period of delirium, followed by exhaustion when Liza and Mrs. Roper and Mrs. Tendergrass, who had nursed him, slowly came into three-dimensional form.

When he was more himself, Lige, no longer the strained vision of the camp, was sitting opposite him by the fireplace whittling out a spoon. Jim, grinning wanly, stretched out his hand for it. "Give it over to me an' I'll make a paddle out of it. Remember what Boone said that time at the licks?"

Lige laughed and passed over the nearly-shaped wood. "Ain't goin' to give you the knife, Jim. First place we ain't got no canoe an' second I don't want you to lose a finger as well as them two toes."

Jim handled the wood for a few minutes while Lige looked into the fire.

"Tell me what's going on. Liza hushes up what anybody says and I want to know."

Lige jerked his head around in assumed surprise. "Why, Jim, you knows it all. None better 'cause you was there. Told you we'd followed the traces until the storms wiped 'em out. Saw nothin'," his spurious cheerfulness dropped from him and he watched the fire again, "nor nobody," he finished heavily.

"Then what's happening here?"

"Nothin' more than spring's a-comin' an' we'll all feel better."

"And the women are grieving. I know that much."

Lige could not keep his mask of cheerfulness. "That's so," he said slowly. "But now that spring's here as I said, there's some that'll be goin' back to the settlements an' we won't be always sorrowful. Times change—an' I hope to God for the better."

Jim saw that he made Lige uncomfortable. The tall young Kentuckian was casting glances at the door. Either he wanted to make his escape or he longed for Liza to come in and take the weight of responsibility off his shoulders.

"Don't run from trouble, Lige. You've never done it . . ."

"Ain't I? Reckon my legs have kept me out'n more of it than my tongue has."

Jim would not follow his lead. "Out with it, then. What's the matter?"

Lige welcomed the excuse. Their friendship was a solid thing, as tangible as the wooden spoon which Jim still nursed on his knees. He wanted to talk, but Jim's weakness had held him back.

"It's what they're sayin', some of 'em at least."

Jim nodded as the best encouragement he could give.

" 'Course we know that there's bound to be backbiters everywhere you go. There's some was jealous of Dan'l . . ."

"Of Boone?" exclaimed Jim, startled.

"Surely. You knows that some of his family favors the King? That he was a Royal officer in Lord Dunmore's War?"

"So I've been told," said Jim, stiffening. He could see what was coming and it made him sick again.

Lige looked at him. "Liza told me not to tell you this, but I reckon you've guessed. Yes, it's true. There's some that says it was all arranged. You recollect that there was no fight? There's some that says he brought down the indins on 'em so's he could get to Detroit an' Hamilton the Scalp-buyer an' cripple Kaintuckee into the bargain."

XXII

As Jim recovered and could take an interest in his surroundings he found much to depress him. After the first stunning effect of the losses wore off, the ever present optimism of the Border reasserted itself and there was a gradual return to normal. Still the normality that was achieved was more a strict adherence to routine than any regrowth of security. There were too many women who might be widows, too many children who might be orphans, and no way of finding out what had become of the saltboilers. The indian country north of the Ohio was as yet hardly known. Chillicothe and Piqua were indian towns, but where they were or how to reach them no man could say. Scouts like Lige and Simon Butler had penetrated to the Ohio, but that stream was a boundary. George Rogers Clark, skilled, daring and masterful, might have given the answer, but Clark was busy on a still bigger concept. Take Vincennes and Kaskaskia in the Illinois country and from them strike at Detroit. If Detroit were captured then the indians would be deprived of the guns, the powder, the lead, the scalping knives and the vermilion for warpaint which the British furnished. Strategically the scheme was sound, but meanwhile the little Kaintuckee forts must hold against the Shawanoes, and their vanished defenders must take their chances among the indians.

There was a decline in the quality of leadership as well. Certain men had become symbols. Harrod at Harrodsburg, Ben Logan at St. Asaph's, Boone at Boonesborough had stood out in the defence. With Boone gone the peril to his settlement became intensified. Callaway was an honest, patriotic, stubborn individual, but he just missed the stature of a great frontiersman. He was too uncompromising, too intolerant of advice to hold together the very diverse individuals who made up the garrison. The issues weren't so simple. There were undoubtedly those at Boonesborough who secretly favored the Royal cause and fought the indians only because those agents of George the Third were prone to use the tomahawk without discrimination. Let a force come headed by white men who could control the warriors and there would be an element inside the palisade which might embrace the opportunity of going to Detroit.

Meanwhile spring brought its changes too. The ground must be prepared for the precious seedcorn, the cattle must go out to pasture in the woods. Battle must be joined with nature if the luxuriantly rioting weeds were not to choke the green sprouts. Above all, the hunting must continue so that there would be food to tide the settlers over the period before the corn would be ready for cutting. In spite of its rich soil, Kaintuckee was eternally just one jump ahead of starvation. The indians had learned to wipe out growing crops. Then too there was always an insufficiency of labor. The hunters and the scouts must be out, the stockade guarded and the workers in the fields covered by a screen of riflemen. When these necessary subtractions had been made from the available total of settlers there were few enough for the work. Before the stark necessities of providing food, fire and clothing, other tasks must wait.

It wasn't consoling to Jim. His strength had largely returned and he was doing his share of grubbing with a hoe, but Liza caught him one twilight thoughtfully examining the west face of the palisade. The knoll on which it was built sloped down to the river and the winter storms had caused a slight landslip which had carried away the supporting earth. Several of the timbers had fallen outward, leaving a four-foot gap.

"Kind of interestin', ain't it?" she remarked. She had withdrawn herself slightly since the days of his illness when he had depended upon her for help and found it forthcoming. "I might also mention that there's another gap even wider just a little further along and neither of the gates'll shut proper. Don't we look like fools?"

"What are we going to do about it? It would take a week's hard work for everybody to get it back into shape and two weeks afterwards to get rid of the weeds that would grow in the meantime. I never saw anything like the weeds here. Nick says that if you stand quietly at sunset you can hear the rustle of them pouring out of the ground. It's discouraging, mighty discouraging."

Liza, having no consolation to offer, remained silent. Jim tried another timber and it moved slightly under his hand.

"No sense my pushing it or it'll fall down. Hear some of the families are going back. Can't blame them for giving up." He struck his fist against the timber and it tilted outwards.

"Needn't knock it over," remarked Liza. She was looking at the bank-full Kentucky. "No news," she continued wearily. "None at all an' I reckon that means the worst."

"You've been mighty brave. Why be discouraged now?"

"You're in the fields most of the day, ain't you? I got to be with Miz Tendergrass an' the younguns. That ain't so easy."

229

"Is she taking it badly?"

"Wish I could do as well when my turn comes. Funny, ain't it, how people'll be deceivin'? I'd never thought it of her. When she first come I was lookin' for her to be one of them washed-out, whiny sort, trailin' along just because her man was goin' somewheres an' she didn't have the courage not to follow. But she ain't, an' I should have known better. Strikin' out on the Wilderness Road when you're carryin' a baby an' your time's not far off is brave enough. She says he's goin' to come back. Fact is, she's right serene about it an' I only wish it wasn't me what's been givin' her false hopes."

"You think they're false?"

" 'Fraid so. Twenty-odd prisoners an' Dan'l Boone will tickle the indins no end. They'll pay Dan'l a compliment—he's been captured before an' though he never talks about it, we know he's killed some of 'em. They'll burn him longer an' with more ceremony than they will any of the others. They'll want to hear him holler but I don't think they can make him do it."

Jim too looked at the rolling river without seeing it.

"The British may ransom some," Liza went on, self-controlled though her voice quivered. "Even if they set the tribes on us, they got some pity. Trouble is the tribes'll only let go them they wants to. But supposin' the British do manage to rescue a few, they're still prisoners and they won't be turned loose until the war's end. And when's that goin' to be?"

"There are exchanges . . ." began Jim without much hope.

"Thinkin' of your father? Still, he's in the east an' that's where the exchanges are made. Our fellers will be up in Canada at best, where the exchanges are few an' far between."

The first spring frogs were tuning up and a whippoorwill cleared his throat in the brush below them.

"I'll send a letter to Grandmother and tell her about Tendergrass. She'd have an eye to his family if they go back. Maybe it'll reach her. Surely somebody who's going to the Holston will carry it that far for me and maybe Colonel Campbell will see it forwarded by a post rider."

"Better'n that, why don't you carry it yourself?"

It was too dark to see her expression. "Do you want me to go?" he asked quickly.

If he was trying to surprise her into an answer, he had failed. Her deep steady tone had lost even that quiver which had been in it before.

"Why should you stay on? There's nothin' you can do about your father's lands. Either they've gone or the courts'll settle up about 'em when the war's over. If we wins it you should get your own grant as a militiaman, but that's pretty well bound to be a swamp or a rocky hill, while them who comes later gets the best pieces. I don't trust no lawyer nor no politician either. Then what you goin' to do with it when you gets it? Stay out here an' hardscrabble while Happy Return goes to rack an' ruin? You'd be a fool if you does."

It was hard to put his answer in words, but he had it ready. He had had a chance to ponder during his convalescence and he had made the most of it. The frogs and the whippoorwill were now in full voice and made an undernote as he spoke.

"You're right, Liza. Reckon those big tracts are gone and what I'd get for myself wouldn't be even worth considering. Still my year's not up an' I'm resolved to spend the rest of it here."

"Why?" she shot at him. "You lettin' your pride an' Mary Raeburn drag you into this? You come near enough to makin' frozen wolf-bait of yourself right recent."

"Hush your clatter!" he exclaimed unreasonably. The words still would not come. How could he find them to express his meaning unsentimentally? In Kaintuckee he had found himself. In Maryland he might be simply the oldest schoolboy in the state; west of Cumberland Gap he was a rifleman, in his own way a respected citizen of Boonesborough. There was no more private jeering about his being merely the grandson of wealth. By God, if there ever were again and he heard it, he'd climb all over the mocker and change his face into something that his own mother would have trouble recognizing. Out here he had friends, and the best one of them was off in the dark and beyond the grim Ohio.

That much he could admit and did so.

"John Tendergrass isn't back yet," he said.

The frogs and that damn whippoorwill were making such a racket he couldn't be sure but he thought he heard the breath of a sigh.

"You allowin' to wait for him?"

"He'd have waited for me."

He felt her lips on his cheek but before he could reach out for her she was gone. He took a step or so after her, then stopped and slowly rubbed the place her lips had touched. His impulse to pursue passed. She had made him think, and not all of his thoughts were pleasant. Liza wasn't Ilcy, to be chased and cornered. Prickly and unpredictable she might be, a pipe-smoking, uneducated frontier girl, but what was welling up in him even he could recognize. He was falling in love with her, and to fall in love with her would raise problems that he shrank from facing. She'd never be happy in Maryland, John Tendergrass had said so and Jim believed him. He'd have to take up that land out here and make Kaintuckee his home. Then a slow smile spread his mouth. Was that so bad?

He walked home whistling softly.

He knew better than to press Liza too far. Indeed, for a while he was even less at ease with her than usual. Her pride had aroused itself and she was over-eager to quarrel in compensation for her yielding. Nor was there much opportunity for sparring. The real labor had commenced and there were four more mouths to feed and one less pair of hands to help. Lige got himself relieved by another scout and joined Jim in the fields, but he was too valuable in the woods to be spared for long. The multiplicity of tasks bewildered Jim, and he might have exhausted himself through sheer wasted energy had not Tom Roper taken a friendly interest and told him what was important and what was not. Farming at Happy Return was quite a different affair from scratching a living among a tangle of tree-roots. A tree could be felled or girdled, but getting rid of the stumps was so difficult that it had to be shirked. However, Jim did not complain. If this back-breaking labor was what was necessary when he came to clear his own acreage, then he'd have to prepare himself for it. He'd begun to feel that Liza would be more than worth it—no small victory for his heart.

There was a draining out of the discouraged, among them Ilcy and her family, and there were a few newcomers; but for the first time since Jim's arrival there were empty cabins within the stockade. The gaps in the palisade were increasing, yet the consensus of opinion was that it couldn't be helped. There was noticeably less joking and merrymaking, men and women wore a serious air, yet a combination of optimism and stubbornness kept Boonesborough inhabited. The indians had had a good licking the previous year, maybe they wouldn't come this year, and when the heaviest of the work was over, the defences could be strengthened.

Then Andrew Johnson returned.

Andrew was a very small, deceptively mild-looking man in an indian blanket coat with a hood that pulled over the head. He arrived in company with Lige, whose long, triumphant yell warned the pickets that they were friends with good news. There was a tone to the cry that brought the women to the stockade gate with their hands at their throats to watch the two of them enter at the border lope. All work stopped and the fields emptied as quickly as if there had been an indian alarm. The space about the Johnson cabin was crowded as Andrew set down his light pack, kissed his wife, mustered his children, and grinned unemotionally. Andrew was a saltboiler.

"We got took," he announced loudly. "Shawanoes. We was carried to their towns. Nobody was dead when we got there an' I don't know of any since, but then we was split up."

He fidgeted a bit under those eager eyes. "Reckon that's the important part. If any of you wants to come in I'll tell the rest of the tale. I'm a mite dry," he remarked to the world in general, and a jug of Monongahela appeared in answer. He set it to his lips and took a hearty swig. "Got away from Little Chillicothe by pretending to be teched in my wits so they wasn't watching me close. Come in, them that wants to."

He dove back into his cabin like a groundhog. There wasn't a crowding to follow him. Kentuckians didn't feel it fitting to display intense emotion in public, but some of the women were weeping in spite of themselves. Callaway and a few of the leaders ducked under the lintel, then Johnson thrust his head out again. "Hey Lige, Flanders, Jim Cheston, you was there. Reckon you might be interested."

The three invited came forward (Jim feeling mightily privileged) and took their places just inside the door. Johnson set out the stools and took another pull at the jug. He looked worn with travel, but no more than other men who had made a wilderness journey. He was worried about his hospitality and made sure that the jug was circulating before he spoke.

"It had been snowin' good, you'll recollect." He turned to the three scouts as if for confirmation and seemed relieved when they nodded. "Springs had got flooded with fresh water an' we was just a-restin' when we see'd Dan'l comin' in without his horse. I recollects we made some remarks but it was his havin' no horse that made us wonder. It wasn't till Levi Mason saw some indins followin' him at a distance that we jumps for our rifles. Yes," he drawled, his eyes upon the scouts, "with Dan'l out an' these three fellers out we reckoned we was safe enough."

Jim flushed hotly, and from the uneasy twitch of his companions he knew they were as uncomfortable as he was. Johnson continued after a moment.

"Boone yells not to shoot, that we was surrounded an' outnumbered an' that he'd had promise that we'd be treated as prisoners of war to the British in Detroit an' used well. We didn't doubt Dan'l, so we gave up our rifles."

The jug had come back to him but he set it down without drinking. "Mebbe Dan'l was right. There sure was a slew of 'em. White men too, mongrel French an' those two bastards the Girtys, Simon's brothers. Simon wasn't there, though, which I reckons was just as well."

There was a deep, universal breath. Simon Girty was gaining the wrong sort of name for himself on the frontier. Even Jim would have rejoiced to have had him in front of his sights.

"They powwows for a couple of hours, talkin' in Shawanoe so's we didn't understand. That is, all except Dan'l. Reckon he followed it, though he can't speak it too well. Then he gets up . . ."

Apparently he noticed the jug at his elbow and tilted it to his mouth. The liquor spilled over and he coughed with a mild apology, but his eyes were hot.

"Mebbe I misjudged Dan'l but he made an awful queer speech. He spoke English an' that nigger Pompey who's with the Shawanoes put it into their talk. Wish I could say otherwise but there's one thing he said still sticks in my craw."

No one tried to interrupt, but Jim saw Colonel Callaway's

234

head nod as if what he had suspected was about to be confirmed.

"He said, 'Brothers, what I promised you we can do better in the spring than now. The women an' children at Boonesborough can travel better then an' we'll all come to your towns an' live as one tribe.' Then he goes on that we had surrendered like he said an' we'd make good warriors an' hunters for them. That's the most of it, but I admits I didn't follow him close after that first bit."

Jim sat astonished and dismayed. Clearly Johnson believed that Boone had sold the saltboilers to the Shawanoes as part of a prearranged plan. Boone was often scouting and hunting in the woods about Boonesborough—what was to have prevented him from having a rendezvous with an emissary from Detroit? The suspicions which Lige had whispered to him, the suspicions held by a certain fraction of the settlers, seemed to be confirmed.

"They listened to it but they still had 'em a council as to whether or not they'd kill us," continued Johnson. "They brought out a warclub. Some of 'em dashed it into the ground and others passed it on. Didn't need no interpreter to tell us what was goin' on. It was close, right close, an' I never counted harder than I did watchin' that damn thing sink into the ground and wondering if my skull'd be the next thing it'd be sinkin' into. Anyway, them that were just for carrying us off won."

Jim could see the shame and anger in the man come to the surface, to be repressed only by an enormous effort.

"Ever been an indin captive? They roped us tight an' then piled loads on top of us. It was real severe weather but they never turned us loose. Some of us was frost-bit a-plenty. Reckon they'd hoped we'd fall so's they'd have the pleasure of tomahawkin' us, but we managed to keep on, though we didn't eat often or well. White oak bark is right unappetizin', though I'm fair to admit that they didn't have much else themselves. They didn't make Dan'l carry no load . . ."

Two or three of the listeners growled. Johnson shook his head.

"I aims to be fair," he said. "First camp they made Dan'l run the gauntlet."

"How'd he do?" asked Tom Roper. The question was automatic. Leadership was based upon courage, and if Boone had failed in his ordeal he need never expect to have a follower.

"He made it hotter for them than they made it for him, I reckon," said Johnson. " 'Twas the only thing made us laugh. A warrior got just a little too eager an' stepped between the lines . . ."

Jim could see it. The prisoner, arms bound behind him, forced to run the length of a double line of warriors armed with clubs and all striking at him.

"Boone butted him in the stomach an' knocked him far an' true. Even some of the warriors laughed too. He did better than any of the rest of us when, stripped to our hides, we had to do the same in the indin towns."

He went on quietly, the emotion now seemingly drained out of him. "I don't like to be dragged by indins, I don't like to be beaten by indins. Reckon I did well enough because I was adopted into the tribe. This here's my indin father's gun and coat. I feels bad about takin' 'em though he took his turn in wallopin' me. I reckons to go back an' make 'em sorry." Once again, he flashed erect and his voice sank to a deadly whisper. "I knows the trails. They can't just hit us now withouten us hittin' back."

The questions began and he answered as well as he could. No, he didn't know what had happened to most of the prisoners. He gave the names of those at Little Chillicothe. Didn't reckon many of them would see Kaintuckee again. He didn't know what had happened to Boone and furthermore didn't care much.

Jim and Flanders Callaway and Lige left together. Jim's doubts were yielding to consideration of the circumstances.

"After all he had to run the gauntlet," he remarked, more as a question than as a statement.

"Don't mean nothin' much," said Lige. "Anybody who's fought 'em as often and as hearty as Dan'l would get in some trouble. The young bucks would see to that."

"But he didn't betray them! Don't tell me that!"

"I'm caught in a cleft stick," said Flanders Callaway. "My uncle'll have it so but Jemima, my wife, won't have it said of her father."

236

"As for me," Lige's voice was as soft as the spring night, "I don't believe it."

"Why not?" asked Jim eagerly, and he could sense that Flanders Callaway was also hanging on the reply.

"Because I've known Dan'l a long time an' it ain't like him. When I've known a feller a long time an' he acts kind of funny I waits until I hears from him why he acted the way he did before I judges him."

"We ain't liable to see him no more," said Flanders heavily.

"True, but I still tells you this. I ain't a-goin' to believe it unless he comes back an' says it's so."

XXIII

One May morning, or rather dawn, Jim was aroused from a dead man's sleep by the steady familiar thumping that meant Liza was pounding the hominy. He thrust his head reluctantly out from under the blankets, kicked Lige awake, and blinked at the fire under the kettle. The gray from the open door was brighter than usual and he realized they had again overslept.

Hearing them stir, Liza turned her head.

"Wakin' up at last? Sun'll be a-scorchin' your eyelids off before long. I'll step outside. Give me a holler when you has your pants on. I'd rather hear you start beatin' the hominy after that but I reckon that's too much to hope."

Jim grinned. He had long since realized that Liza's talk was no more than a rough form of banter which he had grown to enjoy. He had yet to hear her make a real complaint, and the life was hard enough to justify plenty of them.

"If this other turtle will push his head out from under the shell, maybe I'll put in a few strokes."

Liza picked up her yoke with the water buckets and started for the spring, remarking to her brother, "Lige, there's a Shawanoe a-scalpin' you with a dull knife. Open your eyes an' you'll see whether or not I'm lyin'."

Mush and milk were ready for them on the table, but the

milk was low. Lige poured it on, grumbling, "We got to freshen up that spotted cow. If it ain't one thing a-pesterin' you, it's another. An' here's the younguns to make it even truer."

The children came tumbling down the ladder from the loft and ten-year-old Amasa Tendergrass spoke up.

"I'm goin' to get me a mess of squirrels today."

Lige shovelled in another mouthful. "How you reckonin' to set about it? Chase 'em down?"

"Jim's goin' to lend me his rifle."

"I am not," said Jim. "First thing, you can't even pick it up."

"I can so." Amasa left the table, dribbling milk from the corners of his mouth, and with an effort lifted the heavy piece off the floor.

"Set it down," rebuked Jim. "It's got a charge in it."

"But I can pick it up. I just showed you, didn't I?"

"Hush Jim," remarked Lige. "He's goin' to club 'em to death, can't you see? Still even if he can't take your gun he's got a plan. I know that 'cause I can see his ears a-wigglin'."

"Sure have. Take a look at this here." With a great pride Amasa produced a leather strip broadening at the center. "You puts a rock in the middle, swings it around your head, and lets go one hand-holt. Like this."

He followed his words by an example, but the pebble that was supposed to fly through the door went off on a tangent instead and struck Lige a smart blow on his buckskin shoulder.

"Reckon them squirrels is safe," said Lige as he rubbed the spot.

Amasa was regarding his weapon with disappointment. "Maw was readin' out of the Bible an' it says that Ben's slingers were right smart at a mark."

"The slingers of Benjamin," translated Jim. "Reckon they had a little more practice."

Mrs. Tendergrass was coming down the ladder with the baby under her arm and he rose to help her.

"Maw reads the Bible a lot," piped up Amasa, "but I wish it'd tell me how to shoot this damn thing. I aims to get me an indin to pay off for Paw."

Mrs. Tendergrass compressed her lips and Lige, after one look, hastily wiped his mouth.

"I'll be goin'," he said. "Work's a-waitin'."

238

Mrs. Tendergrass didn't seem to hear him. Instead she spoke slowly to Amasa.

"I don't want to hear no more cursin' an' swearin' out of you. But if you aims to get yourself an indin, then some day be sure you gets one."

Jim without comment picked up the hominy pestle. He could hear Liza's voice outside and she sounded excited. A moment later she entered, rebuking Lige over her shoulder for spilling some of the water. Her brother followed her inside, his face flushed.

"What's that? Miz Boone's goin' east?"

Liza gave him an exasperated look, jerked her head towards Mrs. Tendergrass, and lowered the buckets to the floor. Mrs. Tendergrass had heard, however. She smoothed her hands against her homespun skirt.

"Rebecca's leavin', you say? Reckon then she's given up on Dan'l."

Liza went over to soothe her but she broke out again. "Well, I ain't a-goin'. My man'll come back, you'll see, an' he'll find me waitin' right here for him."

"Sure he is an' sure you are," answered Lige instantly.

Mrs. Tendergrass did not relax from her rigid posture though Liza was stroking her head. The baby began to wail and she pacified it without looking at it.

"He's been long a-comin' but he'll come. You mark what I say."

"Andrew Johnson got away, didn't he?" said Jim nervously. Privately he considered Johnson a much better woodsman than Tendergrass. It was over a hundred and fifty miles to the nearest of the indian towns, with the broad Ohio as an additional obstacle. Furthermore Johnson had befuddled his captors by pretending to be a half-wit and therefore had been enabled to equip himself unusually well. The indians would watch more closely since his escape, and even if Tendergrass got away, the chance of his having a rifle or supplies was fairly remote. Involuntarily he shook his head. He more than doubted his own ability to cover the distance, weaponless and foodless.

"You don't believe me," said Mrs. Tendergrass. She was not screaming nor hysterical, but that monotone made their nerves raw.

239

"Of course we does," said Liza, and the tone was the same as that which Jim remembered and treasured from the half-delirium of his illness. Mrs. Tendergrass responded to it in part. She came to herself enough to shoo out the wide-eyed children and sank down on a stool.

" 'Fraid I've been a mite over-anxious. He should have been here before now." Her confidence in her husband was too sublime for them even to smile at it. On the contrary they dared not look at each other. Yet under the calmer, more assured voice was a quivering terror which they had mis-read.

"If he's comin' back at all," she said after a helpless pause. "He used to talk a lot about that time at Ingles' Ferry when he met the feller who'd been captured. It made him wonder why white men would leave their own people an' go live among the indins. He's an inquirin' sort an' he's had a hard time keepin' me and the children in vittles. Mebbe I wasn't always too good to him." Then the terror unmasked itself.

"You don't suppose he's turned indin on us?"

Lige tried to laugh and Jim to scoff, but both laughter and scoffing were hollow. It had happened before and would happen again. The wild freedom of the woods against the daily grind of farm or tavern. They might not believe in the possibility, but they could not in honesty deny it.

It was Liza who answered for them. "He said he'd come to Kaintuckee to make his stand. You heared him an' I heared him. He ain't a man to change."

Mrs. Tendergrass raised her bowed head, her lips relaxed and her expression filled with a queer, steady pride.

"You've done said it, Liza. He ain't one to change."

Then she burst into a flood of tears and the young men made their escape.

The incident, however, brought Jim and Liza closer together. Jim couldn't help but feel that Liza might have acted the same way if he had been missing. In fact he was sure of it. He was getting sure of quite a lot of things about Liza, her deep loyalty, her innate kindness, her sympathy with those afflicted and, what meant even more, the continuing charm of her presence. He was restless away from her and looked forward like a miser to those work-narrowed periods each day which he could spend near her. Not that he did not have competition, for the faithful Nick Watkins might put in an appearance just when Jim had hopes of their being alone. In turn Liza changed towards him, gradually but perceptibly. There were small betrayals, a glance that lingered too long, a dropping of lids when he watched her too fixedly, a notable mellowing of her banter which now seemed directed almost exclusively at Lige and the children. It was a slow process but it walked hand-in-hand with the true rousing of his heart.

A June moon is a June moon, and particularly bright in Kaintuckee. It was inevitable that they should step outside to admire it. Master Blackthorne had not equipped Jim with either a philosophy or a fund of small talk which could stave off its devastating effects. Not with Liza beside him laughing quietly as he traced phantasies on its golden surface. The moon and their old gap in the palisade with the river confiding softly to the reeds combined to bring his arm about her waist and she did not resist.

"Wonder if we could ever climb up there and make a stand?" he said softly. "Wonder what makes it glow like that? Do you suppose it's all gold?"

"I'd rather think that it's a great forest an' what we see is the sun a-glinting on the leaves."

He was a trifle surprised. Her matter-of-factness had masked her appreciation of beauty. He could see her smile glimmering through the soft glow.

"Sometimes I has other things on my mind than poundin' hominy or drawin' water or makin' moccasins. Reckon there's more than me what feels the same. Boone an' Lige an' Simon for instance—yes, an' Maw too. I've caught 'em many a time watching sunrises an' this same moon. 'Twasn't just to see whether or not they could get light enough to draw a bead on a deer either. You ask Simon if he was lonely when he was long hunting all by hisself. He'd laugh at you and ask what there was to be lonely about. That's the trouble with the woods, they can get too close to you an' then you don't leave 'em ever."

His grip grew tighter. His throat was dry but he managed to say what was in his heart.

241

"But you're not that way, Liza. Don't tell me that. You can leave them."

Liza put her head upon his shoulder with a quick, confiding motion.

"I'd carry my moonlight with me always," he said tenderly. "That golden hair of yours."

"It might turn white, Jim," she said in a dreamy whisper.

"So does the moon sometimes but it isn't the less beautiful when it does."

Their lips met in that fierce satisfying embrace that only she could give. He lost himself in it until she pushed him away with a half-stifled sigh.

"There's ten spies a-watchin' us from the cabins, I don't doubt, but Jim, lad, it's worth it."

"What do we care?" His emotion overcame him. "Liza, maybe I'm a fool to ask it but I love you so I've got to. Can you leave Kaintuckee and come home with me?"

He could feel her hesitate and tried to brush aside the hesitation with soft urging. She almost yielded, but then brought her hand up under his chin and pushed away his eager lips.

"That's it, Jim, that's the trouble. I ain't foolin' myself none. I love you. I ain't never felt like this before. It's kind of funny." Her voice had a catch in it. "Me who's always had good sense, me who's always said I'd wait till I saw what I wanted— now I've got it but I can't have it."

"Why not? I'll marry you tonight if you say."

"To go home with you to Maryland? I sure would like to meet your grandmaw, but the others—they'd be some different."

"Not to you they wouldn't. You could handle them."

Her wry frontier humor flashed out in a chuckle. "I've spent the first part of my life keepin' men in order, now you wants me to spend the rest of it tryin' to do the same with women. That's harder."

He was pleading now, refusing to see what she with clearer insight saw plain.

"Liza, you're beautiful. All they could be is jealous."

"That's like sayin' all a bear can do is hug you. Sounds mighty mild until it happens."

242

He thought she was teasing him and grew impatient. "Don't, Liza, don't. I couldn't laugh now if I tried."

Her answer was hardly audible, it came to him like a breath of the June breeze. "I'm near to cryin', lad, myself. Jim, I can't."

"It isn't so much to face, not with Grandmother to help you."

"Aren't you even takin' that for granted? You turn up home with a wife ridin' a packhorse with her skirts tucked up, a bustlin' wife with a peeling nose, stinking of tobacco an' speaking like a backwoodsman—that might make a difference."

"She'd take you," said Jim in utter confidence.

Her fingers fluttered over his face like a blind person making a recognition. Then she shook her head.

"It's temptin' but I can't. It ain't right to burden you an' her in her old age with tryin' to make me different. Because I'd have to be different, Jim, an' that's just what I'm afraid I can't be."

"Then, by God, I'll make my stand here in Kaintuckee."

She flung herself into his arms and covered him with kisses while he rejoiced in his victory. Gone were regrets, gone the memory of Happy Return. Here he'd stay and when the indian troubles were over they'd cabin out in some creek bottom and raise a family. He had her and she was his heart's desire.

She held his face between her hands and looked at him. Her expression astonished him. It was compounded of radiance and darkness like the last moonbeams saying farewell from an encroaching cloud.

"I think that's why I loves you so. You means it an' I knows you does. Let me keep that, Jim, an' I'll sure nurse it strong as long as I lives."

The cloud had swallowed up the moonbeams now. Her voice was all tears. "Only, it can't be."

"Why not, for God's sake?" He was still bewildered.

"Because I won't let you, because I won't let you break your grandmaw's heart an' throw away everything she's labored for her whole life through. You told me what she said. Beads and buckskins fit mighty well into a young man's years but

243

they don't sit so well when he gets older. You ain't born to the life here in Kaintuckee. You're like your Uncle Trev who'd never settle on the land because he didn't love the land enough to scratch a living out of it. Scratchin' a livin' is hard, Jim, an' there'll come the time when I'll lose my looks, what there are of them."

"Do you think I'd care?"

She linked her arm in his and drew him away from the gap. Her innate dignity repulsed him, but only with kindness.

"No," she said quietly. "I do not think you'd care. But I do. I wouldn't, if I didn't love you so much. Hush, now, we've been talkin' around in circles like a lost hunter wandering. All you says is 'why' an' all I says is 'no.' Ain't no profit in that."

Dismally he accompanied her while he tried to reach an equilibrium between the heights and the depths which he had just experienced. She said nothing, but her close grip expressed both her sympathy and her emotion.

At last he could speak. "Will you think it over? Promise me that you will."

She meditated a few more steps, then she answered.

"I promise, but it's goin' to be a long thought before I changes. I shouldn't, I shouldn't," she burst out in despair, "but I loves you mebbe less than I thought I did. Otherwise I wouldn't even say that much. Only don't press me, Jim. I'll answer, 'fore the summer's out an' you goes home."

He had to be content with that.

He went back to the fields again, to the daily grubbing and clearing. He worked the harder to overcome the doubt which he would not even express to himself but which nevertheless existed. Was he just such a one as Uncle Trev, unstable and shifting?

Then one bright morning the word spread, carried by shouts and running feet, to the cabins and the sentries on the far side of the stockade.

"Boone's come in!"

244

XXIV

Jim had to look twice to be sure that it was Boone indeed. His head had been shaved except in the center where the hair had been roached up in the Shawanoe tuft. If he felt at all ridiculous he did not show it, nor was his steady composure shaken even by the sight of his vacant cabin. A little knot of the principal settlers, some of whom showed unmistakable signs of suspicion, accompanied him to Flanders Callaway's, but he greeted those he met with no more emotion than he would have shown upon his return from a hunting trip. He attempted no speech and let the rumors fly without correction, until Jim, knowing he would hear the story in due time, went reluctantly back to splitting rails for a fence. The cattle had been drifting out of the woods and into the growing crops, and an undetected, greedy cow could do a lot of damage. Then Flanders Callaway tapped him on the shoulder.

"Dan'l would like to see you if you got the time."

Jim had time to ask a question as they crossed the clearing. "How did he get away?"

Flanders suddenly smiled. "Indins has always thought that Dan'l would make a mighty good buck if mebbe he had the chance. They aimed to give it to him and adopted him into the tribe. Took him down to a creek and scrubbed the white blood out'n him with sand and gravel. 'Case it didn't come out altogether they keeps a strict watch as well." His grin widened. "Some day when I has the time I'm goin' to bust my sides a-laughin' 'bout Dan'l playin' Shawanoe. They weren't very trustin' of their new brother an' it must have been the same for Dan'l as bein' in a cave with a bunch of panthers an' never knowin' when one of 'em would kill him out of pure cussedness. Meantime he'd got hold of an old busted musket an' fixed that. Then he got his powder by firin' reduced charges, his shot by puttin' two in his mouth when he loaded an' only spittin' one into the barrel. He kept warnin' 'em that he was a-goin' to leave but after a bit they disbelieves him an' they gets careless.

245

Don't pay to get careless with Dan'l. He just takes a horse an' lights out. Rides it till it can't go no further an' then he keeps a-comin' till he's here. Only if I was Dan'l I wouldn't get took again."

Boone was sitting on an upended log near the fireplace while Jemima singed off the Shawanoe tribal badge with the glowing end of a stick. At sight of Jim, Boone wrinkled his nose pleasantly.

"Sooner it was my hair than me a-burnin'," he remarked. "Glad to see ye."

After a pause he inquired casually of Flanders, "Lige ain't a-comin'?"

"Out huntin'," said Flanders and Boone nodded. It came to Jim with a tiny shock of pride that Boone regarded him as being privileged to hear the full story, just as had Andrew Johnson. His expression must have betrayed him, for the quiet man smiled slightly.

"Good I advised you to stay—good for us I mean. Hear you did your full part after we was taken."

Jemima went on singeing his hair and he sat as motionless on the log as if he were an extension of it. Only his lips moved as he told Jim what had happened at the Licks.

By sheer ill-luck four warriors had stumbled on him during the snowstorm. The ambush had not been complete, for he had seen them before they could close in, but his horse had been his downfall. Unable to sever the lashings of the meat he was packing to camp he had been forced to abandon it and run. An indian, at leisure, unloaded the horse and mounted it to cut him off. The snow was too deep for him to get clear. Four to one were long odds. One he could have been right sure of killing, maybe two, but the outcome would have been the same. He had surrendered before they could lay hands on him when their killing instinct might have been uppermost.

The warriors weren't what he had thought at first, a mere scouting party, but part of a band, a regular expedition, of over a hundred led by Blackfish, the most prominent of the Shawanoe warchiefs. They were bound for Boonesborough and they knew about the saltboilers, for the camp at the Licks had been discovered. With such numbers against them, coupled with surprise, the saltboilers could only have been massacred.

Jim found his old admiration for Boone renewed in full strength. The man sitting on the log was merely stating facts as he saw them. Others could draw their own conclusions. When he continued, it was in explanation, not in defence.

The relief party was unsuspectingly marching into the same trap, but of this the indians were apparently ignorant. The white renegades and Canadians were urging a double stroke, an attack on the saltboilers to be followed by a rush on the weakened settlement, much weaker than they knew. Even if the relief ran into them, the disaster could not be staved off, for the odds were still too long. There was nothing to do but give them the prize they already had and hope that they would be content with it.

"I done so," concluded Boone. "I thought I knew indins, but it was the white men that made it hard. They didn't lose sight of the main chance, but all them prisoners were too much for the Shawanoes to pass by. More'n a score of enemies taken without any loss, that's an indin's idee of how to make war. They carried us back, as you knows."

"What if the vote had been different?" asked Flanders.

"That was the risk we took. Bound to be a risk when the b'ar's got you an' your rifle's empty."

"You thought that out just after you'd been taken?" exclaimed Jim in ungrudging praise.

For the first time Boone made a movement. He shifted in embarrassment.

"Sure didn't think of it anywhere else. They weren't givin' me time to set on my hunkers an' hold a council. 'Tain't so much, it was just the way things were."

"You hear anythin', Dan'l, whilst you were a prisoner?" asked Flanders. He too had been absent from the cabin when Boone had met Colonel Callaway and the others.

"They're gatherin' at Chillicothe, talkin' an' hittin' the warpost. That's why you ain't had no raids. Goin' to be more Shawanoes even than Blackfish had at the Licks. Goin' to be plenty of 'em. Capturin' so many prisoners an' horses the last time has made 'em eager. They're comin' down on us after a while longer to brag an' talk. Braggin's like Monongahela to an indin."

"God!" said Jim thinking of the rotten palisade.

Nobody made any comment. Jemima threw the stick back on the fire and blew the last of the fluffy ash from her father's head. Boone gave a deep chuckle.

"Reckon I'm well prepared. 'Tain't nobody goin' to get a grip on my scalp for to lift it." He rose from the log and stretched himself. "Still there's some sachems in Chillicothe who may find they've bitten off more'n they can well chew."

Jim saw that the conversation was over, but before he left he asked a question.

"Do you know anything about John Tendergrass?"

"Taken north, I heard. At least he wasn't one of them who were carried to Detroit and he wasn't long at Chillicothe."

That might be some consolation for Mrs. Tendergrass, thought Jim, and hastened to her and Liza.

The women had obviously heard the warning which Boone had brought. Mrs. Roper turned away with a nod to him as he came up and finished a remark directed at Mrs. Tendergrass. "Well, if you wants to learn how to load a rifle, Liza'll show you. Might come in handy." John Tendergrass' little girl was hiding her face in her mother's apron but Amasa was wiggling in excitement. Before he could burst out, Mrs. Tendergrass put a hand across his mouth and gave Jim such a look of appeal that any discretion he may have had about his answer vanished at once.

"Carried north from Chillicothe, since then no word. He wasn't taken to the British which probably means he's been—" Suddenly a flash of panic reminded him that there was another possibility. Boone had not said that Tendergrass was among those adopted. It might be that he was a tribal gift to another tribe. Such unfortunates had been known to be burned. He tried to cover up the gap by saying quickly:

"Of course he's been adopted."

"Sure he has," said Liza, with a glance at Jim which clearly conveyed her estimate of his tactlessness.

Mrs. Tendergrass was paying no attention. She pulled the wailing little girl into her arms. "You hear, Susie, you hear, 'Masa? Your paw's been carried north. That's why he ain't back yet. He's got further to travel."

She was actually humming as she went to take care of the baby who was howling lustily.

248

"Jim."

Jim and Liza looked down at Amasa whose freckles were prominent in an unlovely face. They had forgotten about him but Jim was secretly grateful to the boy for saving him an immediate scolding.

"What is it?"

"Maw's a mite over-hopeful about Paw, ain't she?"

Jim was fond of the boy but there was a directness to his question which forbade too much evasion.

"Maybe," he admitted. "Best not look on the worst side though."

"Can I load for you when the indins come?"

It wasn't a boyish begging to be in on the excitement. The leather in John Tendergrass had been transmitted to his son.

"I'm loadin' for him," answered Liza. "Lige ain't got nobody though an' he'll likely use that light rifle for a spare. I'll ask him about it."

"I thanks you. If he can't, reckon I'll ask Captain Boone."

He went off sedately to do what others were commencing already—ask Captain Boone.

"Thank you too, my dear," said Jim softly. It was the first time he had used such a term to her and she blushed.

"It just came into my head 'bout loading for you and I said it." She came close to him and gently ruffled the fringe of his hunting shirt. He would have kissed her but she turned her face aside.

"I was awful wrong though. Your year's up, Jim. You needn't stay no longer an' nobody will blame you—much," she added honestly, thinking in Kaintuckee terms.

He laughed at her with a touch of grimness. "Nobody except Jim Cheston and the rest of the settlement. Ready to give me your answer yet, Liza?"

"It would still have to be 'no,' Jim." Her face was muffled on his arm. "By God it still ought to be no whatever happens. I ain't making a game of it, you knows that, don't you?"

He kissed her for answer and she responded eagerly. Then almost in a shout she exclaimed. "Why don't you go? Why don't you go home, Jim? I love you so much it's killin' me."

With a tremendous effort she regained control of herself

249

and with a shade of her old bantering tone told him to get his axe and get a-going.

"You an' me was a-pushin' down that stockade. Serves us both right if now we've got to set it up again."

It was fine to be in love, but not in Boonesborough awaiting attack and desperately busy preparing for it. All the doubters were neither convinced nor silenced, but the great majority believed in Boone and worked under his direction as they never would for Colonel Callaway. Such projects as Jim's fence were discarded; instead there was hacking and hewing, whittling of pegs and drilling of holes to receive them, digging and bracing. Boone was not only repairing the defences but strengthening them as well. The old blockhouses were raised in height and new ones begun at the two exposed corners. Throughout the work the crops must yet be tended, and the hunters must go out so the settlement might not only be provisioned for the expected siege but for the coming winter as well. If only the indians did not come even before the unripe corn could be harvested . . .

A party brought back the salt kettles, another with Andrew Johnson made a quick raid on the Shawanoes and reported with grim satisfaction that they had ambushed some warriors north of the Ohio and done damage. Yet, though they sometimes worked by torch-light, there was still much that had to be neglected.

Cricket and Jim each grew thin, she from helping to snake logs from the woods to be shaped into the timbers of the new blockhouses, he from toil so laborious that he longed for his turn at guard duty, when at least he could rest physically though he must keep mentally alert. From his concealment in the fringing woods he could sometimes see Liza working as hard as any man and adding the cultivation of the corn to the care of the cabin. She had said nothing further, but by tacit consent the decision had been postponed. If she had yielded he would have married her at once, but since her doubts were still upon her he could not bring himself to force an answer.

Such efforts as they made at Boonesborough could not have been long continued had there not been a spur to their anxiety. One July morning a feeble call from the far side of the river brought a sentinel's shouted alarm. A canoe pushing cautiously

250

across ferried in William Hancock, another saltboiler, who had laid himself down to die but had seen his brother's name carved upon a tree and had realized that he was only four miles from the settlement. The attack was coming, he gasped out, but it had been postponed. Then he set himself to go on living, an objective which he achieved with some difficulty.

At last the letters that went back to Virginia calling for help grew more cheerful. Boonesborough stood stark and a little as Jim had imagined it during his boyhood fourteen months before, a wooden fortress lording it over the lowering woods. No military man would have pronounced it properly defensible with its limited water supply and its ragged, rough-hewn logs, but few military men would have had the riflemen who manned it. The pressure slacked off. That is, the ordinary back-breaking labor went on without the additional burden that had made Jim a soiled, brawny shadow with calloused hands.

Late in August Simon Butler turned up. He'd been with Clark to Kaskaskia and he was cheerful, though he looked longer and thinner than ever. He surveyed them with a quizzical expression.

"Ain't summered so well, has you? Lige is the only one what looks hog fat."

"I been scoutin'!" exclaimed Lige indignantly.

"I knows that kind of scoutin'. Lyin' next to a stump with the sun a-shinin' on ye an' openin' your eyes only when a fly lights on your face."

Liza flew to her brother's support. "Don't doubt you a mite, Simon, only it was a Kaintuckee stump that he was leanin' against. He ain't been traipsin' out to the Mississippi—or a-bundlin' with French girls," she added as a hasty afterthought.

"Might have been nice at that, only Major Clark he wouldn't have none of it. 'Keep the goodwill of the people,' he says, though we might have raised a good Kaintuckee generation if we'd had our way. As for traipsin' off—you ain't goin' to have the western tribes down on you. Clark saw to that. By God at dealin' with indins I never met the like—even Dan'l ain't so good."

He did not stay long. Boone was anxious to "flusterate" the Shawanoes, recapture some badly needed horses, and generally

prove to the indians that Kaintuckee could strike back. Though
Colonel Callaway, this time with considerable justice, argued
that to detach eighteen or twenty men now was madness,
Boone had his way in the battle of wills and the party started
for the "Paint Creek Town," accompanied by the indispensable
Simon. Lige was to go too, for the pick of the woodsmen were
taken.

Liza had spent the evening before pouring melted lead into
the bullet moulds while Jim had smoothed them with a knife.
She and he had exchanged only a few words, but Butler was a
better scout than Lige. Next morning before the party assem-
bled he was counting the bright pellets into his pouch as Jim
held them cupped in his hands.

"Found somethin' really nice in Kaintuckee, ain't you, Jim?"

It was spoken in a completely non-committal voice but Jim
bridled.

"If you mean that I'm a trifling sort . . ."

"Don't mean a word of that. You plannin' to marry up with
her?"

"If she will."

Butler seemed absorbed in his count. "You don't find 'em
no finer. Wish I was the marryin' kind myself. Would have
done it with her but I reckon I knows when I've missed a deer.
Don't do no good to run after it. Only, Jim, better be right
sure you plan to do the marryin' or I might come a-lookin' for
you even back in Maryland."

Jim drew his fist back in fury, but Butler caught it with his
powerful fingers.

"Hush, now. That was all I wanted. Liza will settle it for
you both." He smiled wryly. "She sure settled it for me when
I asked her."

He released his grasp, clapped Jim on the back, and went
off to join the group at the gate.

The next few days were anxious ones for Boonesborough,
stripped of its best scouts. Necessity still sent the hunters to
bring in game. This time Jim went, for, with Lige and John
Tendergrass both absent, he must be the provider. Rather
against his better judgment he accompanied Nick Watkins and
Gabe Venable across the river, since the intensive hunting on
the south side had cleared the woods of deer. They crossed in

252

a canoe, concealed it in the reeds, and divided, each to his own ground.

Jim ghosted through the woods, applying all his skill. This was hunting with a bite to it, for there might be warriors flung out ahead of the indian invasion. He realized that the Paint Creek raiders could bring neither protection nor warning, so vast was the country. By now they should themselves be crossing the Ohio. Colonel Callaway's misgivings occurred to him and he even doubted Boone's judgment in going, as he reconnoitred a clearing before he crossed it. He listened to the cry of birds, noted the wind and watched for bushes that might bend inexplicably against it. A squirrel's shrill chirring sent him behind a tree until he could fathom the reason. Patience and wariness were necessities.

He was out possibly a couple of miles from the river before he saw what he was after, a flicker of brown and white in the sunshine. Step by cautious step he worked forward until he could see the buck grazing in the forest meadow. He was downwind from his quarry, so the warning man-odor would not carry. There was no alarm from bird or squirrel. He pushed his rifle forward, took aim, and then released the trigger. The buck was alert, ears pointed, snorting slightly; he was staring in the opposite direction. Not so long ago Jim would have blessed the chance and fired, but Kaintuckee had taught him. Even if he lost the shot, he would make sure what it was that alarmed the buck. It might be a panther, of course . . .

The buck made a mad leap and bounded away while Jim hugged his tree the closer. There was something moving off there beyond the clearing, something that made the portly robin who had been picking nearby, unalarmed by the quiet hunter, take to wing. There was a crackle and a snap as a branch broke. Jim brought his rifle to bear. Buffalo? Unlikely, most unlikely, but it was possible. Bear, perhaps. Certainly no indian would so advertise his presence.

He caught a glimpse of movement and waited coolly until the leaves were brushed aside. Then he lowered his rifle with a gasp.

It was a man, a white man. He could tell, for the figure was almost entirely naked, though the sunburn had red-brushed the exposed skin where normally the clothes covered it. Stag-

253

gering, the man came out into the open, stood and swayed; then, just as Jim thought he would surely fall, he put a foot out in front of him and brought the other up to it, all the time muttering to himself.

Jim broke from cover and ran forward, but the man did not apparently notice. His mind seemingly had lost power to comprehend what was going on about him. Only an iron will, surviving exhaustion, starvation and pain, was bringing those feet into obedience.

Jim reached him and held out his arms. John Tendergrass, still muttering "I advances step by step," fell into them.

It was easy to hoppus him back to the canoe, easy to paddle him with strong strokes across the river. Others came to aid, and they carried him to the cabin. Mrs. Tendergrass was running towards them, and they laid their burden down before her like an offering.

Tendergrass had been muttering softly all the way, the same phrase over and over again, his leg muscles jerking. The gaunt woman put her hand on his forehead.

"Stop marching," she said. "I'm here."

XXV

"Ain't they finished eatin' yet?"

"Just about. Old Blackfish is a-reachin' for another hunk of pork, but the rest of 'em has stopped to belch."

Ambrose Coffer was stretched on top of the northwest blockhouse enjoying the sun and calling down the news. There had been no time to roof the structure, and Ambrose lay along the timber like a snake on a log.

Jim looked up at him without envy. He thought Ambrose was a fool to take the chance. There might be a dozen indian rifles drawing a bead on him from the thickets and no telling when some young buck might pull a trigger in spite of the truce. Still it was mighty boring, and he yawned. Inside the logs against which he leaned were thirty men and twenty boys

254

grown enough to be of service in defending the women and children; outside were nearly five hundred indians, stiffened by French Canadians. He had felt tense enough when they had appeared, with no effort at concealment, but marching in a semi-military order against the skyline and displaying both the British and the French flags, with a fine disregard of France's alliance with the rebel colonies. The line had seemed interminable and he remembered wondering if it ever would end. Lige had grunted but Jim had been surprised at the inflection of the grunt. It had expressed profound relief. "No cannon," Lige had remarked, and had seemed untroubled at the crowding warriors. Then he had grinned at Jim. "I ain't as calm as I seems. We had a glimpse of them at the Blue Licks when we was comin' back from the raid and I got over my shivers then. Mebbe we can hold 'em off but if they had managed to fetch along a gun we'd be out on a limb. Stockade wouldn't stand battering."

John Tendergrass slipped the plug out of his loophole and took a quick glance. He was still tottery, but a rifle rested against the logs and Mrs. Tendergrass sat on a nearby stump handling a second one. There was a chuckle from the men who manned the wall and Lige's drawl floated down from the blockhouse.

"They ain't dropped it yet, John. Never saw anybody so het up about a pewter platter."

"If you'd packed it across the Wilderness Road you might feel anxious about it," said Liza, strolling towards them. Her hair was pulled up in a knot and she was wearing Jim's coonskin cap. She sat down at his feet with a weary sigh. "I'm quittin' for an hour. I've stuck my head over the stockade three times, once wearin' this cap, once John Tendergrass' hat, and the other time a greasy flat thing what Nick give me. That makes three of me they've seen, but unless I cuts me some hair off Cricket's tail and makes it into a false beard they're bound to recognize me."

"But that makes three more men in the garrison, or so the indins think," comforted Lige. "Queerest siege I ever seen. Four days we've been negotiating with them an' now we're feastin' 'em outside. The Holston folks must be a-startin' pretty soon if they're plannin' to come help us."

It was a queer siege, agreed Jim. One of the gates was thrown wide and past it strolled a group of four defenders, casting a casual glance towards the tables and the intermingled frontiersmen and indians who sat at them.

Nick Watkins, a loophole beyond, chuckled. "There's an indin over there on a stump pretendin' to watch a couple of rabbits. He's been cuttin' notches on a stick every time anybody showed themselves an' I notices he's laid it aside an' picked up another."

The party of four, out of the line of sight through the gate, hastily rearranged themselves. Liza tossed one of them the Tendergrass hat she had been using, while Gabe Venable flung on a blanket coat and he and the man with the changed hat walked back again.

"Why that coat?" remarked Liza. "It's hot enough to broil you. Don't seem very deceiving."

"Indins'll think mebbe he's got an ague," admonished Lige. "Just so he don't do it again an' they thinks we've got rampant fever." He laughed softly. "Who's that half-hoss, half-alligator squinchin' over the palisade now?"

"Jemima Callaway. She's doin' us one better. She's got Flanders' spare hunting shirt on an' she looks pretty ferocious from the waist up an' at a distance."

"Below that she's all Jemima," chucked Jim, as he watched Boone's daughter step up on a log lying against the palisade and show head and shoulders to the counting indian.

Jim heard his name called along with others. He picked up his rifle but set it down again when he saw Tom Roper shake his head.

"You an' me an' Nick an' Gabe are goin' out to fetch in the tables. Don't say nothin' an' look as calm as you can."

Jim's overabundant imagination gave him a qualm, but he tried not to show it. John Tendergrass called after him, "Careful with that platter, boy," and he found himself passing through the gateway with squatting men on either side ready to slam the panels together on the first alarm.

"If they has to shut it, run for the cabin on the right. That door'll be open, I've seen to it," whispered Roper.

The well-worn path to the spring looked different this morning. The high weeds, the stumps, the ragged bit of partially finished fence both threatened and concealed. The negotiators had stood back from the table and were standing or sitting around in a replete group. Jim made himself walk without hurry. Major Smith glimmered in his elegant red uniform coat. Technically he commanded the fort by the authority of Virginia, but the real commander was the quiet man with the nearly shaven head who stood between a Frenchman in buckskins and a tall, graven-bronze chief. Jim could have sworn that Boone's eyes twinkled and it put a ramrod in his spine. Mingled with the warriors were other familiar faces, some looking acutely uncomfortable, others as impassive as their schooled wills could make them: Flanders Callaway and his uncle, the Colonel; Squire Boone, Daniel's brother, but darker and bulkier, come over from St. Asaph's to share in the defence; William Hancock, still thin and worn from his recent escape—nine of them in all.

Tom Roper began to stack the dishes and Jim moved to help him. An elderly indian, fiercer in expression than the others, stood wrapped in a blanket and ignored him, though Jim must pass him to do his work. For an instant he hesitated, then jerked his thumb to one side. The warrior stared deliberately and made no move. Jim battled against the recurrent picture of the indian leaping at him down the trail when Uncle Trev and Greasy Pete had died. Then he thrust out his jaw and jerked his thumb again more emphatically.

"How-de-do," said the warrior in guttural English and stepped aside. Jim took hold of his end of the table and started back while Tom Roper carried the front. Just in time he noticed a glimmer in the grass.

"Wait a bit," he said and was surprised at how steady his voice sounded. Tom Roper stopped and Jim picked up the pewter platter. Then, feeling like a general who retreats in good order, he helped lug the table up the path and inside the gateway.

Back at his loophole he might have welcomed a word of praise. Instead Ambrose Coffer, still sunning himself, spoke in mock commendation.

"Rest yourself, boy. You're entitled to it. Your knees was

257

a-knocking together so much that you must be plenty bruised. Thought from here you'd throw yourself like a horse what interferes when he's trotting."

"Yes," spoke up Liza. " 'From here,' you says, Ambrose. If it had been you what went out you'd have interfered so much we'd have had to send somebody out to sit on your head 'fore we could untangle your legs."

"Damn ungrateful, Ambrose is," chimed in Lige. "After Jim has saved us from a disaster."

"What disaster?" asked Coffer.

"Didn't you see or are you sunning out what's left of your brains? They nigh to forgot that pewter platter."

Lige kept savoring the words on his tongue. " 'Pewter platter' —ain't that a fine, well-rounded sayin'? You can make love to a girl with that. 'You're pretty as a pewter platter, ain't I glad your breasts ain't flatter?' " Then, with an utter change of emphasis, "What goes on now? Watch your loopholes, boys."

Jim, peering cautiously through his, had no more explanation than the others. The chief who had stood next to Boone was giving a loud harangue but his back was to the other negotiators.

"Blackfish telling his warriors about whatever's been agreed on," said Nick Watkins.

It was more than probable, though the whole situation had the stamp of unreality. Jim knew of the progress of the negotiations. Blackfish had at first demanded that Boone redeem his pledge given to save the saltboilers, that he would carry the inhabitants of Boonesborough to join the indians. After Boone's unqualified refusal, there had been talk, talk, talk, ending in an offer of a peace treaty, supposedly sponsored by Hamilton at Detroit. Today it was to be signed, a document regularly written out by mutual agreement. Neither side had showed good faith, but Boone had kept the parleying going in hope of gaining time for the Virginia reinforcements—if they were coming. He had fought a double battle, for Callaway and some others had grown increasingly doubtful of his loyalty and he had had to use as much persuasion within the walls as outside them. This should be the crux.

"Nine more indins comin' out of the woods to join 'em. That

258

makes eighteen of them to nine of ours," reported Ambrose, sitting up on his timber. "By God they're all joinin' hands. There's two of 'em to each of our people, one on either side."

Tom Roper ran along the wall. "Remember if they waves their hats, fire."

"They're bein' held!" shouted down Lige tensely. "They can't signal."

Jim thrust his rifle through the loophole and covered the group. Liza came up beside him and Tom Roper bounded up on the log which let him have a clear view over the palisade. The negotiators seemed locked together but there was no struggle.

"Not yet!" called Roper piercingly.

Then Blackfish whooped and a rifle cracked. The frieze of borderers and indians broke into a confused mass. From the forest sounded the high panther-wail of the warwhoop.

"Shoot!" yelled Roper. "Stand by the gate!"

Jim had fixed his eyes on Boone, clearly recognizable at the eighty yards distance. He saw him send Blackfish hurtling to the ground, saw an indian strike with a tomahawk, the tomahawk that was to have been buried had there been any honesty to the proceedings. He fired. Without waiting to see the result of the shot he jerked the empty rifle back and felt another thrust into his hands.

" 'Member it carries high," said Liza and the ramrod clicked in his ear.

There was a roar of firing all about him. The nine were running for the gate under a hail of bullets from the forest. Fortunately the indians in the clearing were unarmed, having relied upon their stratagem to subdue the embattled negotiators, and the shots from the stockade were doing damage. The smoke bothered him, but he saw Major Smith throw a warrior clear and instantly took the target. If Lige and three others subsequently claimed they had done the same it made no difference to Jim's fierce elation when he saw the indian fall. It was all rattling, blending reports and fierce yelling and Liza pushing a reloaded rifle into his hands.

Boone was inside, others were inside, but there were indians close after them—or might be, the smoke was too thick to tell.

"Shut that gate!" roared Tom Roper. The straining men

shoved the panels together and the bars fell into place. Jim saw Squire Boone change direction and charge for the cabin which served as an alternate entrance. The door opened and swallowed him and the smoke began to clear. Only one figure was left outside.

"Get behind a stump!" roared the stockade and the man dove for shelter.

The indian fire continued, but Lige's dry comment was clear in the momentary pause in the racket.

"Best advice I ever heared, only it come too late. He picked his stump his own self."

Boone came past Jim. He was panting a little and a trickle of blood ran down his cheek from a cut on his head. His calm voice governed the excitement.

"We'll get him in soon as it's dark. You in that blockhouse see they don't creep up on him."

He turned away and said quite loudly, "Meat's in the pot, now we got to cook it."

There was a sudden roar of laughter from the blockhouse and Boone looked up.

"No concern," Lige's face showed at a side loophole red with mirth. "Ambrose is a-shakin' bullets out of his clothes. They like to stripped him naked but he ain't got a scratch. The luck of fools."

Jim laughed too and turned to his loophole. As he did there was a sharp smack against the side of it and an indian bullet embedded itself in the wood.

"Have a care!" said Liza with a sharp indrawn breath. "They'll settle down to shooting."

From then on the siege lost its slightly comic aspect and took on the reality of death and wounds. The Shawanoes had plenty of powder and lead, thanks to Detroit, and they used them extravagantly. The loopholes were a small mark, but with a couple of warriors aiming at each there was bound to be a time when a bullet would come through.

An exclamation from Nick Watkins showed that he had been hit.

"Damn splinter!" he said apologetically and pulled from the skin of his forehead a long sliver knocked off by a passing ball.

The blood was running into his eyes and John Tendergrass offered him a strip of linen.

"Thankee for the thought," answered Nick, wiping his hand on his hunting frock and leaving a bloody smear. "Rather have a strip from Liza's skirt. Homespun don't make you a target like linen does. Likewise it would make me feel right sentimental."

Hardly had he bound up his wound when there was a rising crackle of rifle fire and a chorus of yells from the opposite side of the fort. Boone called names in a stentorian shout and Nick and a half dozen others departed on the run for the threatened area. Lige reported what he could see.

"Shawanoe rush! We can't help none less'n they get in over the stockade. Then face around an' shoot fast."

The attack was repulsed, for the fort was spitting flame. Next to Jim's ear, Liza chuckled. "What you aimin' to do, London?" she asked.

The Negro slave was at Nick's vacated post, rifle in hand. He touched his battered hat to her. "If that Pompey can stay out with them indins an' shoot in at us, Miss Liza, I ought to be able to stay in here an' shoot out at them." As steadily as the bravest defender he searched the woods for a target.

The first bright impressions of excitement faded with the coming of night. Night was the time of greatest danger, with the darkness split by occasional rifle flashes and the stumps changing into charging warriors. The indians crept closer and both sides aimed at the spurts of fire from the muzzles. When the dawn broke it brought with it sniping from the treetops that swept the enclosure of the fort.

The indians did not relax the siege as the days came and went, and the defenders were too few for reliefs. They must sleep by their loopholes or snatch a couple of hours' rest in the nearest cabin, flinging themselves down on the trampled floor with children crying fretfully to the beat of the rifles. Jim found, as every fighting man has found, that war is far different from the books. His youthful beard sprouted and made his face itch, his eyes sank in his head, his nostrils were growing sick of the smell of people and animals crowded together. The latrines, the manure, the unwashed bodies and the rank odor of black powder smoke became so strong as to color his

261

thoughts. It was as if he were wearily struggling in the midst of a charnel house, not with high gaiety and courage but with a dogged determination that was wearing down his nature to its bedrock.

Liza was as hollow-eyed as Jim himself. She did not spare herself, for she must help in the cooking, feed the animals, run the chance of the dropping bullets, and then come back to him to help in case of another rush, a rush that was always threatening but never materialized. Yet an attack pressed home would have ruined Boonesborough. Their tenuous hold on their defences depended (and they knew it) on Boone's monumental bluff. That ostentatiously open gate, that parading of numbers had done its work. There had been too many notches cut on the sticks by the counting indian for the chiefs to send their warriors across the littered fields.

London was killed the second night, Gabe Venable the day following, when he came up from working on the new well which they were trying to sink. Jim saw him fall and helped drag him into shelter, with the bullets thucking into the ground as the snipers too hurriedly tried to add to their success. Pompey, the Shawanoe Negro, had jeered at the defenders from what he thought was a safe distance, but Boone had killed him at extreme range. Daniel was a mighty unsafe man to take liberties with, thought Jim, and the rest of the settlers felt the same, though Callaway and others must still keep voicing the old suspicions which should have been dead and dried by now. The snapping and snarling grew as the nervous tension mounted. Even John Tendergrass yielded to it in a totally unexpected fashion.

William Hancock came in to sleep just as Tendergrass dragged himself from under his blanket to go on watch again. Hancock cherished a rancor against Boone and spoke his piece to the weary cabin. John Tendergrass interrupted him, rusty and fierce, his hand on his butcherknife.

"I was saltboiling too an' I tell you you lie! How many times have they taken that many prisoners an' not burned some of 'em? He bluffed 'em then as he's doin' it now. Just yell over the wall to the Shawanoes how many of us there really is an' see if they believes you. They got twenty score more men than we've got but we got Dan'l an' that equalizes things."

262

The owner of the cabin was at the loophole. He fired and drew back his rifle, peering through the smoke.

"I'd have got him if you fellers hadn't been a-shoutin' so you threw off my aim. If you're goin' to grapple, damn ye, do it outside so's I can fight indins in peace."

Tendergrass gave a last snarl at Hancock. "Are you fool enough to think Boone'd surrender?"

Hancock was at least honest in his opinion. "No," he answered shortly.

Tendergrass nodded as if he accepted an apology which had not been offered. "See you don't talk so much, then. You've made us waste a shot."

"Now damn him," said Hancock, open-mouthed. "He was the one that was bellerin'."

This day the watchers reported that the indians had begun to dig under the riverbank where they could not be reached. The Frenchmen with them had counselled a mine that would bring down the stockade on that side. There was no solution except to countermine and force them to break into the tunnel when their own was close enough. The shovels had to be moved if the dirt was to be thrown, and the burden on the defenders was heavier than ever. The weather had turned to a damp clinging mist and the indians closed in with it. When Jim took his turn in the dank, musty depths he sweated until the spade handle slipped in his palms. The distance to be covered by a yelling assault was halved, and the thought of being trapped down here while the fort was stormed shook his courage. Yet he took his turn uncomplainingly while Liza watched his loophole with a rifle.

Seven days of active siege, and this was the seventh night. No sign yet of the Holston relief, and the grim badinage which the riflemen shouted to the warriors had lost its bite. God sakes had Virginia forgotten them? The rest of Kaintuckee could do nothing, even though Simon Butler and another scout were hanging around outside the besiegers' lines to give what aid they could. St. Asaph's and Harrodsburg had sent men to the defence—a few, but all they could spare. No force could be gathered to meet so many indians in fair battle. The taint of despair began to weigh down upon the tired garrison.

Jim was in the blockhouse with Lige and glad that Roper

263

had sent him there, though the mist drifted coldly across the unroofed timbers. Amasa Tendergrass, covered by Lige's blanket, was giving small-boy snores in a corner.

"Thought he'd be a hindrance," remarked Lige, "but he ain't. He don't flinch an' he's managed to load good enough."

"What are our chances?" whispered Jim. He felt that he had to be frank with someone to make the gnawing worry take its teeth out of his nerves.

"Jus' what Dan'l's made 'em," answered Lige equally quietly. "If they believe there's too many of us they won't rush unless the mine brings down the wall. If . . ."

An arc of flame soared from behind a stump and quivered into the ground just short of the stockade. The panther yell came into the fort and sent the cattle wild. Around they stampeded while the screams of terrified children and the shouts of the riflemen mingled with their bellowing. The whole clearing lighted up as warriors dashed forward, crouching low, and hurled torches at the wall and the cabins while the fire arrows streaked the sky. There was a roar of gunfire. No shrinking from the loopholes now. The fort opened on its four sides in reply.

Jim shot at a running indian and saw him fall. Lige fired, tossed the empty rifle back to Amasa, fired his second piece, and started reloading that with blinding speed. Liza scrambled up the ladder and snatched shotpouch and powderhorn. The torches quivered and burned on the cabin shingles. The defenders ripped them off from below and tossed the precious water onto the flames. The mist mingled with the smoke and the lights glared against it. Jim was cursing at the top of his lungs, for his nose brought him the worst of warnings, the smell of woodsmoke, mingling with that of rosin and burnt powder. Liza, shaken for once, dropped an empty rifle as he passed it to her and clutched at his arm.

"Look!" she screamed.

The cabin to their right had received an arrow fairly in the outside door and the tops of the planks were running with small flames.

"Damn them, why don't they put it out?" cried Lige, and ran to the side of the blockhouse, pointing and yelling. In the clamor his warning was unheeded. The men there were either

264

firing or tearing down another torch which had rolled down the slant of the roof and stuck.

Jim dropped down the ladder and sprinted across the open space. The cabin was empty save for a white-faced woman who stood at the entrance to the loft with a baby in the crook of her arm and an axe clenched in her free hand.

"Water!" he yelled, but she only stared at him until he saw the full kettle and snatched it up. He raised the bars and swung the outside door open. Not daring to look at the lighted clearing with its darting figures and its gunflashes, he fixed his eyes on the little, treacherous flames that were beginning to get a grip on the wood. He dashed the water against them and saw them sizzle and fail, then beat furiously at the last of them with his hands. Bullets rapped into the logs, he felt a twitch, and then a heavy blow took his legs from under him and he fell, half inside and half out of the door. He tried to crawl in, but the panther yell shrieked higher still.

Then he felt a jerk under his shoulders, a friendly pressure that gave him the final lift he needed, and he was inside the doorway and rolling to one side. The door crashed shut and the bars rattled down. The woman from the loft was testing to make sure that the bars had gone home, Liza and a rifleman were tumbling into the cabin, and Amasa Tendergrass stopped tugging.

"By God Jim, if you was much heavier I couldn't have lugged you inside."

XXVI

Liza examined Jim quickly while the screeching confusion continued unabated. The rifleman had knocked the plug out of the loophole and was taking quick shots at bold warriors who had tried to take advantage of the momentarily open door. The blockhouses which flanked that section of the wall chimed in to help him and the whipping cracks almost blended. Liza straightened up with a relieved expression and then put her mouth close to Jim's ear to make herself heard over the racket.

"Ball went clear through the calf of your leg, 'nother grazed your shoulder. You'll be reasonable spry. You're not much worse off than Ambrose Coffer an' you an' he can compare lies afterwards. You've got pretty near as many holes in your huntin' shirt as he has."

She bound up the principal wound with a strip from her dress.

"I'd better not be takin' care of any more young men or I ain't goin' to look decent," she said as she ripped the cloth with the point of Jim's knife. There was another crescendo of yowling, this time from another section of the stockade, and Liza patted Jim's shoulder, though her anxiety showed itself in her eyes.

"I'm goin' back to get your rifle an' one for myself. Things is livelying up."

Jim raised himself on his elbow and tried to move his leg, but the sweat ran down his face from the pain. The terrors which working in the countermine had inflicted upon his imagination came back reinforced. The bellowing of the cattle, the pound of hooves, the warwhoop and the shouting of the defenders became magnified each instant into the fall of Boonesborough. He was listening for the crash of the stockade along the riverbank. Surely the indians would not have attacked so fiercely unless their mine was ready to bring down the wall. The room was hazy with powder smoke and the woman had gone back to the loft with her axe and the baby. The rifleman fired again and Liza reappeared, lugging the two weapons.

"Here's your'n," she shouted above the din. "I loaded it." She stared at his involuntary pallor. "You hit somewheres else?" Hardly had she spoken when she must have sensed his ordeal for she covered her slip quickly. "Worst's over on this side, but there's another fire on the east face. 'Tain't catchin', though, the mist has pretty well soaked the logs."

She grabbed at the shoulder of the rifleman. "You hear me? I'll take your place. Dan'l says to get on over to the east face. They're most through here."

"There's one in the dip there, behind that pile of brush. I can't get a shot at him. An' I was the fool who piled that same brush an' meant to burn it," exclaimed the rifleman bitterly and ran out with a reassuring shout to Jim. "They're crawlin' away, now, not closing in."

266

Liza was crouching at the loophole, gripping Jim's spare weapon. A bullet smacked against the logs and in a single movement she thrust the rifle through the hole, aimed and fired.

"Shot at his smoke," she announced, "but I'm afeared I missed again."

Jim got a grip on himself and in spite of that agonizing leg, scrambled to his feet and dragged his rifle over to her.

"Let me have a try," he said between his gritted teeth. Liza gave him a quick look and fetched a stool.

"Sit on this," she said. "I'll call you if I needs you."

"Get back from that loophole." He was leaning heavily against the logs, but he was doing his best to claw himself erect with their assistance.

"You ain't fit to stand at it!" she screamed.

"Sooner it was me than you," he mouthed in return and put his eye to the opening, shouldering her aside. The fires and the torches were dying and the gunflashes becoming more pronounced against the restored darkness. The pile of brush was still distinct, but search as he would he could see no sign of the warrior behind it. It was just as well, for it is doubtful if he could have hoisted the heavy Deckard to his shoulder without his leg buckling under him. Liza put her arms around him and hauled him down onto the stool. The firing was subsiding to a rapid patter and their voices became more audible.

"Sorry, Jim," she said. "You're not fit for the job an' it had to be done. That was all."

The smell of the stockade's interior, the stink of the burned logs, the acridity of the powder, the reaction from combat, made him quick to misinterpret her meaning.

"I'm not fit for this sort of life then! I've got to get a girl to take my place because I'm so damned useless," he burst out. "I've sweated and frozen out here and I've done my best against the Shawanoes. Maybe it's a right feeble best but it's all I've got to offer."

His leg was paining him so much that he hardly noticed her hurt expression. He did not truly mean his next phrase but something inside him made him say it.

"If it wasn't for you I wouldn't stay."

She stepped back from him. The torches no longer sent their

267

wavering light through the loophole and he could not see her face. The cattle had run themselves out and had gathered together, puffing, with clicking of horns; the calls back and forth from wall and blockhouse took on coherence, but he did not listen. Liza dropped her hands and shouldered her rifle.

"Glad you told me," she said. "You took me wrong, though. I'll send Lige an' John Tendergrass to help you over to our cabin as soon as they can get away. Reckon the attack's finished."

She was gone. The baby began to catch its breath between sobs and the mother set down the axe. In a stupor of sullen despair Jim levered himself back to the loophole and peered through it, indifferent to indian bullets. There was a patch of light in the sky and raindrops began to drive the mist away. The wrecked clearing with the trampled remnants of the unharvested crops was empty. Scorched, battered, defiant, Boonesborough yet stood virgin and untaken.

Lige and John Tendergrass exclaimed together when they saw him.

"Want to get yourself killed? Standin' next to that loophole an' makin' a target of yourself?"

They pulled him away and hammered in the plug. Jim didn't care. The structure of his defiance of a life he truly hated had collapsed. He knew that the savor of adventure had been submerged long since in the constant drudgery, the lack of intellectual companionship. There were compensations—Lige's steady friendship was one of them, his acceptance as a borderer was another. Yet those themselves were a satisfaction rather than a fulfillment. He knew it when he saw the fields. Even if Boonesborough managed to hold out when the river stockade was undermined, the year's work had been largely wasted. To start over with no feeling of gain or accomplishment for the expenditure of so much wearing toil, to realize that another indian raid would send up in smoke cabins, fences and crops, was too much for him. If he had not blabbed out in front of Liza his own inner thoughts, he might have hoped that time and her love would conquer his distaste. Possibly determined attention to his stand might have wiped out the recollection of Happy Return, passed on perhaps to the Virginia cousins. He had left to him only the hope that she might have understood the strain he was under when he had spoken, and might still be willing to go on with him.

He lay that day in the bed in their own cabin while Mrs. Tendergrass took care of him. He had time enough for black thoughts, nor was the atmosphere about him conducive to cheer. Jim was still too young to take an objective view of his own situation and to realize that even the most phlegmatic of the settlers was close to nervous collapse. The strains and stresses of the siege, the night attack and the sound of the indian digging, becoming more and more audible as the tunnel approached the wall, cumulated until there were signs of collective hysteria. Women were prone to weep and men to quarrel over trifles. Several of them even lashed out against Boone, who had done all that a man could do to keep the resistance effective. John Tendergrass mentioned it with a worried look when he came in to see how Jim was.

"There's talk of court-martialin' Dan'l when the siege is over," he remarked. "I told 'em they'd better wait until it *is* over before they throws away the crutch they've leaned on."

"Oh God," said Jim wearily. "Still making out that he's a Tory?"

"Just that. Fine friend of King George he's turned out to be. Bluffing the biggest indin army that's ever come to Kaintuckee for three days an' then holdin' out for eight." It was a sign of Tendergrass' tension when, speaking to no one in particular, he said, as he was leaving to go to his post again, "What's keepin' them Holston fellers?"

Liza came in to have a look at Jim, but her grave face averted much talk. She dressed his leg with silent efficiency and when he strove to take her hand, pulled it away.

"Don't mind what I said," he whispered imploring. "Oh Liza, if you'll marry me, I swear I'll make a liar of myself—about leaving Kaintuckee, I mean. I'll make my stand and never go . . ."

"I knows you'd try," she whispered in return and brushed her hand across her eyes.

"Then you will?" he begged her eagerly.

"No." She was crying openly now. "The only hope we had was that you'd really picked up a love for land. Reckon you have, but you knows as well as I do that it's Happy Return

269

you loves—an' rightfully so. 'Fraid that's my last word, Jim, lad."

She leaned towards him, then pulled herself back with an effort.

"I can't kiss you, either. Trouble is I still loves you."

She did not reappear through the long day with the rain hammering on the shingles and the rifles still quarreling. Mrs. Tendergrass made no remark and went quietly about preparing the supper. She gave Jim his, which he could not eat, and she carried a pot to Lige and to her husband. The night came down and Jim felt lonelier than ever. Now was the time for the mine to be holed through and the Shawanoes simultaneously to repeat their attack on the stockade. He thrust aside the blankets and tried his leg. Though the wound had stiffened the rest had done it good. He limped over to the loophole and took out the plug. The ashes still glowed on the hearth but not enough to silhouette him and he saw that his rifle was ready. If the crash and the rush came he would do what he could. The rain kept pouring.

"Jim!" It was a cheerful shout, and Lige and John Tendergrass were clapping him on the shoulders.

"Hark to them drops a-spatterin'!" yelled Lige and whirled him around in a dance until he cried out in pain. "Sorry, but you'll feel better when you hears what I has to say. Their mine's done caved in on 'em. Ground got soaked an' I reckon they hadn't braced it proper. Didn't do the least mite of damage either."

"We got to remember they're still out there around us," admonished John Tendergrass in a cautionary tone. The water dripped from his hat and his hunting shirt was soaked, but he was grinning.

"They won't be for long. If there's anythin' I hate it's squattin' out in wet woods an' I knows the Shawanoes feels about the same. They're back where they started an' they'll be gone tomorrow. That's why Dan'l has let half of us away from the loopholes."

He went across to their own and squinted out. "Rain, bless it! I hope it runs down them bastards' necks an' under their blankets."

John Tendergrass came down the loft ladder from where he

had been reassuring his little daughter. Lige cast a wise eye at Jim.

"Never remarked on it before, but from what I sees of you and Liza reckons you two have had a falling-out. Good thing for you, Jim. Come along with me an' Simon when this is over an' have a look at the country. There's a lot to see an' I aims to see most of it 'fore I dies. Wished I'd been along with Simon an' seen Kaskaskia an' the Mississip. You an' me an' Cricket an' Simon would have a right smart lot of fun." He broke into a roar of laughter as a thought struck him. "Poor Simon, he's out there somewheres beyond the indins an' just as wet as they are. Bet he wishes he could do what I wants to now."

He put his finger to his forehead. "It seems to me that a touch, just a touch, mind you, of Monongahela would be a mighty good remembrance of Simon, wet an' cussin'. Where's the jug?"

John Tendergrass felt for it in its accustomed place. "They've moved it. Question is where?"

Lige lit a candle at the fire and handed it to Jim. "I put in a shelf for Liza couple of weeks ago. Reckon it's up there. Hold the light high, Jim. Now there it is, nestlin' right next the pewter platter. Wise to put our valuables where they're safe."

He grinned at Jim again and reached up. "Here's your comforter, lad. Don't want no girl's arms about me when I can have a little drop of cheer. I'm through with women . . ."

There was a hum, a thwack and a clang. The pewter platter leaped from its place and fell. Lige, still grinning, went limp across the table. He was through with women forever.

XXVII

The indians were gone in the morning, the siege was raised, but Jim sat in bitterness of sorrow. They buried Lige and Gabe Venable and London and those others of their company who had been killed in the siege; buried them deep and concealed the graves with all of Boone's skill, for the indians had been known to dig up bodies and scalp them for trophies. Some more peaceful day a farmer's plough might turn up the bones of the men who had opened the land and given it to those who would follow. In so closely knit a community there were many who realized the full extent of Jim's loss and good friends like Boone and Butler slipped in to assure him that his self-blame was unjustified. They could bring him no relief. He waited for Liza.

His leg had begun to heal, but not even John Tendergrass could make him come out into the sun. Instead he clung to the semi-darkness of the cabin, like a denned animal. Liza had moved over to Tom Roper's, for with Lige dead Roper had taken his place as her protector. There was no provision in border economy for a woman without a man.

She had been in to see him before, but he had said nothing, nor had she, her grief so hard upon her that she had dared not open her mouth and shame herself in her own mind by an undue display of emotion. This time when she arrived she had made a resolution and it showed in her expression.

"Stand up, Jim," she said softly. "You looks better on your feet than moping here. What's the Book say, 'Let the dead bury their dead'?"

He would not touch her, but he arose. "I made a target of him," he answered. "I held up the candle so a Shawanoe could put a bullet through the loophole. Do you wonder I can't talk to you?"

"He saw the plug was out, didn't he? Didn't he go to it an' talk about the rain? John Tendergrass gave me the whole story. He lighted the candle himself and told you to hold it high, didn't he? It was a mighty unlucky shot fired through that downpour that happened to come in the loophole. Even Dan'l couldn't have done it without luck. Well, whyfor are you grieving over it? 'Twan't in noways your fault."

She shook him until he nodded.

"You has to admit it, don't you? There's trouble enough on the border without your brooding over what can't be helped. We loses somebody an' then we shuffles aroun' amongst ourselves an' starts over or picks up where we've left off."

Her voice had begun to tremble and he took her to him.

She burst out crying and hugged him close.

272

"Liza, you've got me to turn to. Isn't it about time you did it? Forget what you said."

Her answer came to him between gasping sobs. "Told you we'd done some reshuffling, didn't I? Jim, I'm a-marryin' up with Nick Watkins."

He could not believe her; he kept muttering, "You mustn't," but she was getting control of herself.

"I told him, Jim. Told him I loved you but I'd never marry you. He said he was willing to take me second fiddle rather than play first with anybody else. I'll make him a good wife, Jim, a lot better wife than I'd make you."

"But, Liza, why won't you try?"

"Ain't no use to try. Don't you think I haven't laid awake nights tryin' to talk myself into it? I knows where I fits an' that ain't in Maryland. Jim, your grandmaw needs you, an' if she don't your paw does. Lad, you don't even know if they're still alive. You've been out here long after your judgement must have told you you ought to have gone home. For me! Yes it was. Towards the last that's all it was. There's some the border sickens, 'cause it's mostly dirt an' blood an' toil. You fit, Jim, don't you ever tell yourself that you don't. Few men can say that they have Daniel Boone an' Simon Butler an' Flanders Callaway to call them friend."

He was still pleading, but in his heart he knew that she had decided. She listened to him, but her face was setting with determination.

"Askin' me what I means? Can't you see it yourself? You fits the border but the border don't fit you. It's like this. If you has nothin' you can come to Kaintuckee an' better yourself. You keep on encouragin' yourself with that thought every time you has the Shawanoes burn you out. Some day we'll beat them Shawanoes an' then we'll have farms, 'stead of backwoods scratchings. But when you got everythin' to begin with it ain't so easy."

She led him outside and sat him on a stump. "That's the answer, Jim. I ain't a-lecturin' you on your duty but I reckons you owes it to your family to go home as soon as you can travel. I'll send John Tendergrass to tell you the same thing."

She was gone almost at a run with her head bowed. It was over and Jim knew it. He'd have to think Maryland now. Then John Tendergrass coughed nearby.

"Glad to see you out an' about. First of the Holston men just arrived an' they're goin' to hold that court-martial on Boone. Those fools like Callaway are still a-stickin' to it."

He knelt upon the ground and spoke softly, his hand clumsily but affectionately on Jim's knee.

"I've come to think nigh on to as much as you do about Liza Bonham. Since I thinks so much of her I believes what she's doin' is right."

He kept on talking without giving Jim a chance to reply. "Mebbe I was a mite disparaging when I first saw her, but I knows now that I was mistook, plenty mistook. Whatever may have happened home take this consolation with you, I thinks you was right in stayin' on until she'd made up her mind. I'm puttin' new shoes on Cricket. We're short of iron but there's enough for that."

He brushed the dirt off the knees of his leggings. "Now I'm goin' lookin' for that William Hancock an' if he says any word against Boone I'm goin' to crawl headforemost down his throat. You'll excuse me, but I'm stayin' on in Kaintuckee and I reckons to have my opinions duly noted."

It was a good fight while it lasted but the Holston men pulled Tendergrass and Hancock apart. Tendergrass had done his best to spoil one witness for the prosecution but he need not have worried. The court-martial was held in the shadow of public opinion and public opinion was overwhelmingly in favor of the man who had saved Boonesborough both by quick thinking and hard fighting. Boone was not only acquitted but was issued a new commission as Major in the militia.

Jim was in a rush to leave now, for it was pure pain to be in Boonesborough with Liza about to marry Nick, and Lige dead. Boone solemnly issued him his discharge from the militia and paid him out of Virginia funds for his days of service. John Tendergrass would have given him more, but Jim refused.

"You taught me how to travel coming out and there's enough to fetch me home. Reckon I wouldn't know how to behave in a respectable ordinary."

"Even the worst of them is as good as we've had this last

year." Tendergrass gave his lip-wrinkling smile. "Who you ridin' back with?"

"I don't know yet," Jim answered wearily. "Reckon I'll have to wait for the first batch of Holston men to go home."

"Wouldn't wait so long as that. There's a feller says he'd like mighty well to ride with you as far as the settlements, if you'll have him."

"Who is he?" asked Jim, with no more interest than was necessary. The choice of a road companion was important, as he knew well enough.

"Daniel Boone. He's fetchin' Rebecca out again from the Yadkin. Leavin' tomorrow mornin', he says. Be a good idea to say what goodbyes you has to."

There were more goodbyes than Jim liked to say, more people to wish him well than he had ever expected. He could have floated himself in Monongahela. Even Nick Watkins came in at the last with a straight look and a wry smile.

"Reckon I ought to be glad you're leavin', Jim, but I ain't." He turned red and shuffled his feet. "Liza asked me to tell you that she'll be waitin' down by the gate when you rides out."

He had that to anticipate during his last night, sitting up a good part of it with Simon Butler and Tendergrass. They were companionably silent until the three were ready to turn into the bed. Then Butler listened to an owl hooting outside the stockade.

"That's just an owl," he remarked. "First we've been able to say that for a good many months. Well, the Shawanoes will be back again. Jim, if you ever gets out this way later, just give a holler an' I'll come a-runnin'.'"

The gray, familiar dawn came and Boone waited beside the horses. Liza was waiting too, in the shadow of the gate. Jim came up to her and tried to make his voice as casual as he could.

"We're leaving now." His studied effort was a failure. "Oh Liza, I do love you."

She kissed him with her old hunger and fierceness. He returned it and for a moment they clung to each other.

"Don't aim to keep you," said Liza. Suddenly her voice rose. She said her farewell, half proudly, half in a wail:

"You'll always remember Kaintuckee."

275

XXVIII

From the Holston to Kaintuckee it had been September, and now from Kaintuckee to the Holston it was September again. The forests and the marching ranges had so much the same appearance and coloration that he had only to glance down the backtrail to feel a recurrence of memory. Not all by any means was grim. There was the spot where Greasy Pete's horse had stirred up the yellow-jackets and they had fled madly with the barred-tailed pests clinging and stinging; another reminded him of Uncle Trev trying to keep up their courage with a hunting yarn. He even recalled the yarn. When he looked ahead again there was Boone riding down the Wilderness Road and he in his company.

They travelled fast but surely, sparing themselves and their horses, each sheltered campsite decided on before the start of the day's journey. The old markers, seen anew from the opposite direction, took on an accustomed look, the Hazel Patch, Cumberland Ford, the rising valley of Yellow Creek. At Cumberland Ford they had met a party of Holston militia moving up for the no-longer-needed relief of Boonesborough, and Jim was hailed by Adam Dobson. "Jim Cheston, aren't you? I've got a letter for you. Colonel Campbell asked me to fetch it along."

Until it was read, Jim had a guilty tightness in his throat. But the news was good. Grandmother Dorsey wrote that his father was home at last. His leg was gone and his health was poor but he was making out splendidly. There was an enclosure from his father, a quiet note from a quiet man. If he still had his row to hoe in the wilderness then let him hoe it, but if he was through then his father would like to see him again.

With that weight lifted from his heart, Jim began to brighten. He stopped feeling that he was retreating from a failure. Perhaps this return was the beginning of more solid achievements.

He could have had no better companion to this fresh mood

than Daniel Boone. A shrewd observer, a wise and kindly advisor, he drew the sting out of Jim's soul at their night camps. He could talk in his low, pleasant way of his own life, cataloguing his failures and what they had done to him. After each he had picked himself up and gone on instead of sitting down to bemoan his ill fortune. Listening to him, Jim could not but recall old Master Blackthorne's advice, "Never be sorry for yourself."

They crossed Cumberland Gap but Jim did not turn his head. If he must give up Kaintuckee he would not look back upon it with vain regrets. Still he could not help but notice that there were people on the road, not militiamen but settlers, and this time the tide was westward. Martin's Station, where they had spent the rainy nights, was occupied again and glad to see them; the bottom lands were gradually becoming repopulated. The Shawanoes' efforts had been concentrated against Boonesborough, and where they had not come the borderers had come instead.

Past Moccasin Gap, past Sapling Grove, to stop briefly at Uncle Trev's group of cabins, now wearing a worn look. The woodmice and the squirrels had played havoc in the living room, but the old chart of the holdings was still above the fireplace. Jim took it along as a remembrance but threw it away before he had ridden a mile. That too was gone and behind him.

At Fort Chiswell Boone parted from him to take the road to North Carolina and the Yadkin. He drew his horse alongside of Cricket, gave Jim a hearty handclasp, and then lingered an instant with his grave smile.

"You thinks too much 'bout what might happen, but if it comes you stands right up to it," he said, then raised his hand, palm outwards, in the border salute and rode away, his old slouch hat shading his face, his shoulders square. Jim looked after him with a great emptiness and set Cricket to the north once more.

At Ingles' Ferry, old Mr. Ingles stumped to meet him when he came in. "I've heared of ye, heared well of ye from Kaintuckee," he said, and would take no fee for his lodging. It was Jim's final parting with the frontier. Beyond New River he became, with the passing days, an object of covert curiosity, a silent, long-bodied young man in battered buckskins, too big for the dusty mare.

Staunton, Charlottesville, Orange Court House, Culpeper—Jim retraced the road to the Potomac, sleeping in the ordinaries with the carriers and the farmers, not with the planters and the lawyers. He was happier with the publicans and the sinners than he was with the pharisees of the land. When he forded the boundary river he thrust the Deckard under his knee, but he watched the country as he rode with an alertness that had become ingrained. At last he saw the maples towards sunset, the maples he had last seen in the dawn.

The house was the same, the copper beech was the same, the colts running in the meadow might have been awaiting his return. A Negro groom came to meet him, hesitantly, then opened his eyes wide.

"That's Cricket, can't tell me it ain't! My Gawd, it's Marse Jim!"

Jim smiled to himself. It was still the mare who was the better known of their pair. Simon the Butler (another double memory) flung open the doors and Juno, in bandanna and apron, made him a fat curtesy, restraining herself visibly.

"I'm a house servant now, suh," she announced shakily. "I'll fetch your grandmother."

Candles burning again, and the long rows of books in the library. His father sipping his wine and still taking stock of him long after the first greetings had been over. Grandmother Dorsey, erect as ever, giving side glances at the mirror to be sure that her emotion was not marring her complexion. This was home.

"You will stay with us for a while at least, I trust, James?" asked his father. Jim roused himself from reverie.

"If you will have me, sir. I want to learn as much as I can of the management of the place. Then next year, if the war continues I shall go into the army."

His father smiled. Jim felt a strong affection for him, an affection made even stronger by the bond that lay between them, a bond forged by their mutual past of hardships and danger. His father understood him and left the decision to him—not to Grandmother Dorsey.

"Morgan's Virginia riflemen I presume would be your choice?"

"No sir, the Maryland Line."

"That can be arranged. Both are good troops."

Grandmother Dorsey had been watching Jim closely.

"Have you left your heart behind you in Kaintuckee, James?"

He tried to turn it off with a laugh.

"No, ma'am. Only two toes."

They laughed with him, but Grandmother glanced at his father and he knew they had guessed. They did not press him and he was grateful to them. Instead they talked of the future and what had been done at Happy Return in his absence. Before long they went to bed and left him sitting in the library.

He stepped out upon the long porch that faced the lawns. The moon was up, and the little brook that ran the length of the front pasture was talking as softly as had the river below the stockade. He leaned against a pillar as once he had leaned against the logs. Time might have reversed itself for the moment, but it would move forward again and carry him with it.

Except that his heart whispered, and the words were clear:

"You'll always remember Kaintuckee."